THE GUILTY

Gabriel Boutros

Although parts of this book are loosely based on actual events, this is a work of fiction, and all names as well as many facts have been changed. As such, names, incidents and characters are products of the author's imagination, or are used fictitiously and are not to be construed as real.

 ISBN-10:1479277754 ISBN-13: 978-1479277759

Chapter 1

At half-past midnight there was almost no traffic on Sherbrooke Street West. A strong wind blew the thin, granular snowflakes horizontally past the streetlights, slamming them into the sides of buildings lining the deserted road. Gazing out a fifteenth-story window, shielded from the storm, Robert Bratt stood alone. He was wearing his favorite silk pajamas on the off-chance that he would ever get to sleep again, and he sipped a freshly poured glass of Chivas in the hope that it would help get him there.

His thoughts were miles away from the Montreal winter that froze the streets below him. For the briefest moment his eyes focused on his own reflection in the window. His tall frame looked thinner than usual tonight in the pajamas that Jeannie had bought him for Christmas. His face was gaunt and tired-looking, his brown hair disheveled.

He blinked a few times and quickly turned his gaze back to the street where he spotted a lone pedestrian braving the cold night wind. Bratt watched the man walk, bent forward, head down into the gale, and wondered where he could be going at that time of night. The distraction was all too brief, though, and he found himself deep in thought again. He drank deeply from the glass in his hand. He was having absolutely no success trying not to think about what had happened that day.

It was a day that had begun well enough, but had turned sour very fast. The stars must have been aligned just right for Bratt to end up in the gallery at Nate Morris's rape trial that afternoon, instead of being the one defending him. It was one of the few times in the almost twenty years he had been a lawyer that he had sat in a courtroom and watched another defense attorney at work.

Nate Morris had been a good client for Bratt, well-connected and willing to pay handsomely for his lawyer's services. Four years earlier, Bratt had successfully defended him against an identical accusation and Morris had naturally begged Bratt to defend him again when he had been arrested last summer. But this time Bratt couldn't get involved because he knew the victim; knew her very well, in fact.

Claire Brockway had been friends with his eighteen year old daughter, Jeannie, since they were both in pre-school. When Bratt's wife had died eight years earlier Jeannie had begun spending more and more time with Claire and her family, and he had been glad to let her find some comfort there. Through their turbulent adolescent years their friendship had survived and grown stronger.

When he had learned that Claire had been raped, he had shared Jeannie's grief for her friend. That the alleged rapist had been a former client only added to his daughter's bitterness and his own sense of responsibility.

Bratt, of course, had refused Morris's request to represent him. But when his partner, J.P. Leblanc, had suggested that they refer Morris to Antoine Perron, the best lawyer they knew outside their firm, Bratt had agreed. Perron was Bratt's former protégé, a lawyer to whom he had taught all the tricks of his trade, before going out on his own five years earlier.

Despite Bratt's connection to the victim his years of training told him that it was only right that Morris should get the best defense that he could afford. Jeannie hadn't really understood that at the time. She had angrily accused him of favoring Morris over Claire. It had taken weeks before the tension between them had eased and, until earlier today, he had thought this issue was behind them.

As for his own caseload, Bratt had spent the previous eight weeks fighting a seemingly endless fraud trial, plowing through mounds of accounting books, questioning tax experts, and generally boring himself stiff. His client was Cooper Hall, a nervous mouse of a man who wore rumpled tweed jackets and constantly ran his thin fingers through his even thinner hair. That those fingers had allowed him to expertly forge enough bearer bonds to buy and sell everyone in the courtroom several times over was one of many confidences that he had made to Bratt, subject to attorney-client privilege, of course.

On this very morning the seemingly interminable fraud trial had finally ended. Judge Smythe had granted Bratt's motion to exclude two very damaging auditor's reports since the auditor who drafted them had not bothered showing up to testify at the trial as he had been subpoenaed to do. It seemed that he had recently come into a bit of money and spontaneously moved to a seaside villa in Costa Rica. Bratt wasn't one to look a gift-horse in the mouth by asking where all that money had come from.

Judge Smythe's ruling had effectively brought the prosecution's case to a close. Bratt did not present a defense because any claim of innocence by his client would have been an outright lie. Bratt had never been above bending the truth when it suited him or even ignoring it now and then, but he wasn't prepared to suborn his client's perjury outright. Hall was such a nervous wreck his testimony would undoubtedly have been disastrous anyway, and that would have wasted the masterful job the lawyer had done of destroying the credibility of the Crown's other witnesses. Bratt knew he had a better chance of winning by relying on his own cross-examination skills than by risking having his client lose his case for him by testifying badly. He always considered the cases as his own. The clients were just there to pay him to do what he had always loved best and to interfere as little as possible with his work.

Sam Brenton, the Crown prosecutor, had asked the judge for two days to prepare his final arguments, not an unreasonable request considering the twenty-six boxes of sleep-inducing documentary evidence he'd be trying to summarize. Bratt, having been left free to do as he wished that afternoon, decided to join Jeannie, who had been attending Morris's trial from the morning. For the most part he had been concerned about how Claire would do on the stand. But another part of him, the part Bratt would never tell Jeannie about, had just been interested in watching Perron at work.

Now Bratt stood alone in his apartment, wondering if he wouldn't have been better off not going at all and not seeing what he had seen. He should have realized how different a trial would seem when he was on the outside looking in. With his daughter at his side, watching her emotions rise and fall with her friend's fortunes, he had seen a side of his profession that he had always known existed, but never cared to think about.

Watching Claire get roughed up on the witness stand was bad enough, but Bratt felt even worse knowing he had trained the attorney who asked all those insinuating questions, manipulating the victim into looking guiltier than the man accused of raping her.

At home now, hours after the trial, Bratt realized that his misgivings went beyond this one particular trial. After all, if it hadn't been Claire, it would have been somebody else's closest friend up on the stand, somebody else's daughter testifying, and she would have come out of the cross-examination looking just as bad, and feeling even worse than she looked. And if Perron hadn't been the one asking the questions, it might well have been Bratt doing the hatchet job. It certainly wouldn't have been the first time.

Such a prospect had rarely bothered him before. In the past he had considered himself a gladiator, looking down at the mangled forms of the helpless victims of his cross-examinations, savoring the taste of victory. He had never spent too much time worrying about the witnesses who had fallen under his attacks. Their fate was the prosecutor's problem.

It was winning that he had lived for, that gave him the rush that nothing else could ever come close to. In his arena there was no room for the softhearted or the weak-kneed, who were forever relegated to pleading shoplifting cases at Montreal Municipal Court.

He had always prided himself on his reputation as a "tough as nails" attorney. It was the only way he knew to do the job that he had loved for so many years. Yet it was now past midnight and he was still brooding over the day's events, events that had shaken his confidence in himself and his work. He wondered if this wasn't some sort of punishment for his years of professional arrogance.

Turning away from the window and from his own reflection he shuffled back into his bedroom, his bare feet sliding along the thick, cream-colored carpet. He swirled the ice in the glass absentmindedly, the soft clinking the only sound in the otherwise silent apartment. He sat down on the edge of his bed and thought that the one good thing about Jeannie spending the night with Claire was that she wouldn't be there to see him drinking again. Then he emptied the glass in one gulp.

I haven't needed a real nightcap like that in a long time, he thought. *This shit has really gotten to me.*

He stretched out on the bed, closed his eyes and waited for sleep to come. But the only thing that came was the sound of Jeannie's voice, yelling at him in the courthouse corridor earlier that day.

"YOU'RE A HEARTLESS BASTARD, JUST LIKE HIM! YOU DON'T GIVE A SHIT WHO'S TELLING THE TRUTH AS LONG AS YOU COME OUT ON TOP!"

He couldn't believe that she had spoken to him like that. He never thought he'd have to defend his chosen profession to his own daughter, as if he was a hired killer, not a respected attorney. But, as harsh as her words were, it was their ring of familiarity and truth that worried him the most.

He rolled over and pulled the comforter over his head, but there would be no sleep on this night. Instead, the day's scene played out in his head again and again.

Courtroom 4.05 had been nearly full that afternoon, with family, friends, and interested members of the public in attendance. Prior to the judge's entrance the rustle of excited whispering had filled the cold, gray courtroom in anticipation of Claire continuing her sometimes-explicit testimony.

Bratt sat in the front row, near the one journalist who was covering the trial. Jeannie had told him that Claire had testified fairly well that morning. Johanne Dulude, the Crown prosecutor, had gently elicited from her the story of the job interview that had ended up with a rape. Bratt was surprised to learn that Judge Dion, a notorious misogynist, had actually managed to avoid displaying his irritation with the sometimes-tearful witness. The jurors, while evidently titillated by the lurid details in Claire's morning testimony, had also seemed sympathetic to her plight.

Finally, the judge and jurors filed in, and a low hum of anticipation filled the room. From where he sat, Bratt could see only part of Claire's profile as she stood in the witness box facing Dion, with her back to the gallery. Jeannie sat at his right, leaning forward, gazing intently at her friend.

Perron stood off to Claire's right, looking like he was waiting for a signal to start his cross-examination. Bratt knew that the hesitation was merely Perron relishing the moment. His incongruously happy smile showed off his bright white teeth, the canines somewhat longer than the norm. With his black lawyer's robe swinging around him like a cape as he moved toward Claire, Bratt thought he looked like a vampire about to pounce on his unsuspecting victim.

However, Claire should not have been unsuspecting at all. At Jeannie's request Bratt spent two hours with her the previous evening going over the kinds of questions Perron would throw at her. Claire was able to answer them about as well as he could have expected, but with one look at her pale and tense face as she stood in the witness stand, Bratt feared that she had forgotten every warning he had given her.

Perron, who was all of five foot five, moved right next to the gangly teen-ager and Claire seemed to tower over him from her high-heeled shoes. He certainly wasn't fazed by the height discrepancy. He held a yellow legal pad in one hand and brushed back his thick black hair with the other.

Dulude sat to Claire's left, tapping her pen nervously as she waited for Perron to get started. When he finally spoke his tone was surprisingly casual and Bratt noticed Claire's shoulders droop slightly as she relaxed.

Big mistake, he said to himself.

"So, Miss Brockway, you had heard about Mr. Morris from one of your girlfriends before you went for the job interview," Perron began, his French accent barely discernable.

"Yes, that's true," Claire answered, her eyes fixed on the Bible she had been sworn in on that morning.

"And you were told that he fancied himself a bit of a lady's man…"

"Yes."

"…and that your obvious good looks would probably improve your chances of being hired?"

Claire blushed at the compliment, and looked up at Perron's face for the first time. "I had heard that he was always flirting with the younger women working there. I didn't expect that it would be any different with me."

"And you certainly dressed in a manner that would show off your best attributes, didn't you?"

"I think anybody going for a job interview is going to try to look their best. That's just normal."

"Well, do people try to look their best when they have totestify in court?"

"I suppose so. Yes."

"So, why is it that today looking your best doesn't mean wearing a short, tight leather skirt?"

Claire opened her mouth, then slowly shut it again, unsure what to make of this question. "I didn't think it was appropriate for a courtroom," she finally answered.

"But it was appropriate for a job interview, wasn't it?"

"I wasn't going to go there wearing my mother's old house dress."

"No, obviously not. And the blouse you were wearing that day, was it buttoned up to your throat as your blouse is today?"

"I don't see what difference that makes."

From his right, Bratt heard Jeannie call Perron a prick under her breath. He understood how she felt, but he could still appreciate the way Perron worked. There was nothing particularly subtle about the younger lawyer's strategy. Bratt could see Perron's questions coming a mile away. Claire was so nervous, though, deep subterfuge wasn't necessary. Bratt fidgeted in his seat, unused to being on the sidelines of this little game, just watching.

A slight grin formed on his face as he imagined himself in Dulude's shoes, jumping up and objecting to every second question that Perron asked, if only to throw him off his rhythm. But he knew there was little hope of that happening. Dulude was the type who rarely made objections, except when she was certain they would be sustained. She was always worried the jury would think she had something to hide.

Bratt turned his head and saw that Jeannie was eyeing him with a critical expression. His grin made a quick exit and, feeling somewhat guilty for letting his mind wander, he turned his attention back to the trial.

"So, a lot more of your cleavage was showing," Perron was saying, "and you could tell that he was having a very good look, couldn't you?"

"Oh yes, I could."

"But you didn't comment about it to him, did you? Or button up your blouse a bit?"

"Well, no, I didn't."

"Did you do anything, change your seating position in any way, to try and make it more difficult for him to have such a good look down your blouse?"

"No, I didn't."

"No, you didn't. And wasn't Mr. Morris's interest also obvious in the things he said to you?"

"I'll say. He wasn't the least bit shy to tell me what he was thinking."

Good old Nate, Bratt thought. *Always straight to the point.*

"He was very complimentary toward your figure," Perron said.

"You mean he made some disgusting remarks about my body."

"What he said disgusted you?"

"Of course."

"And you showed him how you felt."

"Well…I don't know if he could tell."

"Surely you got up and stormed out of the office."

"What? No, you know I didn't."

"Oh. So you stood up and slapped his face."

"I didn't do anything like that."

"Well, you must have at least told him how thoroughly disgusting you found his comments to be."

"No. No, I may have said something, but not that."

For the first time, Perron's voice began to rise, as he leaned even closer to Claire, his expression that of a father scolding a young child. "As a matter of fact, you didn't say anything, did you, Miss Brockway? As a matter of fact you were perfectly happy to see that he was paying so much attention to you, that he was so clearly taken in by your beauty. As a matter of…"

"I object, My Lord," Dulude finally exclaimed, surprising Bratt who had almost forgotten her presence. "My colleague is badgering the witness, not questioning her."

Dion's expression let everyone know that he didn't particularly like agreeing with her, and he slowly turned his eyes toward Perron.

"Perhaps you could rephrase your question," he almost sighed, and then raised an irritated eyebrow in Dulude's direction to see if this satisfied her.

Bratt thought that if Dion had to hide his true feelings any longer he surely would have burst.

The prosecutor was barely seated when Perron took up right where he had left off.

"You really enjoyed his attention, didn't you? You liked the way he looked at you."

"What was I supposed to say?" Claire asked, frustrated. "I needed the job; I wasn't going to piss him off." She turned to the judge, trying to compose herself. "I'm sorry, sir...I wasn't going to insult him in the middle of my job interview."

Perron didn't try to hide the sarcasm in his voice as he continued. "So you giggled like an innocent little schoolgirl, and blushed and said, 'Oh my, you naughty man. You shouldn't say such things.'"

"I never said 'naughty,'" she snapped back, just as Jeannie's clenched fist came down on Bratt's knee. He gave a start, but realized that his daughter wasn't even aware of what she had done. He could see by her intense expression how wrapped up she was in her friend's interrogation. He also couldn't ignore his own growing feelings of unease, although he tried his best to analyze the questions and answers objectively.

Bratt knew it wasn't the lawyer's fault that Claire was so easily goaded into losing her temper. As much as they had tried to prepare her ahead of time, she was making Perron's job look easy.

Bratt glanced at his watch, to see if Claire would be allowed a reprieve from Perron's verbal assault any time soon. It was still going to be a while before the judge called a recess. In the meantime, she was just going to have to try her best to keep her composure, no matter how nasty or embarrassing Perron's questions were. There were moments, Bratt thought as the time crawled slowly by, when nasty was the perfect word.

"Tell me, Miss Brockway, what's your bra size?" Perron asked at one point.

This question caused several of the jurors to gasp audibly. They looked toward Judge Dion, as if expecting him to intervene and perhaps even chastise the impudent lawyer. The judge, said nothing, though, and the prosecutor made no move to object. Bratt had read Claire's statement to the police, and he was aware of how pertinent that seemingly impertinent question was.

Claire's eyes were cast down again as she answered. "I don't think I need to tell you that."

Perron opened his eyes wide in mock surprise. "Oh, since when are you so shy about your measurements? You didn't hesitate to give them to Mr. Morris during your job interview, did you? Don't worry, I won't quote you here."

"I was stupid," Claire whispered, her voice so low now that people sitting behind her could hardly hear her.

"I'm sorry, did you say that you were stupid?"

"I should have walked out when he asked me that. He had gone way too far."

Perron's voice also dropped, until he almost sounded as if he sympathized with her.

"But you didn't walk out, because you really wanted that job. Isn't that right?"

"Yes."

"And his lewd remarks weren't so bad, after all, as long as you got hired."

"I figured I could live with them."

"And the staring down your blouse. You could live with that too."

"Yes."

"I understand that your financial situation at the time was quite precarious."

"It wasn't just that; it was a really good job. Something for the long term."

"A really good job," Perron repeated, walking slowly away from her and nodding his head to show that he was taking in the implications of everything she had said. He stood facing the jury, in a brief moment that Bratt recognized as pure theatre, then took in a deep breath and swung around brusquely to face the witness.

"Miss Brockway, you knew that your chances for getting hired would be improved immeasurably if you showed up in a very attractive outfit, didn't you?"

"Yes."

He strode up close to her again, all traces of his earlier sympathetic expression gone from his face. "In fact, your appearance was quite sexually provocative, wasn't it?"

Claire seemed taken aback by his suddenly aggressive tone and posturing. "It…I guess it was…to him."

"Yes, to him. And that certainly wasn't accidental, was it?"

"No, I guess not."

"And not only did you intentionally dress in this sexually provocative manner, but you went out of your way to be friendly with him, didn't you?"

"I try to be friendly with everyone/"

"You smiled. You laughed."

"Yes. There's nothing wrong with that."

"You flirted."

"He was doing most of the flirting."

"Miss Brockway, are you saying you didn't flirt at all?"

Claire turned her head slightly toward the front row, looking for help, but Perron would have none of that.

"Miss Brockway, I'm over here," he barked. "Could you please answer the question."

"Yes, I flirted."

"And I suppose your own flirtations simply slipped your mind when you made out your statement to the police."

"I didn't think it was that important."

Perron raised his arms in another dramatic gesture, then let them flop back down to his sides. "You didn't think it was important? You didn't think it was important to tell the police the truth about what happened in Mr. Morris's office?"

"I did tell the truth," Claire insisted.

"Did you really? Did you tell them that you went there bound and determined to get that job by whatever means necessary? That you dressed in a way you knew would turn him on? That when you saw he was turned on you flirted shamelessly with him because you wanted to make sure he hired you? Did you tell them any of these things that we both know to be the truth?"

Claire said nothing for several seconds, keeping her eyes cast downward. Bratt felt Jeannie's hand squeeze his as they waited for her to answer. He turned to look at his daughter and was surprised to see a tear rolling down her cheek.

Then he asked himself, *Why should I be surprised? That's her dearest friend getting kicked around up there and I'm sitting here rating the lawyer's work. When did I become such a heartless shit?*

He squeezed Jeannie's hand in return and looked back at Claire. He wished that there had been some way he could have spared her this public humiliation, but it was what every witness had to expect when stepping into a courtroom.

Finally, Claire spoke. "I didn't think…I didn't realize that's how it would seem."

"How it would seem? Miss Brockway, I put it to you that you knew exactly what you were doing. You were perfectly happy to see that he was falling for you. It was exactly what you wanted, wasn't it?"

"I never wanted that to happen."

"Didn't you? Were you really fighting so hard against it?" Perron sneered, even more sarcastically than before. "Tell the court the truth, Miss Brockway, did he seduce you or did you seduce him?"

Claire looked up brusquely, shocked at what Perron was insinuating. Her voice seemed to choke, as she whispered, "No, no." Then her body began to shake as tears spilled from her eyes, and she sobbed, "Nobody seduced anybody! This wasn't a fucking seduction!"

The air in the courtroom was heavy with stunned silence. Bratt could see the jurors were sitting expectantly on the edge of their seats, seemingly fascinated and thrilled at the pitiful spectacle that was being put on for them. Even Judge Dion forgot to scold her for her foul language. The only word that came to Bratt's mind as he looked at the staring faces around him was "bloodlust."

Claire must have felt the weight of all those eyes upon her. Her legs gave out and she sat down hard on the small witness bench behind her. She buried her face in her hands, but couldn't muffle the sound as her sobs burst out.

Bratt looked away, wishing he were anywhere but there. Dulude reached out a sympathetic hand and squeezed Claire's arm, looking toward the judge for some commiseration. Dion, however, simply dropped his pen onto his desk, folded his arms and sat back, rolling his eyes in exasperation.

Bratt couldn't see the expression on Nate Morris's face in the prisoner's box at that point, but on Perron's lips there was just a hint of a self-satisfied smirk. Bothered by the pleasure Perron was taking in his work, Bratt decided that the young lawyer had always been a bit too cocky for his taste.

Finally, Dulude stood to speak. “My Lord, I think this would be a good time for a recess.”

“Evidently,” Dion grunted. He lifted his ponderous weight, as the bailiff hurriedly called out, “All rise.” The jurors quickly stood and began filing out of the courtroom, whispering excitedly among themselves. Dion strode down the stairs from his dais and out the back door.

Jeannie pushed past Bratt to rush to her friend’s side. Bratt also moved toward the anguished witness, then stopped, unsure if he should approach Claire or leave her with Jeannie. Just then Perron turned toward him and flashed a knowing smile at his mentor and fellow defense attorney. Bratt attempted to return the smile but couldn’t.

Claire took the time she needed to compose herself before the jury reentered, but it would make little difference in the end. Bratt found the rest of her testimony that afternoon to be anticlimactic. Although he could see by the expressions on the faces of several jurors that their sympathy for her was still there, he knew that Perron had managed to plant the seed of doubt in their minds.

When the questioning continued after the short recess Claire seemed to lose the will to fight back and was unable to defend herself against Perron’s allegations and insinuations. His questions led her where he wanted, and no matter what she answered Bratt was afraid the jury would end up thinking that she had gone to the job interview ready for some action and she had gotten what she came for.

He thought that people hadn’t changed much, twenty-first century or not. It was still too easy to believe that the woman was a slut and the man had simply done what any normal man in his position would have done.

Bratt knew that, especially with Claire and Nate, these propositions were as far from the truth as black is from white. But when it came to getting that message across in the courtroom there was nothing that he could do about it, and Jeannie should have known that.

He knew it was trite, but he didn't make the rules, he just played by them. Perron, whatever she thought of him, had merely done the same. It was pointless for her to blame the lawyers. But, blame them she did.

When the afternoon session had finally ended, the jury had been left with a dozen questions that Claire could not answer. The questions had ranged from why she wore what she wore, to why she had waited two days before going to the police to lay charges against Morris. Despite his sudden dislike for Perron, Bratt knew these were perfectly fair questions, the kind every lawyer would ask. Last night, with Jeannie and Bratt in her apartment, Claire had been able to provide acceptable answers for all these questions and others too. But her apartment was a million miles away from the courtroom, and was but a distant memory to her that afternoon.

Judge Dion had barely left the courtroom at the end of the day when Claire had rushed out and headed for the nearest bathroom. Bratt tried to put his arm around Jeannie's shoulders to comfort her as they walked out the courtroom's double doors, and that was when she had turned and yelled at him.

"YOU'RE A HEARTLESS BASTARD, JUST LIKE HIM! YOU DON'T GIVE A SHIT WHO'S TELLING THE TRUTH AS LONG AS YOU COME OUT ON TOP!"

Then she turned and ran down the hallway after her best friend.

Bratt was stunned at being blamed, although he knew all too well what Jeannie had meant. He'd had nothing to do with Claire's mistreatment, yet he couldn't shake the sense that he was as responsible as Perron.

He realized, with some embarrassment, that her loud voice had drawn some amused looks from several people who had been leaving the courtroom behind them. He was relieved that the one reporter covering the case had continued to follow Claire as she ran down the hallway, and so wasn't able to record Jeannie's words for posterity. Perron, of all people, had been nearby and had heard her, though, and he placed a hand in sympathy on Bratt's back.

"That's the problem with young girls, Bob," he said. "They can't control their emotions."

Bratt glowered angrily, not particularly welcoming Perron's commiseration just then. He had a strong urge to rip into him, but stopped short when he noticed the crowd that was gathering around the smiling lawyer, and the reporter rushing back to get some pithy comments from Perron for the next day's papers. He suddenly didn't have anything devastatingly clever to say.

"I gotta go, Tony," was all he could mumble, and he pushed his way through Perron's gathering admirers and strode quickly toward the nearest exit.

All that was left of the trial was Morris's testimony, which would start the next morning. Having heard Morris testify with calm and false sincerity four years earlier, Bratt knew that he'd have no trouble getting the jurors on his side.

They would surely waste little time in acquitting him, Bratt thought, all the while clucking to themselves over the naïve young girl who had gotten in over her head and now was trying to hold the older man responsible.

He was as confident of the outcome as if he had pleaded the case himself.

Chapter 2

Sometime during the night Bratt finally drifted off to sleep. When he woke up, after hitting the snooze button on his clock radio three times, it was nearly eight o'clock. A small, vengeful part of him hoped that Jeannie had slept as badly as he had, but he regretted the thought right away. It had been hard enough on both of them to witness Claire being cross-examined. He would try to be a little more understanding about why she blamed him along with Perron for how it had gone. The little voice in his head, which had been quite insistent the night before, woke up just in time to ask him if Jeannie wasn't right to do so.

"Shut up, already," Bratt said out loud.

Great, now I'm talking to myself, he thought as he headed for the shower. *From now on I mind my own business*.

He showered and shaved, and ate breakfast while reading the sports section of his morning paper. He assiduously avoided the city beat where, no doubt, a detailed account of the previous day's courthouse activities could be found. The trials and tribulations of Montreal's once-mighty hockey team were sufficiently aggravating morning fare.

By the time he left for work he had stopped hearing that irritating little voice, or, at least, had stopped listening to it.

Bratt et Leblanc, Avocats. The brass sign in the lobby at 511 *Place d'Armes* in Old Montreal was big enough to be seen from the street. Bratt pushed the heavy steel and glass door open and entered the stately brownstone. It was built in 1888 and, at nine stories, was the first skyscraper in Montreal. He stamped the snow from his feet on the rubber mat at the entrance and headed for the elevators, their doors also plated in shiny brass.

He and J.P. Leblanc had started out together sixteen years earlier, in a much less elegant building not too far from where their offices were now. Leblanc had been spinning his wheels for three years at Legal Aid when he decided to propose partnership to his old law school buddy Robert Bratt.

Bratt had begun his own legal career at the provincial prosecutor's office, but too much internal politics and not enough money were incentives enough for him to jump to the other side of the judicial divide.

At the time his immediate superior was Francis Parent, a Jesuit-educated prosecutor with a nearly religious devotion to ridding his city's hallowed streets of criminals and sinners. He cleaved to the virtuous path of his career as if he was following the Via Dolorosa.

Parent, who was an average trial lawyer of uncommon self-righteousness, looked upon Bratt's departure from the Crown as an act of betrayal to his cause. He was certain that the young lawyer was selling his soul and jumping into a moral cesspool by joining the defense.

But Bratt had seen enough in his three years working with prosecutors and policemen to know that few of them had an exclusive claim to the moral high ground. In law, he learned, it was all a man could do to remain true to his own ethical code.

Heading up to his office in the elevator, Bratt felt the worries of the past twenty-four hours start to melt away. Even more than his expensive apartment with a view of Mount Royal, or his lakeside cottage in the Eastern Townships, this office was his true home.

Here he was among his own kind. Nobody would question his values or try to burden him with guilt. Nobody would criticize him for how he made his living. He was the unquestioned top dog in the firm, and that simple thought put the spring back into his step and brought a wide grin to his face. When he walked through the firm's ornate wooden doors nobody would have suspected the inner turmoil that had kept him up half the night.

Sylvie, the receptionist, looked up at the sound of his voice as he greeted her. She handed him his mail and smiled back a hello while talking into her ever-present headset. Bratt noticed that the door to his office was closed and threw a questioning look in her direction. She covered the mouthpiece with one hand and said, "John's there. I think he had another bad night."

"John" was John Kalouderis, an associate in the firm who, in recent years, had become close friends with Bratt. He had a brilliant legal mind, when it wasn't totally fogged by alcohol, and that was a rare enough occurrence these days. Kalouderis might not have lasted at the firm, even with Bratt's friendship, if he didn't have a particularly large, and largely dishonest, extended family, whose members regularly hired the firm's high-priced lawyers to get them out of their scrapes with the law.

Bratt opened his office door and was immediately greeted by the licorice smell of ouzo emanating from the carcass sprawled across his leather sofa. Kalouderis's snores were the only signs that the inert form held a grip on life. Bratt stood over the prone, slack-mouthed figure and shook it none too gently.

"Hey, Yanni, wake up! You're drooling all over my sofa."

Kalouderis snorted, opened his eyes and looked up blearily at his disturber, rubbing the back of his hand across his mouth. His expression was one of vague recognition, like he was searching his memory to put a name to a face that he hadn't seen in a long time. He quickly gave up trying to remember and turned back onto his stomach, burying his face into the sofa.

"Fuck off, *malaka*! Get your own bed," he mumbled.

Bratt threw his mail onto the pile of sweaty hair that was stuck to the back of his friend's head, but got no reaction. Exasperated, he dropped into the chair behind his desk. Kalouderis's vulgarity, as well as his indifference to Bratt's arrival, irked him.

"I mean it, John. It's well after nine and I've got work to do."

"Go right ahead," replied Kalouderis, "you won't bother me."

"Look, John, I'm damn tired myself and I don't find this the least bit amusing, so MOVE IT!"

That last exhortation finally led to some movement on Kalouderis's part. He began getting up slowly, gingerly putting his stockinged feet onto the floor as if he expected to find shards of broken glass there.

Bratt asked, "Did you spend the night here or did you crawl in drunk this morning?"

Kalouderis scratched his head at the question and tried to keep his gaze level at Bratt while answering. "Both, I guess. I got in about five o'clock, and I've been stretched-out here ever since."

Bratt rested his head on the back of his chair and sighed. Every now and then Kalouderis and a group of his favorite cousins would hit the town and attempt to commit collective suicide by alcohol. This time he looked like he had almost succeeded. Bratt was concerned that his friend was going to embarrass himself publicly one day, which would, of course, embarrass the firm. Still, there was a part of Bratt that felt envy, wishing he could be as irresponsible with his own health and career. But he had too much to lose, in his personal and professional lives, to risk it for a night of uncontrolled drinking.

Kalouderis began awkwardly fishing around with his hands under the sofa, looking for his shoes. Finally retrieving them, he burped and struggled to his feet, a loafer in each hand. Bratt watched the proceedings with a sense of irritation, tapping his fingers on his desk in barely repressed impatience.

Kalouderis swayed slightly where he stood and breathed in deeply through his nose. "Geez, I reek. Mind if I use your shower?"

"As a matter of fact, I insist on it," Bratt replied, thinking of the staff and clientele who would come into contact with Kalouderis during the day.

Once his friend had shuffled off to the partners' private shower area, Bratt turned his attention to his day's work. He had a number of phone calls to make before drafting his final arguments for the Hall trial. Brenton would probably spend all of tomorrow pleading, so Bratt wouldn't have to plead until Thursday morning.

He remembered that Nate Morris was testifying in his rape trial that morning. The jury would probably start deliberating some time tomorrow, and Bratt's experience told him they probably wouldn't have to deliberate very long. If, or when, they acquitted Morris, Bratt suspected that he would be having another heated discussion with Jeannie. He would get as much work as he could done now while his mind was still free from the aggravation that awaited him.

Bratt was less than an hour into reviewing his trial notes when J.P. Leblanc opened his office door without knocking. He walked in and, with an audible grunt, sat down heavily on the sofa that had so recently served as Kalouderis's bed. Leblanc was more than eighty pounds overweight and a heavy smoker. Whenever he sat, it was always heavily. Grunting was optional.

"Who the hell made a mess in the shower?"

"Probably John," Bratt answered, without looking up from his papers. "I found him asleep and drooling all over that sofa when I came in this morning."

"Aw, crap," Leblanc said, trying to jump up from any wet spot he may have sat on, but only managing to shift his position to the middle of the sofa before the exertion made him give up. "That pig," he said, red-faced. "I should fire him, you know."

"Yes, you should. If you go do it now maybe I can get some work done."

Bratt looked up to see if his partner had gotten his point, but Leblanc hadn't moved. Watching him slowly ruminate over whatever it was he wanted to talk about, Bratt wondered, and not for the first time, how such an eclectic group of people had ended up working, and working so well, together. About the only thing the eleven lawyers in the firm had in common was a highly competitive nature and a willingness to do whatever was necessary to win. Over the years this had kept a harmony of sorts in place between them.

Leblanc sat without speaking, although he clearly had something on his mind.

"So, how'd the interviews go?" Bratt asked. "Find any diamonds in the rough?"

"Hm. Oh, yes. I did, actually," Leblanc answered, sounding distracted.

Bratt put down his note pad, folded his arms across his chest, and cleared his throat impatiently.

"Anything else?"

"Oh, yeah. You hear about Lynn Sévigny?"

Bratt was surprised at the topic his partner had chosen to broach. Sévigny was a struggling, but fiercely independent, sole practitioner who rented a small office down the hall from them. Bratt had always admired her fighting spirit and, on occasion, had discreetly sent some business her way. He had been among the first people she had confided in when a cancerous lump had been found in her left breast.

"I heard they operated on her," Bratt said.

"Yeah. She…you know-"

"Don't say it," Bratt interrupted. "I know what they did."

"Yeah, anyway, she's not going back to work for a while, you know, what with the chemo she'll probably have to get and stuff. You know it makes them go bald."

"I'm aware that can happen," Bratt said, uncomfortable about discussing Sévigny's medical problems with his less than sensitive partner.

Leblanc scratched his head, trying to look concerned and thoughtful. "This is gonna be tough on her, financially-speaking. You know if she's off work for a long time she's gonna lose a lot of clients."

"I know. I think she has some insurance."

"Yeah, I guess so, although she probably couldn't afford enough." There was another thoughtful pause from Leblanc. "Thing is, maybe we can help her out a bit."

Bratt had never expected altruism from Leblanc. He had been partners with the man long enough to know that he didn't spend too much of his time worrying about lawyers outside the firm.

"Help her how?"

"She was scheduled to do a murder trial this term. You know, that Small kid who's been in the papers. It's supposed to start in three weeks or so, and now that her guy's going to need a new lawyer I thought we should look into taking over the case from her."

Bratt knew he should have seen this coming. “The woman’s just been operated on and the vultures are already circling! Some help you’re offering.”

“Come on, Bobby. I’m really thinking of her. At least we can take care of her a bit from whatever we get, which a lot of other guys wouldn’t do, you know. Besides, this kid’s been inside for I don’t know how many months. We can’t let him wait until she’s back on her feet to have his trial. That would be unconscionable. She knows that, I’m sure. Anyway, I’m going to see her in a couple of days in the hospital, so I thought I’d speak to her about the case then.”

“Don’t forget to bring her flowers while you’re at it,” Bratt snapped.

Leblanc waved Bratt’s remark away. He slid his bulk back over to the side of the sofa, pushed with all his strength on its padded arm, and slowly levered himself up to his feet with another grunt.

“Look, why should the file end up with Chartrand or Gold? At least we’ve always been friendly, and I’m sure she’d prefer that it was us who took over for her than one of those other guys.”

Bratt didn’t answer, so Leblanc just shrugged and walked back out, his message delivered. He closed the door softly behind him, leaving Bratt to try to get his thoughts back on his trial notes.

He didn’t relish being one of the sharks getting ready to pounce on the remains of Lynn Sévigny’s practice, but maybe Leblanc was right. She probably would prefer the Small murder file going to their office rather than to certain other lawyers.

Either way, it wasn’t his problem. He wasn’t about to jump into a murder trial that was due to start in less than a month. Once he had won over the jury in Cooper Hall’s trial he was going to take some well-deserved time off to recharge his batteries, and maybe mend some fences with Jeannie.

The next day was Wednesday, and Bratt was back in court for the reprise of the fraud trial. As Brenton’s final arguments dragged into the afternoon Bratt received a note telling him that the jury in Nate Morris's trial was still deliberating. He slipped the note into his pocket and tried to concentrate on his own case.

Brenton gave a detailed recitation of the facts that had been alleged against Hall, delivered in the prosecutor's inimitably slow and phlegmatic style. Most of Bratt's mental energy was used up trying to look like he was paying attention while his esteemed adversary droned on and on, reminding Bratt of how painfully dull much of the trial had been.

Bratt let his eyes roam around the courtroom, and they stopped at the long legs of Sergeant-Detective Nancy Morin sitting in the first row of the gallery. She wore a blue suit jacket over a skirt with a fashionably high hemline which revealed that she did some serious running when she wasn't sitting in court.

Her light brown hair was cut just above her ears, revealing a strong, but graceful neck. Once upon a time Bratt might have found her athletic build a bit too muscular for his taste, but in the two months of this trial she had managed to radically change his tastes. Now their mutual attraction was evident to anyone who watched them interact in the courthouse hallways.

His gaze lingered on her legs and a small smile formed on his lips as he recalled the sparks that had flown when he had cross-examined her over a month earlier. He had tried attacking Morin on everything from her personal honesty to her professional competence, but she hadn't backed down an inch. Her pale, greyish-green eyes had flashed angrily at him as she stood her ground against his onslaught. Her defiance had actually excited him, to the point where he lost track of his questions more than once.

His grin widened at that memory, and then he realized that she was looking straight back at him, also smiling. He felt unexpectedly embarrassed and snapped his gaze back to Brenton.

That was really smooth, he chided himself. *She's really gotten to you, Bobby.*

Bratt tried to keep his attention on Brenton's monologue on the off-chance that he might miss something of interest. He had no reason to fear, though. The details and minutiae of the Crown's evidence that was being dumped on the jury seemed to have lost all meaning to anyone other than Brenton himself.

What passed for Brenton's style was anything but dramatic or exciting. His calm, ploddingly analytical arguments betrayed his conservative, English schooling, and Bratt was glad to notice that they did nothing to keep the jury's interest or attention. Among the twelve sworn citizens, some eyes wandered, while others slowly shut, only to blink rapidly open again, as Brenton reviewed the countless graphs and charts that had been prepared by the Crown's best forensic accountants. Yawns were barely stifled as Brenton carefully listed offshore bank accounts and dummy numbered companies, in the hope that the jury would understand how they all linked together like a chain that should come together to imprison Hall.

Bratt had no doubt that this chain of transactions could fatally encircle his client. His arguments tomorrow would aim at the chain's weakest links, those officers of Hall's companies who had testified for the prosecution. For much of the trial's two months he had poked and prodded and questioned them until he was certain they had lost all credibility in the jury's eyes. When it was his turn to plead he would remind the jury, in a much more dramatic and entertaining style than Brenton, of how unworthy of its trust these men were.

Once the testimony of these witnesses was set aside, the Crown's case against Hall became purely circumstantial. Bratt loved that term, "*purely* circumstantial." He was sure some American TV writer must have coined it. Any lawyer knew that circumstantial evidence could often be more accurate and more damaging than a dozen eyewitnesses. Eyewitnesses were notorious for forgetting or misconstruing the most basic facts. They regularly bent the truth to make themselves look more important or their testimony more relevant.

Despite that, most jurors felt only a roomful of eyewitnesses could assure them that an accused was guilty. Show them a solid case made up entirely of circumstantial evidence, and chances were they'd still have lingering doubts.

And Bratt knew that those little doubts were what acquittals were made of.

The following morning a clean layer of snow that had fallen overnight covered the trees on the hillside adjacent to Bratt's apartment building. The previous day's bright sunshine had been replaced by a heavily overcast sky. According to the incomprehensible rules of Montreal winters, that meant that this day would be warmer than the day before. With the rise in temperature all that glistening snow would soon melt into piles of mud-like slush. Municipal snow-clearing crews were in the midst of their seemingly annual work slowdown, and the streets and sidewalks would be an adventure to negotiate.

The taxi carrying Bratt straight to court from his apartment made its way slowly through the clogged and sloppy streets. Despite the depressing weather, his mood remained upbeat. Two months of deathly boredom had been replaced by a feeling of near-giddiness in anticipation of finally addressing the jury. Instead of the countless hours he spent slumped in his chair yesterday, praying that Brenton would pack it in before one of the jurors became suicidal, today Bratt was to be the center of attention.

He saw himself standing, with just the lightest touch of cockiness, in front of the jury and making his brief, but brilliant, final arguments. His well-chosen words would seem to fly by, compared to the previous day's marathon. He would display the casual, self-effacing charm for which he was well-known, seemingly almost embarrassed at his own hard-to-conceal cleverness and wit.

He would guide the jury easily to the conclusion that the Crown witnesses should be ignored and the circumstantial evidence rejected, so that everyone could happily return to their regular lives, feeling good about themselves and a job well done.

Bratt looked out of the taxi window as he approached the tall, featureless building that was the *Palais de Justice*. Its flat, slate-grey exterior matched the dull winter clouds overhead. The taxi pulled out of the early-morning traffic and stopped at the curb in front of the Notre Dame Street entrance. On the sidewalk, pedestrians balanced themselves like tightrope walkers as they stepped across the melting ice and over unplowed snow banks.

Their faces expressed frustration and worry at the precariousness of their footing.

Bratt opened the car door, stretched one long leg out and smoothly stepped over the slush-filled roadway. Then he gingerly stepped across the still-frozen sidewalk and headed in the direction of the courthouse. A city worker was busy salting the cement steps to prevent any potential accidents. Bratt saw several fellow lawyers, over-stuffed briefcases in hand, inching carefully up the stairs ahead of him. He smiled cynically as he imagined all the lawsuits they would gladly file if they ever took a spill on government property.

He gripped the handrails tightly, tucked his chin into his upturned collar against a sudden draft of cold wind and followed the trail of salt up the stairs and through the automatic revolving door.

Once he was inside the cavernous, but dimly-lit, atrium his glasses immediately fogged up from the warm air. The large lobby area hummed softly with the sounds of the usual collection of lawyers and policemen, litigants and witnesses, and unemployed courthouse regulars who depended on the daily drama of the law for some free entertainment on these cold winter days.

He moved forward, resigned to the fact that everyone around him would be nothing but a blur for the next minute or so. He passed the information desk and the Espresso counter, squinting over his now useless glasses, nodding and smiling at the half-seen faces that floated by. He may not have been able to recognize them but he assumed that they all recognized him.

When he reached the escalator a large, blurry figure brushed up against his left arm.

"Better wipe those glasses clean before you get to the TV cameras, Bobby-boy," Leblanc said, breathing heavily from the effort of catching up with Bratt. "They'll ruin your carefully-groomed image of sophistication."

Bratt turned toward the familiar voice, accepting a tissue that the latter was holding out. "J.P. Coming up to enjoy some of my brilliant oratory?"

Leblanc laughed. “Please, haven’t you got enough groupies and hangers-on filling up the courtroom? No, I’ll just worship your greatness from afar.”

Bratt wiped his glasses with the tissue as he stepped off the escalator. “Well, you’ll miss a great show, if I do say so myself.”

“Yeah, but Brenton isn’t exactly a hard act to follow,” Leblanc said, turning to walk away. “I might make it up to see you if I don’t get stuck behind the Legal Aid guy at the bail hearings. Kick ass.”

“You know I will.”

Bratt navigated his way down the crowded hallway. Spotting the TV cameras posted outside the doors of the courtroom about thirty feet ahead he quickened his steps in anticipation.

As he approached the courtroom the cameras turned their bright lights toward him. Microphone-toting journalists stepped up and smiled at him. Bratt smiled back, his warmest, most sincere smile and came to them like a favorite son, home after a long absence. He would gladly pause long enough to answer all their questions, no matter how long it took. Twice during the trial Judge Smythe had needed to send the constable out to drag him away from the cameras.

Once past the media scrum and inside the courtroom he paused, like a warrior looking over the field before a battle. He saw that Brenton was engaged in an all-too-friendly chat with Nancy Morin. As Bratt approached, Brenton smiled stiffly and returned to the prosecution’s table, grudgingly conceding defeat on at least this point.

Morin turned in her chair and looked up at Bratt, smiling unabashedly. She wore a sharp gray suit, which, in Bratt’s eyes, looked anything but business-like.

“Good-morning, Nancy.”

“That’s Sergeant-Detective Morin, sir. I happen to be on duty.”

“If you’re going to be that officious you should wear a uniform.”

Morin smiled mischievously and said, “If you don’t like what I’m wearing I could always take it off.”

Bratt laughed nervously. He was always surprised to find her more aggressive in her flirtation than he was. He was more old-fashioned than he cared to admit and her brashness put him on the defensive.

Morin must have sensed his discomfort, because she quickly changed the subject. “All set to give your big speech.”

Bratt smiled, feet planted on more familiar turf now. “You just wait and see. If you thought I was brilliant earlier in this trial...”

Morin laughed, well-used to Bratt’s vanity as well as his humor. “Well I’m absolutely dying with anticipation. I only hope I can survive the wait.”

“What wait?”

“Oh, nobody told you?”

Bratt shook his head, mildly concerned now.

“Juror number six lives on the South Shore,” she explained, “and he’s stuck on the Champlain Bridge behind nearly half a dozen fender-benders. We’ve got a good hour wait ahead of us.”

Bratt only nodded at this news, trying to hide his disappointment. Despite his years of experience, he always got an adrenalin rush before making his closing arguments to a jury. This unexpected delay was going to be torture for him. Morin was still looking up at him, smiling and unaware of how bothered he was by the interruption in his plans, so he decided he’d make the best of it.

“Well now,” he said, as he sat down next to her, “I’m sure I could find worse company for the next hour or so.”

In room 4.05, where Nate Morris’s trial was being held, the sequestered jurors all arrived together and on time from their downtown hotel. They rendered their verdict shortly after arriving at the courthouse, suggesting that they had held off on giving their verdict the previous day in order to enjoy at least one night on the government’s tab.

About three-quarters of an hour after his own arrival at court, Bratt was still sitting and chatting happily with Nancy Morin when Jeannie walked into the courtroom. Bratt’s back was to the door, so he had no idea she was there until he noticed several people looking toward the rear of the room. He turned and saw his daughter, tears streaming down her face, staring at him from where she stood.

Morin was in the middle of some not so slight sexual innuendo when Bratt suddenly stood up, as if she had offended him. He paused only long enough to take in the scene in front of him, before rushing toward Jeannie. He was unsure how she felt about him at that moment, but his paternal instincts permitted no hesitation. As soon as he got to her he opened his arms and enveloped her in them. She pressed her face into his chest and sobbed, her hands grasping the vest he wore under his robes.

"They let the bastard go, Daddy! They let him go!"

He had no words to comfort her at that moment, so he just squeezed her tighter. After a few seconds it occurred to him that she was there alone and he asked, "Claire?"

He could barely make out Jeannie's answer through her tears. "They took her to the infirmary. She fainted when they…when they gave the verdict. She was on the floor and he just walked out without even looking at her!"

"Christ, I'm so sorry, Jeannie." It sounded trite, but what else could he say? How else could he express how badly he felt at the turn of events? He only hoped that she would recognize the sincerity in his words. She looked up at his face, her sobbing starting to ebb, and nodded.

He wanted to take her somewhere more private, where they could talk without being the center of attention. Out in the hallway, though, the cameramen and journalists would be waiting to swarm all over them. He looked over to the constable and signaled him closer.

"I can't take her out the front door with those cameras out there."

The constable nodded his understanding. "OK, you can take her through the judge's door into the back hall. But you better follow me so you don't run into any jurors back there."

His arm wrapped protectively around Jeannie, Bratt hustled her down the aisle toward the front of the courtroom. Morin was still standing where he had left her, her concern evident on her face. He glanced at her briefly, but didn't know how he could express his myriad feelings in that split-second's look, so he turned his eyes back to the constable ahead of him and hoped she would understand.

Once into the corridor running behind all the courtrooms, the constable directed them to an empty meeting room where they could talk privately, and then left them. Bratt sat facing Jeannie, holding both her hands in one of his, stroking her tear-streaked cheek with the other. He waited for her to speak first.

"This really sucks," she finally said.

"I know."

"I really wish I hadn't come today. I hate this whole place. I hate everything that goes on here."

Bratt feared this comment might signal a renewed attack upon him or his profession, but he resisted the impulse to defend himself.

"I just don't understand," she continued. "You take twelve average people off the street, people that are as honest as anybody else, and then convince them to let a guilty man go. How do you do that?"

Again Bratt held back from answering. Maybe it was a rhetorical question, but he suspected that her comments were directed at him personally.

She cleared up any doubts when she asked him, "Don't you have anything to say?"

"I really wasn't sure what I should answer. I didn't think you would like whatever I had to say, so I thought it better..."

As he let his words trail off, she jumped to her feet. The anger in her eyes reminded him of the look she had given him in the hallway the day Claire broke down on the stand.

"Since when are you afraid to defend yourself, Daddy? You can defend any scumbag that can afford to hire you, so how come you can't come up with a brilliant argument to convince me of how I'm seeing it all wrong?"

"Jeannie, honey, let's not do this now."

"Why not? This is as good a time as any. Aren't you supposed to think fast on your feet? So, think about this, Mr. Defense Lawyer: he raped her and he walked away! You used to give us both piggyback rides, and this creep raped her!"

"Dammit, why are you blaming me for what he did to her?"

"Because you helped him get away with it!"

Her accusation hit him like a slap in the face. He knew that her words applied equally to what Morris had done to Claire as well as to the crime he had been acquitted of four years earlier. An acquittal that had come courtesy of the courtroom tactics of one Robert Bratt, defense attorney to the rich and infamous. Details of that earlier trial tried to force their way into Bratt's mind, but he quickly shoved them back into the recesses of his memory. The sight of Claire crumbling under cross-examination had been reminder enough of how easily a nervous witness could be torn apart in court.

Jeannie didn't give him any more time to think of a reply before lashing out with, "It could have been me that he raped!"

Bratt jumped to his feet.

"Christ, this is ridiculous! Are you going to hold me responsible every time a client goes out and commits another crime?"

"Why not? You're always so quick to hog the credit when you win, but you never think about the consequences, do you? If that bastard had gone to jail for what he did four years ago, he might never have done it again. But you were just too damn good a lawyer!"

"This is insane. I was just-"

"Doing my job," Jeannie cut in, parroting the last line of every lawyer's defense.

She looked at her father defiantly, as if daring him to answer her back. But Bratt did not answer. He wanted to yell out that her accusations, however logical on the surface, were too simplistic and patently unfair to him and to the whole legal profession. He knew this in his mind, but in his heart he couldn't find the words to answer her.

He suddenly felt very old and tired, as if all the life had gone out of him. All his stock answers to Jeannie's questions seemed weak and inappropriate.

The spell that held them both in place, staring at each other wordlessly, was broken when the door opened and the constable stuck his head into the room.

"Sorry to interrupt, but number six just got here. The judge wants you to start right away."

Bratt still couldn't pull his gaze away from Jeannie. He couldn't leave this situation unresolved, yet there was no more time to talk.

"I think we really need to talk about this some more, OK? Tonight, when we get home. Please?"

She didn't answer him. Instead, she silently turned and walked out the door ahead of him and was quickly gone down the corridor. He knew that she could have made some sort of peace with him if she had wanted to, but she preferred leaving him twisting in the wind. Her bitterness would not let her turn back. Now he would have to put all thoughts of this argument behind him and get back to court. They were waiting for him.

A few minutes later, Robert Bratt stood at the broad desk that passed for a lectern in the courtroom, his shoulders bowed under the weight of the guilt his daughter had laid on him. He watched as the twelve jurors, eight women and four men, entered the room and took their seats. Several of them glanced over in his direction. Their cheerful expressions revealed that, having watched him at work for two months, they were expecting him to put on a good show for them this morning. At least two of the female jurors smiled at him, and not for the first time during the trial.

The room was now fairly full. A few journalists occupied the front row. Nancy Morin, whose frown of concern still lingered, sat just behind them. Around her sat various retirees and unemployed types that had drifted in during the weeks of the trial's progress and ended up coming back for each new episode.

Yet Bratt just continued to stand, silent and motionless, totally unaffected by the people in the court or their expectations of him. He stood so impassively, while the jurors entered and the judge settled everyone in the courtroom down, that his client surely felt confident that Bratt was focusing on the job at hand, blocking out all the irrelevant distractions around him.

As it so happened, Bratt's mind was so unfocussed on the case he was about to plead that Judge Smythe had to clear his throat meaningfully twice, and finally call out Bratt's name, ever so politely, in order to get the lawyer's attention.

This finally brought Bratt back from his reverie, and he saw that they were all waiting for him to start. A momentary look of confusion flashed across his face, then it was gone. He was aware of what he was there to do, but a sort of mental inertia was keeping him from getting started, as Jeannie's words continued to ring in his ears.

He looked over the twelve still-patient faces before him and realized that he was going to look like a fool if he didn't say something soon. He tried to will his daughter's tear-filled voice to leave him in peace just long enough for him to get through the morning.

Slowly, a sense of detached calm came over him. He began to feel like a disinterested observer with no stake in what was happening. He felt no pressure on himself at all, and he stood perceptibly straighter. He managed to let all of Jeannie's arguments fade away quietly, until the sound of her voice in his memory was just so much background noise.

Then, as if nothing else in the world could have been on his mind, he smiled the casually handsome smile he reserved for juries and women he hoped to seduce. He greeted the jurors with a bright "Good morning, everyone," and they greeted him back cheerfully, relieved, perhaps, that all was back to normal.

To his left, Sam Brenton shifted uncomfortably in his seat, realizing that his presence in the courtroom had just become superfluous. Bratt's hands, soft and perfectly-manicured, opened his file folder and settled his neatly written notes on the desk in front of him.

He heard a warm, rich voice begin to speak. It was reading some of the words that were written on the pages, and adding many other words. He recognized the voice as his own, and heard in it the confidence and ease he expected of himself at this time.

In his mind's eye he stepped forward and turned around to watch himself give his final arguments. He no longer saw the judge or the jury. He was alone in the courtroom. With total self-absorption, he studied every move that he made: how he turned his head, how he smiled occasionally, how he leaned forward and stood silently, his palms pressed down on the desk in front of him, when the moment called for seriousness.

He was perfectly aware of the impression he was making with his words, his tone of voice and his body language. These all had an unrehearsed quality, a seemingly honest spontaneity about them, as if he was just having a relaxed chat with the jurors, talking off the cuff. Years of practice had gone into refining his technique to get just that effect and he smiled inwardly as he watched it work its magic once more. His timing was perfect. Like a veteran stand-up comic, he knew just how long to pause before hitting his audience with a punch line.

Look at their eyes, he thought. *Look at the expressions on their faces. They're eating up every word I say.*

He was in awe of himself.

Chapter 3

Bratt sat with his feet up on his desk, his suit jacket off, his shirt sleeves rolled up. On the sofa, sitting up this time, was John Kalouderis. Ralph Ralston, who had brought his carceral law practice to their firm back in its third year, sat across from Bratt in a soft, low-backed leather chair usually occupied by clients. Sylvie had brought some mail into Bratt's office and stayed, standing shyly to the side, to listen to him regale his associates with the highlights of his morning's pleadings.

His co-workers smiled and nodded as Bratt told them how he had made Brenton squirm by pointing out to the jury every miniscule mistake and contradiction in the Crown's evidence. They laughed as he repeated the well-timed jokes he had tossed to the jurors, which had allowed him to display how totally confident in his position he had been.

Bratt was on such a high after that morning's pleadings that all of his misgivings about what had happened to Claire, and all of Jeannie's angry accusations, had been consigned to a tiny compartment in the back of his mind that was off-limits for the time being. Once back at the office he had even skipped his lunch in order to treat everybody who approached his open door to tales of the performance he had put on. Other than actually addressing a jury there was little that gave him as much pleasure as bragging about it afterward.

He noticed with dismay that he had less than half an hour before he had to be back in court. Judge Smythe was going to give the jury his instructions that afternoon. Bratt would have to interrupt his storytelling and that was a shame, because there was still so much story left to tell.

As he spoke, Leblanc's corpulent form filled the doorway and Bratt paused in mid-anecdote to invite him to come in and listen. He noticed another man standing behind Leblanc, half-hidden by his partner's bulk.

"Sorry, to interrupt you in the middle of your self-congratulation, Bobby-boy," Leblanc said as he entered the office. "But there's someone I want you to meet."

He turned and motioned to the younger man who had remained outside the door, seemingly hesitant to enter the presence of such greatness. The newcomer was in his early twenties, with dark hair and a thick mustache. He walked in and stood next to Leblanc, looking like he'd found some sort of security in his presence.

"Everybody," Leblanc continued, "meet Peter Kouri. He just finished his *stage* with the Federal Crown, which is probably why none of you have ever seen him in court."

Kouri smiled and ducked his head in embarrassment at the jibe, while the other lawyers grinned knowingly.

"Anyway, he's decided he's fed up being mollycoddled and wants to practice some real law. While our esteemed colleague here," he pointed at Bratt as he spoke, "has been bamboozling helpless jurors with his magnificent oratory, I've been carrying on the job interviews all by myself. In Peter I believe I've found someone who'll fit in with our little family quite nicely, if, that is, we can help him unlearn any of the bad habits he's developed over the past six months."

Kalouderis motioned over to Kouri and said, "If you're going to join us then you might as well get used to an important ritual in this office: listening to Robert Bratt remind us of how great he is."

The lawyers laughed loudly at this, but Kouri held back until he saw that Bratt enjoyed the joke at his own expense as much as the others. Bratt dropped his feet to the floor and stood up to shake his hand in welcome. Kouri's grip was strong, Bratt was happy to see, showing more self-confidence than did his nervous smile.

Kouri almost gushed with enthusiasm as he shook Bratt's hand. "This is a real honor, Mr. Bratt. I've been following your legal career since I was a kid."

Bratt grabbed his stomach like he'd been punched and winced in mock pain. "Ouch! Kid, you're making me feel so old," he complained, nevertheless flattered by the younger lawyer's admiration. "Anyway, I'm glad to have you aboard. I think you'll find we're a fun group of people to work with."

Leblanc stepped up and stood between the two, putting an arm around each one's shoulders. "I'm glad you two are hitting it off, Bobby-boy, because you're probably going to be seeing a lot of each other for the next little while. First thing I told Peter he'd be doing is giving you a bit of a hand in your next case."

Bratt's smile faded slightly as he looked suspiciously at Leblanc. "That so?"

Leblanc's own smile faded entirely, before he turned away from Bratt and began to shoo everyone else out of the office.

"The old brain trust's going to need some time alone, people, so why don't you show Peter here around a little. You too, John," he said to Kalouderis, who still sat on the sofa. "You can have a nap after everybody's gone home tonight."

Kalouderis grinned and flipped his middle finger in Leblanc's direction before getting up and following the others out of the office, leaving the two partners alone. Bratt returned to his feet-on-the-desk position, while Leblanc closed the door.

"So, what's the scoop?" Bratt asked.

Leblanc didn't sit, a sure sign that he was feeling nervous. He ran his fingertips along the back of the chair that Ralston had just vacated, and pursed his lips, before finally answering.

"Well, I spoke to Lynn Sévigny…about that murder case I told you she had."

"I hope you asked about her health while you were at it."

"Geez, Bob, I'm not that much of an asshole. I made sure she was fine, OK? I'm just trying to get to the point quickly because you've got to be in court in twenty minutes."

"You're right there, so let's get to it."

"Right. Bottom line is she'd like you to take the case."

Bratt stamped his feet down to the floor. "Are you nuts? I'm not taking on any new cases, and you know it. I'm exhausted and I'm planning on sleeping in for the next two weeks."

"That's perfect," Leblanc smiled, "you'll still be back a week before the trial."

The weak attempt at a joke only got Bratt angrier, and when he spoke this time he was almost shouting. "I'm not kidding! You can shove your dumb jokes, J.P., because I need some time to myself."

"OK, OK, I'm sorry. Don't take my head off. I never wanted to get you involved in this thing in the first place. I know how hard you've been working, how tired you are. It's just that when I went to speak to Lynn she brought up your name before I even had a chance to ask her about the file."

"*She* brought up my name?" Bratt was surprised to hear this. He had been certain that his partner had decided to drop this hot potato into his lap because Leblanc hated handling major trials himself as much as he hated seeing them go to lawyers from outside the firm.

"Yes, she did. I told you, she knew she couldn't do this kid's trial herself, no matter what the money involved was. She's about as straight a shooter as they come, as you've often said yourself. So, she's been considering who she could refer it to and I guess you've been such a buddy to her all these years that she chose you."

"Well, it was nice of her to think of me, but she's going to have to find someone else."

"You know that's not going to be easy at this late date. You're not the only lawyer with scheduling problems."

"So, if everybody else gets to beg off because there's not enough time, how come I don't? Why am I so special?"

"Because, Bobby-boy, you *are* special. And that's not only your own opinion, by the way, Lynn thinks so too. She said she wouldn't trust any other lawyer with this file. It seems she already told the kid's mother all about you, told her how you were the Second Coming of the Messiah. Now the mother's just bursting to meet you."

"How the hell do you know the mother's 'just bursting'?"

"Because the lady told me so herself. Her name is Jennifer Campbell, and she was with Lynn when I went to the hospital. She's a very spiritual lady and she had some sort of prayer session going on up there when I showed up. Very concerned for Lynn, she was. And you can be sure now that you're in the picture, she's not planning to sit idly by and miss the Second Coming. Not when her son's the first soul that's gonna be saved. So, Mrs. Campbell will be here to meet you at five-thirty today."

Judge Smythe had his hands full trying to keep the jurors' attention as he gave them his final instructions before they began their deliberations. The twelve citizens seemed to be able to smell the finish line at the end of the grueling marathon, and their only thoughts were to get it over with as fast as possible.

Bratt had difficulty concentrating as well, but this time it wasn't because the dry subject matter bored him. Rather, his mind was on the murder trial that he had never intended to take on. Leblanc only had time to give him the briefest details in preparation for meeting the client's mother, despite Bratt's insistence that he had absolutely no interest in doing so. As it turned out the details were more than enough to pique his interest.

Marlon Small, Leblanc told him, was the oldest son of a hardworking Jamaican immigrant and had never been in trouble with the law before. Now he was accused of two counts of first-degree murder and one count of attempted murder.

The shootings had occurred in a Little Burgundy crack den the previous June 14. This small section of town, barely a few blocks wide and tucked into the southwest corner of the city, contained a mix of immigrant families and blue-collar workers who co-existed uneasily with drug-dealers and street gangs.

Small was alleged to have been one of two gunmen who had gone up to the dingy apartment to steal drugs, but took lives instead. The other gunman was an eighteen-year old named Marcus Paris, who, soon after his arrest, had made a deal to testify against Small in return for being allowed to plead guilty to second degree murder. As a result Paris would be eligible for parole after serving only ten years, with a promise by the Crown of a favorable recommendation. Bratt thought that was a small price to pay for the two dead bodies he'd left behind.

The other main prosecution witness was Dorrell Phillips, the surviving victim of the shooting. He had gone to that apartment looking for his older brother, a longtime junkie who often smoked his crack there. Dorrell had ended up with two bullets to the back of his neck that he had miraculously survived.

He would be called on at trial to identify Small as the man who shot him. His brother, Dexter, and the crack dealer known as Indian had not been as fortunate as Dorrell. Their bodies had been found lying face down on the bloody apartment floor by the late-arriving police.

As much as he had not wanted to get involved with this case, Bratt couldn't stop thinking about it. According to Leblanc, Lynn Sévigny had strongly believed in her client's innocence, despite the seemingly overwhelming evidence. This was what intrigued Bratt the most, because the case against Small seemed almost open and shut. Lynn wasn't one of those softhearted beginners who took everything their clients told them for Gospel, and the possibility that there could be such a strong case against a genuinely innocent man made for a challenge that he thought would be worthy of his skills.

Sitting in the courtroom, half-listening to Smythe explain the jury's duties, Bratt mentally kicked himself at the realization that he was actually considering defending Marlon Small, despite his earlier reticence. A gambler by nature, Bratt could see himself defying the heavy odds and riding the long shot to victory. He also thought the subject matter would be much more appealing than what he had lived through for the past two months. Furthermore, the murder trial was scheduled to last only two weeks, which made it a wind sprint compared to the Hall trial.

He balanced the pros and cons of jumping into the Small case at such a late date. Beyond his mental and physical exhaustion, he wanted to spend some time reconnecting with his daughter. They had grown apart recently, as was evidenced by their recent conflicts. Despite how interested he was in the case, he had all the reasons in the world to pass on it.

Bratt entered the front door of the firm just before 5:30 p.m. and Jennifer Campbell stood up to greet him. She was a petite woman wearing her hair in a short ponytail and his first thought was that she must be Small's sister, not his mother. He guessed that she was seven or eight years younger than himself, which meant that she must have been around sixteen when she had had her son. She had a pretty, but harshly-used face which wore the traces of raising four children, usually alone, and often working two jobs to keep the family clothed and fed. She had a proud nature that he could sense just in the manner that she stood straight and looked him in the eye as he shook her hand.

She had been sitting in the waiting area with Kouri, his unexpected assistant. Bratt was less than thrilled to see the young lawyer there. He wanted to be alone with Mrs. Campbell, especially if it turned out that he was going to have to disappoint her. He didn't want the president of his fan club watching wide-eyed as he tried to weasel his way out of an uncomfortable situation.

"Mrs. Campbell," he greeted her, wearing his serious, but compassionate, look. "I'm so glad you came. I've been wanting to talk to you ever since I heard about your son's case."

She clasped both his hands in hers and looked up at him with reddened eyes. "God bless you, Mr. Bratt, for taking our case," she said, her voice revealing a light Jamaican accent. "I had been despairing about our situation, until I learned that you'd been sent to us like an angel of mercy."

Bratt hadn't been prepared for this effusive greeting and, for a moment, he didn't know what to say. Kouri stood behind her, smiling at him and nodding as if to say, "I bet you weren't ready for that." It took Bratt only a brief moment to recover his composure and retake control of the situation.

"Well now, Mrs. Campbell, I don't think there are many people who would consider me an angel, but maybe they're not as perceptive as you are." He smiled and winked knowingly, as if they were the only two people who were in on a secret joke. Still holding her by the hand he guided her into his office. Kouri followed close behind them, carrying an accordion folder that contained Marlon Small's file.

"Oh, thanks, Peter," said Bratt. "Just leave the file on my desk on your way out."

"Actually, Mr. Bratt, I'd be happy to stay. I already had a chance to go through most of the witnesses' will-say statements. I explained to Mrs. Campbell how you've been overwhelmed with work lately, and I thought I should be ready to brief you on whatever you'll need to know."

"I understand this is a very busy time for you, Mr. Bratt," Mrs. Campbell chimed in. "But your agreeing to take our case anyway, well that tells me you're the kind of man who'll help us with all his heart and soul. When Miss Sévigny got sick I prayed and prayed we'd find someone who'd do whatever has to be done to save my Marlon. She told us that we couldn't be in better hands than with you."

Bratt felt that her words were meant to corner him into taking the case. She obviously had her mind set on retaining him and wasn't going to be easily refused.

"Mrs. Campbell, your confidence in me is very flattering, I'm sure. But before I can make a total commitment to your son's case there are some issues that have to be addressed."

"Have no worries about that, sir. I'm not a rich woman, but I have good and true friends in my congregation, and they're going to see to it that you'll get paid whatever you need to get my boy out of jail."

"Oh, no, you misunderstand," Bratt said, hurriedly. "I wasn't worried about the money."

"Why, that's a very Christian attitude for a lawyer."

Bratt stopped again, unsure if she was joking or being serious. Looking at her open face he finally decided that she was being a bit of both, and he managed a hesitant smile. He was trying to at least look at ease in the conversation, but it was hard to get an accurate reading of the woman. He decided to just push on and let the chips fall where they may.

"As I said, Mrs. Campbell, there are issues to consider. First of all, the time element is very important. There are barely three weeks until your son's trial-"

"Peter, here," she interrupted, pointing at Kouri, "told me that it was a pretty straightforward 'their word against ours' case. Not a lot of complicated points of law to study or anything."

Bratt threw an exasperated look at Kouri, whose expression showed that he wished that he had kept his mouth shut. "Well, I don't want to disagree with such an excellent attorney as, uh, Peter, but I'll still have to go through the whole file very carefully before I could give you my considered opinion. And I'm just finishing up what was a very long, arduous case, you see."

"I'll tell you, I don't know how you can do it, jumping from one big trial to the next like that. I'm surprised you're able to keep your head on straight. Mine would be just spinning like a top."

"Precisely my point."

"But, I guess when you're the best lawyer in the country you do things that the rest of us can't even dream of."

Bratt had to squeeze his jaw shut to keep it from dropping open. She was very obviously laying it on thick to win him over, but that knowledge didn't prevent him from taking a certain pleasure from her flattery.

"Well, that's really very nice of you to say. It's obviously very exaggerated, but you still won't get an argument out of me."

They both laughed, but he could tell that as she laughed she was observing him very closely, measuring his reactions and trying to read his thoughts before saying anything further.

"Mr. Bratt," she said, her tone turning serious, "Marlon is my oldest boy, the one I'm the closest to in age. And I know him like I know my own breath. He isn't living his life the way I want him to. He's still got a lot of growing up to do, but he's not nearly as bad as they're saying.

"Now if you have children, you know what they can do and what they can't. You know what's in their heart just by looking at them. I'm not a very educated woman, but I've seen enough things in my lifetime to trust my own eyes and my own heart. I know this much: my boy's no angel, but he didn't kill anybody. Why those two boys say he did, I don't know. I haven't met them. I haven't looked them in the eyes like I did with my Marlon. I don't know what's in their hearts, except that it isn't the truth.

"Now, Miss Sévigny, she's a fine lady. We took her as Marlon's lawyer because she had already helped out my sister Carmela's boy Anthony when he got mixed up in some bad drug business. I'm sure she would have done her very best for Marlon too, but I don't think her best is as good as your best."

Bratt opened his mouth, feeling that he should at least say something in Lynn's favor, but Mrs. Campbell wouldn't let him interrupt, and she waved him quiet with her hand.

"Please, let me continue. Now, I know that the Lord will always do right by us if we believe in Him, and sometimes we have to find His good in the bad that's happening to someone else. I think that's what happened here with the sickness that Miss Sévigny's got, making it so that we had to look for a new lawyer. And now we've found you and you're going to save my boy, I just know it. I don't like using the word miracle too often, so I'll just say that my prayers have been answered."

Bratt was speechless. He thought of poor Lynn Sévigny and the mutilation that she had undergone, and that was just the beginning of her ordeal. Yet, somehow, this woman was able to rationalize this tragedy into the answer to her prayers, and he found that just a bit scary. There were professional spin-doctors out there who would envy her ability to stand in front of him and say what she said with such a sincere expression on her face.

"Once again, I have to say that I'm very flattered by your kind words. It is somewhat daunting, you'll understand, to have to live up to such high expectations. Even my late wife never told me that I was God's answer to her prayers," he joked feebly. This time he got nothing close to a smile from the woman standing before him, her face wearing a determined expression. His earlier suspicion that she would be hard to refuse was being confirmed.

"Mr. Bratt, please understand that if I speak a bit strongly it's because it's my boy's life I'm talking about. I don't wish no evil on anybody, but if I can save him from the lies that have put him in jail, then that's all I can think of. He is all I care about, all I *can* care about, right now. Do you have children? Do you understand?"

"Yes, of course," he replied, thinking that maybe he should be making his own child his priority. But taking on the role of Marlon Small's savior was going to interfere with his plans to spend more time with Jeannie. Then again, much of his life had been that way. He had long ago accepted the long hours that were necessary to properly defend his clients, and his family life had often paid the price.

When he took on a case it had never mattered whether the clients were truly guilty or not, whether they were scumbags, as Jeannie had pointed out, or the people next door. There could be no half-measures in his world. Now this extremely devout woman was standing before him, ready to swear on her soul that her son was innocent, and she was turning to him for help.

Bratt's body and his mind were tired, but like a reluctant action hero in the movies, he was going to have to ignore his own needs and go back into the burning building: there was one more child to save.

That night, feeling exhausted, Bratt trudged into his apartment at 10 p.m. After Mrs. Campbell had left his office he sent Kouri home with a promise to consult with him after he had read Marlon Small's file. He looked briefly through the evidence and found, as expected, that the case against the young man was strong. There were, however, chinks in even the best-crafted armour and he already had an idea of what he would have to do to exploit the case's weaknesses, although he wasn't ready to tell Mrs. Campbell that there were reasons for optimism yet. And he certainly wasn't about to corroborate what Kouri had told her.

Presumptuous little twerp, he thought. *Who told him to go giving his opinion to clients?*

While Bratt removed his shoe rubbers and topcoat he heard some movement from the direction of Jeannie's room. He thought of calling out to her, but stopped himself, afraid of setting off another shouting match.

The hall leading to their respective bedrooms was dark, but light was streaming out from Jeannie's open door, and there were sounds of movement coming from inside. Stepping into the lit square on the hall carpet, Bratt looked into her room and saw Jeannie, standing with her back to him, handing a folded sweater to a young man that he didn't recognize. The stranger stopped in the middle of packing the sweater into a cardboard box full of other sweaters, and looked up at Bratt. Jeannie paused in what she was doing and followed the man's gaze until her eyes rested on her father.

Several other boxes on the floor, as well as the empty walls and bookshelves, spoke volumes about what was happening. Still, Bratt couldn't stop himself from asking a most obvious question.

"What're you doing?"

Jeannie answered without any hesitation and without a hint of emotion in her voice.

"I'm leaving, Daddy."

Hearing her speak the words he had feared the most shocked him into silence. It didn't even occur to him to ask her where she was going. He couldn't believe that she was taking things so far. This was all over an argument about his job, after all. Surely not enough to break up his family. Not enough to make her suddenly hate him.

He had no idea how things had snowballed so quickly, and to such a melodramatic point. But his pride wouldn't let him show her how her words had affected him. He felt he had to say something, no matter how banal, to hide how shaken he was.

He pointed at the man still standing with her sweater in his hand.

"Who's he?"

"André. He's a friend."

As if the mention of his name had broken a spell, André returned to the packing he had been doing when Bratt showed up. Jeannie, though, continued to face her father. Her expression seemed to soften slightly.

"I don't hate you, you know," she said, as if she had read his mind.

Bratt let out a breath that he didn't know he was holding. "Well, I'm glad to hear that, I guess. Sure had me fooled."

"I'm just seeing things differently right now. I know you don't understand."

"Oh, no, I understand perfectly. I've been doing the same job for close to twenty years, a job that many people, including you once upon a time, considered honorable. A job that thousands of people do each day all over the world. And suddenly I'm a pariah that you can't get away from fast enough. So, yes, it seems that I do understand."

"No, Daddy, that's not it at all. I just need time to think about things and try to understand my own feelings. And maybe you should take a little time to step back and look at what you've done with your life too. A little introspection might actually do you some good."

His mouth opened and then shut again. The last thing he had expected or needed that day was to have his eighteen-year-old daughter suggest he try "a little introspection." He was fed up with her youthful insolence.

"Jesus Christ! Do you think *you're* going to judge my life now?"

She shook her head slowly and looked toward André for support. André clearly knew better than to return her look. He just kept on emptying a drawer full of underwear, not wanting any part of this family argument.

She turned back to her father, and softly asked, "How did court go today?"

"What?"

"How did court go?" she repeated, her voice calm but sad.

"If you really want to know, it went quite well…once I got over the little scene you made in the back room."

"Final arguments for Cooper Hall, wasn't it?"

"Yes, it was."

She paused before speaking again, a pensive look on her face, and brought the tips of the index and middle fingers of her right hand up to her lips. Bratt knew that this was how she looked when she was trying to organize her thoughts, putting together her own final arguments.

Softly, she asked him, "He never testified, right?"

"No, I told you about that."

"Probably because he would have lied if he had."

"Yes, that's right," Bratt said, enthusiastically, grasping at the opportunity to bring up his own honesty, while not even paying lip-service to client-attorney privilege. "I told him I wouldn't let him lie on the stand. I could win this case without his lies."

"So what did you plead to the jury? That they shouldn't believe the Crown's witnesses? That they weren't trustworthy?"

"Yes, of course. Their testimony just didn't stand up under cross-examination, so there was no way the jury could find them credible."

"You made sure of that, didn't you?"

"Damn right, I did. I know how to protect my client's rights."

"Yes, your client's rights," she dryly repeated his words. "So you told the jury they shouldn't believe a word these people said, even though you knew the witnesses were telling the truth. You wouldn't let your client lie about what happened, so instead you lied for him."

"What're you talking about? I'm supposed to challenge their testimony, dammit! Why is that so hard for you to understand?"

"Because for you 'challenging their testimony' means tearing apart perfectly honest witnesses. You make them out to be liars, when you know they're not. You make them look like fools on the stand and you humiliate them. Just like what your little lawyer buddy did to Claire."

The mention of what had happened to Claire Brockway was like a slap in Bratt's face. How dare Jeannie compare how he did his job to what Claire had experienced? It wasn't the same thing, wasn't even close. For one thing, he didn't give a shit about the witnesses who had testified against Hall. He hadn't seen them grow up. They hadn't been as much a part of his family as his own daughter. They didn't matter a damn bit to him, but Claire did and that was all the difference in the world. If Jeannie couldn't see that, he wouldn't waste any more time arguing with her. There was nothing more for him to say.

He turned on his heels and headed for his own bedroom, leaving her where she stood. He was angry at the thought of how his day had been full of high points that kept getting abruptly cut short by Jeannie's misdirected attacks. Mostly, though, he was angry with himself for not being able to come up with answers to her accusations.

What am I letting her get away with all this shit for? he asked himself. *I haven't felt at such a loss for words since first year Moot Court. She hits me with a bunch of feeble, adolescent arguments she probably got from one of her brain-dead humanities teachers, and I can't even stand up for myself. Screw it! If she wants to go off and sulk then let her. But she better not come running back to Daddy anytime soon.*

At 8 a.m. on Friday morning the bright winter sun was shining through Bratt's un-shaded bedroom window. He had been awake for nearly two hours, but hadn't yet left his room. He looked out the window while still seated on the edge of his bed, a sense of deja vu coming over him. Lately he seemed to be spending a lot of time staring out of windows, mentally replaying scenes of the confrontations he kept having with Jeannie.

Down on the snow-covered trails of Mount Royal a lone jogger was braving the biting cold. The jogger's breath appeared in regular puffs of condensation through the opening of a ski mask. *It must be 20 below,* Bratt thought. *Health nut!*

He let out a soft sigh and his eyes turned to the framed picture on his night table: Jeannie at age three, sitting on her mother's lap. Fifteen years later she was still as precious to him as ever, despite the feelings of anger and frustration she inspired in him, seemingly at will.

He hadn't gone out of his room yet because he didn't want to pass her open bedroom door again. He couldn't bear to see how empty her room had become. She had taken everything with her: old stuffed toys from her childhood, posters of rock stars and teen actors, her clothes, her books. Just her and this "friend" of hers, André.

Who the hell is André, and how come I never heard of him before?

His eyes moved to his wife's face in the picture, but he looked away quickly, feeling ashamed. He peered back out at the mountain, then let his gaze move up, past the forest trails, to the cemetery where Deirdre was buried. What would she think of him now? Wasn't doing much of a job looking after their daughter, was he?

He had raised Jeannie alone for the past eight years, and had been better at it than many people had expected. Now, over something that was beyond his control, but which was bothering him more than he cared to admit, she had turned away from him.

Last night, for the first time since she was born, he had no idea where his daughter had slept. He had thought to call some of her friends, but then decided not to. He couldn't face the possibility that they might lie to him, at her request, about her whereabouts. The most likely place for her to go, the place where she spent nearly as much time as her own home, was at Claire's and he wasn't about to call there. What in the world could he say to Claire now?

Testifying in that trial had nearly destroyed her. But what was he supposed to do, start hating himself and his job because someone he was close to had gotten hurt? What good would that do now? He had refused to take on Nate Morris's defense specifically because the case had involved Claire, and God knew Morris had paid him well in the past. So, why should he feel guilty about the job the other lawyer had done on her?

Teenagers could allow themselves to be impetuous and to change the paths they had chosen at the drop of a hat. That kind of knee-jerk reaction to everything going on in the world was a luxury that he could not afford.

He fell back in his bed, bare feet still on the floor, and stared up at the ceiling. He tried to clear his mind, concentrating on a small crack in the off-white paint above him, but to no avail.

"Dammit, I gotta be in court in an hour," he said aloud, but there was nobody in the apartment to answer him. There were only his thoughts, and these had become quite repetitive since 6 a.m.

Strange thing about self-pity, he thought. *It never seemed to get boring.*

The rest of the day seemed to go by in slow motion. As Bratt fretted about his daughter's whereabouts, Judge Smythe wrapped up his instructions to the jurors, who then went off to deliberate on the fate of Cooper Hall. Bratt left Hall sitting on a bench outside the courtroom, and wandered the courthouse corridors alone while waiting for the verdict to come in.

He never could stand being in his client's presence for too long, and often had the urge to check if his wallet was still there when he and Hall would part company, such was the effect the shifty con artist had even on him.

As for Nancy Morin, she waited for the verdict with Brenton and the others on his team in the Crown's offices. That was just as well, Bratt decided, since he was in no mood for playing verbal footsy with her just then.

As he slowly shuffled from floor to floor, a Styrofoam coffee cup in his hand, he did his best to avoid crossing paths with any of his colleagues or professional rivals who might have been at court. He dreaded the idea of idle chitchat with his fellow attorneys, or worse, having to talk about his family life. Today he preferred keeping his own company and observing everyone else from the distance that he felt separated him from the world.

As time dragged itself forward he sat down and watched the constant movement of the volume lawyers, those whose careers were spent fast-tracking most of the thousands of cases that crowded the court's dockets each year. They rushed with stacks of case-files under their arms, running from a hastily-prepared trial to an arraignment, to a preliminary inquiry or two, all in the same morning.

He watched a pair of teen-age girls, hardly older than Jeannie, chasing down the corridor after their infants. They were probably waiting for word of whether their boyfriends had gotten bail, or had copped pleas to avoid jail time, or had somehow managed to get themselves acquitted, on those rare occasions when their Legal Aid lawyers had bothered to go through with trials.

Watching these people, the lifeblood of the courthouse being pumped back and forth through its corridors, he felt nothing, neither common bond nor dislike. There was only an ever-growing wall going up around him.

At 12:30 p.m. the jurors were brought their lunches in the jury room, and their deliberations were suspended until two. He was free to return to his office if he wanted to, maybe do some paper work or swap war stories with John or J.P. for a while.

He sat on a bench at the end of a courthouse corridor and tried to muster up the will to go back to his office. But human contact held very little attraction for him just then. He sat alone in his corner and spoke to nobody until the lunch break was over.

A few minutes before 8:00 that evening the jurors came back with a verdict acquitting Cooper Hall on all the fraud and forged document charges. Brenton's face had fallen at the verdict, convinced as he always was that right had been on his side. Nancy looked toward Bratt and gave a little shrug, as if to say *que sera, sera*. They had other things on their minds, after all.

As for Hall, he was nearly overwhelmed with relief, and he burst into tears of gratitude. He ran up to his lawyer and threw his arms around his neck, letting out little woo-hoos of joy between his sobs.

Bratt stood unmoved while his client hugged him. He had no feelings of his own about what had just happened. He had won a complicated and torturously long trial, yet he felt no sense of accomplishment. Neither feelings of relief nor joy had washed over him at the verdict, which he had barely listened to.

His thoughts had been on Jeannie, and now they were tinged with bitterness. With her simple act of rebellion she had managed to rob him of one of the purest pleasures of his profession: the feeling of anticipation before a verdict is read out, followed by the exultation of victory.

Now the verdict held little meaning for him, and he had Jeannie to thank for that. This time she hadn't even needed to be in the same room: she still managed to bring him down from what should have been the high point of his day.

The taxi ride home seemed too short. His workweek was over, but he wasn't ready to go back to his empty apartment. He had no place else to go, though, and for once, he regretted not having asked Kalouderis which bar he would be closing that night.

He didn't bother turning on the lights as he entered his home; he knew his way around well enough, and the dark certainly suited his mood. As he undressed in his bedroom he noticed a tiny red light flashing from the direction of his night table. He walked over, turned the table lamp on and saw that he had two messages showing on his answering machine.

For a moment he considered ignoring them, but then thought that one might be from Jeannie. He sat on the edge of his bed and pressed play, only to be greeted by the sound of his partner's wheezing voice.

"Hey, Bobby-boy. Didja get the verdict yet? I hope you didn't go and blow this case. Think of what that would do to office morale, eh. Anyway, I hope the verdict did come in, so you'd be free tomorrow. Pete-," and for a moment Bratt couldn't remember who Pete was, "-is going up to R.D.P. to meet Small. I gave him the OK on that, in case you're wondering, because time is obviously of the essence, as they say.

"So, maybe tomorrow would be a good opportunity for you to go up and meet the client too. I know you're probably going to be out late celebrating this latest triumph of your glorious career, or whatever, but try to drag yourself out of bed in the morning and go up there with Kouri. Congrats again. You did win, didn't you? Bye."

Bratt's blood had begun boiling from the second he heard Leblanc's voice and was turning to steam by the time the message had ended. He couldn't believe that his partner had the gall to ask him to jump into the Small file without even taking a few days off to recover from the previous trial, as well as from the emotional roller coaster of the past week. He also had no interest in spending his Saturday morning with a rookie lawyer at the detention center. He considered phoning Leblanc and telling him off, when his thoughts were interrupted by the sound of a woman's voice that he had never heard on his machine before.

"*Allô, Maître Bratt. C'est sergent-détective Morin. Ah, merde.* You know: Nancy. Your favorite cop. At least, I like to think so. Sorry I couldn't speak to you after the verdict today, but I think Brenton would have had me kicked off the force if he saw me getting all chummy with you at that point. Besides, you don't really need me to tell you what a great job you did in court, not that I think your client shouldn't be in jail right now. But, hey, that's showbiz.

"Anyhow, you may not have realized this, what with this trial obviously preoccupying you so much, but I've gotten used to seeing a lot of you recently. I hope I don't sound too pushy or overconfident. See what happens when they put a big gun in a woman's hands?"

A light, disembodied laugh sounded from the speaker, and it occurred to Bratt that she might have taken a drink or two before calling him.

"So, I hope you have no plans for tomorrow night because I thought we could get together for dinner or whatever. We were interrupted in our little chat the other day and I think we should finish what we began, don't you?

"I hope you didn't lose my number. *Bonne nuit, Robert.*"

So much for being angry with Leblanc. His earlier thoughts about his partner had disappeared at the first sound of Nancy's voice. Bratt lay back on his bed and looked up at the ceiling, much as he had done that morning, but this time he was in a much better frame of mind. Nancy, he was happy to see, was not a woman who wasted time beating around the bush. She certainly wasn't someone who would let him waste a lot of time on self-pity either.

He decided it was time to forget about the little problems that had haunted him the previous week. He had, after all, just won another seemingly unwinnable case and tomorrow he'd be off to meet the client for his next one. As for Jeannie, she was still just a child and, like most children, she tended to over-react. She'd be back to her senses and home soon enough. And tomorrow night he would finally be able to do something about the courthouse flirtation he had carried on for the past two months.

He reached over and slid out the top drawer of his night table. From inside it he pulled out Nancy's business card, handed to him in a very open and professional manner some three weeks into the trial. Her home number had been hastily written in sharp, bold strokes on the back. That was Nancy all over: sharp and bold.

That was also how he had always thought of himself, at least until his recent bout with sensitivity. But the sensitive male, who knew how to cry and was in touch with his inner child, was definitely not his style. He was quite sure that that wasn't what had caught Nancy's attention either. That guy had snuck out from whatever closet Bratt kept him hidden in over the years and took him by surprise. Now he was going back into the deepest, darkest hole that Bratt could find to bury him in, hopefully for good.

Chapter 4

At 7:15 a.m. the ringing phone woke Bratt up with a start. Peter Kouri was calling to see if his hero was ready to embark on their latest quest.

"Morning, Mr. Bratt. Hope I'm not calling too early."

Bratt thought it would always be too early when Kouri called, but kept his comment to himself.

"Not at all, Pete. It's always a pleasure," he lied, stretching and yawning loudly. "I hear you're going up to R.D.P. today."

"Yes, that's right. Mr. Leblanc said you'd want to come up too, especially if you got your verdict last night. And there's the great news, right in this morning's paper."

"I'll be sure to read all about it."

"So, I was just going to say…um, about going up to see Small today…I'm going to need a lift."

A lift? It was bad enough he was expected to nursemaid the kid, but he didn't think he had to play chauffeur for him too.

Perhaps sensing Bratt's hesitation, Kouri continued, explaining himself. "Um, I really don't know the way up there very well. But, you won't have to go out of your way much. I live in Rosemont, just off the highway. Besides, I think it would be a good chance for us to talk…about the case, I mean. Sort of compare ideas."

Bratt winced at the thought. He knew that Kouri meant well enough, but there was something about the young lawyer's over-enthusiasm that had grated on his nerves from their first meeting and continued to do so.

There was no way to avoid the drive up with Kouri, it seemed, but he wasn't going to be rushed into it. If Kouri meant to compare ideas about the Small case, then Bratt was going to have to take his time this morning and try to develop some of his own, or risk looking unprepared in front of his assistant. And that would never do.

But, first, there was the more pressing matter of a long-delayed phone call that he'd been waiting all night to make.

Nancy Morin answered the phone on the first ring and, in her bright, quick voice, said, "*Allô, Robert*."

Bratt hoped that she had call-display on her phone, and not that he was that predictable.

"Good morning, Nancy. Did I wake you?"

"No, I just came in from my jog. It helped to clear my mind after that long trial."

"I hope you weren't trying to forget everything about the past two months."

"Not *everything*, as I'm sure you gathered from my message."

"Oh, that. Well, it was a bit ambiguous."

Morin laughed, that light, knowing laugh he'd gotten so used to. "OK, so maybe I was pretty straight-forward. No crime in that, is there?"

"Not in the least. Actually, since you don't like wasting time on small-talk, I'd like to discuss some plans for tonight with you."

"Great. Discuss away."

"As it so happens, I have to go to a wedding reception, one of those big Italian events. And, believe it or not, I don't have a date for the event."

"No-o," she answered, in mock disbelief. "How did that happen?"

"Actually, I wasn't planning on doing more than making a brief appearance there. These are old, uh, friends, of mine. I don't usually like big parties, but I felt I had to go. So, my original plan was just to pop in, stay for half a dozen courses or so, then take off. It's not exactly an intimate little evening, but it certainly could end up that way."

"This normally wouldn't be my choice for a first date, but I actually like big Italian weddings. I mean, pizza at midnight, and a band in tuxedoes playing old disco tunes. What else could a girl ask for? What time will you pick me up?"

Bratt hated taking his car out in the winter. It was a 1961 Jaguar XKE sports coupe, one of the first sold in North America, and it was in mint condition. He'd had it since the late 80's and he babied it like he had babied Jeannie in the first few years of her life. But the *Rivière des Prairies* Detention Center wasn't exactly a short taxi ride away from his downtown apartment building, and he felt like showing it off today anyway.

He drove up to the address that Kouri had given him at a bit before 11 a.m. It was a street lined with tall leafless trees, in front of block after block of pink and white duplexes. Kouri was standing in the street, carrying the accordion folder that was stuffed with the Small file, when Bratt pulled up with a dramatic roar of his engine.

The drive up to the Detention Center, hidden away on the northeast edge of the island of Montreal, was ugly and monotonous, a long stretch of highway, past oil refineries and industrial parks, taking them to the middle of nowhere. They passed the occasional evergreen tree struggling to survive in the poison-aired environment. Bratt's good mood, however, was not in any way affected by the bleak surroundings.

Speaking to Nancy that morning had left him feeling positively chipper, so much so that he was even willing to make small talk with Kouri, who had seemed somewhat ill at ease upon entering his car and not in such a hurry to compare ideas after all.

As they rolled smoothly down the near-empty road, the bright sunshine feeling warm on their faces, he broke the ice by asking Kouri what had gotten him interested in criminal law.

"More than any other influence, I'd have to say it was the movies," said Kouri. "The lawyers' lives always seemed so exciting. At the same time they always managed to help out people in trouble."

"Yeah, movies and TV can make our jobs out to be pretty glamourous, but what they show you isn't always reality," Bratt said, never having cared much for Hollywood's portrayals of lawyers.

"Yes, but I still enjoyed them. And the lawyers in them were the kinds of lawyers I always wanted to be like. And, to tell you the truth, Mr. Bratt, you are too."

Bratt blushed at the at the compliment, but said nothing. Once again he felt embarrassed at Kouri's open admiration for him. It was one thing to go around telling everybody how great you were. It was another thing to find somebody who actually believed you.

They drove on silently and soon they saw on their left the large estate that held Pinel, the Institute for the Criminally Insane, letting them know that their own destination was only a few blocks further on. They reached the entrance of the detention center and Bratt turned his car into the long driveway, slowing down as he spotted a police cruiser parked in front of the visitors' parking lot.

"You got your Bar card with you, Peter?"

"Yes, sure. Why?"

"'Cause this guy doesn't know you, and he won't even let us park if he has any doubts about who you are."

Bratt pulled up next to the police car on the driver's side and lowered his window, pulling back from the draft of cold air. The *Sureté de Québec* agent lowered his own window. He wore his standard issue fur hat, with its flaps down over his ears. Bratt recognized him as being the lucky stiff who seemed to always get this patrol, and waved his own Bar card casually past the window, fully expecting the policeman to recognize him instantly. The agent, though, was staring straight past him and at Kouri, who was holding his card out toward him, in front of Bratt's face. The agent reached his gloved hand out and Bratt took Kouri's card and handed it to him. Glove, hand and card disappeared back through the window, which was quickly closed while the policeman punched Kouri's name onto his computer.

"Why'd he take mine?" Kouri asked, his voice betraying his concern.

"You're a new face. They've been pretty jittery up here since that transport bus got shot up, and now they're extra careful if they don't know you."

Kouri leaned forward in his seat to see what the SQ officer was doing, and received a suspicious glare over the walkie-talkie the cop was talking into in reply.

"Geez. He's looking at me like he's ready to throw me in jail."

Sensing some nervousness in the younger lawyer's voice, Bratt couldn't resist having some fun at his expense. Noting Kouri's Mediterranean features, he smiled sarcastically.

"It's not his fault you look like a terrorist."

"Hey! What the hell's that supposed to mean?"

Kouri's angry tone surprised Bratt, who never would have expected his young idolizer to take exception to anything he said. With the ethnic and linguistic mix in his office, Bratt was used to all sorts of slurs and epithets being flung around at will, with nobody ever feeling aggrieved. He looked at Kouri's firmly set chin and pursed lips and burst out laughing.

He laughed so loud that the SQ agent looked suspiciously in their direction through the frost-covered window, and seeing this only made Bratt laugh harder still. Kouri must have begun to feel silly, looking and feeling furious while Bratt was so obviously enjoying himself, because his angry expression faded away until he looked merely confused and somewhat embarrassed.

Bratt's laughter finally died down, and he wiped the tears from his eyes with his sleeve, then looked over sympathetically at Kouri. He shook his head in wonderment and patted Kouri's face with the palm of his right hand.

"God, you're cute when you're angry," he said. At that point the police car window was lowered and Kouri's ID card was wordlessly handed back, the cop looking at them as if they were more crazy than dangerous. *"Merci beaucoup,"* Bratt called out to him, with a big smile and a wave, then drove toward the nearest parking spot.

Kouri took his card back from him without a word, looking as if he knew that there was a joke somewhere that he had just missed.

Once the car was parked they disembarked and set out on foot across the snow-covered parking lot. They had to wait for a sliding gate to open, allowing them passage through the barbed wire fence that surrounded the compound, then waited again to be buzzed through a door into the main building. Overhead, cameras were aimed unmoving at the spot where they stood and waited.

Since this facility had opened half a dozen years earlier, security had always been strict. But once the biker gang wars of recent years began including police officers and prison guards among their victims, security had been tightened even further.

Bratt explained all this to Kouri just before they passed through the steel and glass door to the reception area. Inside, they would have to empty their pockets and open their briefcases before passing through a metal detector. Bratt recalled a time when lawyers were not searched at all, and were allowed to pass ahead of other visitors. But the violence brought on by the motorcycle gang wars had brought such casual practices to a screeching halt.

After going through all the required security procedures, they finally found themselves ensconced in an four by twelve foot interview room that had been divided in two by a low cement wall, topped by a glass partition. Attorneys and clients had to sit on each side of the partition and speak through a thick web of metal wires and bars running along the bottom of the glass. The web muffled and distorted their voices to the point that the contents of all conversations were easily kept confidential, not only from any prying ears, but from the participants themselves.

They sat and waited. Bratt knew that the guards often took as long as they could to bring prisoners down to speak to their lawyers, so he sat back and tried to get comfortable on his thinly padded chair. Kouri stood, squeezed in behind him and looking nervous. He would have paced had there been room enough for it.

"What's up, kid? You're not still mad at me, are you?"

"What? Oh, no. I guess I overreacted before. It's just that this is the first murderer I've ever met."

"Let's not go hanging him just yet."

"You know what I mean. The first guy *accused* of anything so serious. This is the real thing. With the Federal Crown I spent six months working on black market cigarettes, for crying out loud. That's why I couldn't wait to get out of there. I wanted to be a real criminal lawyer, and now that it's really happening I feel a little lost."

"Don't worry about it, Pete," Bratt said, trying to sound paternal. "A very wise man once told me that it would take me two or three years before I really felt like a lawyer. Until then, I'd always feel like I was just faking it and hoping nobody would find out."

"Yeah, that sounds about how I feel right now. Who was that wise man?"

"He was my dad."

"The late Judge Joseph Bratt?"

"Geez, you really do know my life," Bratt laughed.

"We studied several of his rulings back in Criminal Procedure. He was quite a respected judge, of course. You must have been very proud of him."

Bratt grimaced inwardly, regretting that he had mentioned his father. He had once been proud of the man, of course, until the newly-minted judge left Bratt's mother for his much younger secretary. All these years later talking about him was still difficult.

"With a dad like that, no wonder you became a lawyer too."

"How about your dad?" Bratt asked, turning the topic away from his relationship with his own father. "Was he in law?"

"Oh, no. He was just a tailor in Damascus. I'm the first university graduate in the family."

Their small talk was interrupted by the opening of the cell door on the other side of the glass partition. They looked up as Marlon Small sauntered in.

He wore a red bandana tied over his shaved head. He had a gold loop in his left ear and a toothpick in his mouth, which he sucked on noisily. The top of his baggy jeans barely reached the bottom edge of his buttocks, and his torn, sleeveless basketball jersey exposed a series of explicit tattoos on his wiry arms.

Bratt thought that as much as Jennifer Campbell could have

been the poster child for decent, hard-working people, her son had chosen to play the role of a bum, copping a hard-case attitude to cover up for his own probable lack of character. His clothes, his walk, everything about him seemed to be ripped off from some stereotypical depiction of what a street gang member should look like. Small sat down across from them, eyeing his new lawyers with a look of suspicious hostility.

"Mr. Small," Bratt began, smiling his smoothest, silkiest smile, "I'm Robert Bratt, and this is Peter Kouri. We're your new lawyers."

Small just kept on eyeing them and sucking on his toothpick. Finally, he deigned to speak. "Is she dead yet?"

"Uh, is who dead yet?" Bratt responded.

"Lady lawyer; *Seven-yee*. She dead yet?"

"Oh, Miss Sévigny. No, she's not. As a matter of fact, the doctors are pretty optimistic that she'll make a full recovery."

"No shit? She look pretty lousy last time I seen her."

"Well, she's better now. I'm sure she'll be touched by your concern-"

"My concern," Small said, his tone getting louder as he brought his face closer to the glass partition, "is that my ass is in jail, an' I was depending on her to get me out. Now I get you two jokers showing up, saying you're my new lawyers, an' my trial's in less than a month."

"And I'd be pretty worried if I were in your shoes too, Marlon. But we're not here to waste your time or ours-"

"Your time's paid, man, so you're not the one wasting time here."

"What I meant to say is that we're working hard to be ready for your trial in time, so I don't think you have to be worried about new lawyers getting into the file at the last minute, and all that. I explained to your mother that the time constraints would not make our job any easier, but that it was certainly doable."

"Doable don't cut no ice with me. It's winnable I wanna hear about. My momma said you're the best fuckin' lawyer in the world. If you're really that good I wanna hear what you're gonna do for me."

"Your mother actually said that, did she?"

"Those exact words."

"Okay then, let's talk about how we're going to defend you. You told the cops you were in LaSalle the night of the shooting, playing basketball with some friends at Wilfort Park. Now I have some of the names of these friends of yours, but there's only a couple of pager numbers in the file. We've tried them without success so far."

"Yeah, they won't call you back if you don't put the code. They'll think it's just the cops trying to catch them selling weed."

"Your friends traffic in marijuana, do they?"

"Just helping out some friends and neighbors, you know. Everybody smokes pot, nowadays. No big thing."

"No big thing? Okay, we'll worry about that later. What's this code we're supposed to put on their pagers?"

"First time you call you put 007. Then you call again an' put your own number."

"Double-oh seven, eh? That's clever."

"Hey, James Bond, man. That's as cool as you can get an' still be white."

"Ok, we'll use your code. Now, the pager numbers were next to only two names, Ashley Parker and Bernard Clayton, and it seems that Sévigny never got a chance to get their statements."

"Yeah, they weren't always available when she wanted to meet them; but I put the word out that if my lawyer calls they better show up, 'cause time is short. Ash's my little cousin, an' I drove him home about midnight the night those dudes got shot. Bernard was with us in the car too. But when you call him, don't say Bernard. He doesn't like that name. Call him Shoot."

"Shoot?"

"Yeah, short for Shoot to Kill. That's his street name."

"Well, isn't that lovely," Bratt said. He was tempted to ask if Bernard had earned that nickname honestly, but decided to let it pass for now. "Do you have a street name too, by the way?"

"Yeah, they call me Brando, 'cause my name's Marlon. On the outside, I'm just Brando."

"Brando's a bit…uh, old-fashioned, isn't it? For a street-name, I mean."

"Nah. We like doin' things old school, is all."

"Fine. Whatever. If you don't mind we'll stick to real names in court. I wouldn't feel too optimistic if our main alibi witness was sworn in as Shoot to Kill. We'll page them both today and see if we can't meet them tomorrow."

"Ooh, you're working on Sunday. Don't let my mother find out," Small said with a sarcastic grin.

"Well, I'm sure she'd understand that we've got very little time to waste, especially considering what's at stake for you."

"Yeah. She does love me, though, don't she?"

Bratt looked at Small, who was sporting a self-satisfied smirk around the toothpick, and thought to himself, *a face that only a mother could love*. But then, such was the fate of all parents.

"OK, there's something else I wanted to ask you about. The Crown's going to file into evidence a video of your police interrogation. Somehow, in getting the file from Sévigny, it's been misplaced, and I won't get to see another copy for a couple of days."

"So, what's the problem? It's not like I confessed or anything."

"That's exactly what has me worried. Prosecutors don't usually put anything into evidence unless they think it's going to help them. Since you didn't admit your guilt to the cops I can't help but wonder just exactly what there is on it that can hurt you."

"Like I said, I didn't admit anything. I just told them I was in the park. That fat detective kept asking me over an' over why I shot those guys, an' I just kept on denying it. There's nothing else on the tape, so don't worry about it."

"Like *I* said, the prosecutor knows what he's doing. So, we'll wait and see before deciding what we should worry about."

"Suit yourself. You're the lawyer."

"I'd also like you to tell me about Marcus Paris. He used to be a good buddy of yours."

Small jumped up, suddenly enraged, and slammed the glass partition with the palm of his right hand.

"That bitch! He's lucky I'm locked up in here or I really *would* be guilty of murder."

Kouri jumped back in surprise at this unexpected display of anger, but Bratt managed to keep a poker face.

"So, I gather you're not buddies any more," he noted dryly.

"Damn right! He's selling me out just to save his own ass. You know that. Once the cops got that fool Dorrell to pick out my picture, Marcus just went along with 'em. He'd say his mother shot 'em if it got him out of jail early."

"I don't blame you for being angry, Marlon, but we have to take his testimony seriously. You've got to understand that someone who's been friends with you since he was a little kid is going to be carefully listened to by the jury. Especially since he's admitting he was in on the shooting."

"Well, that's why my mother's paying you, isn't it? So that the damn jury doesn't listen to him."

"Listen, I'm a pretty good lawyer, but I don't have time to investigate Paris's whole life. It would be very helpful if you could tell me a bit about him, and especially what issues there may be between you two."

"*Issues*!" Small's mouth opened into a big grin, revealing a large gap between his crooked lower teeth. "The only *issues* we got is that his kid sister, Karen, is my baby-mother, an' he hasn't learned to accept that."

"His *kid* sister? How old would that make Karen now?"

"Just turned sixteen. Saundra, that's my baby, is gonna be a year old on Valentine's Day. An' Marcus just couldn't get around the fact that I made his little sister my woman. If you wanna know why he's so ready to fuck me over, you got a reason right there. That enough of an issue for you?"

Bratt had to admit that this was a pretty fair reason for Paris to hold a grudge against Small, although it meant telling the jury that his client had gotten a fifeen year-old pregnant. But if it was presented the right way, along with the fact that Paris was saving himself at least fifteen years in a penitentiary, the jury could be made to see that the accomplice had all the necessary motivation to lie under oath.

As he sat and looked at Small, though, Bratt couldn't muster up an ounce of sympathy for his new client. He had to admit that between Small's sarcasm and his badass attitude, he simply didn't like the young man. Maybe his not liking him was coloring Bratt's thinking, but he also doubted that Paris was lying about Small's involvement in the murders.

He shook his head. He knew that this kind of thinking would lead him nowhere. It wasn't his job to like, or to judge, Marlon Small. Objectively speaking, he knew there was ample room for a doubt about his guilt, and his job was to lead the jury to that doubt. They wouldn't be able to convict Small if they only got as far as deciding that he *probably* killed those men. People weren't sent to jail just on probabilities.

He did his best to wrap up the discussion with Small as fast as possible, explaining what had to be done over the next few days and promising a return visit to update his client later in the week. Small seemed to have lost most of his interest in the conversation after venting his feelings about Marcus Paris, and hardly paid attention to what Bratt was saying, so getting out of there and back on the road was easily done.

Once in the car and heading for the highway, Bratt turned to ask Kouri his impression.

"Well, it was really something," Kouri opined. "It's amazing how the cards seem to be stacked against this poor guy, but it just goes to show you how far the cops are willing to go to get a conviction."

Bratt kept his eyes fixed on the road in order to avoid staring at Kouri, who seemed to be talking about a very different client. There was little doubt in Bratt's mind that he wasn't going to be fighting for some pathetic, unjustly accused soul. He had developed some fairly reliable instincts over the years, and they told him that the cops didn't have to go far out of their way to gather evidence of Marlon Small's guilt.

The Buffet Dolce Vita was in a quiet, middle-class and mostly Italian neighborhood in the eastern suburb of St. Leonard. Bratt looked up at the long white columns fronting the building and the marble lions standing at attention alongside the entrance. He thought this was one of the few neighborhoods on the Island of

Montreal where this building wouldn't stand out like a sore thumb.

He drove his Jaguar up the long circular driveway and stopped, waiting his turn while a tuxedoed valet took the keys of a 1983 Cadillac Eldorado that was as shiny as the day it had rolled off the lot. The car's driver, a short, hugely fat man in a long suede coat with a fur collar, slipped the valet some cash for extra care, then escorted an equally fat woman, with blue hair curled high over her head, through the large glass doors of the building.

Bratt turned his eyes away from the woman to look at Nancy in the passenger seat next to him. She would definitely look better than most of the women they would see that evening, and this gave him a sense of security and triumph.

He was glad that for this evening they had agreed to be just a normal couple and put their respective professions aside. Bratt had admitted to previously defending the groom, although he didn't tell Nancy the charges, but tonight this was supposed to make no difference. There would be no cops and robber talk at the table.

As beautiful as she looked right now, Bratt could hardly believe that she was a police detective. Surely nobody else at the reception would either. Under her lambskin winter coat she wore a straight, black, sleeveless gown that showed off her well-formed arms and neck and most of her back. The slit reaching halfway up her thigh reminded him that she had legs worth showing off too.

Bratt thought that he looked quite good when he had finished dressing earlier that evening. When Nancy greeted him at the door of her apartment he knew that he had more than met his match. At that moment his heart had begun beating like a teenager going to his graduation dance, and, instead of coming up with anything clever to say, all he could do was stand there with a dumb grin on his face. The look in Nancy's eyes told him that if there was ever any self-doubt in her mind, it had just disappeared. She knew he was a beaten man.

The valet approached the Jaguar and held the door open for her. He looked impressed both with Bratt's car as well as his date. Nancy slipped her hand through Bratt's arm as they headed for the entrance. She looked up at his satisfied face and asked him, "Which one of us are you showing off?"

He laughed with unabashed glee.

Inside the building they found themselves in a large foyer, filled with sofas and leafy potted plants. Several guests were in line at one of two cloakrooms at the rear of the room and they joined them.

Once rid of their winter outerwear they headed for the large, circular staircase leading up to the main hall. Chandeliers glistened over their heads and the lights reflected brightly in ceiling-high mirrors lining the staircase. Bratt had ample opportunity to admire the handsome couple they made as they walked up the stairs, mentally comparing himself and Nancy to the other guests.

At the door to the main hall there was a large rectangular table with name cards spread across it in alphabetical order. Guests were slowly filing in, many of them sipping from punch glasses as they waited their turn. A tall, heavy-set man with a face like a boxer stood taking people's names and methodically finding them their cards. Nancy looked at him for several seconds, trying to remember where she had seen him before, then followed Bratt inside the hall. Once through the door they found themselves in the hands of one of several young ushers who were efficiently weaving their way in and out of the lavishly-decorated tables, leading the wedding guests to their appointed seats.

They had arrived at the reception after the cocktails, and most guests were already seated, awaiting the arrival of the wedding party. Their table was in the middle echelon, not as far back as company employees or neighbors, but not quite up with the cousins and childhood friends. The hall itself was impressively large, easily holding over four hundred guests, with room to spare.

Nancy looked around, wide-eyed, at the well-dressed crowd. Low-cut gowns and heavy make-up were the order of the day for most of the women, some of whom were well into their golden years. Girls in their early teens wore the latest designer dresses, with hairstyles that had taken them all morning to get done and probably cost a small fortune. The older men were all in black tuxedos, the younger men in Armani and Boss suits.

Nancy leaned over to Bratt and whispered, "Somebody here must have hit a Brinks truck."

"Now, now. Don't go making any slanderous remarks. Besides, we're both supposed to be off-duty tonight."

"Sorry. I couldn't help noticing that everybody in this place is dressed very expensively. Some of the weddings I've been to there were more jeans than tuxedos."

"Not with this family. Weddings are a big thing for them. I'm sure a lot of people blew their budgets just trying to outdo each other."

"Now I regret not having gone to the church too. They must have had a beautiful ceremony."

Bratt looked at her with a bit of surprise. "I didn't think you'd go for that kind of thing: the bride in white, choirs singing and all that."

She smiled back at him. "That goes to show how little you know me, Mr. Bratt. I'm just an old-fashioned romantic at heart."

As she spoke there was a sudden rush of movement near the entrance to the hall, and several photographers and a cameraman appeared, trying to make themselves some space in the crowd. The wedding party had arrived.

On the stage, the band stopped playing and the master of ceremonies took the microphone. He began talking effusively in Italian, and Bratt, not understanding a word that was being said, thought that he had never heard Italian spoken any other way. The crowd seemed to be enjoying whatever he said, and laughed and clapped frequently.

Nancy smiled too, clearly enjoying the extravagance of the whole production. Bratt looked at her and imagined her as a young teen, full of enthusiasm and curiosity.

I guess she hasn't been a detective that long, he thought, wistfully. *The cynicism still hasn't set in.*

The band began playing again, although not too loudly. Bratt didn't recognize the tune, but it was full of dramatic flourishes offset by low drumrolls. While the music played the front doors opened wide and, two by two, the members of the wedding party entered as their names were announced.

The young ring-bearer and the flower-girl, each maybe five or six years old, were first, and they looked around the room nervously as they walked in front of the large, applauding crowd. They looked like they were ready to bolt for their families, but they managed to keep up their courage and climbed up to their places at the head table.

A half-dozen ushers then escorted in the same number of bridesmaids wearing long lavender gowns, several of them looking like they were rehearsing for the day they would be the center of attention. Everyone waved enthusiastically as they made their way to the front, then split off to sit at two tables set aside for the young singles. The best man and maid of honor followed them, arm in arm, and joined the two younger children on the long dais.

Nancy was happily clapping along in rhythm to the music. She poked Bratt in the side and encouraged him to do the same. Reluctantly, he joined in, feeling a bit embarrassed but not wanting her to think he had no sense of fun.

The two sets of parents were announced next and Bratt wasn't sure which ones were his former client's. The men were both fairly tall, with thin, graying hair. The women had slightly heavier builds, hidden under sparkling dresses that seemed to have magically sprouted flowers. They strode proudly to the head table and stood behind chairs that were placed on either side of two thrones, covered with flower garlands and waiting to receive the newlyweds.

Finally, there was a long drumroll, then the M.C. shouted out his introduction of the bride and groom. The clapping and cheering got even louder as the young couple entered, and Nancy grabbed his arm to tell him how beautiful she thought the bride looked.

He turned to hear what she was saying and saw her suddenly freeze up, her eyes locked on someone or something across the hall. Bratt looked at her curiously, wondering what had caught her attention in such a dramatic fashion. He was shocked to see that all the blood had drained from her face, taking her smile with it. He tried to follow her gaze through the milling crowd, but couldn't see whom she was staring at.

"Do you know who that man is?" she asked him, pointing at a short, neatly-dressed man who had discreetly slipped into the hall and was heading for a seat just to the right of the head table. "That's Nick Tortoni. I'd recognize him anywhere."

Bratt said nothing. He had been aware the well-known crime figure might be present, but had hoped Nancy wouldn't have recognized him so easily.

Looking confused, she asked him, "Did you know he'd be here?"

Bratt picked up a bread roll and tried to look casual as he buttered it. As much as possible he wanted to show her that the man's presence was not something to get worked up over.

"Well, of course he's here. He's the groom's great uncle."

Nancy stared at Bratt, an expression of disbelief on her face. "You told me the groom's name was Joe Capelli."

"Mm-hm," Bratt managed with a mouthful of bread. "But his mom is a Tortoni. Angelina Tortoni, Nick's niece. It's not that big of a deal."

The expression of disbelief on her face quickly turned to anger.

"What do you mean, not a big deal? You know who he is-"

"Look, Joe's got nothing to do with the old man's business. They're not even particularly close. But he's family, so he had to be invited, that's all."

"And you just had to invite me," she stabbed a finger at him, accusingly. "I'm a cop and no matter how much you try to act like it doesn't matter, you still brought me to a wedding in Nick Tortoni's family. You must have known I'd never come if I had known; that's why you never mentioned the family connection."

"Come on, Nancy. You're not supposed to be a cop tonight, remember? We're just at my old friend's wedding. I wasn't exactly planning on introducing you to the old man."

"Christ, I hope not," she almost yelled, indifferent to the stares this attracted from the other couples sitting at their table. "If you brought me anywhere close to him I'd spit in his face.

That man ordered the shooting of two cops last year, so you must be nuts to think that I might want to meet him."

Bratt's lawyer's instincts took over and, before he'd had a chance to think about it, he found himself arguing in the old man's defense.

"You guys never could pin that on him, so why won't you forget about it?"

As soon as he had spoken the words he realized that he couldn't have chosen a worse thing to say. Nancy made that clear when she grabbed his forearm tightly and spoke through clenched teeth, tears of anger beginning to well up in her eyes.

"Are you really such a thoughtless jerk? Just because we can't prove something in court doesn't mean he didn't do it, and you know it. It's not bad enough that he's a crime boss, but he's a cop killer to boot, and you're stupid enough to think that not being able to pin it on him makes the least bit of difference to me?"

For several seconds he sat there in stunned silence. He realized that her reaction should have been totally predictable. What surprised him most was how he had managed to convince himself it might be otherwise.

Earlier that day, when Nancy had agreed to attend the wedding of his former client, he had decided to not mention the Tortoni connection. He thought that once they were here, happy to finally be together, she wouldn't care who else attended the reception. He thought that she might even find some sort of humorous irony in attending a Tortoni wedding. He had clearly thought wrong.

Nancy turned her face away from him and picked up a glass of water, bringing it to her lips with a trembling hand. She sipped from it slowly, then turned back toward him, clearly still angry, but in better control of her emotions.

"I'd like to go home now, please."

He began to speak, to present further arguments in his defense, but the little common sense he had left told him it was pointless. It would have just made things worse, if that was at all possible. In the space of less than a minute their perfect evening had come to a sudden, crashing end.

Moving quickly to avoid looking at the amused stares of the other guests at their table, they got up and slipped out of the hall.

Chapter 5

Kouri had managed to reach the two alibi witnesses and they were coming to the office at noon that Sunday. Bratt spent the morning reading through the preliminary inquiry transcripts, doing his best to forget the previous night's debacle. When Kouri arrived a bit before 9 a.m. he was surprised to find Bratt already hard at work, unaware the lawyer had gotten to bed early following the abrupt end of his date with Nancy.

Bratt jotted down notes as he read the testimony of the two main Crown witnesses, trying to get a feel for how Paris and Phillips reacted under cross-examination. To Bratt's way of thinking, Paris, the accomplice turned stool pigeon, couldn't help but come across as untrustworthy and the lawyer didn't worry too much about how he was going to handle him in court.

Phillips was another story, though. By some sort of miracle he had survived two gunshots to the back of his neck, just at the base of his skull. He had no criminal record. He didn't know nor have anything against Marlon Small, whose picture he had picked out of several dozen photos in a high school yearbook. It wasn't even the same high school that Phillips attended. For all these reasons it would be very hard to get a jury to believe that he was lying about who shot him. He had no reason to lie, to intentionally blame the wrong man.

But that's what I'm going to have to show, Bratt thought. *The jury's going to have to think that either he's a liar or his powers of observation are so weak as to be worthless. That kid's the biggest obstacle to our winning this case. Too bad about him getting shot, but I'm just going to have to knock him down a peg or two.*

Phillips's testimony at the preliminary inquiry had been fairly solid, but Bratt had been able to rattle better witnesses than him before. He knew this was precisely what Jeannie was angry about, why she had suddenly turned against all criminal lawyers. But there could be no self-doubt now. Time was short and he had a client who was relying on his skill and experience to be saved from a lifetime in jail. Bratt's personal feelings about Small and the skepticism he felt about his innocence were irrelevant.

At the same time, Bratt knew it would be hard to predict which way a jury's sympathy would go. Attacking a shooting victim on the stand could easily backfire if he wasn't careful. For that reason as much as any other they would still need some solid alibi witnesses to raise the precious doubt they needed to win. And that's what had him sitting in his office on this Sunday morning.

Just then Kouri knocked at his office door. "Mr. Shoot to Kill is here to see you," he announced, clearly reveling in the chance to call Bernard Clayton by his street name.

Bratt pushed the transcripts aside and asked, "What about the Parker kid?"

"Oh yeah, he's here too," Kouri answered, with a smile. His head disappeared from view for a few seconds, then he returned, leading two heavily muscled young men into Bratt's office.

The pair shuffled in nonchalantly. Their style of dress was identical to Small's. They wore the same baggy, low-slung pants, sleeveless sports jerseys under puffy winter jackets and matching red bandanas on their heads.

Uninvited, they dropped themselves, side by side, onto Bratt's sofa, and looked up at him with totally inexpressive faces. Bratt doubted that either one was going to be any more personable than their friend Small. He didn't get up from his own chair to greet them, as this simple civility seemed superfluous. He just turned to a fresh page on his legal pad and picked up his pen.

"Which one of you guys likes to be called Shoot to Kill?"

The two glanced at each other, then the taller one spoke. "Who wants to know?"

"Ah, you would be Bernard Clayton then," Bratt surmised. He felt he needed to show he was in charge of this interview right off the top. "I'll call you Bernard because I'm old enough to be your father, and I'll only call you Mr. Clayton in court. You'll call me Mr. Bratt all the time."

The two young men continued to wear their blank expressions, as if Bratt were a boring TV show they had watched so often they knew the words by heart. He turned his gaze to Parker.

"I guess that makes you Ashley, right? If you'd be so kind to wait outside the office, we'll talk with Bernard here first and then get your statement later."

Ashley, unsurprisingly to Bratt, didn't move from his place. He didn't turn toward Bernard either, but just stared blankly in Bratt's direction. Kouri shifted uncomfortably in his chair and Bratt cleared his throat before trying again.

"Ashley, if I'm going to take your witness statements I have to speak to each one of you alone, so that you can both tell me just what you remember, without influencing each other. I'm not trying to pull any fast ones on you guys. In court you won't be allowed to listen to each other's testimony, so you better get used to telling your stories independently."

Parker didn't move at first, but Clayton turned his head toward him and whispered, "It's OK, man, go."

Parker slowly stood and walked out of the office. Bratt turned to Kouri and signaled with his head that he should follow the witness, resisting the temptation to warn him about making sure Parker didn't steal anything.

Once they were out of the office, he turned his attention to the remaining witness. Clayton's face wore several scars that attested to the violence of the life he lead. Under the bandana, his hair was short, except on one side where he wore it dreadlocked.

"Ok, Bernard. You know I want to talk to you about the night the Phillips boys and a drug dealer named Indian were shot, late last summer down in Little Burgundy. It was in an apartment on Carrier Street. According to the reports of gunfire by the neighbors, the shooting took place at approximately 11:25 p.m. Can you tell me where you were that night?"

Clayton's tone of voice was flat and disinterested. He sounded like he was reciting a boring script.

"I was with Brando and Ash at the park in LaSalle, shooting hoops. Brando drove us home around midnight, so he was nowhere near Little Burgundy when the guys got shot."

"Fine. Now what makes you say you left the park around midnight?"

Clayton's expressionless face displayed the slightest hint of confusion.

"What you mean?"

"Well, you said that Brando, Marlon that is, drove you home around midnight. How do you know what the time was?"

Clayton shrugged. "'Cause that was the time."

Bratt took a small breath and decided to start again. He knew that for some witnesses certain facts, such as time and place, were so self-evident that questioning them made the witnesses feel defensive, as if they thought they were being tricked. Clayton's new expression of wariness let him know that such was the case now.

"I'm sure that you're right about the time. It's just that in court you may be asked how you knew what the time was. So, I want you to be ready to answer that question. Now, can you tell me why you think you left the park around midnight."

"'Cause it takes me twenty minutes to get home and I got home around twenty after midnight."

"Excellent. Now, why do you say you got home at twenty past midnight?"

"I know what time I got home."

"I'm sure you do. I just want to know why you say that it was twenty past midnight."

"'Cause that was the fuckin' time, man!"

Bratt felt a growing sense of exasperation. If the most basic questions were so hard to answer in his office, how would Clayton handle the pressure cooker of a jury trial? He had no choice but to be very suggestive in his questions, almost to the point of explaining to Clayton what kinds of answers he should give.

"Look, Bernard, I'm really not trying to trick you or anything. When somebody knows that something happened at such and such a time, usually it's because they either saw the time on their watch or on a clock, or maybe somebody told them the time. Sometimes, it's just because they were watching their favorite TV show, so they might know the time that way. OK? So, let's try again: how do you know at what time you and Marlon left the park."

Clayton sat up and pointed his finger angrily at Bratt. "Now you're trying to trick me. I left the park with Marlon *and* Ashley, not just Marlon alone!"

With that he sat back in the sofa, an expression of satisfaction on his face. Bratt had no idea what his own expression was just then. He only knew that it would be anything but satisfaction. He thought that if he were in a comic strip he'd be pulling tufts of his hair out of his head by now.

He sat quietly for several seconds, his mind as blank as Clayton's earlier expression, before reviving himself with an idea for a fresh approach.

"I notice that you're not wearing a watch today, Bernard. Do you remember if you wore a watch that night in the park?"

"I don't got no watch," Clayton answered sullenly.

"Do you remember if you saw the time on the clock in Marlon's car?"

"Clock in his car don't work."

"All right then. Did you see the time on a clock at your home after he dropped you off?"

"No. I didn't put the lights on 'cause I didn't wanna wake up my mom."

"That's very commendable. So did somebody, anybody, mention the time to you when the three of you left the park?"

Clayton seemed to think through this one for a couple of seconds before answering. "No. The park was empty when we left. Everybody had gone home a long time before."

"I see," Bratt said, thinking that he had gotten his point across to Clayton, who would now have no reason to misunderstand his meaning. "So how do you know what time it was that you left the park?"

"Shit, man," Clayton yelled, jumping up in frustration. "I thought we already settled that. How come you don't believe me? I tell you over and over I know the time we left. It was *around* midnight. It wasn't exactly midnight, so I didn't have to check the second hand on nobody's watch or nothing. It was just *around* midnight."

"So it could have been before midnight?"

"Well, yeah. It could have been before midnight. Maybe it was. That would still be around midnight, right?"

"Could it have been 11:30?"

"I suppose so. I wasn't wearing a watch, like I said. An' it's been a long time."

"Could it have been close to eleven that you three left?"

"I dunno. Maybe it was. We just left when we got tired of playing, you know? We didn't have a schedule to keep or nothing."

"If you left at 11 P.M. and drove to Little Burgundy, what time would you have gotten there?"

"We didn't go to Burgundy. Ash an' me live up in *Cote des Neiges*."

"If. Just if."

"OK, '*if*.' I dunno. It's not far. Maybe ten past. Maybe 11:15."

"So, that would still have made it possible for Marlon to commit the murders at 11:25 p.m. And it might indicate that you and Ashley were his accomplices."

Bratt sat back and watched as the implication of what he said sank into Clayton's none too thin skull. Clayton looked lost at first, then began getting angry again.

"What the fuck're you trying to pull? You're supposed to prove that Brando didn't do nothing, not that I helped him kill those guys!"

Bratt was equally angry now. He sat forward in his chair as he spoke, his hands gripping its armrests. "Yes, that is what I'm supposed to prove. And the least bit of help from you or any other so-called alibi witness would be appreciated. So far, though, you haven't given your friend much of an alibi, have you? Your 'around midnight' seems to give him all the time in the world to go to Burgundy and shoot those guys."

He stared at Clayton who had gotten up and begun pacing around the office in obvious agitation. Finally, Clayton turned to him and said his first intelligent words since he and Parker had arrived.

"OK. Maybe I gotta talk to Brando a bit about that, see if there's maybe something I forgot."

"Yeah," Bratt said, trying to keep the sarcasm down to a slow drip. "Maybe there are a couple of small details that slipped your mind."

Clayton sat back down slowly, nodding his head. "Yeah, some small details."

"Fine. There is another important question that I have to ask you, and it's along the same lines as the last one. How do you know that the night Marlon drove you and Ashley home was the night of the murder?"

"What you mean?" Clayton asked timidly, obviously concerned about where this question might lead.

"Well, are you sure you guys were playing basketball at the park the night of the murders?"

"Yeah, of course. We spent every night at that park. It was right next to where Brando's baby-mother lived, and he was always by there. We shot hoops every night during the summer."

"Great. So, if you guys spent all your evenings last summer hanging around that park, playing basketball, how do you know that the night Marlon drove you home "around midnight" wasn't the night before the murders, or the night after? In other words, how can you be sure you're talking about the same night that I am?"

The blank expression on Clayton's face gave Bratt a sinking feeling of deja vu.

They spent the next thirty minutes determining that Clayton knew nothing more than the most superficial details of his story and wasn't even able to explain why he knew those. Finally, Bratt threw his hands up in disgust and asked him to wait outside.

It was just possible that Clayton had been playing basketball with Small on that fateful night. It was also just possible that the Easter Bunny was Santa Claus's bastard son. Now Bratt dreaded talking to Parker. Was it too much to hope that one out of the two alleged witnesses might not be a total, and totally obvious, liar?

From where he sat Bratt could hear Clayton whispering angrily to Parker before the second witness entered his office.

Parker came to the office door and hesitated, looking at Bratt with an expression that was a mix of defiance and trepidation. *Funny*, thought Bratt. *They hardly had any expressions when they first showed up, but they didn't take long to acquire a broad range of looks.*

Kouri came into the office and mentioned that Clayton had left, so Bratt motioned to him to sit down with them. He said nothing to Parker, however, waiting to see what the young man's first move would be. Finally, Parker headed for the sofa, trying hard to look disinterested in the proceedings. Bratt began the questions without any preliminaries.

"Ashley, what's your relationship to Marlon Small?"

Parker hesitated, obviously trying to think ahead to where the traps lay in this question.

"My cousin," he finally answered.

"Do you think your cousin shot those guys in Burgundy?"

"No way, man."

"Tell me why not?"

Parker was obviously ready for this kind of tricky lawyer's questions, because he answered right away.

"'Cause he was with me an' Shoot, at the park. No way he could have shot those guys."

"Good," said Bratt. There was no point in wasting time with this witness. Either he knew more than Clayton or he didn't. "Now tell me about the park. Tell me what time you got there, what time you left. Tell me who was there."

To Bratt's total surprise, Parker told him. Detail by detail, all the relevant names and times were listed. He knew they had left the park just after midnight because a public security car had driven by and told them the park was off-limits at that hour. He knew it was the same night as the murders because he had heard about the shootings the next morning and called Marlon to ask him if he knew any of the guys. He knew who was there with them, what time they had arrived at the park and how everybody had spent their time. In short, and in comparison to Clayton, he was a revelation. Bratt listened and smiled to himself. One excellent alibi witness wasn't so bad after all. It was certainly better than two below-average ones.

When Parker finished recounting their comings and goings on the fateful night, Bratt looked back over his notes and read a logical, credible story. As much as possible at this early stage, Parker had been able to answer every question that Bratt foresaw might be asked of him on cross-examination. The difference between Clayton and Parker was staggering. There were only a few personal details left to cover with him.

"Ashley, I want you to be straight with me, because the police are going to pull out your criminal record as soon as we give them your name this week. You've been in trouble with the law?"

"Yes, I have. But nothing heavy like murder, or anything violent at all."

"Good, good. Tell me whatever you've been found guilty of. Adult or juvenile."

"Ok. Well, I passed a few bad checks a couple of years ago."

"What's 'a few' mean?"

"About forty, I guess. It went on over a year. They were checks from where I worked."

"Oh, I see. About how much were those checks for?"

"About? Oh, about thirty thousand dollars."

Bratt felt his earlier feeling of elation start to die down just a bit.

"So, you defrauded your employer for thirty grand. Was any of it recovered?"

"Naw, man. I blew it all on coke."

Just like that, Bratt's feeling of elation was a thing of the past. Queasiness had quickly taken its place in the pit of his stomach.

"Coke? You got a coke problem?"

"Not any more," Parker smiled proudly. "I did a cure while I was in the pen."

"You were in the pen? Of course, you were sentenced. What did you get?"

"For the thirty grand, or for the credit cards?"

Queasiness now had total command of his internal organs. It thought about inviting frustration and depression in for a visit.

"What's the story with the credit cards? No, wait." Bratt resisted the urge to throw his legal pad across the room in frustration, needing to get all the details of Parker's criminal past straight. "Tell me everything, about all your convictions, from the beginning."

Parker took a deep breath in preparation of telling the epic story that was his life as a criminal. First, there were a string of petty thefts as a juvenile. Then, he began stealing credit cards from his neighbors' mailboxes and passing their spending limits as fast as he could. At the same time he was running various scams among area merchants, smooth-talking several of them out of thousands of dollars in merchandise. Most of the money he stole or conned people out of went to pay his growing drug habit. He had been in and out of jails for two years when his mother had found him a regular job with a construction company in the illusory hope of keeping him out of trouble.

"I was still on probation when I got caught signing my boss's signature on those checks. They added three years to my sentence for those checks. I got out on day parole, and was in a halfway house for two weeks when those guys got shot."

"Tell me, did you have a curfew to keep at the halfway house?"

"Sure, eleven o'clock. But, hey, I never worried about that."

Bratt sat quietly, musing on the little ironies of life. Ashley Parker spoke well, had his facts straight and was able to think quickly on his feet. But that should not have come as a surprise, considering he was an experienced fraudster. A full-time, professional liar. On top of that, he had been violating his parole at the time he was supposedly being Small's alibi.

Nothing came easier for an experienced lawyer than discrediting a witness whose whole life had been predicated on successfully lying to people. No matter how credible the witness sounded, the jury would always ask itself if that wasn't just because he was such a good liar. As a matter of fact, witnesses like Parker often ended up bragging on the stand about what great liars they had been all their lives and how many people they had been able to defraud. First that idiot, Clayton. Now, Parker, who was clearly too clever for his own good. Bratt gently put his legal pad down on his desk, his hands shaking slightly from his frustration.

"Thank you for coming to talk to us, Ashley. Peter, could you please see him out?"

Once the witness had entered the elevator and headed for the ground floor Kouri returned to Bratt's office.

Excitedly, he asked, "So, what do you think? He seemed to have his facts straight."

Bratt didn't answer right away. He stood now, looking out of his window at Notre Dame Basilica across the street. He watched the tourists and the churchgoers intermingle on the massive church's front steps. A light snowfall came down, rendering a postcard quality to the whole scene. All those people spending their Sunday with such peace of mind. None of them would suspect that from a window above them they were being watched by a man struggling to formulate a plan that would let a murderer go free. *Alleged murderer,* thought Bratt. *Yeah, fucking alleged!*

"We're screwed."

"Oh," Kouri's voice was small, hesitant. "I had gathered from Clayton that you weren't very impressed with his answers"

"No, not very impressed," said Bratt, his anger building. "The kid's an idiot and a liar, and both those facts will be very evident ten minutes into his cross-examination. As for Parker, he's no idiot, he's just a plain liar. Who the hell does Small think he's kidding, telling me these two are his best alibi witnesses? And Jesus Christ, why do these kids all have to dress and behave like, like…"

"Like they're auditioning for a Spike Lee movie," Kouri suggested.

"What? Yeah, whatever. Can you imagine how they'd look in front of a jury?"

"No, I-"

"You know the make-up of an English-speaking jury in Montreal? It's a bunch of West Island retirees and Toronto expatriates. You think these people have a clue about the latest urban dress code? They'd take one look at Mr. Shoot to Kill and go hide in their suburban cellars."

Kouri opened his mouth to speak, then stopped, waiting for any further rants from Bratt. When none were forthcoming he jumped in.

"Maybe they wouldn't look so bad if we could get them dressed a bit more conservatively. You know, and tell them to watch how they speak. Then they wouldn't come across as being too…different, to the jury."

Bratt felt totally exasperated. As if Small's alibi witnesses weren't bad enough, now Kouri thought he'd come up with a plan.

"We've got less than three weeks. You think we can turn these two guys into brilliant, cultured gentlemen in that time? Maybe that works in the movies, but in my version of reality, which you're welcome to join at any time, you try that and you look like a fool. Do you have any other brilliant ideas?"

Kouri shook his head, looking embarrassed. His face was flushed red, as if he took personal blame for the witnesses' lack of credibility.

Bratt had no time to worry about that now. His defense had a huge hole in it, and he should have been prepared for that eventuality. It probably hadn't been realistic for him to expect Small's friends to come across as perfect witnesses, although he couldn't have known how unrealistic his expectation was.

He sat down again, trying to envision how the trial would unfold. Even if he were able to rattle the Crown witnesses, would it be enough to win? Two young men were dead. The jury would surely expect the accused to say something in his own defense. But Small probably wouldn't make any better impression on the jury than his two buddies. If the jury found him as unlikable as his own lawyer did they might not listen to anything he had to say.

Bratt's frustration grew as he wracked his brains to find a way to defend a man he seemed to dislike more with every breath. While he knew he was competitive and his desire to win would always keep him going, it didn't hurt to occasionally have a client that he felt a trace of sympathy for. Once in a while he liked thinking his motivations weren't entirely self-serving or mercenary. The truth was, it had been quite a while since he had cared much for any of the people that he defended, and that thought saddened him.

"Listen, Pete. I'm going to go home and forget all about this case for today. I recommend you do the same. Tomorrow I'll call whoever the hell's the detective in charge and arrange to get a copy of that tape. Then, in a couple of days we'll go have another visit with Small, and discuss what we can do to salvage this case. In the meantime get the message to him through his mother that these witnesses were a waste of time."

Bratt picked up his briefcase and headed out of his office. Kouri had hardly moved, and the look on his face made Bratt wonder if his assistant saw the case, and their client, in quite the same light as he did.

It didn't matter, Bratt thought. *Sooner or later he'd learn what every criminal lawyer eventually found out: this was a great job, if it weren't for the clients.*

Monday morning at the office all the other lawyers came by to congratulate Bratt on his successful defense of Cooper Hall. While he tried to maintain his usual outward appearance, bragging and laughing about the trial, on the inside he felt there was little to celebrate. It wasn't long before John Kalouderis poked his head through the door, catching Bratt staring off into space.

"Hey, great leader and shining beacon of justice, you don't look as happy as you're supposed to be."

Bratt considered briefly telling him to get lost, then decided that a friendly ear to listen to his tales of woe might not be such a bad thing.

"Come on in, doctor, and bring your notepad. I've got a lot of venting to do."

Kalouderis came in and sat down at his favorite spot, stretching his legs out along the sofa.

"I thought the patient was supposed to be the one lying down," said Bratt.

"You didn't call dibs," Kalouderis responded with a smile. "So, tell me your problems, and please make them interesting.

I'm usually not a very good listener when I'm sober."

Bratt wondered where to begin. He wasn't quite ready for an existential discussion about his role as a lawyer or the morality of his courtroom tactics. As for the conflict that these tactics had caused between him and Jeannie, he had never liked talking about family problems, always keeping a clear demarcation between work and home.

He considered talking about the problems he was facing preparing Small's defense, but these were the kinds of things that came up fairly regularly in a criminal practice, and were probably too commonplace to keep his friend's interest.

That left Nancy. He looked at Kalouderis's slightly sarcastic smile and decided that this was about as far as he was ready to open up.

He told his friend about the wedding reception, while tending to paint himself as a surprised innocent in the whole matter. He wasn't used to being dumped on the first date, and his ego fought with his heart over what his next step, if any, should be.

"She really had no business taking her anger out on me. We could have just left and gone somewhere else," he said.

"Do you think she was reacting as a woman or as a cop?"

"That's the problem. Those are two species I've never been able to understand. So, imagine how inscrutable they become when they're combined."

Both he and Kalouderis chuckled.

"Well, maybe it was to be expected," said Kalouderis. "After all, two fellow police officers were killed. You couldn't expect her to turn a blind eye to what the guy did."

"Why not? It's not like she even knew them. They were anti-gang and she works white-collar crime. Besides, remember that nut, Castle, the guy who shot Dougal McDonald? I didn't have any problems defending him. It's not like I said, 'Oh, no. You shot another lawyer, so I can't have anything to do with you.' And I knew McDonald fairly well."

"Yeah, you knew him just enough to hate his guts. What if it had been a lawyer that you liked? What if it was somebody from this office?"

"I guess that would depend on how much he was billing."

The two friends laughed again, able to enjoy the tasteless joke in the privacy of Bratt's office. Bratt wondered why they could make jokes over what had happened to McDonald, while Nancy had been brought close to tears just by the sight of Nick Tortoni.

Maybe we do need a bit of sensitivity training, Bratt thought. *Then again, maybe laughing at some of the less pleasant aspects of this job is the only way we can do it.*

"Anyway," continued Kalouderis, "from what you told me she really had the hots for you. So, if you already told her how sorry you were and you got her out of there right away, I don't think she's going to continue holding it against you. Why not call her? Even apologize again."

"Maybe I should forget about her. I don't want her thinking I'm desperately chasing after her."

"No, you certainly wouldn't want her to think *that*," said Kalouderis, sarcastically. "Anyway, maybe you *should* forget about her. But, if you're not going to, then call her, for Christ's sake, and quit pining over her like a lovesick teenager."

They talked for a while longer before Kalouderis went back to his own office, waving his finger at Bratt, who was still considering whether to take his friend's advice. Bratt opened the top drawer of his desk and pulled out a little plastic folder full of business cards. He flipped it over to the back, to a separate section for various police officers whom he had dealt with on occasion, some of whom he actually liked.

He pulled out S/D Philippe St. Jean's card. The lead investigator in the Small case wasn't a personal favorite of Bratt's, although he held a grudging respect for the veteran detective. St. Jean had conducted Small's videotaped interrogation and Bratt had an idea of what it had been like before even seeing it. Where other cops often tried bullying and intimidation to extract confessions, St. Jean put on a much more amiable face. He tried building a rapport with suspects, getting them to like and trust him and, hopefully, admit their crimes once they were convinced it was in their own best interests to do so. Those who knew the detective were aware there was little similarity between the easy-going, almost warmhearted guy who conducted the interrogations and St. Jean's true bulldog personality.

Bratt held St. Jean's card in front of him, but his mind turned to the card that rested in the front pocket of his shirt. Nancy's card.

It's almost noon, he thought. *I guess if I call her up now I won't look too desperate.*

He dialed the number of the fraud squad and punched in her personal extension, unsure if she was even on duty. It rang several times, then she picked up.

He sensed some hesitation on the other end of the line before she finally said, "*Bonjour, Robert.*"

I'm really going to have to get call-display, Bratt thought.

"Good morning, Nancy," he said tentatively. "How've you been?"

"Well, my weekend was a bit of a bust, if you'll pardon the pun." There was silence for a few seconds, as if she were deciding whether to continue the conversation. Finally she asked, "How about you?"

"Mostly I've been feeling pretty bad about the other night. I realize it wasn't the best idea I've had."

He waited for her to respond, but was met with more silence. *Well, she hasn't hung up yet; that must mean something.*

"I guess it was more than just a bad idea. It was totally, *ridiculously* stupid of me. And I, I guess I was hoping you'd forgive me."

"Wow, Robert. I don't think I've ever heard you grovel before. You actually sound sincere, too."

"I guess I'm even surprising myself," he said. "So, what do you think? Can you forgive me?"

"I don't know," she said, her voice sounding suddenly perkier. "Maybe I should let you grovel some more."

"If that's what it takes."

"No, dear Robert," she said with the light laugh he so enjoyed hearing. "That's enough groveling for you. I can't stay furious with you forever."

"You had every right to be furious."

"Oh, I know. Of course what really made me angry was sitting through that God-awful trial for two months having naughty little fantasies about you. Then you almost went and ruined everything."

"*Almost?* So things can be fixed?"

"Yes, things can be fixed. Anyway, I was probably too hard on you. After-all, you've been a defense attorney all your life, so you just didn't know any better."

"Ouch," Bratt said jokingly, feeling the weight of the past two days slide off his shoulders.

"So," she continued, "if we just pretend that whole evening never happened, I suppose I wouldn't mind trying again."

"How about tonight," he suggested.

"Tonight would be nice, but I don't know if I should trust you to decide where we'll go."

Bratt tried to think of the best spot to take her. He quickly ruled out the many chic, self-important eateries lining St. Laurent Boulevard that he usually frequented. Unlike other dates, he didn't think it was necessary to try to impress Nancy with all the members of the trendy set that he knew. What he wanted now was to finally be alone with her.

"I know a quiet little place on Park. We'll probably have the place to ourselves on a Monday night."

"Some place quiet for just the two of us sounds perfect. There's hope for you yet, Robert Bratt."

A few minutes after Bratt got off the phone, Kouri arrived carrying plastic-wrapped sandwiches and cups of coffee. He went straight toward Bratt's window and motioned for him to join him there, but Bratt didn't move. With his mind full of thoughts of that night's dinner with Nancy, he wasn't curious about whatever it was that Kouri wanted him to see.

"Some sort of demonstration," Kouri said, motioning out the window. "They're heading for the courthouse."

Their office was a long block away from the *Palais de Justice*, down Notre Dame Street, and Bratt had seen many a group of demonstrators march in that direction. He found the whole thing much less fascinating than Kouri seemed to. The junior lawyer continued to gawk out the window.

"Unless there's a whole bunch of naked women taking part, Peter, it's just another demonstration. They get them all the time at the courthouse."

Kouri turned away from the window and brought the two lunches that he was still carrying to Bratt's desk.

"Well, there are a lot of women out there, but none of them are naked."

"The day the nudists' rights group storms the court gimme a call. Until then, forget about it and let's get back to work on the plight of our friend, Mr. Small."

Around four that afternoon, the two lawyers sat down in front of a small TV in Bratt's office to watch the videotape St. Jean had couriered over to them. On the tape, the homicide detective and Marlon Small entered a pale-yellow room which contained two chairs and a small table bolted to the floor.

Kouri, to whom everything seemed to be new and exciting, noted that the chair St. Jean sat on was soft, padded vinyl, while Small's chair looked like hard, molded plastic. Bratt retorted that this was a clear example of the psychological gamesmanship the cops resorted to in order to break down their suspects. Kouri didn't seem to catch the sarcastic tone.

On the screen, the lawyers saw a wide-angle view of the room at first, but as St. Jean spoke the wall-mounted camera's focus closed in on Small. Bratt noticed that his clothes were nearly identical to those he had worn when they met at R.D.P., except that the police had removed the bandana before taping. Small held on to it now like it was a security blanket and throughout the interview he nervously twisted and pulled at it. He didn't look nearly as cocky as he had when they met him the previous Saturday.

St. Jean spent several minutes making sure that Small understood his rights before beginning the questioning. Bratt knew this detailed procedure was not so much for the suspect's benefit as it was for any judge who might view the tape later. Small wasn't paying much attention to St. Jean, his eyes flitting nervously around the room.

"If you are eligible," St. Jean read from a small plastic card, "you may also apply for legal assistance through the Provincial Legal Aid Program. Do you understand that, Marlon? You can get a lawyer for free."

Small said nothing in response, so St. Jean continued reading.

"This part is really important, so pay attention. You may retain free of charge and immediately, a duty counsel-"

"I need a smoke, man," Small interrupted. "Can't somebody get me a smoke?"

St. Jean looked mildly exasperated with Small's indifference to what was happening to him.

"Like I was saying," he continued, "you may retain, free of charge and immediately, a duty counsel, and obtain preliminary legal advice without charge."

"Great, can I have my smokes now?"

"In a minute, Marlon," St. Jean said. "Just let me finish this bit. You want to know your rights, don't you? You haven't even spoken to a lawyer yet."

"I don't need a lawyer, I need a cigarette. What the fuck do I need a lawyer for, anyhow?"

St. Jean exhaled slowly, as if he had some bad news to tell Small, but couldn't figure out how to do it.

"Just let me get this done, OK? It'll be a couple of more minutes, then you can have your cigarette."

This didn't seem to assuage Small much, and he continued to fidget in his chair, looking wide-eyed at the bare walls around him and rubbing the bandana in his hands. St. Jean went on to explain Small's right to silence, and Bratt's mind lowered the volume on his words to concentrate on the face of the agitated suspect. He continued to scribble notes, describing Small's expressions and body language. Bratt suspected that, more than anything Small might say, it would probably be how he looked and behaved that a jury would find incriminating.

Having taken great pains to make sure that Small understood his rights, St. Jean finally turned to face the camera and asked that somebody bring in some cigarettes and two cups of coffee.

For the next few minutes the detective quietly wrote onto his notepad, hardly paying any attention to Small, and this seemed to make the suspect fidget even more nervously than before. There was eventually a knock from off-screen, and St. Jean got up and walked to the periphery of the camera's field of vision to open a door.

Bratt heard some whispering in French, then the door closed and St. Jean returned to his seat and handed Small a Styrofoam cup of coffee and a pack of cigarettes. Small quickly pulled out a cigarette from the half-empty pack and St. Jean leaned over to light it for him. He then placed his lighter on the table near Small to demonstrate how much he trusted his suspect.

After Small began smoking the cigarette and had a sip or two of coffee, St. Jean began asking him a number of questions about his personal and home life that were intended to make him feel at ease. Small looked barely interested though, and his answers were rarely more than mumbles.

"What's St. Jean doing?" Kouri asked, sounding impatient. "Playing 'This is Your Life?'"

Bratt said nothing for a few seconds, then answered him like a man spelling out the obvious.

"Watch and learn. This man is very good at what he does. He doesn't have to get a confession before the next commercial break. If he spends three hours doing this it'll be because this is his best chance to get what he wanted."

Kouri scrunched down into his seat and turned his eyes back to the TV screen, looking unconvinced.

On the screen, St. Jean eventually got off the subject of home and family and began filling Small in on the case that the police had against him.

"Your friend Marcus was only too happy to tell us it was you that went to that apartment with him. He's going to be a very damaging witness against you, you know."

Small's face briefly registered an expression of disgust at the mention of his ex-buddy's name, then recovered its previous sullen look.

"He knew the best thing he could do for himself was admit what he did. He knew we had him cold, just like we have you. And Dorrell Phillips picked your picture right out of your high school yearbook. Lucky we got our hands on it, since you've never had a mug shot taken, eh? So, over-all I'd say we've got a pretty good case against you, don't you think?"

Small didn't respond. He tugged harder at the bandana and looked away from St. Jean, his eyes continuing to dart around the room as if trying to find a way out.

"The truth is, Marlon, I don't even need to talk to you. If we arrested you it was because we have all the evidence we needed. You know we're not allowed to arrest people just because we suspect them. We've got to have solid evidence to charge them. So, if I'm asking you to tell me what happened, it's only because I want to understand you. Why would a decent kid like you do something terrible like that?"

Small's eyes looked briefly up at St. Jean before dropping to the floor.

"Your mom seems like such a nice lady. Think of what this is doing to her. She must be wondering why too. She believes in God very deeply, more than most people these days. Imagine how this must feel to someone who's that religious. She must have taught you a little of her religious beliefs. She told me you used to sing in the children's choir at Christmas. Is that true?"

St. Jean's head tilted, as if he wanted to look up into Small's downcast eyes.

"See, I just want to understand why? You must believe in God too. A good kid who believes in God doesn't go killing people for no reason. Maybe these guys did something to you. Is that it? Did they provoke you? Maybe they threatened you?"

Small continued refusing to respond to St. Jean's repeated invitations to talk. At times he kept his eyes glued to the floor. Occasionally, when St. Jean seemed to strike a nerve, his head would jerk up, then his eyes would dart around the room again. His expression showed anger and fear, but the only thing that came out of his mouth was the smoke from the cigarette that fluttered nervously between his lips. St. Jean was undeterred.

"I know you don't want to look like a squealer, you want everybody to know how tough you are. But you don't have to be tough with me. I'm not being tough with you, am I? Am I, Marlon?"

Small's eyes met St. Jean's again, and his head shook almost imperceptibly.

"No, that's right. So, why do you feel you have to be tough, hold out, don't say a thing? Marcus wasn't tough. He told us everything we need to know about what you did, about how you killed those guys. Were you being tough when you did that? Was that it? Did you have to prove to somebody how tough you are? Hm? Tell me, Marlon, was this how you were going to make your name on the street?

"You know, nobody in your neighborhood, not even the cops who patrol there, had ever heard of you, you were such a good kid. Maybe you didn't like that, eh? Maybe you wanted people to know your name. Maybe even be a little scared of you? Was that it? You didn't like being a choirboy? You were going to be the toughest kid on your block?"

St. Jean sat back in his chair and just looked at Small for a few moments. Bratt knew that the detective had enough patience to calmly repeat the same questions over and over, all in the hope that cracks would eventually start showing in Small's silent façade. Three hours of this would not make for exciting viewing, yet Bratt found their interaction fascinating.

"Let me tell you, Marlon," St. Jean took up again, "I'm not here to figure out if you did it. I know you did it. Everybody knows you did it. We're going to have no trouble proving it in court. All I want to know is why it happened. You'll be surprised how good you'll feel when you tell me. I know you want to tell me, to make me understand what's going on inside your head, inside your heart. Show me what you know. You can even show me if I'm wrong. I won't mind."

Bratt saw Kouri check his watch after about an hour of repetitive questioning and barely stifled a yawn of his own. By this point, even the study of human interaction had lost its appeal. The afternoon dragged toward the evening, with St. Jean constantly repeating his entreaties while Small wordlessly squirmed.

Then, near the end of the three hours, Bratt saw a slow but noticeable change in Small's demeanor. He couldn't point to anything in particular that St. Jean had said to bring it on, but Small's face showed that his resistance was getting low. His eyes started glistening from tears he was holding back, and his lips moved in silent anguish, as if he was struggling to get some painful words out into the open. St. Jean must have noticed these signs of weakness because he leaned closer, turning up the pressure.

"You don't want to go through a trial, Marlon. You don't want to make your mother sit there and listen to those boys describe what you did. I'm sure you don't want to relive it either. It would be awful for you. So, just let it out. You'll feel so much better. You know you'll feel better. Confession is good for the soul, right?"

Small turned his face away, but his lips kept moving, and his hands were working overtime on the bandana. His breathing became labored and he wiped his face with his sleeve. In Bratt's eyes he looked the epitome of a man grappling with a guilty conscience, needing to relieve himself of a great burden, but afraid to take the next step.

"Why do you want to keep this pain inside you? Let it out, Marlon. Share it with me, that's why I'm here. You'll feel so much better. Everything will go so much smoother for you and for your mom. I can almost hear it coming from your mouth. Just say it and all this will be over. Nobody will bother you about it anymore, if you'll just get it off your chest. You want to say it, so-"

St. Jean was interrupted by an anguished yell from Small.

"I want my lawyer!"

On the tape the detective leaned back in his chair and let his shoulders slump, and Bratt did the same thing in his office. Bratt knew there was no way he could let a jury see this. After almost three hours of silence in the face of a constant stream of accusations, Small had clearly come close to cracking. He'd saved himself by asking for his lawyer, effectively putting an end to the questioning. Bratt knew his client had finally realized why he needed a lawyer: it had become impossible to keep his guilt hidden any longer.

In the interrogation room, St. Jean began stalling, still trying to get Small to crack before he was obliged to call a lawyer for him.

"Of course you'll get your lawyer. I'm the one who told you to speak to one before. But don't forget, your lawyer doesn't feel what you feel. He doesn't know what you and I know. And he's not the one who's going to do the time for what you did. I respect your choice entirely. If you want me to call a lawyer we'll stop the tape right now and get you a phone. But a lawyer isn't going to help you feel better, Marlon."

"Fuck you! I feel fine. Just get me my lawyer!"

Bratt leaned his head back and stared up at the ceiling.

"He really screwed himself," he thought out loud. "He was looking bad enough for three hours, but at the end he really screwed himself."

"Is it really so bad?" Kouri asked. "After all, he's just exercising his right to a lawyer."

"You think that's what a jury will see? They'll see a guy who looks, acts, and feels very guilty. He said it himself at the beginning: why does he need a lawyer? Unfortunately, he spent three hours giving us the answer."

Kouri nodded his head, letting the implications sink in. Finally, as if to avoid admitting defeat for their client, he said, "At least St. Jean's tactics didn't get him the confession he wanted."

"You don't think so, kid? I think St. Jean got all he could have asked for."

Bratt looked at his watch. It was almost 7 PM. He still had to get home and shower and change before picking Nancy up at 8:30. He had been looking forward to seeing her tonight, but the combined monotony and tension of the interrogation had drained him, and romance was now the furthest thing from his mind.

What the hell, he thought. *I'm not going to let Small ruin what little social life I have. He's probably screwed, no matter what he says. There's not much I can do about that tonight. Tomorrow, I'll go see him at R.D.P, but for now I'm going to forget he exists.*

In the small Greek restaurant he had chosen near the corner of Park and Mount Royal there was only one other couple on this cold Monday night. Robert Bratt and Nancy Morin sat quietly, at times looking away from each other, at other times gazing into each other's eyes.

Between them there was an open-mouthed glass bulb, wrapped in red plastic netting, holding a small wick with a flickering flame. They held hands between their glasses of wine like teenagers and hardly spoke.

When they had sat down at the table it felt like they were strangers meeting for the first time. The past two months of flirting and game-playing no longer existed. Neither one mentioned their previous date. They had to discover each other all over again, but words hardly seemed necessary.

Occasionally, the waiter brought them food: hot, fresh bread and a small slab of butter; salad, covered with feta cheese and black olives; a large plate of calamari, piled high. He was the only intruder into their private little world, but he disappeared from view as soon as he set down their plates.

Bratt hadn't thought it possible, but he almost forgot that Marlon Small existed. The earlier stress and aggravation he had felt was a vague memory now. In contrast to the weight that had seemed to constantly hang around his neck in recent days, his spirits felt light.

From the moment he had picked Nancy up things had felt different between them, but somehow better than they had before. Unlike all the other occasions they had been together, he no longer felt he had to be "on" for her. Tonight, he didn't need to be witty or overly charming to impress her. He could let his mind rest from its constant race to find the next clever line.

In her calm, happy gaze he could see that it was more than enough for him to just be there with her. They were two rivals who had gone head to head for two months and now were able to relax together over some good wine, and share the bond they had forged in battle. He no longer had to compete, whether it was with her, with other men or with his own reputation.

At some point during their evening he began telling her about himself. Not the usual bragging about his courtroom wizardry, but about who he was when he got home, when he was alone or with Jeannie. Part of his mind told him not to disturb the silence that protected him, especially if it was only to bore her with his life story, but he felt compelled to let her see a side of himself that he rarely showed.

"About a year ago she told me she'd like to study law when she got to university," he said, talking about his daughter.

"That must have made you very proud."

"Well, only a bit. I actually discouraged her from following in my footsteps."

"That's surprising. Were you feeling a bit down on your profession at the time?"

Must have been a prelude to this week, Bratt thought. "No, just thought she could do a lot of different things. She doesn't really have the temperament to be a lawyer. She's a lot more like her mother: more artistic. Artsy-fartsy I used to call her."

"That can't have been easy for you, raising a daughter by yourself."

"No, I guess not. I could have made it easier if I accepted a little help or advice along the way. But you know how I am; nobody can tell me anything. I'd rather screw things up my way than admit I can't do something. Unfortunately, that's one of the few traits Jeannie inherited from me."

"It's not such a bad trait," Nancy said, squeezing his hand tighter. "A little stubborn self-assurance can get you through a lot in life."

"Oh, it's all just a sham," Bratt laughed, without admitting to himself how close to the truth those words were. "I'm just trying to cover up my insecurities, you know."

"Of course I know," she smiled. "But everyone has insecurities. The ones who get anywhere in life are the ones who cover them up the best."

"Why, are you covering up any?"

"Why do you think I carry a gun all the time?"

Bratt laughed, but Nancy just smiled a bit nervously, then cleared her throat.

"Do you have any idea what it takes to be a female detective in Montreal?" She paused, gathering her thoughts. "It's hard enough getting there, but once you're there everybody's got seniority on you. They can shunt you around from place to place, filling whatever gaps they have and they never take into account what you might actually be good for."

"I didn't realize things were still like that here."

"It's the same with all police forces. They're just boys clubs that they defend from female intruders."

Bratt squeezed her hand sympathetically. He had never spent much time worrying about how cops treated each other before. *Face it,* he thought. *I never spent much time thinking of cops as people, either. Not until Nancy showed up in my life.*

"I'm sorry," she said. "I hadn't planned to start venting my frustrations."

"No, that's all right. Sometimes it's good to do that."

"Anyway, I'm probably exaggerating. It's really not so bad," she said, but Bratt thought that it probably was. "I'd rather hear about how you manage to carry on your practice and be a single parent at the same time."

"Well, it's not always so easy. Sometimes, one role takes up all my time to the detriment of the other. And that can be hard to make your child understand, even when they're no longer little children." Bratt reconsidered what he said and decided it needed to be corrected a bit. "*Especially* when they're not little children, because then they ask all the questions that you have no answers to."

"Is that what happened with your daughter?"

Bratt sipped from his wineglass, unsure how much detail he should go into about what had happened with Jeannie.

"I was there at court that day she showed up, remember," Nancy went on. "After you came back from talking to her, you looked…well, you looked pretty shook up."

"Things have gotten a bit screwed up between us." He sipped again at the wine, then dabbed nervously at his lips with his napkin. He was suddenly aware of how much Jeannie's departure had hurt him, despite his efforts to pretend that it was just a minor tiff.

"To tell you the truth, I don't know how I messed things up so much." He paused again, then looked up at Nancy. "She moved out a few days ago."

"Really?"

"Yeah. It seems she suddenly realized the terrible thing I do for a living and found she couldn't be around me anymore."

Nancy smiled, then quickly covered her mouth.

"Sorry, Robbie. I know it's not funny. But you have to admit it is, um…"

"Ironic?"

"Very ironic. What brought this on?"

"It's a bit of a long story." He wondered how he was going to explain things without making himself look like the villain Jeannie claimed he was. "A friend of hers was raped by a man I'd represented several years ago."

"Uh-oh."

"Yeah. Anyway, the girl was really roughed up on the stand, made to look like she went after the guy herself. And, of course, he was acquitted, which didn't sit too well with my daughter."

"No, I guess it wouldn't. Who was the lawyer?"

"Antoine Perron. Know him?"

"I've heard of him. Is he anything like you in court?"

Bratt knew she was teasing him when she asked that, but it struck a nerve because it had been one of Jeannie's main complaints about the way he did his job.

"Actually, I trained him myself, about seven years ago."

"So he doesn't exactly use kid gloves."

"No, he doesn't. And he's an arrogant little shit to boot."

Nancy looked at him closely and asked, "You're angry at him, aren't you? He did his job too well, and it all ended up on your doorstep."

"Hey, you're pretty smart for a cop."

"I've gotta be. Twice as good for the half the pay, eh?"

They sat quietly for a few minutes, each contemplating where their lives had gotten them. Bratt sipped at his wine. He was making sure he didn't overdo the drinking tonight, but he longed to be able to forget all his troubles again. He had needed to talk about Jeannie with Nancy, but he had also felt a lot better earlier on, when she hadn't been on his mind.

Nancy pulled at his hand lightly as if to get his attention.

"Robbie. Do you ever think about your job? You know, about the things that Jeannie says?"

Lately, that's all I seem to be thinking about, he thought.

"Hey, I thought we weren't supposed to talk about our jobs tonight."

"I know, but this isn't really shoptalk."

"It's close enough. Besides, I don't know how we got into this whole gloomy discussion anyway. Being with you, I should be feeling anything but gloomy."

"Fine," she said, with doubt still lingering in her eyes. "We'll talk about something else, for now."

Thank God she's not pushing the subject too hard. Another time, though, I can see myself lying down, with my head on her lap, unloading all that's been weighing heavily on me.

Bratt smiled to himself at the warm image, and Nancy reacted to the smile. Pulling his hand toward her and leaning closer to him, she reached out and lightly caressed his cheek.

"I'm glad to see you smile again. You're right, there'll be other times and places, but tonight we'll keep things happy."

He brightened up completely at her touch and looked around for the waiter.

"What say we go someplace else? Maybe something a little more noisy and upbeat."

"Oh, Robbie, I think I'm getting too old to drink and party all night. Maybe you could just take me home."

Bratt was surprised and disappointed at her suggestion.

"Home? Oh, I thought…"

She put her hand up to his lips to quiet him, and looked softly into his eyes.

"Your home, silly."

The drive downtown to his apartment took about twenty minutes on the snow-congested streets, but it seemed to fly by. She had tried to hold his right hand as he drove, but had to let go when he shifted gears, so she placed it lightly on his thigh instead. A few minutes after she had gotten into the car she turned the radio dial away from the all-oldies station he kept it on, finding a French soft rock station.

They were soon turning into the indoor garage of his building and pulling into his parking space. Their timing was perfect. The love song she had been humming came to an end, and the hourly news bulletin was taking its place. Bratt turned the key in the ignition, cutting off the radio announcer as he was mentioning that a number of demonstrators had been arrested at the courthouse that afternoon.

Must have been while we were wrapped up in the Small video, Bratt thought. *Pete'll be sorry he missed it.*

On the slow elevator ride up to his fifteenth floor apartment Nancy lay her head on his shoulder and gazed up at him. Looking down into her eyes, Bratt believed for a moment that all could be made right in the world again. He reached down and gently kissed her lips, forgetting that world for a while at least.

In his apartment, there was no need for words. He thought he should ask her if she wanted a drink first, but kissed her instead. They let their coats fall to the floor where they stood, just inside the door. They were still wearing their shoes. Over his he wore ankle-high winter rubbers. He knew it was going to be awkward taking them off while maintaining their passionate embrace, and wondered how they managed to do it in the movies.

As if she had read his mind, Nancy pushed him back gently, their wet lips holding on until the last second. Once they were apart she reached down and removed her shoes, placing them neatly on a rubber mat beside the door, all the while never uttering a word.

Following her cue, he began removing his shoe rubbers. The process was more involved than hers. The zippers on the rubbers were encrusted with street-salt and he struggled to open them. Once these were removed, he hurriedly pulled off his tight leather shoes without untying them, almost losing his balance as he did so. When they were finally off he tossed them aside, then turned to look for Nancy.

She had gone a few steps deeper into his apartment, toward the living room, and now stood waiting for him in a patch of pale light that shone in through the window. He could just make out that the long object trailing from her hand and onto the floor was her dress. All she wore now was a dark camisole, which made her skin glow even whiter in the dim light.

"Robert, which way is your bedroom?"

Wordlessly, he pointed down the darkened hall. Her eyes looked in that direction, but she didn't make a move. He hesitated at first, confused by her inaction, then stepped toward her. He put an arm around her waist and kissed her again. She let him walk her down the hall to his room, leaving her dress on the living room floor.

His large bed was still unmade, and his pajamas were strewn across it. Nancy let out a small giggle at the disorder, then stepped forward, picked up the edge of his comforter and pulled all the bed sheets to the floor. She turned, sat on the edge of his bed, and looked back to where he still stood, her hands folded almost demurely in her lap.

Bratt paused briefly to look at her, then, with an abrupt movement he reached up and tried to pull off his tie, almost strangling himself in the process. He laughed self-consciously, but Nancy did not laugh with him this time. He watched as she pushed herself a bit further up on his bed, and then lay languidly back on his mattress.

The tie finally lost the tug of war and he flung it over-dramatically to the side of the room. He quickly unbuttoned his shirt, and it followed in the tie's direction. Finally, his pants still on, he moved to the bed and lay down next to Nancy. Her bare left arm was stretched out above her head and he reached down and kissed it just below the shoulder. Her other hand reached up and stroked his hair for a few seconds, then pulled his face toward her. Their lips and tongues found each other again, while her left arm wrapped around his neck and held him close.

As his hand reached up to cup her breast through the silky material of the camisole, her right hand slid down to his pants' zipper and pulled it down. Working together, their lips never parting, they got his pants and briefs off, until only the thin lingerie was between their bodies. Gently pushing him away, she sat up and slid it over her head, then dropped it to the floor.

She lay back again, pulling him toward her. He rolled on top of her, feeling her firm muscles underneath him, effortlessly bearing his weight. He could feel her heart beating against his as her breath came short and fast through her parted lips. His own lips caressed her face and, as he entered her, a sudden, involuntary breath escaped from her mouth, blowing into his ear.

They slept in each other's arms, like children huddled together during a thunderstorm. Bratt had tried to remain awake, just to listen to her soft breathing, but his body and mind craved sleep. Soon, his breathing fell into step with the calming rhythm of hers.

A bit after 2 a.m. the phone on his night table rang, jarring them both awake. Bratt stretched his arm instinctively to his right to pick up the receiver from the night table, only to find he was sleeping on the far side of the bed. Nancy had already picked up the phone and reflexively answered, "S/D Morin."

"Yes, this is the right number," she said into the phone. "Never mind, he's right here."

She turned and handed the cordless receiver to Bratt, who was leaning up on his elbow, watching with a bemused expression on his face.

"Well I've just embarrassed the hell out of myself," she said to him.

Smiling, he leaned over and kissed her, totally unconcerned about whoever it might be calling him at this late hour.

"Bratt here," he said into the mouthpiece.

"Bobby, it's Kevin Geary at *Centre Opérationnel Sud*."

Lieutenant Kevin Geary was in charge of the night shift at the downtown police operations center. He had known Bratt since the lawyer had been a young teen, hanging around his father's office during summer vacation. In his younger days, Geary had been a bonafide hard-drinking, hard-hitting Irish cop. On one occasion those two predilections had led him to hire then-attorney Joseph Bratt to defend him. Since then, the Bratts had always gotten special treatment from him.

"What's up, Kev? One of my guys get arrested?"

"Well, uh, kind of…" Geary's voice trailed off.

"What do you mean, 'kind of?' What'd you wake me up for then?"

"OK, it is an arrest. But, Bobby, listen, it's…it's not one of your clients. Shit, it's Jeannie."

Bratt instantly sat up. "Jeannie? What're you talking about?"

"Looks like she's been here since this afternoon. She was with those crazy broads in front of the courthouse today."

Bratt remembered Kouri telling him to look out of the window at the demonstration going by, and his own indifference to it. Maybe, if he had looked…

"So why am I just being called now?" he barked angrily.

Nancy grimaced at his harsh tone, then reached out a comforting hand to touch him, unaware of what had happened. Bratt pulled his arm roughly away from her and jumped out of bed, reaching for his watch and glasses as he did so.

"Sorry, Bobby," Geary said. "But I just got on duty at midnight and nobody else here knew who she was. She didn't tell anybody. I mean, they let her call a lawyer of course, but I guess she was too embarrassed to call you. She called the Legal Aid phone service. I just now saw her name on tomorrow's Municipal Court list. I called right away. I'm really sorry, Bobby."

As Geary spoke Bratt dressed hurriedly, his mind racing. He tried not to think of his precious teenage daughter locked up in a police holding cell, with all the junkies and prostitutes who were regularly scooped up in the downtown core of the city.

"Look, just keep an eye on her for me, OK? I'll be there in ten minutes."

With that he hung up, finally remembering Nancy's presence.

"It's Jeannie," he said, unable to say more. The look on Nancy's face showed that she had understood immediately. "I've gotta go."

"Of course, go. Don't worry about me, I'll take a cab."

Haphazardly dressed, he headed for the door, then turned to look back at Nancy, regretting his earlier reaction when she had tried to comfort him.

"I'm sorry. About being…"

She waved him off. "Just go to your daughter."

"Thanks," he said, then turned and ran out the door.

As he impatiently waited for the elevator he thought what every father thought at times like these: *God, I hope she's all right. I'll kill her for this.*

Once he reached his Guy Street destination, Bratt stopped his car in a tow-away zone right in front of the police station and rushed in through the glass double-doors.

Geary was standing just inside the doors, waiting for him. At the sight of Bratt rushing in, his face showed concern and even a touch of fear.

"Take it easy, Bobby. Just calm down."

"Where is she? Is she all right?"

"She's fine. She's in the holding cells, but she's fine."

"Jesus, couldn't you at least take her out until I got here?"

That last remark drew the attention of some officers who were within earshot, congregated at the front desk. Geary pulled Bratt aside.

"For cryin' out loud, Bobby; you're gonna get me in trouble. Listen, I went down there just now and tried to get her to sit in an office until you came, but she wouldn't hear of it."

"What do you mean, 'she wouldn't hear of it?'"

"Just that. She said she was going to stay with her girlfriends, and she didn't want any special favors just because she's your daughter."

Bratt tried to pull away from Geary. "Is she nuts?"

"Calm down," said Geary, holding on tighter. "She's just got a bit of her father's mule headedness in her, that's all. I'll tell you what I can do for you: I'll take you down to speak to her and if you can convince her, she can still wait out the night up here."

"Why should she wait out the night? Can't I take her home?"

"I'm afraid not. She's gotta appear in the morning with the rest of them."

"That's bullshit!" Bratt pushed at Geary's hands, which still gripped his upper arms tightly.

"That's not bullshit, Bobby. That's the way it is. They're all being charged with armed assault."

"Armed assault? Why? What're you talking about?"

"Geez, where you been all day," Geary asked, as he tried to discreetly walk Bratt past the front desk and toward the elevator that would take them down to the holding cells. "The problems began when some demonstrators started hurling snowballs at lawyers going in and out of the courthouse. Then they all got in on the act. That's when our boys moved in." Geary shook his head and laughed to himself. "Snowballs! Only dames would do that."

"I had no idea. I don't even know what they were demonstrating about," Bratt admitted.

"Oh, the usual stuff that pisses women off. They're some sort of victims' rights group, and I guess they think the courts aren't protecting them enough, or something."

Bratt tried keeping himself calm as they rode the elevator down to the basement cells. He knew that making any more scenes wouldn't help Jeannie, and would only embarrass Geary. He wasn't the least bit surprised to find out that Jeannie was one of the demonstrators throwing snowballs at his fellow lawyers. If it hadn't been his daughter, he would have found the idea quite funny.

Once in the detention area, Geary directed Bratt into a small interview room and closed the door behind him as he went to get Jeannie.

Bratt stood nervously, his back to the far wall of the room, thumping his head lightly against it. He had been in a near-panic when he heard that Jeannie was in jail. Now she didn't want any favors because she was his daughter. *Well, want them or not,* he thought, *you're going to get all the special treatment I can possibly get you.*

The door finally opened and Jeannie stepped into the room, Geary closing the door behind her and waiting outside. Her face sported a nasty bruise above her right eye and her lower lip was slightly swollen, making Bratt wonder what she had gotten herself into. He wanted to run to her and hold her protectively, but she let him know right away that she had other ideas.

"What're you doing here?" she demanded.

"What do you think I'm doing here? For Christ's sake, I'm your father."

"Nobody else was allowed a visit from their parents."

"Well, you are allowed to see a lawyer, you know."

"I already *have* a lawyer. I don't need you."

"Dammit, Jeannie, I know you're pissed at me, but I'm trained to help people in these situations. This is what I do for a living, so why not just let me do it? You can't say you're pissed at all lawyers if you've got Legal Aid representing you."

"I'm not pissed at *all* lawyers, Daddy."

"Can you at least be consistent," he said, trying to control his frustration. "How come what I do is so bad, but you're willing to be defended by another lawyer anyway?"

"Because I'm not going to ask him to lie for me," she spat the words out.

"Is that what you think I do? You think every other lawyer can't be accused of the same thing? You're going to be in for some big surprises when your lawyer starts defending you in court."

"Fine, I'll be surprised. But I'll find out for myself, and not with your help."

"What the hell is it about getting my help that you won't accept?"

"Because you think you're so goddamned important that you can just walk into a police station and all your connections will get you whatever you want. Well, I'm not a child anymore. I make my own decisions and I take the consequences for them. I believed in what we were trying to do out there, and I'm not looking to take an easy way out."

She turned her back on him, opened the door and stormed out, turning to Geary as she passed him. "I'd like to go back to the cell now, please."

Geary gave Bratt a pained look and shrugged his shoulders, then ran after Jeannie, key in hand.

Chapter 6

Bratt tossed and turned, trying to block out the constant ringing in his ears, until finally his eyes snapped open and he realized he was back in his bed and the ringing was his phone. A vague memory of Nancy's warmth faded quickly from his sleep-deprived brain as he reached out and grabbed the receiver.

"Hello."

He was surprised to hear the familiar voice of Senator Roger Madsen on the other end.

"Robert, did I wake you?"

Bratt glanced at his watch and saw that it was well after nine. He quickly sat up, like a slouching student who was surprised by the entrance of the school principal into his classroom. Roger Madsen was an old classmate of his father's, as well as Bratt's godfather. His family was one of the oldest and richest in Montreal, and he had been an elder statesman in the Liberal Party ever since Bratt could remember. He was one of the few people in the world, other than his late father, in whose presence Bratt felt anything akin to intimidation, and he had always addressed him as "sir" because anything else was inconceivable.

"No, no," he lied. "Just, uh, just going through a file. How are you doing, sir?"

"Doing well, thanks. I tried you at the office."

"Oh, I was just finishing up here before heading off." He thought of the trip down to the police station that had cost him most of his night's sleep, and, with an inward groan, he dropped his head back onto his pillow. Trying to keep his voice as casual as possible, he asked, "How's the Senate these days?"

"Same as always. A bunch of spoiled, old men playing at government, pretending to themselves that they're relevant."

"Don't say that, sir," Bratt protested. "You've always been very important in the party."

"I suspect my money was more important than my opinions, but that's neither here nor there. I'm coming in to Montreal today, Robert. I'd like to see you when I get in. Perhaps tonight."

This was a distraction Bratt didn't need, and he tried to find a way out of it.

"I've got a lot of work to do on this trial that's coming up. I don't have much time, I'm afraid."

"I won't take too much of your time, Robert. And I think you'll find this visit particularly pleasurable."

"Well, I-"

"See you at my home tonight, Robert. Make it about nine. Goodbye."

Madsen hung up and Bratt moaned out loud. He was going to have to make at least a courtesy call. He wondered what Madsen had meant by 'particularly pleasurable.' He was a fairly staid and conservative gentleman by nature, not given to surprises, so the enigmatic comment piqued Bratt's curiosity, although not enough to make him look forward to the visit.

He jumped out of bed and quickly got dressed. Jeannie would be appearing at the Municipal Court later that morning, and this made any surprises that Madsen had in store for him irrelevant.

Once at the office he told Kouri he wouldn't be able to go see Small that afternoon, they'd have to go the next day. Although they could have gone to the detention center right after Jeannie's arraignment, with all that was on his mind he just couldn't stomach facing this particular client.

As for Jeannie's arrest itself, as much as he could have used the advice and consolation of his friends just then, he didn't mention it to anyone. He was embarrassed and angry about her rejection of his help, and he didn't relish having to try and explain her decision.

He was heading out the office door at 11 a.m., on his way to the Municipal Court for the arraignment, when Sylvie told him there was an S/D Morin on the line for him. He felt a small, empty ache in his heart. He regretted how he had run out on Nancy in the middle of the night, but there was really no time to talk to her now. After Jeannie's court appearance, when he was sure his daughter was out of jail and doing fine, he'd be in a better frame of mind to talk to Nancy and make plans to spend some more time with her.

Maybe if I don't get stuck at Madsen's too long tonight, he told himself.

He mouthed to Sylvie that he'd call Nancy back later and quickly strode to the elevators without telling the receptionist where he was going. If he had told her that he was headed a few blocks east to the Municipal Court it would have raised more than a few eyebrows in the office and questions would definitely have been asked.

Robert Bratt going to Municipal Court was something that few of his colleagues had witnessed in recent years. Despite the court's physical proximity it might as well have been in a different time zone as far as he was concerned. Every other attorney in the office, even Leblanc, went there from time to time. For him, though, it was a point of pride and ego to refuse to take on what he considered to be the less-important cases that came before that court.

On this day, however, he wasn't going there as a lawyer, but as a concerned citizen. His services were not wanted, but if Jeannie knew him as well as she claimed to, she wouldn't be surprised to find him sitting in the courtroom at her arraignment.

Struggling along the icy sidewalks it took him a quarter of an hour to get to the Municipal Court of Montreal, an aging yellowish-beige building, five stories high, that used to house police headquarters.

When he entered the building he was struck by how much things had changed since he had last tried a case there. Back then, the building was rundown, dimly lit, bleakly furnished, and had all the technological advantages of the Stone Age.

He was surprised to find computer terminals lined up along the side of the brightly-lit corridors, freely available for lawyers and members of the public to check on the state of their files. New offices had been built for the various organizations that had set up shop there, such as AA, Legal Aid, and Social Services. Gone were the thin-walled cubicles that had provided all the privacy of an open-window to the people who had gone in seeking help of one sort or another. In the courtrooms themselves, the city had clearly spent the most money, putting in new benches, desks and chairs, and buffing and sanding the marble walls.

All the external changes held Bratt's attention for just a few seconds as he walked toward Room R30, where the group of protesters was scheduled to appear just before lunch. Once inside the large courtroom he sat at the back, and spoke to no one.

Most of the defense lawyers here were much younger than he was, just beginning their careers, looking to make names for themselves in the hope of moving on to bigger things. As for the prosecutors, he didn't recognize any of them either. The ones he had battled with in his day had either been named judges, moved up to higher courts, or been burned out by the heavy workload and lousy pay.

He wondered which of the lawyers gathered near the front was going to represent his daughter. The logical side of his brain told him that there was little chance for anything to go wrong; after all she was an eighteen year-old first-offender. He doubted the prosecution would be objecting to her release, probably even on her own recognizance. The more emotional side of his brain, however, fretted about the million things that could result in her further detention, although he was hard-pressed to come up with one.

The sight of Jeannie appearing in the prisoner's box a few minutes later with a guard at her side brought sudden tears to his eyes. He wiped them away with the palm of his hand, unconcerned about who might see him in this emotional state. His daughter looked haggard, as if she had hardly slept, which he presumed to be the case. For a brief moment, she made eye-contact with him from across the courtroom, then she turned away, stubbornly keeping the wall up between them.

As was the case with all the other protestors, she was released upon a promise to abstain from taking part in or attending any further public demonstrations. It had taken less than two minutes for Jeannie to appear in front of a courtroom full of people, be arraigned and disappear again. She would be released from another door later that morning, and then she'd go join her protestor friends, or go find Claire, or go see that André guy, whoever he was.

Bratt sat there a while longer, feeling lost and trying to find somebody to blame for the way things had turned out. Dejected and knowing this was pointless, he got up and walked slowly back to his office.

Once back in his office, Bratt dumped his coat onto the sofa and turned to find Leblanc walking in, a half-eaten chocolate donut in his hand and some jelly from another donut still staining his lips.

"Hey, Bobby, we all just heard," Leblanc said, a look of concern on his face. "Why didn't you tell me about it?"

"Tell you what?"

"About Jeannie. It was on the radio. You know, 'daughter of noted criminal lawyer, Robert Bratt,' blah, blah, blah."

Shit, Bratt thought. *So much for keeping this quiet.*

"I just didn't want to talk about it, J.P.," he said. "I didn't know how I was going to explain it."

"I know, I know. Stupid kids, always getting themselves in trouble. Hey, it's better than getting busted for drugs."

Bratt nodded, aware that Leblanc was referring to his own teen-age son's arrest, two years earlier.

"You didn't represent her, did you?" Leblanc asked.

"No. Legal Aid."

"Why didn't you get someone from the office down there for her?"

"Oh, you know," Bratt searched for an answer other than the truth. "I figured since I was in a conflict of interest being personally involved, it would be the same for the whole office. Besides, it's good for her to learn a little independence."

Leblanc nodded thoughtfully, unaware of how Bratt had almost choked getting those words out. They both stood there awkwardly, unsure what to do or say next. Bratt moved to pick up some papers from his desk.

"I'm going to head home," he said. "I hardly slept last night. Peter can draft the motion to exclude the videotape on his own. I'll review it in the morning."

"Yeah, sure," Leblanc said sympathetically. "Let me know how things go with her, OK?"

Bratt nodded wordlessly, stuffing whatever papers he could get his hands on into his briefcase. He picked up his coat and walked quickly out, fighting the urge to break into an outright run to the elevator. All of a sudden, his office had begun to feel quite claustrophobic.

Once at home, Bratt trudged into his bedroom to change out of his suit and tie. The red message light was flashing on his answering machine. *Not much chance that would be Jeannie,* he thought. *Then again, she did see me in court, so maybe...*

It wasn't Jeannie, but Nancy, whom he hadn't had the chance to call back after going to the arraignment. He managed to feel both glad and disappointed at hearing her voice.

"Robert? Are you playing hard to get? Don't forget, I know where you live," she said, followed by her soft laugh. "Listen, I hope everything's OK with your daughter. Please call me as soon as you can and let me know. Also, it looks like we're going to be seeing a lot of each other the next little while, so I really have to talk to you."

Yes, we will see each other a lot, he thought. *But first, I'm going to have to get my head together and figure out how the hell to get off this emotional roller-coaster I've been on.*

Upper Westmount's steeply-angled streets wound along the side of Mount Royal and the midwinter snow narrowed them to a barely passible width. More than once in his life Bratt had wondered how the horse-drawn carriages, the main mode of transportation at the time the stately mansions were built, had been able to make their way up these icy slopes.

That night he took a cab to Senator Madsen's home rather than risking the pristine condition of his beloved sports car by driving it on the narrow and slippery roads.

Madsen didn't think there was anything fashionable about being late, so Bratt made sure the cab arrived at the large, wrought iron gate at a few minutes before nine.

At the front door he was greeted by Maria, a tiny, gray-haired woman who seemed to have been with the Madsen family since the War of 1812. She greeted him so quietly he hardly heard her voice and, just as quietly, she ushered him into the study. She asked him to wait there a moment before she headed back out of the room with small, mincing steps.

Bratt looked around at the large room and thought that the word "study" had never done it justice. The walls were lined with ceiling-high mahogany bookshelves that held countless ancient, leather-bound volumes he doubted anybody had ever read. There were two long, brown leather sofas facing a huge fireplace where several logs were burning fiercely. Prominently displayed over the mantelpiece was a large portrait of the first Madsen to land on the shores of North America, a man who had made his fortune by buying beaver and fox pelts from native tribesmen in exchange for worthless trinkets.

There were also a large oak desk, armchairs, end tables, and floor lamps placed neatly about the room. All the furniture gave off the odour of the wax and polish with which it was regularly treated. It was a smell that distinctly said, "old money."

It wasn't long before Senator Madsen strode into the room. He was a small, trimly-built man, whose robust health belied his seventy years of age. He stepped quickly forward, his hand outstretched toward Bratt, a large smile on his face.

"Bobby. It's so good to see you again," he said in a slightly British accent. He gave Bratt a firm handshake and a squeeze on the arm, which were the extent of the displays of affection that he allowed himself toward other men.

"Good to see you again, sir."

The senator directed Bratt to one of the deep sofas next to the fire, then headed straight to the well-stocked bar.

"Something to warm you up?"

"Yes, please. Whatever you're having."

"Some brandy, perhaps? Your father, God rest his soul, was always fond of a snifter on these cold winter evenings."

"Yes. My mother often mentioned that," Bratt answered none too warmly.

Madsen paused as he poured the drinks, his eyes briefly getting misty, before coming back to himself with a shake of his head.

"He was a fine man, your father," he said, clearing his throat. "Despite it all."

"Yes sir," Bratt replied, not nearly meaning it, and feeling a little embarrassed at witnessing Madsen's momentary emotional lapse.

"Well, enough of that. I didn't ask you to come here so that we can act like a couple of weepy old women. There's some news you need to hear."

This must be the "particularly pleasurable" part he had mentioned, Bratt thought, taking his drink from Madsen while hiding all outward signs of curiosity.

"I understand you applied for the opening on the Superior Court last year," Madsen said, straight to the point, as always.

Bratt sat up in surprise. "That's supposed to be confidential."

"Of course it is, Robert. I'd never mention it to anybody else."

That didn't tell Bratt how the senator had heard about it, but he supposed the man had his connections.

"The selections take so long before they're announced," Bratt said, "I pushed it to the back of my mind. I applied when I heard Mike Dickson was stepping down. His kidneys are shot, I think, and the timing seemed just right for me."

"And timing is everything, because since Dickson retired they'll want another Anglo to replace him in Quebec City."

Bratt felt his pulse quicken at the news. He didn't want to jump the gun, but what Madsen was saying was obvious: they were going to make him a judge! For just a moment all memories of seeing Jeannie in the prisoner's dock were pushed aside.

"The Judicial Selection Committee has a list of likely candidates, of course," Madsen continued. "And it has come to my attention that your name is number one-A on it."

"One-A? Is there a one-B, then?"

"Allen Schneider; with Roux, Perreault."

"Oh," Bratt said, trying to hide his disappointment at learning there was a strong rival for the appointment. "I know who he is. Does mostly family law."

"That's him. They haven't really decided if they need another criminal man on the bench or not. Not many English jury trials in Quebec City these days. Still, it wouldn't look good if they didn't have any English-speaking judges for the criminal side out there, would it?"

Bratt took a deep breath in order to keep his thoughts rational and his voice calm.

"So, what's their next step?"

"They're going to give their recommendation to the minister next month. So don't do anything stupid the next few weeks."

"Don't worry, I'll keep my nose clean."

"Of course you will, Bobby. I wasn't really worried. Tell me, are you working on anything interesting right now?"

"A murder case. Double murder, actually."

"*Double* murder, eh? Sounds gruesome. Your client, not some sort of society big-wig, by any chance?"

"No, nothing like that. A working class kid; maybe in a street gang."

"Street gang? Dear Lord, Robert, the people you represent!"

Bratt couldn't help but laugh.

"I'm sorry, Senator. Westmount doesn't have a monopoly on criminals."

Madsen grunted, obviously not appreciating the joke. "Well, I guess your clientele hasn't been held against you, or they wouldn't even be considering you for the position. You think you're going to win this one?"

"The kid's in tough, but I'll certainly give it my best."

"Give it more than your best, my boy. You never know what'll tip the scales in your favor when it's time for them to make a selection. Better to win it, and win it brilliantly. Believe me, you'll leave that Schneider fellow in your dust, if you do."

"I've had a twenty-year career. Is this one case going to make such a difference?"

"It sounds shocking, but it just might. It's all such a show now, you know, especially political appointments. Everything's slanted for the media, and the papers don't care who you are or what you've done in the past. It's all 'what have you done for me lately.'"

"I've done a lot of work for the Party…"

"Much appreciated, you can be sure, Robert. But so has Schneider. All things being equal, and they really are between you two, you don't want to have them make their pick just after you've blown a murder case. Everyone loves a winner, especially politicians."

Bratt looked down at his drink, unhappy that the Small case could have any kind of role to play in his future. He wondered if he could muster up enough enthusiasm to win it, especially with the sorry excuses for alibi witnesses he'd met so far. He gulped down a bit too much of his drink, burning his throat as he did so and setting off a series of jagged coughs.

Shit, he thought, as his eyes watered and Madsen came forward to vigorously slap his back. *This trial's like some sort of a curse on me.*

His coughing finally began to subside and Maria appeared seemingly out of thin air, a glass of water for him in her hand. He reached for it gratefully and drank slowly, cooling his throat and being careful not to choke again.

"Of course, Bobby, you've got to do more than worry about your own image," Madsen continued. "Any, how shall I put this delicately, 'family scandals' could damage your chances."

Bratt honestly had no idea what he meant. "Family scandals?"

"Dear boy, I'm referring to Jeannie's arrest. It's put your name on the radio all day long."

The memory of Jeannie in court that morning came rushing back to Bratt's mind, accompanied with not a little feeling of shame at his having replaced it with thoughts of his career ambitions.

"Of course, it's not a big deal for you now," Madsen said. "Just a little embarrassment you can laugh off at the office. But the Committee might not like it in a candidate for the bench. Naturally, if she were to be acquitted, all a big mistake, something like that, then they probably wouldn't hold it against you."

Great, now I'm supposed to worry about how her arrest affects my future, instead of hers, Bratt thought. *I wonder what she would think of that.*

"Well, there's no way she'll have her trial before the Committee makes its choice," he said. "The court dates are months away, if not longer, so there's not much I can do."

"No, no, I guess not. Hmm." Madsen pondered the situation for a minute before speaking again.

"Nothing to be done about it, I suppose. If you're ever quoted on it you just say that you're behind her one hundred percent, you've always been very proud of her, that sort of thing."

That's a relief, Bratt thought, relaxing the neck muscles that had involuntarily tensed. *For a while there I thought he was going to suggest I disown her.*

Madsen took no notice of Bratt's discomfort. He returned to the bar and began refilling Bratt's glass.

"Here," he said, "try not to choke on this one."

Bratt took the glass, but only looked into it.

"I'll be more careful, sir."

Madsen stood over him and allowed himself another emotional display by squeezing Bratt's shoulder.

"You know Bobby, I can't tell you how happy I am for you. And proud, too."

Bratt looked up and tried to smile appreciatively, squeezing the older man's hand in thanks.

Madsen came around and sat on the sofa across from him

"I only hope you won't miss your clients too much," he teased. "You realize you won't be dealing with any more of those upstanding citizens like your double-murderer."

"No sir, I guess I won't," Bratt answered in a slightly surprised tone. He hadn't really thought about that part of the equation. He would no longer be at the beck and call of people like Marlon Small. Murderers and rapists would no longer be calling him at all hours of the night.

Better than that, he'd no longer have to twist and torture the truth each day in order to get a guilty client off. Whatever second thoughts he'd had about his work lately, being named a judge could solve his problems.

Funny, he thought. *Until about a week ago, it never occurred to me that what I was doing was so terrible. From the perspective of a future judge, though, nothing would be better than washing my hands of my criminal clientele once and for all. And Jeannie would sure be happy about that.*

Bratt swished the amber liquid around in the glass, almost forgetting about Madsen's presence as he became wrapped up in his thoughts. Getting named to the bench had been something he'd hoped for, even if only as a vague future ambition, for a long time now. But he had never imagined that reconciling with his daughter would be a major side benefit.

Still, as much as he had wanted this, something was holding him back from the elation he should have felt at the news.

This is what I've wanted for the longest time, he told himself, *but the timing isn't very good at all. I've got to worry about looking good in a trial I regret taking on, and even "winning it brilliantly," as if just winning it weren't going to be hard enough. Plus, Jeannie's life has suddenly become other people's business. She's not going to be too happy about that. Even the best news comes with strings attached.*

Early the next afternoon Bratt and Kouri were back at the R.D.P. detention center. He had told nobody about his visit with Madsen the night before, although he knew he'd have to speak to his partner about it sooner, rather than later.

As he sat in the interview room, Bratt wondered if the seat on the Superior Court was really going to hinge on winning the Small trial. If so, what could he do to turn this losing case into a winner?

"I don't think he's going to like what you have to tell him," Kouri said, breaking the silence.

Bratt's mind had been drifting, and he didn't catch Kouri's meaning.

"Small," Kouri went on. "He seemed to have put a lot of faith in those two friends of his, and he won't be happy when you tell him that neither one is going to testify."

"Well, he insists he was with a lot of people in that park, so he's going to have to find a few others who can testify, and fast."

"I know, barely two weeks until the trial."

"Faster than that even. Lynn Sévigny was supposed to give in her list of alibi witnesses but she got sick. I gotta meet Parent this afternoon to beg for more time."

They were interrupted by the noise of metal sliding on metal, as the door on the prisoner's side opened and Marlon Small walked in. He was dressed in the same clothes as the last time they had met, and Bratt hoped he was at least familiar with the prison laundry.

Small gave no words of greeting, but sat with his usual surly expression. Bratt assumed that Parker and Clayton had informed him of how their interviews had gone.

"Marlon, I'm afraid those two witnesses you gave us were less than overwhelming."

Small sat staring at them through the smudged glass partition, as if he was waiting for Bratt to explain himself, but Bratt had decided that the ball was in his client's court.

Finally, Small spoke up. "They're a bit light in the brains department. That ain't their fault."

"I don't begrudge them their lack of brains," Bratt said, "just their lack of honesty."

"What's your problem with their honesty?"

"Well, they seem to have misplaced it on the way to my office."

Small's expression became even surlier than before.

"I don't like the way you say that, like you think you're funny. My friends ain't lyin'."

Bratt paused before answering. He knew that antagonizing his client wasn't going to do either one of them any good, however much he may have enjoyed it. He'd have to keep his tongue in check and show Small that he was just trying to be objective for the good of their case.

"OK, sorry for the sarcasm. The problem is you've got one witness who gets confused by the simplest questions, and another one who's a born liar. I'm a defense attorney and it's second nature for me to give everybody the benefit of the doubt, but that was almost impossible to do here. If *I* think your buddies are bullshitting, what do you think a jury is going to think?"

"No sweat. I'll just call 'em and get 'em to straighten out their stories."

"No, that's not what I meant."

"Talk to them again, they'll have all their answers right. The jury'll believe them, you'll see."

Bratt felt frustrated with where this conversation was headed. He had no doubt that both witnesses were lying about being with Small on the night of the shooting. It wasn't enough for them to just "straighten out their stories" because then *he* would still know how dishonest they really were, even if the jury somehow believed them. And it was his knowing that made all the difference in the world, whether Small understood this or not. More than anything, he just wanted Parker and Clayton to disappear from view, so he could start fresh with new witnesses. As for where Small got those other witnesses, that was a problem in itself. But it wasn't Bratt's problem.

"You just don't get it, do you," he said, beginning to feel irritated.

Small jumped up and slammed the glass partition with his open hand. "No, *you* don't get it! I was in the park that night! Ask anybody an' they'll tell you. I didn't go to no damn apartment in Burgundy, an' I didn't shoot no one! So don't tell me I don't get it! It's *my* ass sittin' in a fuckin' jail-cell for the past eight months an' I'm looking for someone who's going to get me out! Do *you* get *that*?"

Bratt said nothing, trying to keep his cool. At the same time he wondered about Small's dramatic glass-slamming routine, which he had just seen for the second time in as many meetings. He thought that Small, in his own way, might be as good a performer as he was.

"Why don't you just sit back down and chill, Marlon," Bratt said, folding his arms and waiting for Small to take his seat. As he watched Small make a show of regaining his composure, Bratt found himself questioning his own motivations. Was he more concerned that the witnesses might lie on the stand or that they might get caught in those lies, despite Small's certainty that they could get away with it? Winning this case was going to be hard enough and, if Madsen were to be believed, winning this case had just become the most important thing in Bratt's life.

"It happens to be my job to get your ass out of that jail cell," he said, "and it's a job I usually do pretty well. But it's not going to happen just because you say everyone knows you were in the park that night, not when the only two witnesses you give me are liars and everyone who hears them will know it the moment they open their mouths."

Bratt paused to clear his throat. He pulled at a frayed string that had once held a button to his silk shirtsleeve and wondered where he had lost the button and why he hadn't noticed its absence until now. Small sat quietly, waiting for him to go on with his little speech, his dislike for his attorney obvious in his face.

A quick glance by Bratt to his side showed him that Kouri was also watching him and he knew he had to choose his words carefully. He was aware that there was a fine line between telling his client he needed better witnesses and asking for better liars. Over the years he had convinced himself that he had never knowingly crossed that line, although his definition of "knowingly" had gotten narrower with the passage of time and the growing imperative to win.

He hated Small for making him walk that line again, and he hated himself for closing his eyes as he gingerly took the first steps. But what choice did he have? The need to win guided what he had to say.

"You have to understand that I don't do this job for you," he said, "I do it because I like to win. It just so happens that when I win, you win. I couldn't care less where you were that night, whether you shot those guys or not. That simply isn't part of my job."

From the corner of his eye Bratt saw Kouri's body stiffen. *Leave me the hell alone,* he thought, directing the thought both at Kouri and at his own conscience.

"You couldn't pay me enough to care," he continued. "But you also can't pay me enough to lie for you in court, nor to call witnesses that *I know* are going to perjure themselves, like your two buddies."

He paused again, to see if there was any light of understanding in Small's eyes. Almost, but not quite yet, so he went on.

"If you want a jury to believe you were in the park, then you can start by coming up with some *other* witnesses who can convince *me* first."

Small's expression softened almost imperceptibly as he nodded, looking Bratt straight in the eyes, finally letting Bratt see what he was looking for.

"No problem, Mr. Bratt," he spoke slowly. "I know what you want. I'll get the word out right away. I know who else was with me that night. I'll get you their names and phone numbers later this week."

"I'm going to need them as fast as possible," Bratt said, suddenly feeling like a junkie desperately waiting for his next fix. At the same time, he assiduously kept his eyes away from Kouri, who continued to sit motionless at his side.

"No problem, Mr. Bratt," Small said again, and Bratt marveled at the tone of respect his client had suddenly begun using with him. "And no bullshitters this time."

In the car later, driving with Kouri back to the office, Bratt did his best to look and act casual. He could feel Kouri's eyes constantly on him, as if the junior lawyer were waiting for some sort of sign from on high, but he had no words of explanation or of wisdom to give him. He had said and done what was required in order to give them the best, if not the only, chance to win this case, mostly in the hope that it would be the last case he would ever have to plead. He had carefully chosen his words and could defend each one of them if he ever had to. How Small interpreted them and what he did about them was not his problem.

They parked in a lot a block away from the office, and trudged through the snow in silence. At one point Bratt's foot slipped on some ice hidden under a thin layer of snow and he lost his balance. Instantly, Kouri reached out and grabbed his arm before he fell. At that moment their eyes met, and he saw that Kouri's questions still lingered. Bratt mumbled his thanks and pulled his eyes and arm away, continuing along the frozen path.

He began to wish that Kouri would just ask what he was obviously dying to and get done with it. At least then he could defend himself and set the record straight. But he couldn't broach the subject himself, because that would look like he was just trying to assuage his own guilty conscience.

Not much chance of that being the case, he told himself, and tried to push all thoughts of the subject out of his mind.

His appointment with Parent that afternoon was at 3:00 and he headed straight to the courthouse while Kouri went on up to their office. At five to the hour Bratt was standing in front of a receptionist as she advised Parent of his arrival before buzzing him in. He wondered what he was going to say when the prosecutor asked to see the names of the proposed alibi witnesses. "I think my client is interviewing actors for the roles as we speak," was one possible answer, although perhaps dangerously close to the truth.

He walked through the maze of corridors of the Crown offices, following the numbered signs and arrows on the walls until he arrived at Parent's office. As associate chief prosecutor for nearly twenty years Parent had a much larger office than most of the other Crown attorneys. Despite his family connections Parent had never accepted the judge's robes that had been waved at him from time to time, preferring the moral certitude of his sworn oath to prosecute the hell out of every petty thief and jaywalker that had the misfortune to cross his path.

Bratt knocked lightly on the open door and stepped in. Parent sat behind his large melamine desk, on a standard-issue gray-cloth civil servant's chair. Across from him and with his back still to Bratt sat Sergeant-Detective Philippe St. Jean, and next to him, turning in her seat to face the door, was Nancy Morin.

Bratt stared at her from just inside the doorway, unsure how to act. Parent, to Bratt's relief, broke the ice by speaking first.

"Hello, Robert. Come on in. You know Philippe St. Jean. And, of course, this is S/D Morin, whom you've become intimately familiar with recently, I believe."

Bratt was stunned, suddenly certain that she had already revealed their affair. Nancy must have recognized the expression on his face, because she smiled at him reassuringly as she said to Parent, "After the past two months in court I'm sure he hoped it was the last he'd seen of me."

"Nonsense," said Parent. "How could any man get tired of the presence of such a lovely lady? Now, sit down, Robert, and please shut the door."

The prosecutor pulled a yellow legal pad closer and pushed his thick glasses up higher on his long, thin nose, peering through them at Bratt.

"Well, Robert, I've been waiting expectantly for this moment ever since I heard you took over for Lynn Sévigny. What do you have for us?"

Bratt didn't answer right away. He still hadn't decided what to say about the alibi witnesses and Nancy's presence had thrown him for a loop. He turned his head and stared at her again, asking himself, *What the hell is she doing here?*

Parent answered this question as if Bratt had asked it out loud.

"Miss Morin is going to assist me during the trial, Robert. You probably weren't aware she was being temporarily assigned to homicide, since Philippe is taking his retirement. Well-deserved, I might add."

"Oh, I see," Bratt replied, although he clearly didn't see at all.

It was taking several seconds for what Parent had said to sink in. Nancy was going to be working the Small trial? Her message had said they'd be seeing a lot of each other, but this wasn't what he had expected.

Bratt turned toward St. Jean, trying to keep the surprise from his voice as he spoke.

"Retired, Phil? At your age?"

"I've put in my thirty years, *Maitre* Bratt. It's time to move on."

"Well, winning this case won't be half as much fun without you."

Both St. Jean and Parent reddened and frowned at the remark. Only Nancy smiled, turning quickly to the window when she did so.

"He'll still be there to testify about the accused's statement, of course," Parent said. "You had a chance to watch that Oscar-winning performance by Mr. Small, Robert, I'm sure."

Parent raised one bony hand up to his forehead and leaned melodramatically back in his chair, as he mocked Small's words.

"*F you*," he said, deleting the expletive in deference to Nancy's presence. "I feel fine. Just get me my lawyer. And get me my mommy while you're at it."

St. Jean roared with appreciative laughter, while Parent favored Bratt with a slow, snakelike smile. He clearly had little fear about being on the losing team, with or without St. Jean at his side.

Bratt didn't rise to the bait, even though he found Parent's self-satisfied arrogance hard to digest. He surprised the prosecutor by smiling right back. He may have thought as little of his client's videotaped performance as the others did, but he had his own ideas about who was going to see it.

"You'll be served my motion to exclude the tape tomorrow, Francis. We'll be among the privileged few who ever have the chance to see it."

Parent's smile turned icy. "Well, that will be for someone else to decide. In the meantime, I believe you have something for us."

He held out his hand regally, as if he expected an alibi witness to materialize in thin air and be instantly within his grasp. When Bratt didn't respond for several seconds he slowly lowered his outstretched hand.

"Am I missing something, Robert?"

"No," Bratt squirmed uncomfortably, "I am. I haven't had a chance to interview all the alibi witnesses yet. I've been a little squeezed for time."

Parent turned to St. Jean with an exaggerated wide-eyed stare, as if incredulous that such a thing could happen. “If you didn’t have the time you should never have taken on the case, Robert. We’re not talking about shoplifting here.”

Bratt winced inwardly, but said nothing. Being treated like a rookie by the older prosecutor was old hat, but it was getting tiresome.

Parent waited, looking disappointed that he hadn’t been able to goad Bratt into anger. He shrugged indifferently at the lack of a response and continued.

“Well, if you haven’t seen all the witnesses you can give me the names of the ones you have seen. Monsieur St. Jean can begin contacting them-”

“No,” Bratt blurted out. “Sorry, Francis, but I prefer giving you the names of the witnesses that I’ll call only after I’ve interviewed them all.”

“I was supposed to have their names before today.”

“Shit happens,” Bratt growled, unable to think of a better way to explain his dilemma.

“Well, that’s a novel argument. Like to try it in the Superior Court?”

“Just name the time and place,” Bratt snapped back, a little too loudly. “I’ve got nothing to hide.”

Parent’s eyebrows arched as if he had just discovered something fascinating.

“Oh, Robert, you know as well as I do that we all have something to hide, most of all the ones who proclaim the loudest that they don’t.”

Bratt held back an angry retort. Parent wasn’t missing a beat today and he was going to have to watch what he said.

“Here’s an important lesson for you, my dear,” Parent said, turning toward Nancy. “The lawyer who says the least is usually the one hiding the most useful information. Certainly the most interesting.”

Parent was trying hard to impress Nancy with his clever observations. Bratt didn’t like being talked about in the third person while he was sitting in the same room. He felt his face redden in anger, but this only encouraged Parent to continue his analysis.

"Robert here is usually much more discreet, but look how he's blushing. What is he hiding, I wonder? Why not tell us, Robert? Relieve your conscience of whatever burdens it."

Parent had come too close for comfort with that last remark. Bratt suddenly felt like an open book that the prosecutor was able to read from at will. He needed to end Parent's game, but without revealing what was eating at him.

"Quit playing the father-confessor, Francis. That bullshit hasn't worked on me for twenty years, so give it a rest."

"You're usually not so easy to read, Robert."

"And quit telling me what I'm like, or what I do or don't have on my mind. You don't know me as well as you think"

Parent stood up abruptly and walked to the window, stretching as he did so. He spoke while keeping his back turned to Bratt, certain that this would irritate the defense attorney.

"Fine, fine," he said, sounding bored. "Deprive me of my little pleasures if you must. Anyway, Robert, you go and see your witnesses, whoever they might be. Take all the time you need making sure they know their lines well. It won't make much difference for Mr. Small in the end, will it?"

Now the son of a bitch is patronizing me, Bratt fumed to himself. *And he keeps dropping hints about my alibi witnesses as if he smells something fishy.*

"Don't be so smug," Bratt said, trying hard to maintain his own mask of self-confidence. "It's been a lot of years since you put one past me in court."

"Thanks for coming by, Robert," Parent said, with a dismissive wave of his hand. "We'll call you if we need anything else from you."

At this last indignation Bratt's temper, to his own surprise, as much as Parent's, snapped. He was used to being treated with more respect than Parent was showing and he found being talked to like a child in front of Nancy to be particularly galling.

"You can shove your pompous crap, Francis!"

"Oh my, I've hurt Robert's feelings."

"You can patronize me all you want, but you know I'll kick your ass in court, just like I always do."

"Is this what it's all about, Robert? You beating me in court? That doesn't leave much room for the client, does it? But, as long as you win…"

"Don't twist my words!"

"No. That's your specialty."

"I've had enough of your smug self-assurance for today. I'll fax you my alibi witnesses when I'm good and ready."

With that, Bratt stormed out of the office. As he stamped down the hall, he could hear Parent's voice calling behind him.

"All good things come to an end, Robert. Don't take it so personally."

When Bratt got back out on the street the air was thick with heavy, wet snowflakes. He didn't want to go back to his office until he had cooled off from his sour mood and he decided that a mid-winter stroll would help lower his temperature. He headed down St. Laurent Boulevard, toward the Old Port, two blocks south of the courthouse.

As he walked, he tried to figure out exactly why he was angry, and how he had gotten there. Parent's insolence was nothing new. He'd been treating Bratt like a schoolboy since their days together at the Crown, and Bratt had always been able to shrug it off before, chalking Parent's attitude up to professional jealousy.

Bratt had always prided himself in keeping cool and maintaining his composure in the most heated battles. In any argument it was usually his own smug self-assurance that rubbed his opponents the wrong way. Lately, though, he was flying off the handle at the slightest provocation. Parent was probably in his office right now, gloating with St. Jean about having gotten under his skin so easily.

Frustrated over his lack of self-discipline, Bratt kicked at a small chunk of snow and sent it skittering down the icy sidewalk. Walking as fast as he dared on the slippery surface, he got to the Old Port and headed west along the waterfront. The cold wind blowing in off the St. Lawrence River dug into his bones and set his teeth to rattling. The river was still frozen solid, weeks away from the spring thaw that would allow the first ships to get through.

Bratt walked briskly, his hands shoved deep into his coat pockets, alone with his thoughts. There were no other pedestrians foolhardy enough to travel so close to the wind-swept piers. Only the occasional car passed him, looking for a parking space in the shelter of one of the large, converted sheds that lined the river.

Shit, you're going to freeze to death, he scolded himself, making no effort to move farther inland.

Bratt thought back to the day Leblanc had suggested he take on Marlon Small's defense. He had rejected the idea outright at the time and yet he had ended up taking the case anyway.

Just couldn't back down from a challenge, could you? Particularly when people are telling you what an amazing lawyer you are. Vanity, thy name is Robert Bratt. Now you've gotta win it, and not only to satisfy your damn ego.

After walking for a few more minutes, he'd had enough of the cold wind that was whipping around him. He quickly crossed the street again and headed a block north to St. Paul Street, where the narrow, cobbled road would give him some measure of protection. Once there, he was able to slow his pace down somewhat and he took the time to gaze into the windows of the tourist-empty souvenir shops that he passed. He continued his ongoing internal debate as he window-shopped along the Old Montreal street.

Now that I've taken on Small's file I'm regretting it, he thought. *That fact alone is cause for worry. I haven't survived this long in the game by being wishy-washy. Lately, though, I've been constantly second-guessing decisions that used to be so easy to make. Who'd believe Robert Bratt would have so little taste for a good murder trial?*

So I hate my client, so what? When was the last time I really liked one of my clients? That's never been important before. And if I think he's guilty, again so what? That's never been important before, either. At least this one claims to be innocent, unlike a lot of other people I've represented, like Mr. Cooper Hall, 'cash please, no checks from fraud artists.' It's not my job to judge him, after all.

But you can't deny that these things are important now, can you, Robert? You just can't rationalize everything like you used to. Things feel very different, ever since...well, since Claire got beaten up on the witness stand, of course. So now, you're just pissed off every day and at everything, especially if it has to do with the Small case. And it sure didn't take much of a shove to make you go off the deep end back in Parent's office.

He was beginning to tire of the never-ending debate.

What's the point of beating yourself up over this? Just do your best and in a few weeks it'll all be over. Who knows? You'll probably win, anyway. That'll solve everything.

He had walked several blocks west by the time he got a semblance of control over his thoughts and emotions. Despite having escaped the strong wind that came in off the water his cheeks were beginning to burn and he decided he had cooled off enough. He took a right at the next corner and headed back up to Notre Dame Boulevard, then turned back east, approaching his office from the far side of the Basilica that dominated Place d'Armes. As he neared it he could see several tour buses parked in front of the huge church. In the middle of winter it was one of the few tourist destinations that still drew crowds.

Maybe I should go in there and seek some sort of guidance, he thought, half-jokingly. *No, better not. After twenty years as a lawyer, I might not get out of the confessional until spring.*

He reached the parked tourist buses and then crossed the large square, maneuvering through the slow-moving traffic. His pace quickened as he got closer to his destination, until he was nearly jogging by the time he entered his office building.

Safe, he thought to himself, as he came in from the cold.

Tired and cold from the long walk, and mentally drained from the argument he had been having with himself, Bratt sought refuge at his law firm. All he wanted was to be alone with his thoughts for a little while longer.

When he stepped into the firm's waiting area he saw several of his associates standing around in their shirtsleeves at the top of the corridor, drinking coffee and talking loudly. Leblanc and

Kalouderis seemed to be holding court, while the others looked on, smiling at their stories.

They turned to him as he removed his rubbers and coat, and waved him over.

"Bobby, come here. You'll remember this one," Leblanc called out.

Bratt approached the group, puzzled at this unusual mid-afternoon gathering, and hesitant at getting dragged into any kind of group discussion.

"What's up?" he asked. "Nobody got court?"

"Geez, where you been the last hour? They got another bomb alert," Kalouderis said. "Pete here thinks the whole thing's very exciting."

Kouri smiled, but said nothing.

"So, anyway, while we're killing time we thought we'd just fill him in on some of the office folklore."

"Uh-huh," Bratt replied, unable to muster up any enthusiasm. The others didn't seem to notice his lack of interest and continued their conversation as they gravitated into his office after him, not allowing him the peace and quiet he had hoped to find there.

Leblanc sat on the edge of Bratt's desk, dragging him into the conversation.

"Bobby, you remember when John was defending that Haitian kid? What was his name? Edson something or other."

"Horacius," piped in Kalouderis. "He was a small-fry in one of those Montreal North gangs that were shooting each other up, back in the early '90s."

"Yeah, him," Leblanc said, laughing, then turning toward Kouri to continue his story. "So, it was the trial and this one kid who'd had his arm almost blown off is testifying, telling everybody what a murderous bastard this Horacius kid was."

"And he was, too," Kalouderis chimed in again, from his usual seat, stretched out on the sofa.

Bratt sat expressionless and gazed out the window at the blowing snow, barely tolerating their presence, totally indifferent to the topic of conversation. He had no idea if he had ever found this story humorous, and now it simply grated on his nerves.

"So, John's cross-examining the kid," Leblanc went on, "and he's going at him with a sledgehammer, really trying to make him look like shit. And this kid's trying to put up a brave front, right? He doesn't want to give John anything, but pretty soon John's got him twisting in the wind."

"Must have been one of his sober months," a voice to Bratt's left said, getting a laugh from the others, including Kalouderis. Bratt couldn't be bothered to turn to see who spoke, but it sounded like Ralston.

Leblanc waved his hand to hush him so he could go on with the story.

"So, finally this kid speaks up and says, 'Geez, Mr. Kalouderis, if you worked this hard at my trial there's no way they would have found me guilty.'"

Kalouderis laughed loudly, gleefully kicking his feet on the sofa, but Kouri only looked confused. Bratt just wished they would all go away. If John wanted to laugh at his own screw-ups, couldn't he find somewhere else to do it?

"The kid doesn't get it," Leblanc said, pointing at Kouri. He spoke slowly to the new lawyer, as if explaining to a small child. "The witness that was testifying against Horacius just happened to be another one of John's clients. John had lost a trial with him a couple of months before that and he didn't even remember him. He was cross-examining him for an hour and it never clicked that he's representing one client against another, for crying out loud."

"Do you have any idea how frustrating it is when one of your clients shoots another client," Kalouderis complained. "You end up losing two clients out of the deal. Very bad for business."

Leblanc continued as if Kalouderis had said nothing. "He's got no idea that he's in a serious conflict of interest and in the deepest of shit with the judge."

"Yeah, which was too bad because I had Sauvé on the bench," Kalouderis said. "Now that was a good judge. He even acquitted one of my black clients against some cops once."

"I guess you weren't so sober after all," said Ralston.

Kalouderis ignored the last remark, adding his own details to the story.

"Let me tell you, Pete, I had to do some of my best pleading to convince him that it was all just an honest mistake and I wasn't trying to pull a fast one on the court."

"Yeah, he had to convince the judge he really could be that stupid, and it wasn't as easy as it sounds."

"Shut up, Ralston," Kalouderis snapped at him, smiling nevertheless, as were the other lawyers listening to the story.

At this point Bratt had had enough. In the past few days, and despite all the roadblocks that seemed to have been thrown up in his way, he had been trying his best just to do his best. Listening to lawyers joking about their own incompetence now was like a slap in the face.

He turned from the window and roared, "Just because all your court cases are on hold doesn't mean that I've got time to waste listening to your pathetic stories!"

The other lawyers stopped in the middle of their bantering. Their smiles were still frozen on their faces, but all the joy had gone out of them, and they looked at each other in silent embarrassment. Leblanc cleared his throat and spoke tentatively.

"Uh, Bobby's pretty busy guys. Maybe we really should let him and Pete get back to work."

The others nodded to each other and then sheepishly began to head out, all except Kalouderis, who eyed his friend carefully, concerned about what might have brought on that little explosion. Bratt's eyes met his, but they held no invitation to stay and talk, so he reluctantly shuffled back to his own office.

As Leblanc headed for the door, he turned and looked at Kouri, who had remained behind to do his work. Kouri's face held a look of terror, so Leblanc shook his head silently, letting him know he shouldn't worry. Then he spoke to Bratt.

"Sorry, Bobby. I know it's been a really tough week, and time's tight with this Small case. Then again, that's no reason to behave like an asshole."

Bratt's throat constricted as he held his rising anger in. He knew he would regret his outburst later, but right now he had no time to waste on remorse. Once Leblanc was gone he saw that Kouri was just standing in the middle of the room, like a soldier caught in no-man's land, looking worried about his fate. He glared at him accusatorially, as if he held Kouri to a higher standard than he did his associates, but he said nothing. Finally he opened the Small file and sat down, rifling through its pages.

"Did you draft the motion?"

"Yes," Kouri answered, without moving from his spot.

"Did you make copies of the jurisprudence on this point?"

"Yes," Kouri repeated, still unmoving.

"Oh, for Christ's sake. *At ease*, private," Bratt drawled sarcastically.

Kouri's face reddened, and he came forward tentatively to sit across the desk from Bratt.

"Make sure the bailiffs serve it today, so we can argue it on Monday. Just in case the judge decides to let that video in, we'll still have a week before the jury's called to come up with a backup plan."

"Any idea what plan B would be?"

Bratt thought of the tourists and pilgrims lined up to enter Notre Dame that afternoon and briefly pictured himself among them, praying for help.

"Plan B is to make sure that plan A works," he said. "So, let's see what you have for me."

The rest of the afternoon they spent reading the case law Kouri had gathered on the admissibility of statements. Bratt had to admit that in the few hours that he had had available to him, Kouri had done a very thorough job.

They would have to convince the judge that the contents of the video only served to make Small look bad by drumming up suspicions against him, without actually containing proof of anything. After all, saying that Small *looked* guilty on the tape was purely a matter of opinion. And as for St. Jean's crowing during the questioning about how strong their case was, that also proved nothing, but it was dangerous because a jury could easily buy into his claims.

They read the jurisprudence, and wrote notes, and discussed the strengths and weaknesses of their position. Kouri played devil's advocate, arguing against every point that Bratt tried to make, forcing him to think fast on his feet and preparing him for Parent's probable counter-arguments. Once again, Bratt had to admit that Kouri was quite good at this. Once the young lawyer got rolling, his shyness and diffidence seemed to disappear, and they were replaced by a sharp, confident intellect. Bratt wasn't ready to go so far as saying he liked the young man, but he was beginning to dislike him a lot less each day.

By seven o'clock that evening they had argued and analyzed their motion every conceivable way and Bratt was ready to head home. Kouri disappeared into the little cubbyhole that was his temporary office to gather his coat and scarf, and Bratt wondered if it wouldn't be a good time to let him know what he thought of his work. He hesitated, unsure how to go about it. Handing out compliments didn't come easily to him, but he told himself that he would need to keep the young lawyer happy and interested in their work if he wanted him to be at his best in court. Bratt also appreciated the fact that, since his return to the office, Kouri hadn't tried to bring up their earlier meeting with Small.

When Kouri came out into the corridor, he saw Bratt waiting for him, an awkward smile on his face.

"Listen, Pete, before you go," Bratt hesitated, suddenly afraid of seeming over-sentimental. "I thought you should know, I think your work's been pretty good so far. First rate, really. You've been a lot of help."

The two men stood facing each other, both clearly embarrassed by what had just been said, although both seemed happy that it was. For a few painful seconds Bratt wondered if Kouri might try to hug him.

Finally, Kouri smiled and said simply, "Thanks, Mr. Bratt."

"No problem, kid," Bratt said quickly, trying to preserve his gruff exterior. "I just call 'em like I see 'em."

He felt that he should say something more, maybe let Kouri know that he no longer looked on him as an outsider.

What the heck, he thought. *I've got nothing else to do tonight.*

"Got any plans this evening," he asked.

Kouri looked a bit embarrassed and surprised at the question, clearly never having expected it.

"Uh, as a matter of fact, yes. I've got some…friends. I'm meeting them for supper now."

Of course, the little shit would have a social life, Bratt thought, as he smiled and said, "No problem. We'll go for drinks or something, sometime."

Again, there was that moment of awkwardness, then Bratt turned and walked quickly out, hoping against hope that Kouri wouldn't race after him and join him on the slow elevator ride down to street level. Perhaps sensing the older lawyer's discomfort, Kouri lagged behind until the elevator doors slid closed on Bratt.

At home that night he dropped back into the soft leather sofa in his living room and rested his stockinged feet up on his glass-topped coffee table. Remote control pointed at the TV, his eyes half-closed, he flipped aimlessly through the cable universe. He was feeling quite relaxed now. His mind was less preoccupied than it was earlier that day, after the scene he'd made in Parent's office. The time he had put in with Kouri had been very useful, not just in preparing Small's defense, but in getting himself concentrated and thinking straight again.

The ringing of the telephone roused him from his drowsing state and he grabbed at it instantly.

"Bratt here."

He was surprised to hear the voice of Jennifer Campbell on the other end.

"Good evening, Mr. Bratt. I'm sorry to disturb you at home, but I needed to speak to you."

Bratt paused before answering. The last people he wanted to talk to that night were those connected with Marlon Small. But Campbell was the one footing his bill, and she deserved at least the time of day from him.

"Hello, Mrs. Campbell. I'm afraid you've caught me at a bad time. Is there anything I can help you with?"

"I just had a long talk with my boy, Marlon. He's a bit hot-headed and doesn't always know what's good for him, but I think everything's going to be fine."

"What do you mean?"

"He was a bit upset that you didn't think much of his two friends. I told him that you're the expert here and we have to trust in your opinion in such matters."

"Thank you, Mrs. Campbell."

"Well, I certainly wouldn't have hired you if I didn't have total confidence in your abilities. I told Marlon to forget all about the past for now and to concentrate on what has to be done to get him out of jail. He told me you want him to find some other people who will say he was in the park that night. Is that right?"

"Yes. The original list I received from Lynn Sévigny had eight or nine names on it. Most didn't have addresses or phone numbers. If he could help me get in touch with some of them that would be the best place to start."

"That's what I thought as well. I'll make sure he gets you somebody in a few days. I told Marlon that we're putting our faith in God and in the talent that He's given you. So, you go back to what you were doing and I'll see to it that you get the witnesses you need to get my boy freed."

After she hung up Bratt felt a sense of relief. Jennifer Campbell was so straight, so obviously honest, she would make sure that any potential witnesses her son came up with would be on the up and up. This would spare Bratt from possibly having to cross the line that he was so familiar with and had come to dread. Surely she wouldn't allow Marlon to step through the door that Bratt had opened so widely for him when he had implied that he didn't care if the witnesses perjured themselves or not, just as long as they could convince a jury.

Shedding his clothes, he headed to the bathroom and turned on the shower. Totally isolated from the outside world, he was able to think most clearly there. He wondered how his clients would feel if they knew that many of the brilliant arguments he had used to save them from jail had popped into his head between rinse well and shampoo again.

Too bad shower stalls didn't come in a portable, laptop size, so I could take them everywhere with me. Maybe I could stay out of trouble that way, and not have to depend on my client's mother to save what little integrity I have left.

Chapter 7

Thursday around noon they got news from Small about his alibi witnesses. Kouri had just returned from some doctor's appointment and he and Bratt were poring over ballistics reports when Sylvie's voice came over the speakerphone. She announced a collect call from "Mr. Marvin Ball."

Close enough, Bratt thought, as Kouri moved quickly to pick up the receiver. He talked quietly into the phone for a few seconds, his back to Bratt, then turned and passed him the receiver. Bratt looked at him quizzically, wondering what that was all about, before turning his attention to Small.

"Marlon, it's about time. I've been waiting for your call."

Small replied sarcastically, "Yeah, I figured there was no hurry, right, so I took as much time as possible."

"OK, OK. I just meant that I was starting to worry. Time is tight, you know. So, what do we have?"

"I got a couple of guys for you to meet. They been out of town a while, and now they're back I reached 'em. They were shooting hoops with me at the park that night, and they'll swear to it in court. And these guys ain't no fuckups. You're gonna like 'em."

"Well, I hope so, because they're the last, but most important, piece of the puzzle. Can they come see us tomorrow morning?"

"Yeah, I gave my man Pete their names and numbers. I talked to them an' they're waiting for his call."

"That's fine. If they're any better than the last two, I'll send their names on to the cops tomorrow afternoon."

"They'll do. I'm sure of it. Catch you later."

Small hung up, and Bratt thought that his final words made for a chilling prospect.

"Well," Kouri asked. "Feel better?"

"I'll tell you tomorrow. Wanna go call them from your office? I need the phone."

"Sure," said Kouri and, as he left, Bratt wondered when exactly Small had begun referring to the young lawyer as 'my man, Pete.'

Once Kouri was out of the office Bratt reached for the receiver. Feeling a bit better about how the trial preparation was going he thought he'd give Nancy a call and see if he hadn't made a total fool of himself at Parent's office. The day ahead didn't look too busy, so he could afford to get away from the office for a couple of hours. He only hoped she was available, and willing, to see him.

He dialed and when she answered her voice sounded distant and scratchy.

"Oui, allô? Nancy Morin ici."

"Hey, you didn't know it was me calling," Bratt joked, feeling an illogical twinge of disappointment nevertheless.

"Oh, Robert, hi. I'm on the road and talking on this wire they gave me."

"I can tell. There's a lot of background noise, and your voice is pretty scratchy."

"I'm headed down to your part of town now. I've got to pick up some things from Parent's office, get up to speed on the file, so I can at least make myself useful."

"Parent's gonna need all the help you can give him," Bratt joked. He couldn't make out her response, however, as her voice seemed to fade away for a moment before coming back a bit more clearly.

"Robert, are you there?"

"Yeah, Nancy, but your voice is really breaking up. Why don't you call me when you get to the courthouse?"

"OK. Maybe we can have some lunch if you didn't eat yet."

"Lunch sounds great. Call me when you get down here."

Lunch was not quite the intimate tête-à-tête he had hoped for. Nancy only had enough time to grab a quick muffin with him at a crowded coffee shop across the street from the courthouse. There were no seats available, so they stood wearing their coats at a counter, drinking decaf and trying to make themselves heard over the din of the lunchtime crowd.

Bratt felt a certain little boy excitement about seeing Nancy again, even in a crowded café. While he had waited in his office for her to call back his mind had drifted back to their time together Monday night. He hadn't thought of the sex, or even the dinner conversation. Rather, he kept reliving those minutes he had been able to stay awake while lying next to her, feeling the warmth of her breath, touching her cool, soft skin. It had been many years since he had been so at ease, so unguarded in his thoughts and actions when alone with a woman. Not since Deirdre.

He was happy to find that this thought hadn't come with a little pang of guilt.

Now, standing in the crowded coffee shop, Bratt gazed happily at Nancy while he munched on his muffin. She wasn't eating hers, only picking it apart slowly, seemingly deep in thought. He noticed that she wasn't as flirtatious or as self-confident as she usually was with him.

Bratt leaned over to speak directly into her ear, to make sure she heard him clearly and to prevent others from overhearing his uncharacteristically sentimental words.

"I've missed you," he said.

Nancy pulled her head back with a jerk, but he knew that his voice hadn't been too loud. The expression on her face showed reticence at being too close to him. She didn't respond to what he said, and was clearly having difficulty looking him in the eye.

"Is there something you want to tell me?" he asked her.

He didn't expect her to have trouble getting her words out, but she clearly did.

"I guess…I guess I'm just not comfortable about, you know, being seen with you in public."

The way she kept glancing nervously around her made that very clear.

"Hey, it was your idea to have lunch," he said, sporting a wolfish grin as he leaned closer again and touched her hand. "I had much more intimate plans."

She didn't return his smile, and she pulled her hand back from his touch.

"OK, what is it, Nancy? You've never had trouble telling me what's on your mind before, so tell me what's going on now."

She took a deep breath before looking up at him, as if this simple gesture required a great effort from her.

"Robert, this case is very important for me."

"I know it is. It's important for me too."

"Of course, and that's a big part of the problem. Don't forget we're on different sides here."

"What? Does my defending this guy bother you?"

"Frankly, that does bother me…a bit. But I'm not your daughter, and I didn't just wake up and discover you're a defense lawyer. I knew what I was getting into from the beginning. I decided from the moment that I…well, began to feel anything for you, that I wouldn't hold your job against you."

"Gee, that's very big of you," he said, sourly. "So, what's the problem now?"

"Like I said, this case is very important. If I want to get anywhere in this job, I can't have anybody questioning my loyalty."

"You spent two months openly flirting with me during the Hall trial. You didn't seem to care what people thought then."

"It's different now."

"Why?"

"I don't know, it just is. Maybe it's because this is my first murder case, and all I've ever wanted to do was work homicide. Maybe it's working with Parent. He's so straitlaced he acts like we're on some sort of holy crusade."

"And I'm the hated infidel, right? You shouldn't take him too seriously."

"I take him seriously because he can influence my career, and he's made it clear he can't stand you. Look, this case just fell into my lap all of a sudden and I'm really scared that I'll blow it. All I want is for the two of us to slow things down a bit."

"Slow things down? We've barely gotten going."

He placed a hand around her waist and pulled her closer, but she turned her face away when he tried to kiss her.

"Robert, please! We're not kids here."

"You didn't think I was a kid the other night."

"But things have changed, and you need to realize that."

"Fine, but for how long? Don't tell me until the trial is over."

She glared silently back at him. Clearly she didn't like being pushed into a corner, but his stubbornness was preventing him from seeing her side of the situation.

"*At least* until it's over, Robert," she said defiantly.

"At least? What do you mean by that," he came close to shouting, his temper flaring up suddenly, as it had done so often of late.

Nancy looked around, embarrassed at the turned heads and raised eyebrows that his voice had produced.

"Can you please keep your voice down?"

"Oh, I'm sorry," he said, clearly not meaning it. "I forgot how embarrassing it is for you to be seen with me."

"Well, you seem to take great pleasure in putting me in embarrassing situations, don't you? Can't you just for a minute see things my way?"

"I would, but I didn't think your way meant sticking so closely to the rules, living so safely. I thought you liked taking a few risks in your life."

"Oh, that's so easy for you to say," she said, her exasperation evident in her voice. "Who signs *your* paycheck? Who do you have to answer to? Your whole career is based on doing whatever the hell you like. You can go ahead and be a rebel against society, and your clients will love you for it. I'm sorry to be so boring, but my job is to enforce the rules and sometimes that means I have to obey them too. And if that means I don't get to live my life doing just anything I please, when I please, then that's a price I'm willing to pay."

"Christ we're two adults here. I can't believe you're letting Parent decide how you should live your life."

"Don't be so sure it's all him, Robert," she said, her eyes flashing now with indignation. "I'm a big girl and nobody's forcing this on me. Sorry if I suddenly seem like a stick-in-the-mud. Maybe being close to you for so long made me take risks that I normally wouldn't have before. But that has to change now. I don't have the same control over my life that you do. I'm perfectly willing to accept that fact and I've learned to lead my life accordingly. Maybe you should learn to accept it too."

With that she turned and made her way through the crowd and left the café, leaving Bratt feeling stunned, unsure what he was supposed to do next. It had been many years since he had allowed anybody to pull the strings on his emotions the way she did. He had been willing to allow her that privilege, but now she didn't seem to want it.

He found it ironic that she seemed to think his career allowed him some sort of freedom that she lacked, and that she was holding this against him now. Maybe he could come and go as he liked, but that was about the only real advantage there was to being his own boss. Otherwise, as anyone who watched him get totally wrapped up in his work could have told her, he was a slave to his cases.

He wanted to blame Parent for this turn of events, but he knew he also had to respect Nancy's independence. He shouldn't have implied that Parent was dictating her life. Although that probably wasn't far from the truth, there was no point waving it in her face. It was clearly important for her that he accept the choices she made. This had never posed a problem before, when her decisions had meshed quite nicely with his.

No, he thought, *lunch sure wasn't what I had hoped for.*

The next morning Bratt was in the office early, waiting for Leblanc to come in. He needed to discuss the future, both his and the firm's, with his partner, and he yawned sleepily as he waited.

He had spent another largely sleepless night, unable to drive the thoughts of Nancy, Jeannie, and Madsen from his head. Now it was time to tell Leblanc about the opening on the Superior Court, yet he was finding it hard to muster up a great deal of enthusiasm for the fulfillment of his life's ambition.

Leblanc finally showed up about quarter after nine. He came rushing in, as he so often did, his face flushed. He carried his heavy briefcase in one hand, and a paper bag carrying his breakfast from the McDonald's around the corner in the other. He expressed surprise at seeing Bratt sitting in front of his desk, reading a newspaper.

"Bobby-boy, what's up?" he huffed, dropping his large frame into his chair.

Before Bratt had a chance to answer Leblanc opened the bag and pulled out his meal. Bratt winced at the sight of the three egg and bacon sandwiches, with hash browns, that came out of the bag. He almost forgot to speak as he watched Leblanc slurp his scalding-hot coffee and then pull out and light a cigarette.

Leblanc took a deep drag on the cigarette, dropped it into an ashtray full of butts from the day before, and then bit off half the first sandwich. He looked up at Bratt as he chewed and raised his eyebrows, still not having received an answer. Bratt dragged his attention away from Leblanc's stuffed face, remembering what he had come to talk about.

"J.P, I need to talk to you. I've got some news, some big news."

"Mm-hm," Leblanc responded, managing to get equal amounts of food, coffee, and cigarette into his mouth without missing a beat.

"They're going to make me a judge. Maybe. Probably, I guess," Bratt laughed at his own equivocation.

He was glad to see that Leblanc stopped chewing and was now looking at him, openly surprised. He cleared his throat, then continued.

"I have a friend who's very close to the committee that nominates people for the bench. Superior Court. They still haven't replaced Mike Dickson. And it looks like they're going to choose between me and Allen Schneider. You know him?"

Leblanc nodded and then slowly began to alternate once more between the sip of coffee, the drag on his cigarette, and the mouthful of food. He did all this without taking his eyes off his partner's face.

"Anyway," Bratt continued, "they're going to be making their decision in the next few weeks. It seems I gotta get through the Small trial looking good and I'll be a shoo-in."

Leblanc was picking up all of Bratt's signals despite the concentration needed for his display of hand-to-mouth agility.

"This has got you worried," he stated what was an obvious fact.

Bratt nodded, saying nothing.

"Tell me about it," Leblanc said, pushing his food away.

"Winning the Small trial…it's far from a lock." Bratt paused, choosing his words carefully. "And, frankly I'm not sure if I'm going into it at my best."

"Still worn down by that Hall case?"

"No, not that. I've just been kind of, well, questioning things the past couple of weeks."

"Questioning what things?"

Bratt had intended to discuss only his possible appointment to the bench and not the existential mini-crisis that he had been in of late. But, they went hand-in-hand it seemed, so he decided to get his inner conflict out in the open, even if it made him feel like a naïve law student.

"I've been asking questions about what we do for a living. What I do."

"You've been asking who these questions?"

"Me," Bratt nearly shouted, his irritation suddenly rising as he feared that he was going to have to spell every embarrassing detail out for Leblanc.

"Sorry," Leblanc raised his hands in a sign of surrender. "I'll try to keep up."

"Anyway, just before you dropped this murder trial in my lap I was thinking about taking some time off, to think things over. I also needed to patch things up with Jeannie. She left home, you know."

"No. You never told me."

"Yeah. She's been pretty angry with me since the Nate Morris trial. It was her best friend who was raped."

"I heard the girl got worked over by Perron in court."

"Oh yeah. He did quite the job on her. Somehow, Jeannie managed to pin the blame for that on me. I guess it wasn't entirely unfair of her. All this crap's been weighing on my mind since then, and I can't seem to shake it."

"OK, let me get this straight. You're feeling guilty about what happened to Jeannie's friend. Would that be the rape or the cross-examination?"

"Both, really."

"Both? Oh, because you defended Morris a few years back, right?"

"Right. I got him off then too."

"And because Perron did what you taught him to do in court, which is what any lawyer worth a damn would do for his client?"

Bratt nodded, relieved at how fast his partner had understood his situation.

"What a load of self-indulgent horseshit," Leblanc spat out. "I thought you had some sort of serious problem."

"This isn't a joke," Bratt protested.

"No? Well it oughta be. You know why we never take on cases that involve our friends or our family? Because we lose our objectivity, and that's what's happened here. Even if you weren't directly involved in that trial, you've lost whatever objectivity you're supposed to have as a lawyer."

"I don't need lessons-"

"Yes, you do. Otherwise you wouldn't be getting in the way of this unhealthy breakfast I'm trying to have. Listen, Bobby, I know all about the Morris trial. I actually had a long talk with Johanne Dulude a couple of days ago, and, by the way, she wasn't Claire Brockway's biggest booster."

"You're kidding," Bratt said. He had been certain that the prosecutor had been very supportive of Claire.

"No, I'm not. If you hadn't been so close to the girl you might not have thought that what Perron did was such a terrible thing either. She wasn't exactly an angel, you know. Even Dulude told me she went to that job interview dressed like a tramp. OK, now she says she got raped, but she didn't lose a button off her skin-tight skirt when it happened, and she didn't even break a fingernail fighting Morris off. Then she only calls the cops two days later, *after* she finds out that she didn't get the job.

"I have no doubt that Nate Morris is one manipulative son of a bitch, and for all I know he did rape her. But are you telling me that twelve reasonable people, who probably don't like defense lawyers any more than the next guy, should have been convinced beyond a doubt just on her say-so? Are you willing to throw a guy in jail just because he *might* have committed a crime? Believing everything the Brockway girl says is your privilege, but don't expect the rest of the world to join her fan club."

Bratt bowed his head, acknowledging the soundness of Leblanc's reasoning. In his heart he was still sure that Claire had been telling the truth, but maybe he had lost his objectivity, and that's something he should have been aware of from the start.

"Unfortunately, I'll never get Jeannie to see things that way," he thought out loud. "She blames all lawyers, and I'm front and center."

"So what," Leblanc answered. "Imagine that: a teenager is pissed off at her father and runs away from home. Like it's never happened before."

"She's not just pissed at me. She rejects my profession, my whole career."

"Let me tell you something, Mr. Perfect Parent. The meanest judge I ever met, someone who would've been a hanging judge if we still had the death penalty, was your old man. He wouldn't give the benefit of the doubt to the pope on a Sunday. His son, and that's you by the way, ended up spending his life defending the undesirables that his father-"

"Please let's not bring up my dad now," Bratt interrupted.

"OK. Whatever. It just looks to me like Jeannie's just following in the family tradition of going against whatever her father stood for."

Of all things, Bratt didn't want to think about his father right then. But he knew that Leblanc had a good point, although he was afraid that if he conceded too easily his concerns would seem superficial. Besides, his recent worries went beyond Claire and Jeannie.

"OK, smart guy," he said. "That's all well and good for this specific case. What about on a broader scale?"

"Broader scale," Leblanc moaned, putting back the slice of hash brown he had been about to swallow. "What's that supposed to mean?"

"I mean, other than just me and Jeannie and Claire. I mean, what we, me and you, do in court all the time. Do we go too far, really twist around the truth so that nobody can tell it from the lies? Isn't that what we do to get criminals out of jail?"

"Holy shit, I'm back in first year law school! '*Please sir*, how can you defend a man when you know he's guilty?'" Leblanc mocked, waving his hand like a student in class. "I can't believe you'd even worry about such an infantile point of view with your years of experience."

Bratt felt the heat rise in his face at Leblanc's sarcastic words.

"OK, so I'm supposed to know better, right? Yet Morris may have committed not one, but two rapes, and he still walks the streets. Cooper Hall definitely defrauded dozens of innocent people of their life savings, and *he* walks the streets. Shall I go on?"

"Sure, and don't forget to mention Chantal Boucher while you're at it."

"Who?"

"Chantal Boucher. Remember her, back in eighty-five? She was a young hooker, had a couple of kids to support. A real sob story."

"The name's vaguely familiar. What about her?"

"I guess my memory is better than yours, or maybe you've tried to forget her. They charged her with robbing one of her johns at knifepoint, but you were sure she was innocent. So sure you took her case even if she was on Legal Aid."

"I think I do remember her now."

"Of course you do. I don't remember the prosecutor's name, but he made her look like a worthless slut on the stand."

"Pierre Caron."

"Ah, your memory's not so bad, after-all, Bobby-boy. She got two less a day, and her kids cried their little hearts out as they took their innocent mom away in handcuffs. That's exactly how you described it to me, way back when."

"OK," said Bratt, bothered by having to relive this unhappy memory, "what's your point?"

"My point is it doesn't matter what side you're on. You think Crown prosecutors lose any sleep about sending people to jail? They do their job, the system works more often than not, and the results are usually just. We're human, so the system isn't any more perfect than we are. Sometimes the guilty walk, but believe me, most crooks out there can't afford Robert Bratt or Antoine Perron, and they do their time.

"And every now and then even Robert Bratt loses a case, and, who knows, maybe his client was innocent anyway. But, believe me, he didn't lose Chantal Boucher's case because he was too hesitant to do whatever he had to do to win. And no lawyer should ever lose a case just because he chickened out or was afraid to hurt somebody's feelings, or ruffle some feathers. We can only give it everything we got. No quarter asked and none given, right? After that it's up to the judges and juries to screw it up or get it right."

Bratt sat quietly for a few seconds. He felt like a boy who'd just been lectured by his father. After all these years he shouldn't have needed this kind of speech. Then again, maybe Leblanc's pep talk would get him out of his doldrums. Even star players needed an occasional kick in the pants.

"Boy, you've got all the answers today, don't you?"

Leblanc grinned and reached out for his breakfast, ice-cold by now. "That's why you came to see me, Bobby-boy. You're way too smart to waste your time barking up the wrong tree. Now, get the hell outta here and let me harden my arteries in peace. I gotta be in court in ten minutes."

Bratt got up and walked slowly back to his own office, all the while letting Leblanc's arguments percolate in his head. There was no doubt that his partner had made his point well. Now it was up to him to get back into the game and lead his team to the winning touchdown.

Rah-rah, he thought wryly.

The first thing he had to do was get his mind back on the defense he was preparing for the upcoming murder trial. He joined Kouri in his office and waited for the arrival of the two new alibi witnesses. He didn't know what to expect from them. One of them wasn't even on the original list of witnesses he had gotten from Sévigny, and he wondered where Small had come up with him.

He would have to put his doubts aside for now. As long as he didn't know for sure that these two witnesses were lying, he would keep his opinion to himself and do his job. He crossed his fingers and hoped that Jennifer Campbell had been involved in the selection process.

While he waited he mused about the recent changes in his life that had driven him to Leblanc's door. There had been a time, an eternity ago, or perhaps it was only a week or two, when he had been able to do his job without second-guessing every decision he made, when he spent more time fighting in court than he spent fighting his own conscience. He longed to get back to that level of certainty.

His thoughts were interrupted when Kouri stuck his head in through the door to announce that the witnesses had arrived. He told him to show them in and Kouri's head disappeared from view again.

Bratt picked up the notepad on which he had written notes of his interviews with Clayton and Parker, whom he mentally referred to as two out of the Three Stooges. He turned it face down on his desk in disgust. He recalled how nervous and unsettled they had been when he had questioned them. If the two new witnesses were anything like the first pair, they would need every bit of help he could give them. He decided to interview these two together. Of course that would let them listen to each other's answers and maybe even change their stories accordingly, the most basic no-no for a lawyer meeting with potential witnesses. But if that helped them keep their stories straight, then he was all for it. Time was running short, and if a lawyer wasn't willing to bend the rules a bit, then who would?

Kouri re-entered the office and Bratt was surprised to see two clean-cut young men follow him in. He couldn't believe that either of them had anything to do with Marlon Small. They were dressed in casual slacks and sweaters that actually fit them. Their hair was cut short, without being shaved into any gang insignias or initials. They stood politely in front of his desk, waiting to be introduced, neither slouching nor fidgeting. Bratt thought they could be poster boys for some middle-American college.

Kouri stepped forward to carry out the introductions.

"Vernon Sims," he said, pointing first to the taller of the pair, "and Everton Jordan. This is Robert Bratt."

"Good morning, Mr. Bratt," Sims said, stepping forward and reaching out to shake his hand. "It's a pleasure to meet you."

Bratt stood and shook Sims hand, and then did the same with Jordan.

"The pleasure is mine," he said wholeheartedly. "Please, sit down, gentlemen."

The two sat down in the chairs across the desk from him. They sat straight and looked at him with pleasant but serious faces.

"We'll dispense with the preliminaries," Bratt began. "Marlon Small informed me that you two were with a group of people, including him, at a park in LaSalle last June, the night of a shooting you may have heard of in Little Burgundy."

"Yes, the double-murder on Carrier Street," Sims answered. "Everybody was talking about it the next day."

"And at the time of the shooting you were…"

"We were all at Wilfort Park, in LaSalle. We were there pretty much every night last summer."

"Is there anything special about that particular day, Vernon, which would let me be sure we're talking about the same date?"

"Oh, sure. I had spent most of the day at McGill. I wanted to change two of my electives, and that was the cut-off date."

"McGill? As in McGill University?" Bratt asked, surprised to learn that this witness was attending his alma mater.

"Yes. I'm in second year engineering."

Sims reached into his sweater and pulled out an envelope with the McGill crest on it. From inside he pulled out some sheets of paper that he handed over to Bratt. Looking at them Bratt saw they were authorizations to change two physics courses. The date stamped on each sheet was June 14, 1999, the date of the shooting.

Bratt began getting a warm feeling about Sims. Everything Clayton and Parker had not been, he seemed to be.

"Then what happened?" he asked, beginning to feel optimistic.

"Ev picked me up at the LaSalle Metro and we drove to the park together."

Jordan looked over at Sims and raised a finger as if to remind him of something.

"No, wait," Sims said. "First we stopped for a hamburger, because it was almost six o'clock by the time he picked me up. We got to the park at nearly seven."

Jordan smiled and nodded his agreement.

"OK, so far so good," Bratt said. "Did anything special happen at the park itself? Something that makes that day stand out."

Jordan, who had not said a word until then, spoke up.

"I vomited on the basketball court."

Bratt was so surprised at this reply, and the casual way in which Jordan stated it, that he burst out laughing. The two witnesses laughed along with him. Bratt saw that even Kouri was smiling, looking on almost proudly at the two men.

So far so good, Bratt thought. *Still, there's always the chance that...*

"Do either one of you have criminal records?" he asked abruptly, turning the jovial meeting deadly serious again.

Both young men looked at each other, then turned back to Bratt.

"No sir," they answered in unison.

"Have you ever been arrested, even as juveniles? Even things they never convicted you for?"

"No sir," they said again.

"And you, Everton," Bratt was tempted to call him Mr. Jordan, "Neither I nor Marlon's first lawyer had your name on a list of possible alibi witnesses Marlon had given us. Why is that?"

"I'm studying at the U of T and I was only in Montreal for the summer. I left town on the sixteenth, before Marlon was arrested, so nobody ever asked me about who was in the park. I hardly knew Marlon, and he probably never thought about me when he had to find alibi witnesses. Recently, when I learned what was happening from Vernon, I called Mrs. Campbell and told her that I was definitely willing to testify on his behalf. So, here I am."

Bratt's earlier smile returned to his face as quickly as it had disappeared. There would be no surprises from left field with these two fine, young men. He could go on listening to their story with his mind at ease.

"OK, Everton. You were saying you threw up."

Looking a bit embarrassed, Jordan explained what happened.

"I shouldn't have had those hamburgers, I guess. They weren't very well cooked. Then I was running all over the court for a couple of hours, and it was still pretty hot, even at that hour. Next thing I knew…well, they had to stop playing for a while, to hose the court off."

"I drove him home in his car," Sims said, still chuckling at the recollection. "His mom lives a couple of blocks away. I stayed with him and figured that was it for that day, but around 11 p.m. he said he felt better and wanted to get some fresh air. So we went back to the park to see who was still there."

"Are you sure it was around 11:00?"

"Sure. I wanted to watch the sports at eleven-"

"But I convinced him to go to the park, instead," Jordan cut in.

"How long did it take you to get back to the park?" Bratt felt the nervous excitement beginning to build in his stomach, like he was watching the horse he had bet on take the final turn with a growing lead.

"Not even five minutes."

"And who was at the park?"

"Oh, pretty much everyone was still there," Sims answered.

"Including Marlon, of course," Jordan added. "And his cousin, Ashley."

"You're sure of that?"

"Yes sir. We stayed there until midnight, and then Ev and I left."

"Why do you say you left at midnight?"

"There's a curfew at that park, because lots of kids used to go hang out there all night, and get in trouble. So, there was always a security car that comes by a bit after midnight to make sure the place is clear. We left just before that. Most of the others had already gone. Only Marlon, his cousin and Bernie Clayton stayed behind after we left."

"Why did those three stay longer?"

Sims smiled apologetically.

"Well, sir, Marlon was always a little brash when it came to dealing with the security people. He was never one to back down from an authority figure."

I'll bet, Bratt thought. *Brash, indeed.*

He looked at the two surprisingly credible witnesses and told himself that Small had managed to find what he really needed. He couldn't wait until St. Jean and Parent got a look at these two in court. He would have the pleasure of watching their visions of a conviction shatter like glass.

He asked them a few more questions, more as a formality than anything else. He was already sure he had the witnesses he'd been hoping for. They had probably been told ahead of time about all the different questions that they may face, but that was not a problem. They looked good, they spoke well, and their story was believable in its simplicity. He was sure they were telling the truth about never having been arrested before, so he was unconcerned that St. Jean might be able to dig up anything prejudicial about them. Bratt's instincts told him they would be clean as a whistle. It was almost too good to be true.

Sims and Jordan spent less than an hour in his office. When they left, Bratt remained seated at his desk, watching Kouri putter around, straightening out files, with a big goofy grin on his face. As he watched, and thought about the two witnesses, a line from an old cartoon came to mind: "my spider-sense is tingling."

"What aren't you telling me, Peter?"

Kouri stopped his paper shuffling, but didn't turn to look at him.

"I'm sorry?"

"I can feel it in my gut. There's something you're not telling me."

"What wouldn't I tell you?"

"Those witnesses were perfect. Too perfect. There's no such thing in my book."

"Well, OK, I did tell Small, tell them actually, to dress nicer than the last pair."

"So you met with them before today."

Kouri nodded. "And I also went over some of the questions with them."

"Did you go over the answers, too?"

"What do you mean?"

Bratt stood up and walked over to Kouri, then walked back again. The answers to his questions seemed to be staring him in the face, despite Kouri's pretense at innocence, and he could only repeat to himself, "too good to be true, too good to be true."

"They're just too perfect, dammit. Too clean cut. Too polite. Too well-dressed. Their stories match too well. They were finishing each other's sentences, for God's sake."

"Well, they were told what to expect. What's wrong with that?"

"You told them?"

"Yes."

"'My man, Pete'," Bratt quoted Small. Kouri said nothing, but his earlier blank expression was quickly turning to fear and guilt. "What have you been up to?"

"I was just trying to help."

"Just trying to help," Bratt thought. *If that isn't an admission of a fuck-up, I don't know what is.*

"Listen, Pete. You were the one who looked so shocked when I spoke to Small the last time we were up there. Like you couldn't believe what I told him."

"Why should I have been shocked? All you told him was that if you didn't think the witnesses were any good then the jury wouldn't either."

"Is that what I said?"

"That's what I heard."

"Is that what I meant?"

"How should I know what you meant? Am I supposed to read your mind now, too?"

Everything Kouri said made sense, but it still sounded like he was making excuses. He wondered if he was just being paranoid. Before he had a chance to question Kouri further, Sylvie burst into his office, her face constricted with fear and grief.

"It's J.P! Something happened at the court."

Bratt jumped to his feet.

"What? What happened?"

"I think it's his heart," she blurted out the words, the tears following instantly after. "There's a constable on the phone. Oh God, he says it's really bad."

Bratt rushed to his desk and picked up the phone, having to try twice before he found the blinking button to get the line.

"Bratt here. What's going on?"

"It's Constable Lefebvre. Your partner is in bad shape. It looks like a heart attack. The ambulance is on its way."

"Where is he now?"

"He's still at 3.07."

"I'm on my way."

Bratt hung up and rushed out of his office, grabbing his coat as he passed Kouri. All thoughts about the Small trial and the too good to be true witnesses had disappeared.

He didn't bother to stop to put on his shoe-rubbers and as he got out of the building and ran down the snow-covered sidewalk his feet constantly threatened to slip out from under him. He jumped over snow banks and jostled slower pedestrians, but eventually made it to the courthouse, panting heavily.

An *Urgences Santé* ambulance was already parked on the sidewalk in front of the main entrance. Ahead of Bratt, two technicians were wheeling a stretcher in as fast as they could, a large black medical bag teetering precariously on top of it.

Out of breath, Bratt struggled to catch up with them, but they crossed the main mezzanine quickly and disappeared around the corner. As he ran, he saw other people heading in the same direction, some looking concerned, others just curious.

He turned the corner in front of Room 3.07 and had to stop abruptly to not run right into the large crowd that had gathered. A constable, he presumed it was Lefebvre, spotted him and pulled him aside.

"You'll have to wait here," he said, speaking slowly to make sure that Bratt understood what he said. "The technicians cleared the room. I'm sure they're doing all that can be done for him."

Bratt nodded wordlessly, still breathing heavily from the run. His mouth was dry and he briefly wondered about his own physical condition. The constable may have had the same concern, because he led him to a nearby bench and sat him down.

"I'll get you some water," he said, before turning and disappearing into the crowd.

Struggling to catch his breath, Bratt tried to stop his mind from racing out of control so that he could think clearly about what was happening and what this all meant. He had long been concerned about Leblanc's health, but there was no way he could have prepared himself for this. Now, it was a question of how serious the attack had been. To his knowledge this was the first time that Leblanc had had one. He only hoped that this lessened the chance that it would be fatal.

Shit, what the hell do you know about this? He could already be dead for all you know. And if he does die, after nearly two decades together, what then?

Bratt bowed his head, his face buried in the palms of his hands. He hated himself for being selfish, but he couldn't chase away the thought that Leblanc's heart attack had come at the worst possible time.

Chapter 8

The intensive care unit at the Montreal General was probably not much different than that of most other major hospitals. Bratt felt a small sense of gratitude for not having been in enough of them to know the difference.

The last place he had expected to find himself on that Saturday morning was there, at Leblanc's bedside. His partner was heavily sedated and breathing with the help of a respirator. The doctors had told Bratt that the first forty-eight hours after the attack were the most crucial. If he got through those all right his chances for recovery improved dramatically.

When Bratt had shown up at the ICU the attending nurse had asked him if he was part of Leblanc's family. It seemed they were still waiting for someone, anyone, who was a relative to arrive. Leblanc had divorced over ten years earlier. His ex, Sandy, a mean-spirited bitch who Bratt had despised from the get-go, had remarried and moved out west somewhere. There was also his junkie son, Luc, but Leblanc had had no news from him for nearly a year. Bratt had never heard his partner mention any brothers or sisters in the time he had known him. He thought he might be the closest thing Leblanc had to family.

Over-all, he thought it was a pretty sad state of affairs. No matter how closely he worked with someone, Bratt knew it wasn't the same thing as real family. He looked down at Leblanc's peaceful face, and wondered if it mattered to him that he had no relatives to come see him, perhaps mourn for him, at this time.

He turned to look at the other beds in the unit. Three were occupied, but only around one of them had the curtain been pulled shut, and no nurse went in there to check on a pulse or to adjust the I.V. He tried not to think about what the reason for that might be.

As it was, he still couldn't believe that Leblanc, who seemed to be sleeping comfortably in front of him, was halfway between life and death. He touched his old friend's hand, tentatively at first, then more firmly, squeezing the chubby fingers together.

It occurred to him then that he had not done as much for his own father. Few of his friends were aware that he hadn't spoken to his father during the last seven years of his life, not since Bratt's heartbroken mother had drunk herself to death. When his father entered the hospital for the last time in 1994, paralyzed by the second stroke he'd had in a year, Bratt only went because Jeannie had begged him to, certain as she was that her grandfather's final hour was near.

Earlier that year, when the first stroke had occurred, Bratt had refused to even call the hospital to see how his father was doing. He had only found peace with his father once they had become strangers and he wasn't ready to face him again, even in a hospital bed, for fear of reopening old wounds.

After the second stroke, he gave in to his daughter's tear-filled pleading, if only partially. At the hospital, he stood outside the private room that would be the final home of Joseph Bratt, and occasionally looked in through the small window in the door while Jeannie sat for hours on end at her grandfather's side.

She never understood how Bratt could have refused to be with him in his final hours. It was many years before he himself had been able to understand that he had no longer been angry with his father, but with himself. The stubbornness he had inherited from Joseph Bratt had led him into defying both common sense and his own heart, and by the time his father was close to death he felt it was too late to repair their relationship.

On this day Bratt came to see Leblanc wondering if it would be for the final time, but found himself stuck in the past and feeling sorry for himself. He looked down on the large, inert form and wished that it was his father's hand that he was holding.

A movement behind him brought Bratt back to the present and he turned to find Kouri standing diffidently near the door.

"It's OK, Pete. You can come closer."

"Sorry. I thought you were praying," Kouri whispered as he approached.

Praying for Leblanc, Bratt said to himself. *Now that's something I never would have thought of.*

"Any news?" Kouri asked.

"Nothing overly bad, I guess. He's stable."

Kouri looked down at Leblanc's still form, then quickly around the room.

"There's nobody? Family, I mean."

"No. None."

"I faxed Parent the names and addresses of Jordan and Sims this morning. I know I was supposed to do it yesterday, but I forgot. You know…"

Bratt nodded. He didn't want to think about Jordan and Sims just then. He felt that his friend's precarious condition should take priority over any work-related issues.

Kouri nodded back solemnly and looked around again, his expression showing a touch of embarrassment. Then he stepped closer to the bed, nudging Bratt off to the side in the process.

"Do you mind?" he asked quietly.

"No, not at all," Bratt answered, and he stepped back a couple of feet, having no idea what it was he was supposed to mind.

He watched wide-eyed as Kouri bowed his head and crossed himself, the thumb and first two fingers of his right hand pressed together.

S*on of a gun,* Bratt thought. *He wasn't kidding.*

He stood still, unsure if he should stay or go. He watched as Kouri prayed silently, crossing himself again as he finished, then wiping a tear from his cheek as he stepped back from the bed.

"I feel bad because I hardly got to know him," Kouri explained, turning to look back at Bratt. "Now I wonder if I'll ever get the chance."

I've known him for over twenty years, Bratt thought. *How bad am* I *supposed to feel?*

He was surprised to see Kouri take a hesitant step toward him, looking at him with a strange expression, then advance quickly, his arms opening to hug him. Bratt stiffened for only a second at Kouri's touch, but he let himself be hugged as he felt his own hot tears rolling down his cheeks.

Bad enough, he answered himself. *Bad enough.*

The rest of the weekend wasn't much more upbeat. The somber weather matched Bratt's mood as he waited for news of any improvement in his friend's condition. He only made a desultory effort to reread his notes for Monday's motion, having lost all ability to concentrate.

Unable to work, he spent several hours at the hospital on Sunday, the lonely keeping company with the lonely. Occasionally, some of the other lawyers dropped in for a few minutes. Ralston and Kalouderis stayed a little longer. But, eventually they all moved on. Unlike their senior partners, most of them had families to be with, lives to lead.

In a moment of desperation, sensing how alone he and Leblanc both were, Bratt tried calling Claire to see if she knew where his daughter could be. The taped message from the operator telling him that her number was no longer in service left him feeling despondent.

By Sunday night he had to admit to himself that the only person he could talk to about what had happened was Nancy. He only hoped that, once she heard about his partner, she'd at least be receptive to talking to him.

Before he had the chance to reconsider he picked up the phone and dialed her number. It rang several times and, as he waited, he tried not to picture her on the other end, seeing his number on her call-display, and walking away from the phone.

After several rings, his heart sank as her voice mail came on. Even the sound of her recorded voice did nothing to cheer him. He wasn't sure if he should hang up or leave some sort of message. Before he could decide, the greeting ended and he heard the beep. He looked at the phone in his hands, unsure of how much or how little to say.

Then he realized that he was leaving nothing more than dead air and this would be the worst kind of message.

"Hi Nancy," he blurted out, unsure what was going to come out of his mouth. "It's me, Robert. Obviously. I, uh, just wanted to say hello. And good luck; in the trial of course. I hope Parent appreciates what he has in you."

God, this sounds pathetic, he told himself. *But just now I really don't care if that's how I sound to her.*

"So this is me," he continued, "asking for forgiveness again. For the last time we met, I mean. I feel pretty bad about how that went. Um, I know I can be a bit stubborn, and I don't usually worry too much about the other person's feelings. Well, I guess until now. So, admitting guilt is the first step toward rehabilitation, right?

"Anyway, I guess I'll be back to gazing longingly at you across the courtroom again. Kind of looking forward to it, actually. Keep well."

He paused again, then decided that anything else he said was going to be superfluous, and he hung up.

It wasn't until much later that he realized he'd never mentioned Leblanc.

When Monday morning dawned, it was as if the weekend's feeling of despair had slipped away with Bratt's bad dreams. He felt a small surge of excitement because he finally had something to do other than mope around his home. He was going to appear before Judge Benjamin Green, perhaps the sharpest and most experienced judge on the Superior Court. That meant being on his toes and ready to defend every argument and allegation he had made in his motion to exclude the damaging videotape.

Green was known for holding everybody, defense lawyers and Crown prosecutors alike, in the most obvious contempt, and delighted in peppering them with sarcastic comments. Bratt figured that as long as he had blood pulsing in his veins he'd be able to get up for such a courtroom confrontation. Nothing would get him out of his doldrums faster than butting heads with the old warhorse.

He and Kouri walked the block and a half from his office to the court, arriving a few minutes early for the hearing on their motion. Bratt carried both their robes in plastic suit bags, while Kouri was laden with their two bulging briefcases.

Bratt could feel his blood beginning to pulse stronger than it had for days. When he stood in the hallway, looking at Parent sitting inside the courtroom, he smiled in anticipation of the upcoming battle.

Kouri did a double take at this shark-like grin. He hadn't seen Bratt in battle before and so didn't recognize the expression that showed his mentor at his happiest.

As Bratt strutted through the doors Kouri followed silently, like a slave carrying his general's standard onto the battlefield.

Bratt spotted Nancy as soon as he entered, but managed to not miss a step as he advanced to the defense lawyers' bench. He was going to have to concentrate on the work before him today.

Parent looked coldly in Bratt's direction, and gave him a small nod, barely acknowledging his presence. Bratt nodded back and flashed a smile that exuded fake warmth. He allowed himself a quick peek in Nancy's direction, but she seemed to be deeply immersed in a stack of documents in front of her, never even looking up at him.

He turned to the prisoner's box as two guards led Marlon Small into the court. Small was dressed in an old jacket and tie that his mother must have dug up for him in a church rummage sale. Bratt leaned over the rail and smiled at his client.

"Now it begins," he said.

Small said nothing. His usual arrogant look contained just a touch of apprehension.

Good, Bratt told himself. *Maybe he'll lose that cockiness totally by the time we're in front of the jury.*

At precisely 9:30 a.m. Judge Benjamin Green entered and took the bench. He was a small, thin man who walked with a slow, careful step, leaning tentatively on a cane. His body had reached retirement age, but his mind had retained the vigor of youth and it allowed him to wield his tongue as if it were a sword.

Both lawyers bowed slightly in his direction and murmured their good mornings. He flipped open the file in front of him, not responding to their greetings. He wore his half-moon glasses near the end of his nose, and licked his index finger in a deliberate manner before using it to turn each page.

After what seemed an eternity he finally peered over his glasses in Bratt's direction, seeming to have noticed the lawyer's presence for the first time.

"Well, Mr. Bratt. What can we do for you this morning?"

Bratt grinned back, showing that he wasn't in the least put off by the judge's indifferent manner.

"And how are you today, My Lord?"

Green winced, as if Bratt's false cheeriness pained him.

"You do have a motion to present, don't you?"

"Right there in your hands," Bratt answered. He then pointed to a television set, which was placed up on a high stand at the side of the room. "And to get your week off on the right foot, we're going to watch a little video first. About three hours' worth."

Hardly moving his head, Green's eyes slid from Bratt to the television, and he raised his eyebrows.

"I hope you brought the popcorn," he commented dryly, then leaned back in his chair and crossed his legs to get comfortable. He raised his hands and wiggled his fingers in the air. "Roll'em."

Bratt, still grinning, pulled the TV stand closer to the middle of the room and facing the judge, then slid his copy of the tape into the VCR.

The interrogation room sprang into view on the screen and soon they saw Marlon Small and Philippe St. Jean enter it. The parties to the hearing all settled back into their seats for the viewing, while those in the gallery had to get by with disembodied voices.

Bratt's eyes constantly traveled between the screen and the judge's bench, observing Green's reactions to what was happening, at which times he took notes and when he sat with his eyes half-closed, almost dozing. He knew better than to think the judge was falling asleep at such times, though. Green's eyes may have gotten tired, but his mind soaked in everything.

As for Parent and Nancy, their eyes stayed constantly glued to the screen. Bratt tried to watch her from the corner of his eye, to see if she would ever look his way, but she never turned her head an inch.

Occasionally, he heard somebody from the gallery whisper a derogatory comment about Small a little too loudly, usually when they heard him refuse one of St. Jean's invitations to confess his crime. This would cause Green to flash a fiery look in the general direction of the public, and the whispering would end quickly.

At eleven o'clock, almost halfway through Small's interrogation, Green sat up abruptly.

"Cut," he said sharply. "We'll take ten minutes to stretch our legs, and I mean exactly ten minutes. Then we'll watch the rest straight through until the lunch break."

He used his cane to slowly push himself up to his feet.

"I hope the second reel's got a little more action than the first," he said to nobody in particular as he limped out of the courtroom.

Once he was gone, Nancy picked up her purse and headed out into the hall, her eyes fixed straight ahead of her. Bratt followed her with his gaze from where he sat, but his view became obstructed by the presence of Parent standing in front of him. In his hand he held the papers that Nancy had been poring over earlier.

"Here," he handed them to Bratt. "I'm sure there's nothing in there you don't already know."

Bratt took the stack of case law and turned to hand it to Kouri who sat at his side. When he turned back to speak to Parent, the prosecutor was already heading out the door that Nancy had just taken.

That's fine, Bratt thought. *No reason to start playing nice now, anyway.*

He sat there, looking at the door long after Parent had disappeared through it, and brooding over the cold shoulder treatment that he was receiving. After a minute or two, Kouri tugged his robe and handed him back one of the photocopied judgments.

"I think you should read this one. And not just the headnote."

Bratt felt a touch of surprise as he took the document, wondering what Kouri may have found that they didn't know already. He turned over the first page to get to the body of the decision. On the second page someone had stuck a small, yellow Post-it note. He read the familiar handwriting that was on it.

"You grovel very well. And I miss you too. N."

He kept looking at the note, rereading the words as if they were written in code, while their meaning sunk in.

I guess my message got through to her. Maybe things will work out well this week, after-all. As long as I keep my big mouth in check.

He slowly pulled the sticky square off the page, folded it and slipped it into his shirt pocket. Kouri only glanced at him briefly, a slight smile on his lips, then walked out of the courtroom, leaving Bratt alone with his thoughts.

He realized that Nancy had taken a big risk that Parent might discover her note. He also realized that once more he had underestimated her, and he wondered if she was having as hard a time dealing with her feelings as he was.

Most of the ten-minute break was over, but he never left his chair in the courtroom. It was going to take him longer than that just to get his mind back on the case at hand. His heart began beating faster when he saw Nancy follow Parent back into the courtroom. He thought of giving her a smile or a wink, any sign to let her know that he had gotten her message, but decided against doing anything that might compromise her.

Green was back on the bench exactly ten minutes after he had left it.

Bratt stood to address him. "Act two, my Lord?"

"You wouldn't have a musical ready to go, by chance?"

"I'm afraid there's no singing in this one, My Lord," Bratt said, throwing a dirty look at Parent as he answered.

The last hour and a half of the video was only slightly more interesting to watch than the first. Green's eyes and ears only seemed to perk up at the point that Small, seemingly wracked with guilt and near the breaking point, called out for a lawyer. Otherwise, the judge showed little reaction or interest in what he was watching.

As the tape concluded with St. Jean leading Small out of the interrogation room, Green slipped off his glasses and rubbed his eyes.

"I'll hear your arguments at two-fifteen," he yawned. "I've already read the jurisprudence you've both submitted, so if you would both do me the favor of being a touch more succinct than you usually are I would be very beholden to you."

He stood up and the lawyers jumped to their feet, then he slipped his glasses into a small leather case. He hesitated before leaving the bench, as if he might have something further to say. Finally, he sighed and looked at Parent.

"I can't for the life of me imagine what purpose it would serve to inflict that boring drivel on a helpless jury. I look forward to the Crown enlightening me this afternoon. *Bon appetit*, gentlemen."

Once Green's back was turned, Bratt couldn't help but smile hugely at Parent, who was clearly miffed by the judge's comment.

It looks like things just might go my way today after-all, he thought. *Nancy still cares and Green's obviously leaning toward not admitting the tape. If nothing changes by the end of the day it'll be one of the few times of late that everything didn't turn into crap.*

Lunch hour at the office was fairly quiet. Without Leblanc's loud, huge presence, the place held a mournful emptiness for Bratt. He munched on a veggie submarine sandwich that Kouri had gone out to buy, one of those low-fat, low-flavour things that he'd suddenly had the urge to eat, what with the picture of Leblanc's last breakfast still fresh in his mind.

He looked out the window, saw the usual groups of tourists gathered in front of Notre Dame Basilica and the occasional lawyer or court clerk that he recognized heading to one of the many nearby lunch spots, and he felt a silent contentment. He had seen enough, and not just in the last two weeks, to know that he could never predict how things were going to turn out, either in court or in his personal life, yet he felt a small dose of optimism.

At two o'clock he called Kouri from his office and they headed together to the courthouse, walking with brisk, confident steps.

"You think it's going to go well, don't you?" Kouri asked.

"I guess I don't have much of a poker face. Yeah, Green can already see my point, but that doesn't mean Parent can't get him to change his mind."

"If we get the video thrown out, we've got those two good alibi witnesses ready to go. This case is beginning to look like a winner, don't you think?"

Bratt nodded wordlessly. He had been trying to think as little as possible about those "two good alibi witnesses." He had decided to trust his client, which was what he was supposed to do anyway, and call them for the trial. Just as long as he didn't have to spend too much time thinking about them.

Green took the bench at precisely 2:15, and Bratt was already standing before him, ready to present his arguments. He opened his mouth to begin, but the judge cut him off.

"Mr. Bratt, you write in your motion that the videotape is highly prejudicial, yet of little probative value."

"Yes, My Lord."

"You think the conclusion your colleague will ask the jurors to draw, that your client looks and acts guilty during the interrogation, is too subjective and not necessarily warranted on the facts."

"I'm glad to see you've read my motion, My Lord."

"Yes. It was a model of concision and clarity. You must have had help on it."

Managing a smile, Bratt waved a hand in Kouri's general direction.

"My assistant drafted it. I don't think you've met Peter Kouri."

"Spare me the introductions. This isn't a social occasion. I was merely pointing out that all your arguments seem to have been included in your written motion and unless there's something vital you think you've left out of it, I fail to see why you're standing there."

Bratt struggled to maintain his polite smile.

The bastard's obviously going to grant me my motion, he told himself. *But he won't even let me have the satisfaction of arguing it first. Hell, I wouldn't be surprised if he tells Small that Kouri won it all with the written arguments he drafted and that my own role was superfluous.*

Bratt opened his mouth to make a final comment, found he had nothing left to say, and sat down, feeling totally frustrated.

Green turned to Parent and glared at him over his glasses. Parent merely stood up and bowed slightly toward the judge. Whether the judge had made his mind up already or not, he was still going to have to listen to Parent make his point.

"Mr. Parent. I am obviously tottering on the precipice, at risk of agreeing with your adversary before you've had a chance to say something, which you may be sure I am loath to do. Please throw me a rope if you can, and pull me back to your side before it's too late."

"Well, My Lord, since you obviously recognize the danger of granting my colleague's motion, I feel it is but my duty to save you from this grievous mistake."

Green smiled like he felt nauseous, lay his pen down on his desk, and sat back in his chair, his arms folded.

"Clearly, the Crown feels the statement of the accused is admissible," Parent began. "It was not coerced from him in any way. It was given with full knowledge of his legal and Charter rights-"

"What is given?"

"Why, his statement, My Lord," Parent answered, taken aback by Green's unexpected question.

"From what I read, his entire statement concerning the shootings is, and I quote…Oh, wait. My mistake. Mr. Small actually never says a single blessed thing about the shootings, does he?"

"Well, perhaps not in so many words…"

"In how many words then?"

"There is a great deal of non-verbal communication on his part."

"Are you planning to call in experts on body language, Mr. Parent?"

"No, My Lord."

"You're certainly not planning to comment on his silence in the face of your detective's verbal assault are you?"

"Well…"

"You know, people do have the right to silence in this country. At least since the Inquisition, if my memory doesn't fail me."

Bratt smiled to himself at that comment. *That's hitting a former Jesuit where he lives.*

"He does react verbally at the end, and what he says may be very informative to the jury."

"Such as?"

"Such as when he's feeling cornered by the detective at the end of the interrogation. He calls out for a lawyer because he knows he's going to be caught otherwise."

"Ah yes, that inconvenient right to counsel. In this example we see how cleverly a criminal can use it in conjunction with the previously mentioned right to silence. Really mucks up a policeman's job, doesn't it? But if I let you stand up in front of the jury and make the slightest comment about a suspect asking for a lawyer, how long do you think it would be before Mr. Bratt gets the Court of Appeal to order a new trial?"

"Not long," Bratt said in a stage whisper.

"I wasn't talking to you, Mr. Bratt."

Parent was clearly not getting anywhere with Green, and his displeasure about the judge's constant interventions was evident. Nevertheless, he sucked in his breath and tried again.

"Proof of consciousness of guilt is admissible as evidence. I respectfully submit that the jury can interpret the accused's behavior during the interrogation as evidence of his guilty conscience."

"Well, to me he doesn't necessarily look like he feels guilty, he just looks scared. And I think he'd have just as much reason to feel scared, if not more so, if he were innocent than if he were guilty. Furthermore, the very fact that how he looks and acts is open to these two interpretations leads me to conclude that his alleged actions are too ambiguous to constitute consciousness of guilt. The tape in question has very little probative value, particularly in comparison to the great prejudice that many parts of it can cause the accused."

Parent was beaten, but he remained unbowed. He dramatically slammed his file folder shut and sat down, head still held high. Green looked on with a sour expression.

"I gather you have nothing more to say. I couldn't agree with you more."

Green turned to Bratt, who had been looking on with a sense of empathy for his embattled rival, if not sympathy.

"I'm going to grant your motion, Mr. Bratt, with one proviso. I will review the tape again, in order to see if we may not excise the most obviously prejudicial parts and show the jury the rest. Considering the detective's every sentence was either an inadmissible allegation or outright hearsay, I don't hold out too much hope that there would be anything of value left for the jurors to see. But, I'd rather err on the side of caution and thoroughness. Tomorrow morning at nine-thirty, gentlemen. Have a good afternoon."

After he had gone Bratt turned to Kouri, who looked back with a big grin.

"Thanks for showing me up, kid," Bratt joked. "Now I can't even take credit for winning this thing."

"I'm just trying to justify my high salary."

"Well, you've more than earned it today. Just how much are we paying you, anyway?"

They laughed together as they headed out, Bratt allowing the younger lawyer to feel a sense of belonging. He was more than happy to let Kouri get his share of the credit. The most important thing was that things hadn't all blown up in his face after all. His fears had all been for naught.

He couldn't wait to get back to the office and he speeded up their pace. Once arrived, they burst through the office door like conquerors coming home to receive the love and admiration of their countrymen. They both stopped cold at the sight of Sylvie, sitting on a sofa in the waiting area with her head on Ralston's shoulder, sobbing uncontrollably. Ralston's eyes were also red. He looked up at the two lawyers and shook his head slowly.

"J.P," Bratt whispered, instantly understanding the meaning of what he saw.

This time Ralston nodded, and squeezed Sylvie tighter.

Bratt's knees suddenly went weak.

"DAMMIT! HE WAS SUPPOSED TO BE STABLE!" he yelled, hating the feeling of powerlessness.

The first forty-eight hours had passed uneventfully, although Leblanc had remained sedated, and according to the doctors the prognosis was supposed to be good. Bratt had allowed himself to believe that his partner had turned the corner and was out of danger. That had been the only way he could keep his mind on the motion he had presented today, but things had turned to crap after-all.

J.P. Leblanc had died early that afternoon. He had another massive coronary, which killed him almost instantly. The doctors all were quite sorry of course, but there was nothing they could have done to prevent it, they said. Ralston was the first one to get the news, when he swung by the hospital after lunch, and he returned to the office to tell the others. Had there been less congestion on the downtown streets, he would have arrived before Bratt and Kouri returned to court for the afternoon session. As things turned out, the only person in the office upon his arrival had been Sylvie, and she had not taken the news well.

As the other lawyers returned from court, Ralston gave them each the sad news. Bratt and Kouri were the last ones to hear it.

Ralston had taken care of arrangements for the body and for Leblanc's personal property at the hospital. Until that point, Bratt had been unaware that Leblanc had set out detailed instructions in case of his untimely death, and that Ralston was the executor of his final wishes. Bratt felt, unreasonably, he knew, that his longtime partner had somehow snubbed him by not putting matters into his hands, but he had enough sensitivity to hold his tongue.

He stayed late at the office that night, ostensibly to go through Leblanc's files and figure out what was to be done with them.

Mostly, though, he just sat in Leblanc's chair and gazed at his late partner's personal possessions, somewhat surprised by how calm he had been since that afternoon, yet feeling a touch guilty that his tears had not yet come.

Maybe I've known he was dead since I saw him in the hospital, he thought. *Maybe they'll come later. Who knows?*

His eyes scanned the walls of Leblanc's office where he saw the mementos that a man uses to define his life. There were his degrees from Laval and U. of M., gotten ages ago it seemed. A group picture of Leblanc's graduating class showed that he had neither gained nor lost a pound since Bratt had met him. A large black and white photo of the Brooklyn Bridge dominated the wall next to the door. On his desk there was a picture of his estranged son, Luc, when he was just a boy of six, wearing a soccer uniform and posing with one foot resting on a ball.

Leblanc had rarely spoken about his son in the past few years. Bratt surmised that he had preferred remembering him as he was as a child. When it came to Jeannie, Bratt knew that he would also always think of her that way. That was a parent's privilege, and sometimes his misfortune.

John Kalouderis popped his head in unexpectedly, surprising Bratt in the midst of his reverie.

"I thought I might find you here."

"Were you looking for me?"

"Yeah, I was heading toward Brandy's and I didn't feel like going out alone. All my usual drinking buddies are busy tonight, watching Monday Night Football, or something."

Yeah, in late February, Bratt told himself, aware that his friend was lying.

"I'm not as much of a drinker as I used to be," he said.

"You will be tonight. We're both gonna get piss-drunk."

"That's the best damn idea I've heard yet," Bratt said, getting out of the chair and heading for the door.

Close to midnight on a Monday, the bar was barely half full. Bratt and Kouri sat at a small table in the corner, mixing their drinks indiscriminately. After all, they had reasoned, what's a little mourning for an old colleague if there were no consequences to suffer later? They were both well on their way to their stated goal of getting piss-drunk, and that was fine with them.

"What a fucking world," Kalouderis intoned, as if he had just understood the meaning to all existence. "Am I right? What a fucking world!"

Bratt nodded wordlessly. Each time he tried to speak he found that his tongue, thick with alcohol, kept tripping him up. He finally gave up, concentrated on the glass of he didn't remember what in front of him, and let Kalouderis have the floor.

"He won such a beauty of a case last week," Kalouderis said of their late friend. "In front of that prick, Xenopolos too. That's probably what killed him in the end. Poor J.P., having to listen to that Greek prima donna pontificate all damn day. Like he was on the Supreme Court, instead of the pathetic Provincial Court."

"You're Greek," Bratt noted with some difficulty.

"Damn right I am! That's why I can say what I want about him. But you can't. I don't wanna hear any ethnic slurs out of your mouth, young man."

Bratt ignored him and waved to the waitress, who sat on a barstool watching them with a bemused look on her face. He held up his empty glass and pointed at it, asking for the same of whatever it was he was having, hoping that she would remember the potent potion that was going down anything but smoothly.

"Hermes Xenopolos," Kalouderis stated with finality.

"Who? Oh, the judge. What about him?"

"He's a prick."

"So you said."

Kalouderis pushed himself up from his slouched position. Sitting ramrod straight and clearing his throat, it was obvious to Bratt that he was about to do a little pontificating himself. Fortunately, Bratt's drink arrived just in time to help drown out his friend's voice.

"He thinks nobody knows he's off the boat," Kalouderis said, loudly. "He thinks the boat's way gone, it's history. But I know the village where he was born, the peasant.

"He married a rich Jewish widow from Cote St. Luc, so he acts like he's hot shit. But you get close up to him you can still smell the sheep farm."

"That can't smell too good."

"Don't interrupt me."

Bratt silently waved his rambling friend on and Kalouderis continued as if he had never stopped speaking.

"Who's he think he's fooling? He can't even hide his damn accent. You can still hear the *kha* this and the *kha* that. What a snob! As off the boat as the last group of Chinese refugees and he avoids the rest of the community like we've got the plague. He never even would have gotten where he is, which is no big deal anyway, if he wasn't balling that rich princess with all her daddy's connections to help him"

"That's the one he married?"

"Shit, Bobby. Weren't you listening?"

"Not more than I had to."

They looked at each other and then burst out laughing, drawing curious looks from the few other patrons in the bar. Kalouderis put his arm around Bratt and leaned his head on his shoulder.

"Hey," Bratt tried to push him off. "Is this some sort of Greek thing?"

"Shut up, you racist! I just need a shoulder to cry on for a while."

Bratt thought back to when Kouri had unexpectedly hugged him in the ICU. The timing then had been just right, although he never would have admitted it. He let Kalouderis keep his head on his shoulder and patted him on the back as he glared around the bar, daring any of the other patrons to make a remark or give him a funny look. Nobody looked his way, though. They all had their own concerns.

It was nearly twelve-thirty when two men in their mid-fifties entered the bar. Bratt recognized the pot-belly and white hair instantly. It was St. Jean. He groaned inwardly, hoping they wouldn't be noticed, and gently removed Kalouderis's head from his shoulder, letting his half-asleep friend rest it on the table in front of them.

St. Jean did spot them, though, and he and his companion slowly made their way toward them. Bratt cursed his bad luck. Talking to the detective, especially about the Small case, was definitely last on the list of things he wanted to do that night.

"Well, well, Robert Bratt. Imagine finding you here."

"If you found me, that must mean you were looking for me."

"You always were pretty quick, Robert. I thought you wouldn't mind having a little talk with me."

"Thanks, but no thanks. I got other things on my mind just now."

"Yeah, I heard. Too bad about Leblanc. He wasn't a half-bad guy."

"I hear that's what they're putting on his headstone," Bratt snorted, pulling down most of his drink.

"Hey. I'm just trying to say something nice about the guy."

"Keep trying. You'll get it right eventually."

"All right. Be like that if you want. But there's still something I'd like to ask you about."

"It's kind of late. Call me during office hours."

"This is office hours for me. I'm doing a little overtime."

"Didn't you retire or something?"

"This is my last week, actually."

"So why aren't you, you know, doing something safe, like riding a desk or something?" Bratt pointed the index finger of one shaky hand at St. Jean and made a shooting motion with it. "In the movies cops always get shot three days before retirement."

"Didn't think you had time to catch many films, Bratt."

Bratt gave him a dirty but bleary look, swilled down some of his drink, then burped none too discreetly.

"Sorry," he said, covering his mouth with one hand. "I couldn't think of anything more clever to say."

"I didn't really notice the difference."

"Oh, touché, Phil. You did get your revenge there."

"OK, can we cut the crap?" St. Jean moved closer, leaning his face in next to Bratt's, his elbow planted on the table, inches from Kalouderis' head.

"I've spent an interesting evening chatting with your supposed witnesses, Sims and Jordan. I hope that doesn't surprise you."

"Considering that was the whole point of my giving Parent their names, no, I guess I'm not surprised."

"Where'd you get those two guys?"

"Through an Eaton's catalogue."

"Eaton went belly-up."

"Bankruptcy sale, all witnesses were half-off."

St. Jean straightened up and looked at his partner in disbelief.

"What is this, comedy night? I'm trying to be straight with you, Bratt, so quit the sarcasm for a while. Your witnesses are crooked, and if you know about it you're in deep trouble. I'm giving you a chance to help yourself."

Bratt's brain was just lucid enough that the threat managed to register. He had difficulty keeping the panic off his face as he asked himself, *How the hell did St. Jean know they were crooked? Shit, I wasn't really sure they were, myself.*

He downed the rest of his drink to calm himself, and noticed that St. Jean's partner's face showed surprise.

He was just as surprised at hearing that as I was, Bratt realized. *St. Jean, you old bullshitter, you almost bluffed me. But I'm still faster than you are, even with a bucketful of poison in me.*

"If they're crooked go ahead and charge them," he said, feeling braver now. "And if you have anything on me, feel free to accuse me too. Otherwise, get out of the waitress's way. You're interfering with my drinking."

St. Jean's face reddened. He knew he'd had his bluff called.

"Oh, I'll charge 'em all right. I'm not just sitting on my ass getting drunk till the trial, you know. I know these guys aren't straight and I'm going to prove it. I hope you *are* involved in this little game, because you won't be so clever sitting in a jail cell."

Bratt jumped up, almost tripping on the chair leg as he did so, then struggled to right himself, only to find he was nose to nose with St. Jean, like an umpire and an angry manager during a baseball game.

"Hey, what're you implying? You better watch what you go around saying in public, *mon hosti*, or I'll sue your fat ass."

"Go ahead and sue me. I'm going to prove everything I've been saying."

"Boy, you're really good with your little threats and innuendo, aren't you? Maybe you're getting worried about losing this case."

"You're the one who should be worried, Bratt."

"I am worried," he said, surprising himself by his admission. "Even drunk I've got enough brains to worry about a case like this. But I don't go running around saying the first dumb thing that comes into my fat head, just to see what cards the other guy's holding."

"No, you keep your cards close to the vest, especially when it's about these great witnesses you found, that look like they've been fed a Hollywood script for their testimony."

Bratt's unsteady forefinger was quickly up in St. Jean's face, barely an inch from the detective's nose.

"You son of a bitch, that's…that's slander. If you didn't have a badge, I'd-"

"I'll gladly take it off. Right now, outside."

Before Bratt could reply to the challenge he felt his arm grabbed and dragged down, pulling him back into his seat. He turned, furious at being interfered with like this, only to find that it was Kalouderis, wide-awake now and grinning broadly, who was holding onto his sleeve.

"Whoa! You boys gotta learn to play nice together."

"Let go of me, John. That prick's trying to fuck with my reputation and I'm the only one who gets to do that."

Kalouderis laughed and held Bratt tighter.

"Easy there, big fella. Look," he said and pointed out that St. Jean was also being pulled away by his own partner, and was now almost out of the bar. "It's over, forget it."

"Shit, I really would have liked to punch his lights out."

"Geez, Bobby, you're too much. Like trying to beat up a cop's such a good idea. Forget about him and have another drink. If you can still stand there and shout it out with him, you're not nearly as drunk as you need to be."

Far from satisfied with the conclusion of his argument, Bratt sat down anyway, grabbed Kalouderis's glass, and downed it.

"What is that shit you're drinking?"

"Same shit we've both been drinking for two hours. Waitress calls it her kamikaze special, and that's good enough for me."

He waved at her and she smiled, turning back to the bar to order two more of the near-lethal drinks. Bratt tried to brood over St. Jean, but the arrival of the drink helped him quickly forget the detective.

Somewhere in the back of his mind, as the hour approached three and last call was sounded, he thought of the court hearing he was supposed to attend at nine-thirty that morning, and wondered what condition he was going to be in, if he made it there at all. It was probably a good time to hit the road.

He patted Kalouderis's arm as a sign that it was time to go, then unsteadily got to his feet, looked around for the men's room and stumbled as he tried to walk toward it. He righted himself, but then quickly forgot all about the next day's court appearance as he vomited all over the barroom floor.

The next morning Bratt laid his head back in the slow-moving taxi that was carrying him to court from his home and closed his eyes against the incessant pounding caused by the blood rushing to his brain. With a trembling hand he wiped the sweat off his cold forehead and moaned. How he had managed to get out of bed that morning he didn't know.

When he had stepped out of his building he discovered that the winter sun was the brightest in recorded history and, of course, his sunglasses were nowhere to be found, probably lost under some piece of furniture or other. It was only to be expected, he supposed, that God should turn the screws a little tighter and try to blind him as punishment for the previous night's drunken revelry.

The taxi speeded up with a lurch as traffic opened up, causing Bratt's stomach to jump and sending bilious gasses up his throat. He covered his mouth with his hand and willed himself to keep everything down. Throwing up at the bar at closing time had been the ultimate humiliation. The two other times after he got home were just gut-wrenchingly painful. He only hoped he could get through the morning without wearing his insides on his robes.

Finally arrived at the courthouse, Bratt stepped carefully out of the taxi, squinting uselessly against the sun's searing rays. He slogged his way through the snow, dragging his feet, then headed up the stairs and into the courthouse's main lobby, where Kouri stood waiting for him. Kouri's face showed his obvious concern for his boss's condition. He had received an early-morning phone call from Bratt, sounding like he was at death's door and asking Kouri to meet him at the courthouse with his robe and vest.

"Mr. Bratt, is it all right if I say you look like shit?"

Bratt could only look weakly at him, too nauseous to reply. Opening his mouth for any reason seemed to be a bit risky just then, so he kept his words to a minimum. He reached out for Kouri's arm and shuffled like an old man toward the elevators, hoping his legs wouldn't give out in public.

"You don't want to take the escalator? The elevator never comes," Kouri said,

Bratt imagined the dizziness that surely awaited him if he were to watch the courthouse lobby slide past him while he stood on the rising stairs and decided to stick to the slow-moving elevators. He shook his head no, instantly causing it to spin anyway.

Somehow they made it to the elevators and got on with several other people, a few who smiled at Bratt in greeting, while looking somewhat surprised at his haggard appearance. When they got off just one floor up, Bratt felt their eyes following him.

They got to the courtroom door and Kouri held it open. Bratt slowly made his way to the defense bench and saw Nancy sitting across from him, with her eyes glued to a police report on the desk in front of her. This time he was glad she didn't look up at him as he entered.

Standing off to the side was Parent, engaged in a whispered conversation with none other than Philippe St. Jean. Bratt looked away, feigning indifference to the detective's presence.

He wasn't in court yesterday, he told himself. *I wonder if he showed up today on his own, or if Parent had ordered him to report on last night's "meeting."*

Bratt remained standing, leaning on the front of the prisoner's box, while he waited for Judge Green to take the bench. He didn't want to sit just yet because that would only mean having to stand up again when the judge entered. If it was at all possible he wanted to limit the number of times he would have to struggle to his feet, unsure that he'd have the strength to rise when called upon to do so.

Just before Green entered, St. Jean turned to Bratt and sneered openly. Parent, on the other hand, didn't look his way at all, but on his face Bratt could read his disapproval over whatever St. Jean had whispered to him about the night before.

"All rise," the bailiff called out, getting Bratt's attention.

Green made his way slowly up the dais and into his seat and Bratt thought that the judge looked the way he felt. Bratt slowly sat down as well, his shaky legs almost giving way at the last moment. His stomach gurgled loudly enough that even Nancy couldn't stop herself from looking his way. He gave her a sickly smile and received a puzzled frown in reply.

"Good morning, gentlemen," Green began, ignoring Bratt's audible intestines. "First of all, Mr. Bratt, I'd like to extend my condolences for the passing of your partner yesterday. I'm ashamed to say I was unaware he was in the hospital."

Bratt nodded in thanks, hoping the pained expression on his face would be attributed solely to his grief.

"You'll be glad to know that I won't keep you here too long this morning. I'm sure there are other places you would rather be just now."

Like a bathroom, Bratt thought, pulling out a kleenex to wipe his sweaty face.

"I reviewed the tape carefully," Green continued, "and the fact is that over ninety percent of it is nothing more than a running monologue by the detective. A not too subtle and ultimately fruitless attempt to get the accused to make a statement. None of what the detective says is particularly relevant to the issues in this trial, nor do his opinions on the state of the evidence against Mr. Small actually prove anything. So the jury certainly won't be hearing any of that.

"As for the rest, the few verbal exchanges that took place between the accused and the detective are of no probative value and may even mislead the jury into making the wrong inferences of fact. So those would have to go too.

"As a result, the few individual phrases by the accused that are left, those which I can say with confidence would not infringe on his right to a fair trial, are so disconnected as to be meaningless. I prefer limiting the jury's exposure to meaningless phrases to what they'll hear in the lawyers' final arguments. Therefore, none of the tape will be admitted into evidence."

Kouri whispered a triumphant "yes" at Bratt's side, while Bratt himself felt only a slight sense of relief trying to make its way past his stomach cramps.

"I'll see you gentlemen Monday morning for jury selection. My sympathies again, Mr. Bratt."

Bratt had to quickly cover his mouth against a burp that tried to escape, earning an understanding look from Green in return. The judge slowly got to his feet and Bratt managed to stand by pushing heavily down on the desk in front of him.

Once Green had left the courtroom Parent came over to where Bratt stood, extended his hand and whispered solemnly, "God rest his soul."

Bratt's limp, clammy handshake caused the prosecutor to wince involuntarily in disgust and wipe his hand on his robe as he turned to walk out. Bratt let Parent and the two detectives leave first because he didn't want them watching him wobble unsteadily out the door. Once he was sure they were far gone he grabbed Kouri's arm again and was slowly led into the courthouse corridor.

The block and a half walk back to their offices seemed to take an eternity for Bratt, who felt that mother nature had teamed up with his own body against him. Pedestrians stared or smiled cruelly at his obvious discomfort when he had to stop to catch his breath, leaning on a storefront window as he did so. He thought he heard Kouri whisper "march or die."

What the hell does he mean by that? he wondered, although he felt too sick to get angry.

"It's the title of a movie," Kouri said, once again seeming to read his mind. "All these soldiers marching in the desert, day after day…"

Bratt interrupted the movie account by placing a trembling hand to Kouri's mouth and giving a slight shake of his head. Right then, silence was all he could stand. Leaning against Kouri again, he continued his painful trek to his office.

By late afternoon, after a long nap on the sofa in his office and a couple of mugs of warm tea, Bratt's body seemed ready to show him some mercy. As for Kalouderis, to whom Bratt would have liked to give a swift kick in the pants for bringing him along on his drinking binge, there was little news. Sylvie, still red-eyed and now dressed in black, told Bratt that she had received a cryptic fax from his drinking partner, stating simply, "Please don't call."

Once he began feeling better, Bratt noticed the unhappy faces of the lawyers in his firm. Beyond the passing of the senior partner, there was also a sense of uncertainty about their future. Leblanc, on the morning of his heart attack, had mentioned to some of them the possibility that Bratt would be named a judge. Now the associates found themselves contemplating a major shift in the structure of the firm, if not its possible dissolution.

Bratt had given little thought to the future of the firm or of his associates. The proposed seat on the bench, as far as he was concerned, was far from a lock, especially if it was in any way dependent on his handling of the Small trial. Unsure of the path he wanted to take for his own life, he was in no position to advise others on how they should plan their careers.

Kouri knocked lightly on his door at around three that afternoon, then opened the door a crack and peeked in to see if Bratt was conscious. He saw him sitting up at his desk, sipping the tea that Sylvie had made him.

"Feeling better?"

"Yeah, getting there."

"You really had me worried this morning. I don't think your body can handle alcohol very well."

"Thanks for the insight."

Kouri still stood in the doorway, clearly debating whether to enter or not.

"You can come in, Pete. I won't break."

Kouri came in and sat on the sofa, trying to look comfortable. Something was bothering him and it occurred to Bratt that as surviving partner it now fell to him to take on the role of a paternal figure that Leblanc had played so well. Fortunately, the pounding in his head had for the most part subsided, and he was confident that a short talk wouldn't be fatal.

"What's on your mind?"

Kouri paused before answering, as if trying to make up his mind whether to go on or not.

"Is it always like this?" he finally asked.

"Ah, good question…What're you talking about?"

"Law. The practice. Are things always so, I don't know, ambiguous?"

Bratt thought the choice of words was interesting, and quite appropriate.

"It depends on how much time you spend thinking about things. For some guys, it's all black and white. They don't think too much about what they're doing, and there are few gray areas in their approach to the job. It's always us against them. Maybe that's the best way to be: just do your job and leave the bigger questions to priests and philosophers."

Bratt contemplated his own words, feeling the need to somehow explain, if not defend, his own doubts of late.

"But let me tell you something," he continued. "When you're in court, you really can't have any doubt that that's exactly what it is: us against them."

"And when we're not in court?"

"It's still us against them, only the 'them' includes a lot more people."

"Like who?"

Bratt knew what Kouri was looking for from him and he thought it was a good idea the young lawyer found it out early in his career.

"Like our own clients."

Kouri nodded his head, as if he had expected this answer from Bratt.

"That's the part I've been wondering about."

"Why now?"

"It's not just now. I've been wondering about it for a while. Especially since I've seen you talk to Small, or talking about him when he's not around. You really don't believe him, do you?"

"You know the answer to that."

"Yeah, I know. What I don't know is, why not? I mean, am I so naïve?"

"You are naïve. Not about Marlon Small so much as about the nature of our profession. So, here's rule number one, and if you only remember this rule you'll be ahead of most new lawyers. When you take on a criminal case, every single person you deal with, every cop, every opposing lawyer, every witness, and absolutely every client you ever take on, will lie to you without hesitation when they think it's in their best interests to do so. In the game of law you can't depend on anyone to help you and you can't trust anyone, especially your client."

Bratt stopped to catch his breath and squeezed his eyes shut briefly.

Shit, that took a lot out of me, he realized, opening his eyes again and blinking rapidly.

Kouri asked, "Isn't that pretty cynical?"

"If cynical is the opposite of naïve, then it certainly is."

"How do you live your life not knowing who to trust?"

"No, no. That's not what I said. You do know exactly whom you can trust, and that's yourself. As long as you don't lose that, you'll be OK. When you stop trusting yourself, that's when you're in trouble, because then you have to rely on your client instead. And that's never a good sign for a lawyer."

"Maybe I'm slow, but why would a client lie to his own lawyer? How would he expect the lawyer to properly defend him?"

"Most clients are too dumb to know what's in their own best interests. If they weren't so dumb they wouldn't need a lawyer in the first place, because they wouldn't get caught."

"Or maybe they just wouldn't commit the crime."

"My point exactly."

He sipped at his tea, closing his tired eyes again, and both lawyers quietly contemplated what had been said and where the conversation still might go.

Kouri leaned forward. His hands clasped together made him look like he was begging for the truth, although he didn't look Bratt in the eye when he spoke.

"If you knew, really knew, that a client was innocent, would you do anything at all to save him?"

Bratt lay his head on the back of his chair, eyes still closed, and asked himself, *Is he interviewing me for a newspaper exposé, or is he investigating me on behalf of the Bar? What a question! I never expected to be the one having to add salve to his conscience.*

"Look, Pete. Every lawyer starts out trying to obey the law to the letter. Nobody graduates law school thinking I'm going to be dishonest, or lie in court. I'm sure that's exactly how you are, too. Then comes the first day you're pleading and you realize that you can say the exact same thing in two different ways. The first way sounds bad for your client. The other way, which is still pretty close to the truth, just makes him look a little better. Let's call it a euphemism.

"So, you tell yourself, 'hey, quick thinking.' You're all happy with yourself for coming up with a way to show your client in a better light. But the fact is there's a world of difference between the truth and 'pretty close to the truth.' You may well be on your way to being a good lawyer. But you're also on your way to learning how easy it is to bend the truth when it suits you. And each time you plead, you'll bend it a bit more, and you'll be amazed how far you can bend it and still think it isn't broken. The truth, in the right hands, can be a very flexible tool.

"So, if you want to know how far I'd go to defend a client, *guilty or not*, I don't have the answer. I'm not sure I've reached my limit yet. I'm a little worried about that, to be honest with you. Not knowing how far I'd go, I mean. Does that answer your question?"

Kouri said nothing, but just gazed solemnly at the floor. He took a deep breath, looking like he had just come to an important decision, then he wiped his palms on his pants and stood up.

"Even if we never trust any of our clients, the odds are that some of them are going to tell us the truth."

"You're right. Just don't spend too much time worrying about which one it is. It'll get in the way of defending them."

"I think Marlon Small is telling the truth," Kouri said firmly. He paused, looked briefly at Bratt's face, then quickly away again before continuing. "I don't have any problems defending him."

He turned and walked slowly out of the office. Bratt sipped his tea as he watched him leave, wondering what had brought that on.

Chapter 9

That Thursday morning was the funeral for Jean-Paul Leblanc. Bratt stood at the entrance of Ste. Marie des Anges Church in Outremont, and read his partner's name, written with white plastic letters on a grooved blackboard behind a pane of glass.

He entered through the heavy double-doors, and saw that the church was full. Over his twenty years in practice, Leblanc had made many friends and near-friends, and the legal community was always ready to come out to remember one of its own.

In the front row of pews instead of Leblanc's family, who may have been as dead as he was for all anyone knew, the lawyers from his firm sat. Bratt walked down a side aisle, past row upon row of ornate, hand-carved wooden benches, and looked over the assembled mourners, checking who had come, who sat where, who spoke to whom.

It occurred to him that there was a certain hierarchy at funerals. The closer to the front you sat, the closer you could claim to have been to the deceased. He wondered if people showed up at funerals to show not how much the deceased had mattered to them, but rather to display their own importance. By their presence they put themselves among the privileged few that were allowed to claim a special place in the life of the dearly departed. They displayed their grief like a medal of honor, as if to say, "*I* was his close friend, *my* feelings matter." Others could look at them and say, “Look how sad they are. Their loss is so heavy.”

Bratt’s rambling thoughts stopped abruptly as he spotted Jeannie standing next to Kalouderis in the front pew. He suppressed an inappropriately happy smile and walked solemnly toward her. Kalouderis saw him approach and made room for him on the bench.

Bratt briefly worried that she may not want him to sit closeby. His moment of fear turned out to have been for naught. Jeannie turned her sad eyes to her father as he approached and gave him a welcoming look. Once he was next to her, she stretched up and kissed him lightly on the cheek. He allowed himself a small smile of gratitude, feeling a little less forlorn than he had been since the day Leblanc entered the hospital.

As the priest stepped away from the altar and began reciting the funeral prayers in French, Bratt’s thoughts lingered on his daughter. All his troubles with Small and all the doubts he’d been having about his vocation were linked to the things that Jeannie had said to him and had been aggravated by her absence from his life. He hadn’t been conscious of how much her leaving home had affected him until he saw her again. For all intents and purposes, she was the only family he had left.

He did have an older brother who was a social worker, or something equally altruistic, in Toronto. And a sister who taught English to spoiled, rich children in the South of France. There were cards on birthdays and phone calls at Christmas, but they both had their own careers and families to worry about.

In Montreal, it had been only him and Jeannie for the past eight years. How ironic that he should see her again at a funeral where not a single relative of the deceased was present. He imagined himself lying where Leblanc lay, and thought that he didn’t need a church full of colleagues and acquaintances to see him off, just his daughter.

My God, Bratt, he told himself. *You are becoming one maudlin old man. Good thing nobody can read your weepy thoughts.*

Despite this self-reproach, he couldn’t deny his feelings. He turned to look at Jeannie, who was paying more attention to the priest's words than he was, and slid his hand along the back of the pew in front of them until it was touching hers. Her hand moved almost imperceptibly away, then, after a moment's hesitation, moved back until it was touching his. As he tentatively took her hand in his, he realized he was acting more like a shy schoolboy on a first date than a father.

How come I can't just grab her and tell her she better get her butt home right now, before I take her out to the woodshed or something? What a generation of wimpy parents we are, afraid of hurting our children's feelings and desperate to have them like us.

He thought back to his own father, who had never in his life mistaken himself for his son's best friend. Joseph Bratt had not been one to spend a lot of time worrying about whether he was liked or not, not at home, and certainly not at court. *Just as well,* his son thought. *That way he was never disappointed.*

Bratt knew that if he wanted a closer relationship with his daughter than he had had with his father, especially in those final years, these worries and self-doubts were the price he had to pay. It was too late now to question how he had raised her. Besides, that she was stubborn and had a mind of her own was part of what he loved most about her.

The funeral seemed to end soon after it had started. Bratt had hardly noticed the passage of time, almost forgetting the friend he was there to mourn, preoccupied as he was with thoughts of reconciling with Jeannie.

As the coffin was wheeled slowly out by a group of attendants from the funeral home and the small choir began singing a rather plaintive "Ave Maria," he waved Kalouderis on to join the others, signaling that he would join them later at the cemetery. Jeannie stayed behind with him, clearly willing to talk to him again.

Once the mourners had drifted out into the street and the singers began putting away their hymnals, Bratt took her hand again and pulled her down next to him on the pew.

"How've you been?" he asked almost casually, afraid to scare her off by a too obvious display of emotion.

"Good," she nodded. Her eyes flitted around the empty church, and now she looked unsure that she wanted to be there. Finally, hesitantly, she said, "I've missed you."

Bratt was relieved that she had said it first, freeing him of any lingering uncertainty about her feelings.

"Christ, Jeannie. You've got no idea how empty our place is without you."

She smiled now, a warm, almost maternal smile that reminded him of how Deirdre used to look at him in the early days of their marriage, when he had been struggling to get his practice up and running and got by only with her loving support.

Crap, he thought. *My practice. I still don't know how she feels about that.*

He asked her, "Jeannie, what are your plans?"

He wanted to kick himself for asking such a feeble question, but he couldn't think of a better way to approach her. This had been his basic concern for days, so he had no choice but to ask it as directly as possible.

"Are you planning to stay away a lot longer?"

"I don't know," she said somberly. Then, as his smile faltered at her words, she added with a mischievous smile, "Well, probably not. Although being independent's not so bad."

She shifted in her seat to face him squarely.

"You know I love you, Daddy," she said not too warmly.

Bratt said nothing in reply, waiting for a "but." She had that look he had learned to recognize, the one that told him she was putting her arguments together in her head, trying to be logical. He waited patiently to see where they would take her.

"I realize that I can't hate you for the job you do," she said. "That doesn't mean I like your work any more than I did before. Since Claire's trial."

Bratt realized that he had also begun to think of it as "Claire's trial," rather than Nate Morris's.

"I just can't pretend to like it," she continued. "I can't even be indifferent to it. I guess that's my biggest problem right now: reconciling how I feel about you with how I feel about your work. But I'm at least going to try to distinguish the man from the lawyer. That's not such a bad deal, is it?"

God, he thought, somewhat disheartened. *The wording she uses to express her affection: I'm afraid there's a bit of a lawyer in her, too.*

"What if I didn't do this job anymore?" he blurted out, seeing a solution to both their problems. The news that Madsen had given him now seemed like a godsend.

"What're you talking about?"

"Listen, honey," he said, feeling a growing excitement about what this news would mean to both of them. "Not a lot of people know this, but I might be named a judge."

"A judge?"

"Yes. Superior Court, just like granddad."

"Daddy, that's wonderful," she said, seeming sincerely happy for him. "It's what you've always wanted."

"I know, but it's more than that. It's what you've wanted too, because it means I won't be defending those…well, those *scumbags* anymore."

He felt a pang of self-reproach at using the same word that she had once used to describe his clientele. But he wanted to show her that he was truly going to separate himself from his past life and from his clients, that he might even be ready to see things her way. *Besides,* he told himself, *isn't that exactly how I feel about my most recent client?*

"Daddy, you said you *might* be named a judge. You don't know for sure?"

Aye, there's the rub, he told himself. *Do I tell her about the Small case or not? And do I tell her I almost have to win it at all costs?*

"It's all but in the bag," he answered, looking away briefly as he fibbed. "I just have to finish some litigation I'm working on. They'll probably announce it within the month."

Jeannie reached out and squeezed his hand, then let him pull her closer and hug her. Again, there was that brief hesitation, then she hugged him back.

Bratt held her close, rocking her gently back and forth. He wanted this to be a new beginning for both their lives, yet he was worried that things seemed to have worked out too easily. Recently, nothing had come that easily and he only hoped she'd be this happy for him when the murder trial was over and Marlon Small was back out on the street.

That afternoon the office of *Leblanc et Bratt, Avocats* opened its doors to receive condolences from judges, lawyers, courthouse staff and the occasional client. Bratt had wanted to rent a large restaurant for a mercy-meal, but Ralston insisted in keeping things as simple and low-key as possible, in accordance with Leblanc's final wishes. When Bratt complained that he seemed to have been totally left out of the loop when it came to executing Leblanc's posthumous desires, Ralston calmly explained that this had been intentional.

Leblanc had made Ralston his executor and had left specific instructions about how much pomp and ceremony was to be bestowed upon him after his passing. He had fully expected Bratt to pay no attention to what he wanted and to just do whatever he felt was appropriate, probably going overboard in the process.

As the afternoon wore on, lawyers from both sides of the legal divide, a few judges, and even some court staff made the short trek from the *Palais de Justice* to their building. As they entered, Sylvie greeted them, acting almost widow-like as she received their condolences and allowed them to kiss her tear-stained cheeks.

Trays of party sandwiches and cheese-slices were strategically placed in the various rooms and along the wall in the main corridor, and the end of a long conference table had been converted into a modest bar. The mood occasionally teetered on the verge of breaking into a cocktail party, but Ralston, wandering amongst the guests with his dour face, made sure that no undue levity was allowed to uplift the gathering.

Bratt snuck off to his own office, and only came out when Kouri announced the arrival of a judge or some other eminent jurist. Jeannie had left him after their talk in the church with a promise to call him soon. So he sat alone now behind his desk, drinking only mineral water and vacillating between contentment over the recent turnaround in his personal fortunes and sadness over his partner's demise.

Kouri's head popped in through the door again, but his announcement this time took Bratt by surprise.

"It's Mrs. Campbell. She didn't know about J.P. She wanted to talk to you."

Bratt swore under his breath. "OK, ask her in here, would you?"

He forced the displeasure from his face as Jennifer Campbell stepped through the door, holding a handkerchief to her face. She wore a plastic rain bonnet to keep the snow from ruining her hair. She looked at him with a pained expression and came toward him as if she was going to hug him, but then caught herself and stopped.

"Mr. Bratt, I am so sorry to barge in on you at this sad, sad time. I had no idea that Mr. Leblanc had been called to the Lord. May He rest his soul."

Bratt stood and took her hand in his. His face effected sadness combined with appreciation for her kind words, but in his heart her presence left him void of any true emotion.

"Mrs. Campbell, I'm sure if you came down here unannounced it was for a very important reason. Please sit down and tell me how I can help you."

"I just wanted to be sure you met the Sims boy and Everton Jordan. Marlon and I feel their testimony is what you'll need to get him out of this terrible mess."

"Don't worry. I met them and I think they're going to be of great help."

"Thank God for that. I was so worried that you might find that they weren't any better than the first two boys."

"No, I was very impressed with them. I'm sure the jury will find them to be very believable witnesses."

"Thank God for that," she repeated. "That's what matters most, I suppose. I must say I was quite disappointed when the other two didn't work out. But that's why we're putting our trust in you, to guide us through this court system, which sometimes makes no sense to us at all."

Bratt nodded politely, saying nothing and wondering where she was going with all this. He was sure they had already had this conversation not so long ago. Then she suddenly switched topics, taking him a bit by surprise.

"Mr. Bratt, are you a religious man?"

"I have been in my life."

"Don't answer like a lawyer when you're talking about God," she snapped.

"I'm sorry. I just wasn't sure what to make of your question."

"Only the devil asks trick questions, Mr. Bratt. And lawyers, of course. When I ask a question it only means what the words say."

Now there's a novel idea, Bratt thought, remaining quiet.

"I'm sorry if I sound a bit harsh," she relented, "especially during this time of mourning. But, then, we are all suffering a loss right now, aren't we?"

Bratt nodded, still saying nothing but admiring how quickly her temper could flare and then be calmed again.

"My loss is only part-way complete, as you know. There's still time to prevent it from being finalized. There's only a few days left until the trial, and I've been very unsettled in my soul. I'm sorry to come to you now, but you have so much experience in these matters. I thought if we could talk a bit, it would reassure me that justice will be done to my son."

Bratt thought that she had probably meant "justice *for* her son," but he found the grammatical slip ironically appropriate.

"That's fine, Mrs. Campbell. Maybe we can comfort each other."

She smiled gratefully and went to sit down on the sofa. Bratt swung a chair over and sat facing her.

"Can I offer you something to drink?"

"No, that's kind. I'd rather keep a sober mind and a sober tongue right now."

"Don't worry," he tried to smile reassuringly, "I'm not going to ask you any trick questions."

She smiled back and took a moment to compose herself.

"What did he die of?"

It took Bratt a second or two to realize that she was talking about Leblanc.

"Uh, his heart. I'm afraid he wasn't in the best of health."

"Nonsense, he was a fine specimen of a man. But, when God says it's your time, then it doesn't matter what the doctors say."

Bratt shrugged noncommittally. He didn't like the idea that his friend could have been taken so arbitrarily, but he wasn't about to debate the issue.

"In a way, that's what I want to talk to you about, Mr. Bratt. As much as I pray for enlightenment, I just don't know God's will in this case. I don't know why He's testing Marlon, or if maybe He's testing me with this terrible trial. I worry that maybe in His greater plan, we may not be meant to win."

Bratt was unsure how to answer her. The first time they had spoken she had called him God's answer to her prayers. Now, she was wondering if God was going to pull this trial right out from under him. He didn't want to offend her, but he wasn't ready to accept that the outcome of this case depended solely on divine intervention.

"Mrs. Campbell, please don't take this the wrong way. Since you don't know what God wants, all you can do is what you think is the best thing for Marlon. That's why you came to me in the first place, remember?"

She nodded fervently, and Bratt suddenly had an image of her at Sunday prayers, nodding and clapping her hands to her preacher's exhortations.

"I guess, if I were a truly religious person," he continued, "I'd say that you can't worry, you can't even wonder, about what God wants. You just have to have…faith, I guess, that what He wants is what's best for your son. So, you do your best and I do my best, and we hope that in the end it all works out."

"You are a wise man, Mr. Bratt."

If only, he told himself, but to her he replied, "Like you said, I do have experience in these matters."

"Do you ever think that you might be doing God's work?"

"Oh, I really wouldn't go that far," he said, almost offended by the idea. "I doubt that my clients would even think so, and they're-"

"But you are," she cut him off. "You see, you don't seek the truth of man. You fight against the very judgment and condemnation of man, because in your heart you know that here on Earth, we're all just biding our time. In God's great plan, what does it matter what a court's verdict is? In the end, it's only God's own judgment that every man has to face and to fear. Man is so vain, thinking he can replace His judgment with courts and jails.

"A guilty man may walk away, or an innocent may be convicted, and we'll say that justice was done. But only God knows the truth, and no amount of lawyering can stand in the way of His final judgment. So, whatever reprieve we might get here on Earth, we had better enjoy it while it lasts, because in eternity it might just be another story altogether."

Amen, thought Bratt, wondering what exactly she was trying to get at. *I can't figure out if she's depending on me to save Marlon or telling me that whatever I do for him is pointless in the end. And how exactly am I doing God's work, anyway? I still don't get that part.*

"Would you pray with me, Mr. Bratt?"

"Well…um, yes, of course, Mrs. Campbell."

She knelt down in front of the sofa and took Bratt's hand, pulling him down next to her. He looked at the door, wishing he had thought to lock it when she had come in. From the deep recesses of his memory he remembered reading somewhere that Nixon had asked Kissinger to kneel and pray with him during the Watergate crisis. And look what that got him!

"We can recite the Lord's Prayer together, if you like," she suggested.

Bratt nodded, fairly sure that he remembered all the words.

"Our Father, who art in Heaven," she began.

"Hallowed be Thy name," he joined in, keeping his voice low for fear that anybody might be listening at the door.

They prayed solemnly and when they had reached the end, Bratt gave a quick "amen" and began to get to his feet, only to have her squeeze his hand and keep him down on his knees.

"Dear Lord," she continued, "this is your dutiful handmaiden, Jennifer Campbell. I beseech you, take good care of my boy Marlon. Give strength to his lawyer, Mr. Bratt here. He likes to talk like a non-believer, but I know his heart is true. Speak to the jury through him, oh Lord, and guide his every action in this terrible trial that You have inflicted on us in Your wisdom.

"Bless us and forgive us all, Lord. We are all sinners, and I am chief among them. Help me to do Your will, and let Your will be to see my boy home and free at last. Amen."

With that she let go of Bratt's hand and raised herself up, straightening her skirt as she did so. Bratt whispered a small thank you to God for not having allowed anybody to walk in on them while they were praying. He brushed off the knees of his pants, trying to look casual, but he found that her words had rendered him more nervous, rather than reassuring him.

She shook his hand formally and gave him an appreciative smile without saying another word, then walked slowly out of his office, her head held proudly erect.

What was behind all that? Is it just her religious devotion, or is there something deeper worrying her? The hell with it. I know what I'm doing, at least, and I know what I'm going to have to do. If she feels better for having prayed with me, then more power to her. But I have the defense that I want to present and I'm not going to worry about whose side God might be on.

The last few days leading up to Marlon Small's trial were spent putting the final touches to the pre-trial preparations, with little in the way of the ups and downs that had marked the previous weeks of Robert Bratt's life. He and Kouri spent some time with Small at R.D.P., reviewing the testimony he would give.

Their client was filled with nervous excitement about the upcoming trial, raring to go to battle, yet constantly asking Bratt if he felt good about their chances. Bratt's answers always seemed to be tinged by a mild pessimism. There was a stubbornly petty part of him that refused to give his client any of the hope that might have eased his mind before the trial.

Kouri, on the other hand, was positively brimming with confidence. When he spoke with Small, Bratt almost felt left out, as they both refused to share his negative views about the trial. They had decided they were going to win it, and he could go along with them for the ride if he wanted to. Bratt felt a twinge of jealousy at the ease with which the two younger men communicated, but knew that his feelings about Small, obvious and unchangeable, would always act as a wall between them.

As for his witnesses, Jordan and Sims, Bratt ignored the nagging feelings that arose whenever he thought of their too-perfect alibi. He had too many other things to do to spend time honing their testimony, so he asked Kouri to meet with them again on his own. He was relying on Kouri more and more for the preparation of the defense, preferring to concentrate his own time on finding holes in the Crown's case.

Bratt read and reread Paris's and Phillips's preliminary inquiry testimony and compared it with the written statements they had given to the detectives in the early stages of the investigation, looking for inconsistencies and contradictions between the various accounts.

Bratt thoroughly cross-referenced every change in the fact-patterns, no matter how small or banal it may have seemed to an outsider, whether it was how many seconds Phillips had to observe his assailants, or how many inches the gun was from his head. He knew that the weight of these numerous differences, piled one on top of the other, as well as the inability of Phillips or Paris to satisfactorily explain them away, could be the witnesses' eventual undoing.

All these natural human errors were like nuggets of gold for the experienced lawyer to dig up and wave under the noses of the duly impressed jurors. The witnesses rarely realized there were any inconsistencies in their testimony, until Bratt began pointing out these little glitches in their memories and holding them up for everyone to gaze at and wonder over. Then the witnesses would look like they were getting caught in their own lies.

He had tried to teach Kouri that a good cross-examination did not simply mean asking questions in the hope of finding out some unknown information. A lawyer had to have a clear idea of all the useful information a witness could give before he asked a single question. And he certainly had to know the answer to every question he asked, or risk the kind of embarrassing surprises that were the staple of TV shows and second-rate movies. If there was ever one thing that had turned him off from watching the spate of legal dramas on television, it was the sight of lawyers constantly getting ambushed by answers they didn't expect.

No, cross-examination meant letting the jury in on what the lawyer and the witness already knew. It meant inducing that witness to reveal facts he may have preferred keeping hidden, or the relevance of which he was often unaware. The jurors might think they were witnessing some dramatic courtroom revelations, but if he had done his job right, then Bratt would have scripted the whole scene for them ahead of time. That was how he liked to think of what he did: he was writing a play, scene by scene. If everybody played their parts well and read their lines like they were supposed to, then it was sure to be a big hit.

The weekend passed quickly for him and then it was Monday morning: time for jury selection.

"Unfortunately, jury selection," Bratt told Kouri as they got ready to head for court, "isn't half as interesting in real life as it is on TV. At least not in Canada. We don't use jury consultants; we don't do mock trials or market testing."

Kouri only half-listened to his mentor's rambling exposition as he put on his coat. Bratt could hardly contain the excitement he always felt on the first day of a trial, and all his nervous energy seemed to have been concentrated in his mouth that morning. He had put aside all thought of Leblanc's death. He had forgotten about Claire's humiliation on the stand. He was singularly focused now on the task at hand.

"We don't even get to ask them any questions as a general rule," he continued. "Just peremptory challenges, take 'em or leave 'em, and that's all just a guessing game anyway. All you get is a quick first impression and about two seconds to decide.

"For our case, though, we're *real* lucky. Since there was some newspaper coverage of the shootings last summer, Green is going to let me ask the jury candidates two whole questions: did you read about the shootings, and did you form an opinion as to who did it? That's it. If they answer no to either question, that's the end of my challenge for cause."

Bratt pulled his winter coat on over his robes and picked up a large document case. They headed onto the elevator with a few other tenants of their office building and Bratt let his motor-mouth idle a bit. His dissertation was for Kouri's benefit alone. Since he had first met the young lawyer his opinion of him had changed a great deal. He no longer worried about having to be his nursemaid, and in fact enjoyed giving him the benefit of his experience on just about every topic under the sun.

Out on the street again, he picked up where he had left off as they moved briskly along the sidewalk.

"We'll try to get you some good-looking young ladies on the panel. That'll make the next couple of weeks a bit more enjoyable."

"Seriously, other than good-looking women is there anybody else we should try to get on this jury?"

"Oh, sure. But it's unlikely we'll get twelve of Small's peers up there, and that's the only thing that would make a real difference in this trial."

They got into the courthouse and headed left from the main lobby toward the corridor leading to room 3.01. As they turned the corner Bratt heard Kouri let out a sudden rush of breath at the sight of over a hundred potential jurors crowding the hallway. He looked over and saw the nervousness etched on the younger lawyer's face.

"Buck up, me lad. You've dreamed of this moment ever since you saw Perry Mason on TV. These are your future fans, so give 'em a confident smile and keep walking."

Kouri managed a tight grin and they moved forward again, politely pushing through the crowd. Many of the jury candidates turned to look at them as they passed, several of them whispering comments to their neighbors. It was a gauntlet of sorts that Bratt had run many times. Once through it, they passed through the doors and into the arena he had once thought of as his second home.

The courtroom was quiet and empty and, as they walked toward their side of the lawyers' benches, Bratt kept looking over at Kouri, trying to see it all through his inexperienced eyes.

I guess I'm just an old whore, he told himself. *My first time is just a faded memory. I hardly remember if I was scared, if it hurt. I can't even picture my client's face, there have been so many since then.*

"What's so funny?" Kouri asked, having noticed a little smile forming on Bratt's face."

"Oh, nothing, nothing. Just try to remember this day, OK? Your first time. Hang on to the memory as long as you can."

"You're a sentimental old fool, Robert Bratt." Kouri smiled at him.

"So I've discovered. Let's keep it our little secret shall we?"

"What secret is that?" a woman's voice asked from behind them.

Bratt turned and was surprised to find Nancy Morin standing there, laden with an armful of file folders. He reached out to take them from her.

"Hey lady, need a hand with those?"

"Sentimental and chivalrous," Kouri noted, then quickly got out of the way.

Bratt turned to give him a mock-angry glare, but couldn't suppress the smile he felt coming on as Nancy came closer and put her hand on his arm.

"That's what I liked about him in the first place."

"What about the second place," Bratt asked, jauntily.

"That I won't answer in public. I just came by before Parent got here to wish you luck, Robert."

"Really?" Bratt stood closer to her and whispered, "Aren't you afraid to be seen consorting with the enemy."

She smiled and pulled back a couple of steps.

"Yes, I am. So I'm going back to the safety of the Crown bench…for now."

Bratt smiled and restrained himself from going after her. There was a time for everything, and their time would come later, he was glad to see.

Parent made his entrance soon after her, accompanied by St. Jean, whom Bratt now thought of as the prosecutor's guard dog. They both nodded perfunctorily in Bratt's direction before joining Nancy.

Bratt was tempted to say something sarcastic to St. Jean in retribution for the policeman's allegations in the bar the week before. He looked over at Nancy, who was looking worriedly at him from behind a file folder, and decided that for once he'd keep his big mouth shut.

Getting the verdict he wanted would be the best retribution he could ask for.

At 9:25 a.m. the court clerk announced over the intercom that all jury candidates should enter the courtroom. The hundred-plus people filed in slowly, almost hesitantly, and began looking for seats.

There were not enough places for all of them in the gallery, so some of them sat next to the lawyers, others filled the jury box, and four nervous souls were directed to sit in the empty prisoner's dock behind the defense bench. Looking worried, they constantly glanced over their shoulders at the locked door leading to the cells where Small was being held, almost expecting him to suddenly appear and be let loose among them.

At 9:30 precisely, just as the last candidates were seating themselves, a bailiff entered and told them to rise again. Judge Benjamin Green entered immediately after him and over two hundred eyes, most of them wide-eyed with curiosity and nervousness, focused on the small, fragile-looking old man as he slowly took his place.

"You may be seated," the bailiff said, and everyone sat down at once, with an almost palpable sense of relief.

"Good morning, ladies and gentlemen," Green said in a somber voice, "and thank you for being here. As you know twelve of you will be chosen to form a jury in the trial we are beginning today. Now, being on a jury may seem like an inconvenience to some of you, and we all understand that. However, it is also one of the most important civic duties that you will be called on to perform in your day-to-day lives."

Bratt half-listened to Green's traditional welcoming speech. The actual words mattered little to him, but he felt a sense of comfort at the familiarity of the occasion. He was always a little nervous before the start of a trial, and doubly so when the stakes were so high. But it was a happy nervousness, one that reminded him of what it was that he loved about his work.

He let slip a small smile at the realization that he had been able to use the “L-word” about his job again, something he wouldn’t have thought likely a week or two earlier.

He looked across at Parent, who seemed to be wrapped up in Green’s words, but was probably making a last-minute review of his own strategy in his head. As much as Parent disliked him personally, Bratt knew the prosecutor had a healthy respect for his courtroom skills. He didn’t reciprocate the feeling entirely, but he wasn’t taking the veteran prosecutor lightly either.

Green came to the end of his short speech and asked all the potential jurors to step out into the hallway. This allowed Nancy to recover her now-vacated seat next to Parent and sit down directly across from Bratt, from where she kept her attention focused on the judge.

Those candidates who wished to seek exemptions were called in next, to give their reasons why they should not have to serve on the jury. Only once this sometimes-lengthy proceeding was over would the actual jury selection begin.

As the first candidate re-entered the courtroom, Bratt looked across at Nancy to see if she would continue to avoid eye contact with him. He was sure she looked at him occasionally from the corner of her eye, and he was equally sure that a small movement on her lips from time to time was a smile meant for him. Happy memories of their cross-courtroom flirtation during the lengthy Hall trial came back to him, and he was more optimistic than ever about the way the next two weeks would unfold.

One by one, men and women came in to petition for their release from the burden of jury duty. Some looked defiant, while others were obviously intimidated by the moment, but it seemed like everybody was looking for a way out today.

It took over two hours to listen to the litany of reasons for exemption and for the judge to rule on them. The morning crawled to an end with less than half the jury selected. Everyone got up and stretched, then went for lunch. Kouri looked a bit disappointed that his first murder trial had gotten off to such a stuttering start. He had been looking forward to some dramatic action. Bratt smiled and reassured him that things would pick up soon enough. He would have to be just a little more patient.

"This is just the salad," Bratt said. "They make you wait a bit for the steak."

Chapter 10

To Kouri's chagrin, the main course was not served until Wednesday morning, March 15. Up to that point the trial's preliminaries unfolded pretty much as expected.

On Monday afternoon the last jurors were chosen with little fanfare. Only one candidate had been refused for having read about the shootings the previous summer and forming an opinion as to the guilt of the accused. Soon after Parent gave his opening statement to the jury and Bratt found it somewhat uninspired.

"Young men with guns," Parent had intoned in the gravest of voices. "Children, almost, playing at grown-up games with toys that kill. This, ladies and gentlemen, is the sad story that you will be hearing in this trial."

Bratt noticed that Jennifer Campbell made her first appearance at the trial that afternoon. She listened to Parent's opening speech from the back of the room, staring coldly at his back. She had quietly slipped into the room during jury selection and then left quickly when court broke for the day, without saying a word to Bratt. He felt no particular need to speak to her either, but he couldn't help wondering why she no longer seemed to need to speak to him.

As for Small, he behaved as well as could be expected. He didn't glare menacingly at anyone in the room, although the expression on his face was less than friendly. Most importantly, he listened attentively to Bratt's instructions and did what he was told.

The first witness, the crime-scene technician, was called on Tuesday morning. He filed into evidence three small albums containing a hundred-odd pictures of the shooting site, including some fairly graphic ones of the two deceased lying in pools of their own blood. Several jurors of both sexes squirmed at the sight of these photos and cast quick, awed looks in Small's direction, seemingly amazed that he possessed the ability to commit such mayhem.

The witness presented a floor plan of the apartment, with distances and angles of fire that had been determined by the location of bullets found imbedded in the walls and in the victims' bodies. This map was key, Bratt thought, as he hoped it would show that from where the surviving victim, Dorell Phillips, had sat he couldn't have had as good a look at his assailant as he had claimed.

The rest of Tuesday had been spent listening to two young patrolmen who took turns describing in detail how they had been first on the scene of the crime, had secured it to prevent the loss or destruction of evidence and had stayed with Phillips, placing pressure on his bleeding wounds until *Urgences Santé* had arrived.

Phillips's injuries had prevented him from speaking at that point, they said, or they surely would have gotten a description of the gunmen from him. As it was, they made it clear that their timely arrival had saved his life.

Then, finally, on Wednesday morning the jurors got what they had been waiting for: Dorrell Phillips himself, with two small mounds of flesh protruding from the lower left side of his neck, where the miraculously non-fatal bullets had exited his body, took the stand.

He was in his early twenties, with a short, wiry build. His eyes, behind his rimless glasses, flitted about the courtroom nervously when he first took the stand. However he quickly fixed them on an imaginary point on the countertop in front of him. When he answered questions he rarely looked up from that point to face his questioner, and he spoke with a soft, sad voice, as if retelling the story was something he would have preferred not doing.

The faces of the jurors betrayed their evident sympathy for him. He had passed within millimeters of losing his life and then regained his consciousness just in time to find his older brother's bullet-riddled body. That he should have recovered, at least physically, from such a trauma merited him that sympathy, Bratt had no doubt. He only hoped that it didn't render his testimony beyond reproach in the jury's eyes.

Parent began the young man's testimony by guiding him through a detailed description of how he had spent the day of June 14, 1999, letting him get comfortable on the stand, while allowing the jury to observe him and get to know him as a person. Phillips described whom he had been with and what he had done in the hours leading up to his arrival at the apartment on Carrier Street, where he had gone looking for his brother Dexter.

He had found him there that night, getting high on crack cocaine, as he knew he would. He wanted to take his brother home before their father went looking for him. Even though Dexter was his senior by three years, it was Dorrell's lot in life to be his brother's keeper.

"Now, Mr. Phillips," Parent said, sounding like a solicitous *maitre d'* directing a client to his table, "please tell the jury what happened next. And please let me remind you to speak loudly, so that everyone can hear your testimony."

"Well, at that point I told Dexter that I'd had enough. I wanted to get home because I knew my dad was going to be angry. He said he had to go take a…go to the bathroom first, so I sat on the sofa, waiting for him."

"That sofa we see here, in the living room, on Exhibit P-3," Parent noted, pointing at the floor plan of the apartment that had been taped up on a blackboard for all to see.

"Yeah, right here on the near end. Indian was sitting watching TV, next to me, here. Then somebody rang the bell from downstairs. I didn't even pay attention, 'cause there were people coming and going there all the time.

"So Indian went to the door, it's to the left side of the living room, and buzzed them up. Then, he opened the door to see who it was."

"You saw him do this?"

"Yeah, kinda outta the corner of my eye, 'cause mostly I was looking at the TV. After a bit I heard him talking to somebody at the door. I couldn't hear what they were saying, but Indian sounded angry. I really wasn't paying much attention up till then."

"Go on."

"So, suddenly I hear the door slam real loud. I turn to look right away and I see Indian standing inside the door and there's two other guys with him. Indian looks surprised, and one of the guys, the taller one, grabs him by the shoulder and pushes him face down onto the floor. That's when I notice that these guys, not Indian I mean, these two other guys, they had guns in their hands."

"Do you remember in which hand they carried the guns?"

"I remember the tall one. I know he had it in his left hand, because he pushed Indian down with his right hand. So he was waving it around in his left hand."

Bratt knew, as Parent surely did, that Small was left-handed. He scribbled a note and slid it over to Kouri.

"I thought left-handedness was a sign of genius."

Kouri gave him a wide-eyed look, shocked that Bratt would be passing notes in the middle of the trial. To Bratt's amusement, he slid the note furtively into his pocket.

"Now, tell me, Mr. Phillips. Did anybody say anything at this point?"

"Yeah. The tall one spoke. When he pushes Indian down he yells out, 'I'm here for your shit, so nobody fuckin' move.' That's exactly what he said. I'll never forget that."

"No," Parent nodded solemnly, "I'm sure you won't."

"Thing was," Phillips went on, "it made no sense, 'cause as soon as Indian was down on the floor he shot him. So, I mean, why did he tell us not to move? Nobody moved, nobody had time to do anything, and he killed us."

Phillips paused, head now hanging even further down, and wiped a tear from his eye. Bratt could only look on admiringly.

"He killed us," he thought. *That's a pretty good turn of phrase. I wonder if Parent came up with it.*

As for Parent, he looked on quietly while his witness composed himself, a priest waiting patiently for a penitent to unburden himself.

"When you're able to continue, Mr. Phillips."

The witness nodded, sniffling softly, then turned his red eyes up to the jurors.

"Like I said," he continued, "as soon as Indian was on his stomach the tall guy shot him twice. Bang, bang! Real fast."

"Could you describe how the two gunmen were standing and exactly what they were doing at that point."

"Sure. The little guy was just in the corner, all kind of squeezed into it, like he didn't want to be there. He didn't point his gun at Indian. He kind of held it at his hip, pointing straight, but not really at me or anybody.

"The tall guy was standing over Indian. His feet were next to Indian's head, one on each side. When he shot, he pointed the gun straight down, between his feet, at Indian's head. Like I said, he took two shots, real quick."

"Go on."

"Then he looks up at me, and I'm still sitting on the sofa."

"You didn't get down on the floor when he told you to?"

"No, I was too surprised. I didn't know if it was really a hold-up or just a joke, or what. He just yells it out and I'm still thinking, what's he mean by that? Then suddenly, bang, bang, he's shot Indian. And I'm still sitting there 'cause I can't believe this is real. I never saw nobody die before. I didn't think it was so easy. I wasn't even thinking that he might want to shoot me. I don't know what I was thinking.

"Then he pointed the gun at me and began walking at me, staring at me. And he yelled, 'Get the fuck on the floor or I'll shoot you too.' That's when I got off the sofa. I didn't even think that he was probably gonna shoot me when I'm lying down anyway. I just got down real fast."

"Which way were you facing?"

"I lay down straight ahead of me, with my feet at the sofa, on my stomach."

"Could you get a good look at him at this time?"

"Oh yeah. He was looking straight at me when he walked this way, pointing the gun. Then, when I lay down, I sorta got on my knees first, then on my stomach, and the whole time I was looking at him over my left shoulder.

"When I lay down I turned my face so I was looking right into the carpet. I couldn't see him or anything then. I thought maybe if I don't look at him he'll just go away."

"But he didn't go away, did he?"

"No sir. I heard footsteps coming at me. Then from just behind me I heard him ask me if I got a gun. At the same time, I felt somebody pull on the back of my pants, on the belt, like they wanted to check if I hid a gun there or something. That's when I turned my head and looked up at him again. He was down low, leaning over me and I could see his face from real close. He was grinning and I saw there was something wrong with his teeth."

"What do you mean, 'something wrong'?"

"On the bottom, the middle teeth were all sorta bent, like an opening between them. That's how I knew for sure that it was him when the cops showed me his picture."

"Yes, good. We'll get to his picture later. Please continue with what happened after you saw his face."

"That was it."

"That was it?"

"Yeah, that was the last thing I remember. After a bit it was like I was waking up from a dream. I felt my head really hurting me and I had trouble breathing. I was swallowing something hot each time I took a breath. The doctor told me later it was blood from where the bullet come out of my throat."

Phillips tentatively reached up and touched the protrusions at the side of his neck, like a doubting Thomas checking to see if the wounds could possibly have been real. Parent's eyes followed Phillips's hand as it lightly touched his neck, a look of approval on his face.

"Did you hear anything else at that point?"

"No, I don't think so. I remember hearing some footsteps running further away, maybe in the hall going to the kitchen. But I'm pretty sure that was just before I got shot, or, at least, before I blacked out."

"Of course. You didn't hear the gun go off when you were shot, did you?"

"No, I don't remember hearing anything after he asked me if I had a gun."

"And did you feel it when you were struck by the bullet?"

"No, nothing, until later when I woke up."

"I see. And this corridor to the kitchen, is that the way your brother Dexter had gone when he went to the bathroom?"

"Yeah. I think the bathroom was down the same hall. When I woke up, I didn't even know I was shot, I just knew my head hurt a lot. Then I thought of Dexter, 'cause I didn't see him when the two guys came in. I wanted to know if he was OK, and I remembered the footsteps, so I tried getting up and kinda crawled across the floor to the hall.

"There's a little corner there, where you go out of the living room, and when I went around it, that's when I saw him. He was lying face down next to the bathroom door. There was blood on him everywhere. I couldn't see his face, because of the blood."

Phillips swallowed hard and stopped his recitation. He bowed his head again and put one hand over his eyes, as if to block out the sight of his dead brother. Bratt didn't look toward the jury, but he could sense how their breathing had quieted and their note-taking had stopped. They were clearly hanging on every word of Phillips's testimony, and more than likely were sitting forward on the edge of their seats.

A minute or two passed while Phillips sobbed quietly into his hand. Bratt wanted to feel true pity for the young man who was mourning his brother, and he hoped that his face showed at least a trace of it. His mind, though, was darting around the room, trying to pick up the reactions of both the judge and the jury, weighing how their obvious sympathy for the witness would affect his eventual cross-examination.

Kid gloves, he told himself. *Firm, persistent questioning, but sensitive to his tragic experience. This is going to be a hell of a balancing act.*

Phillips cleared his throat and put his hand down, signifying he would try to go on, although his eyes were still brimming with tears.

"I, I crawled toward him, toward my brother, Dexter. I guess I said his name, maybe a couple of times. I tugged on his arm a bit, but I was scared to touch him more. I knew he was dead, but I was scared to touch him more…"

His voice trailed off, Parent nodded ever so slightly, and Bratt heard several throats being cleared, as well as a nose or two being blown, from the direction of the jury. Softly, gently even, Green spoke up.

"I think this would be a good time for our morning recess. Ladies and gentlemen, I'm afraid I can only give you fifteen minutes."

Bratt put his hands on his lower back and stretched as he walked toward the men's room halfway down the long courthouse hall. Kouri walked next to him, silent for one of the few times since Bratt had known him.

They had seen Mrs. Campbell come in just as the trial had begun that morning, and then quickly slip out again when Green had adjourned. Once again, as had been the case since Monday, she had said nothing to either Bratt or Kouri.

They entered the bathroom and found Parent already occupying one of the three urinals there. Bratt sidled up to him, while Kouri, looking a bit embarrassed, headed for a stall.

"How do you like the boy?" Parent asked, without turning to look at Bratt.

"He's good, I have to admit that. I don't know if it's real or if it's just a put-on, but he is good."

"You don't know if it's *real*!" Parent exclaimed, offended. "After what he went through that night, what is there to doubt?"

"Take it easy, Francis. We've both seen stranger things in our time."

"Really? Considering the loved ones that you've lost in your lifetime I would have expected a bit more understanding from you."

He zipped up, backed away from the automatic-flushing urinal and turned toward a sink as he spoke.

"Don't let the jury see how cold-hearted you've become, Robert. They're probably feeling very protective of the young boy right about now."

This is a tough enough job as it is, Bratt thought, saying nothing in reply. *Getting all mushy about a witness's misery won't make what I have to do any easier.*

Once Parent had left the restroom Kouri approached, finally ready to share his thoughts and impressions about his first murder trial.

"Boy, this is really something. I don't know if it's all an act or not, but a couple of times today it was all I could do not to cry."

"Et tu, Brute?"

"What? Why?"

"Nothing, nothing. I was hoping you'd be the one person who didn't think Dorrell Phillips was a wonderfully tragic figure, just one step away from being canonized."

"I know what you mean. I was trying to dislike him, but it isn't easy. And he sounds convincing when he identifies Marlon. He seems to have had a really good look at him…at the shooter, I mean."

Now Bratt smiled his "I told you so" smile.

"Wait a minute. Is this Peter 'Marlon is Innocent' Kouri talking? Don't tell me you're beginning to have doubts about your main man. You knew what Phillips was going to say before today, so why are you having doubts only now?"

"I'm not having doubts. I'm just saying that when you hear him in person, I could imagine that the jury would find him very believable."

"Oh yes, he is very believable. But that doesn't change what we have to do, it only makes it harder. Come on, let's get back before they start the show without us."

After the break Phillips picked up the narrative when he was in the hospital, recuperating from his wounds. On June 20, a few days before he was eventually released, S/D St. Jean had shown up with an armload of high school yearbooks for him to look through. An anonymous phone call to St. Jean's office the day before had suggested that one or both of the shooters had attended Dorset High School in the Cote des Neiges District, several kilometers north of where the shooting had occurred. The police had never been able to trace the source of this information, but they were certainly glad to have gotten it.

"I remember this was the first day they had taken the tube out of my throat, so I could talk a little," Phillips explained. "But Mr. St. Jean still asked me to write most of my answers down."

"And what did he ask you to do?"

"He said that maybe the guys who shot me had no criminal records, so there would be no police pictures of them. He wanted me to see if I recognized any faces from the yearbooks."

"So you didn't identify anybody from the mug shots?"

"No. There was one guy who looked a bit like the tall guy, the one who shot me. But it wasn't him. So Mr. St. Jean showed me the yearbooks, I think there were ten of them. At the time, he didn't tell me about the call saying the two guys were from Dorset, so I didn't know why he had chosen those books."

"Did you ever attend Dorset?"

"No, I never lived up there. I always went to school in Burgundy."

"So, tell us about the yearbooks."

"I looked at them in order, from 1989, I think. There were a lot of pictures of young black guys. And in two of the books I found pictures of the guys who shot everybody in the apartment."

"Do you remember from which years?"

"I think the tall guy was 1995. And the short guy was in the last year, 1998."

"Can you describe for us exactly how it happened, what you did and said when you spotted these pictures?"

"Yes. The procedure was pretty much the same for each yearbook. They handed them to me in the bed and I flipped through the pages on my own. Nobody said anything to me, nobody asked me any questions. Sometimes I made a comment, like if I maybe knew a guy or if somebody looked like somebody else. I wrote those comments down on a piece of paper that Mr. St. Jean gave me.

"When I got to 1995, it was the same way. In the beginning of the book there were lots of pictures of school activities and stuff. Poems and stories too. Then there was the big part, which had each student's picture. Each one said something about himself under it, you know, their best memories and stuff. That's where I saw him."

"Mr. Phillips, can you tell the jurors the name of the person whose picture you chose?"

"Marlon Small."

"Did you know Mr. Small before?"

"No sir."

"Had you ever seen his face anywhere before?"

"Yeah. The day he shot me."

"Yes, of course. I meant before *that* date, had you ever seen Mr. Small's face?"

"Oh, no. Never."

Parent coolly reached his hand out to Nancy and she handed him a thin green book, with some sort of gold inlay on the front of it. He showed it to Phillips.

"Mr. Phillips, do you recognize this book?"

"Yes. It's the 1995 Dorset yearbook."

"Can you open it to the page that's been marked and tell the jury what you see there."

"It's the picture that I ID'ed."

"What is written under it?"

"The handwriting part? I wrote that. It says, 'guy who shot me.' And I signed my name and the date, June 20, 1999."

Parent slipped the book from Phillips's hands and handed it to the court clerk.

"Please file this under Exhibit P-7."

He stepped back a few steps from Phillips now, so that the jury's attention would be focused entirely on the witness.

"Mr. Phillips. I'd like you to look around this room and tell us if you see the person whose picture you identified for the police last June 20."

Phillips began turning his head slowly around. When his gaze came to Small it stopped and held there for a few seconds. He turned back to face the jury and stretched out his right arm, pointing straight at Small in the prisoner's box.

"Him. He shot me."

Parent turned to the judge, a serene smile on his lips, and bowed.

"We have no more questions for this witness, My Lord."

Green turned to address the jurors before Bratt had a chance to say anything.

"Considering the time, I think we'll put off the cross-examination until after lunch. Two-fifteen, Mr. Bratt."

Bratt stood and politely bowed. He said nothing, not wanting to give the jurors the impression that he felt in any way unnerved by Phillips's identification of his client, as if he had ever doubted it. He could see the jurors' eyes passing from him to Small, and the question they all seemed to be asking in their hearts came through loud and clear:

"What do you have to say for yourselves now?"

That afternoon, Bratt's cross-examination took Phillips through his story once more, making sure the witness stuck to what he had testified to that morning. Phillips never backtracked. He insisted on every fact as if it had been set in concrete, and that suited Bratt just fine.

"I'd like to go back to the moment the two gunmen entered the apartment," Bratt said as he walked over to the floor plan on the blackboard.

"If you wanna talk about it again."

"I'll try not to bore you. You said you heard the door slam and you turned your head to look at the group that was standing just inside the doorway."

"Yeah," Phillips replied, showing some irritation at having to go over the facts yet again.

"You pointed to this sofa and said you were sitting at the near end, here. I believe you said you were leaning your head on the back of the sofa."

"That's how most people watch TV."

"I gather the TV show didn't have you sitting on the edge of your seat."

"No, it didn't."

"You didn't lean forward at all? Not even when the door slammed?"

"No," Phillips answered with a shake of his head, not even trying to hide his exasperation now. His soft, hesitant attitude of that morning had disappeared quickly once the cross-examination began.

"Fine, fine. Now you drew an 'X' next to the door where the taller of the two assailants was standing when he shot Indian. Standing right over his head."

"Uh-huh."

"And from the pictures in P-2 we can see Indian's body, and where his head is in regards to the entrance, and your 'X' is really very accurate."

Parent stretched his long frame up and raised his hands, as if pleading for mercy, toward Judge Green.

"My Lord, is my colleague planning to get to some sort of point?"

"Why," Green growled, "do you have a train to catch?"

Parent was clearly surprised at the judge's response, but not nearly as surprised as Bratt was. Bratt looked at Green's face and thought, *The old fart's caught on. Now if only I haven't lost the jury yet.*

"Go on, Mr. Bratt," Green said.

"Thank you, My Lord. Mr. Phillips, would you be so kind as to take this ruler and draw a straight line from where your head was as you sat on the sofa to where the taller of the two assailants was standing."

Phillips hesitated and looked over to Parent, suspecting some sort of trap, but the prosecutor did not return his look. Shrugging, the witness took up the ruler and the pen with which he had been marking the floor plan and did as Bratt asked. He then stepped back and looked indifferently at his questioner.

Bratt couldn't resist letting a little smile come to his lips as he saw an expression of discomfort appear on Parent's face.

"You must have X-ray vision, Mr. Phillips."

"Huh," Phillips responded, turning to look again at the floor plan. Then he looked confused, as if someone had changed the picture without his noticing. The line he had drawn passed from his position on the sofa and through part of the living room wall, before ending at the "X" near the apartment door.

"You did say that as soon as you heard the door slam you just turned your head and saw the taller one push Indian down and then shoot him?"

"Yes," Phillips replied, hesitating slightly now even though this was the fifth time that he had been asked some variation of that same question.

"And you also said you never leaned forward, nor sat on the edge of your seat. Yet, as you can see on this very accurate floor plan, from where you were sitting this wall sticking out here would have totally blocked your view of the entrance. Isn't that puzzling?"

Phillips's hand reached out to the floor plan and he ran his finger along the straight line he had traced, looking for some sort of explanation.

"I know what I saw, okay?"

"So you say. What I want to know is how you saw what you say you did?"

Phillips didn't answer, but just folded his arms across his chest, half in defiance, half as a defensive reflex.

"You've told the jury that you had a perfectly clear view of the taller assailant's face from the moment he entered the apartment. You said you could see his face when he spoke, when he pushed Indian to the ground and when he stood over his head and shot him. Is that not what you have been saying all day?"

"What's the difference? After he shot Indian he walked right up to me and I could see his face clear and up close."

"So, are you now telling us that you didn't see his face when he came into the apartment, when he spoke and when he shot Indian?"

"No, that's not what I'm saying."

"Well then, just what are you saying?"

Phillips looked over at Parent again, but once again received no assistance from that corner. He squeezed his lips tight, afraid that an unwanted answer might slip out. After a few seconds Bratt looked at his watch and saw that it was 4:25 p.m. *Might as well end it here,* he thought. *At least the jury's got a little bone to chew on until tomorrow.*

"My Lord, may I suggest we give the witness the night to think up, um, I mean, think about his answer, and continue tomorrow morning?"

"That's fine by me, Mr. Bratt. Ladies and gentlemen, we'll continue with Mr. Phillips tomorrow at nine-thirty sharp."

"I don't get it," Kouri said as he sat on the sofa in Bratt's office. He was feeling the exhaustion of being in court all day, although he himself had done nothing but take notes. "I thought he was doing so well. How did he let himself get painted into a corner like that?"

Bratt blew into a cup of hot coffee that Sylvie had made for them before she left for the day, feeling content about the way the trial was unfolding.

"His hatred blinded him," he replied.

"I guess so, although I'm not sure-"

"He hates Small," Bratt interrupted. "Not that I blame him. And I'm Small's lawyer, so naturally he hates me too. Maybe more so because I'm questioning the terrible things that happened to him. So he spent most of the day hardening his position, making sure every answer he gave was carved in stone, when there was really no reason for it. Now he can't back down from anything he said before for fear he'll come out looking the worse for it. But that's what'll happen anyway because he's too inflexible to admit to making any mistakes, or to being unsure about anything. And nobody's that perfect."

Kouri nodded his head silently, letting it all sink in.

"It's funny, but if you had mentioned that part of the wall to me before the trial I wouldn't have thought it was such an important point."

"It's probably not that big a deal. I don't expect to score any big points with Phillips. His story doesn't allow for that. But I'll just keep chipping away at his memory and hope the jury doesn't lose interest. I don't expect them to think he's a total liar, just wonder a bit about how reliable his memory is and how much of his story they should take with a grain of salt."

"So, tomorrow you'll ask him if he has an answer to your question."

"Hell, no. He just might come up with one that the jury could buy. I'd rather it stayed unanswered and just be one of many unexplained holes in his story."

"Something so terrifying," Bratt said the next morning, "it must have seemed like an eternity before it was over."

Phillips scowled back at his questioner, as he had been doing all that morning. He was less confident in his answers than the previous day and Bratt wasn't giving him much room to breathe.

"It took the time it took. People didn't move in slow motion or anything. I didn't think I was dreaming. I knew exactly what was happening and exactly how long it took."

"And, 'exactly' how long was that?"

"Ok, so I didn't look at my watch. But I could tell."

"Then *around* how long did it last?"

"A few minutes."

"A few minutes? Could it be four to five minutes?"

"Yeah, maybe."

"Mr. Phillips in one of your written statements to the police, this one dated June 23, 1999, at a time when your memory of the events was probably quite fresh, you said that from the time the door slammed to the time you lost consciousness was four to five minutes. Do you remember that?"

"Yeah, I remember."

"Do you remember saying the same thing in response to a question posed by my learned colleague yesterday morning. Four to five minutes?"

"Yeah, what's your point?"

Green's head jumped up from his notebook and he rapped his knuckles on his desk.

"Mr. Phillips, I will ask you to answer the questions in a courteous manner while you are in my court, is that understood?"

Phillips bit his lip, clearly seething over having to answer what seemed to be an endless string of trivial questions that somehow always ended up with him unable to explain himself. He nodded in the judge's direction, but said nothing. Green waved Bratt on with a snort, then bent his head to continue his copious note-taking.

"I remember you had mentioned the time it took yesterday and you said you were able to see the face of the taller assailant quite well during the whole incident, a good four or five minutes. Do you wish to revise that estimate today, Mr. Phillips?"

"No. Four to five minutes sounds about right. Like I said, I didn't look at my watch at the time. I was worried about other things. But it's about right."

"Of course, I understand. So it might have been a little more or a little less than four or five minutes. Right?"

"Right."

"Could it have been as short as three minutes?"

Phillips's hatred for Bratt came through loud and clear in his silent glare. Bratt managed to keep an expression of patient equanimity on his face, while under his black vest his heart was beating like a jackhammer. He was thoroughly enjoying every minute of this. He knew he was about to corner Phillips again, and felt a sense of childish glee overtaking him.

After another of the long pauses he had gotten into the habit of taking before answering, Phillips nodded his head curtly.

"I'm afraid we'll need a verbal answer, Mr. Phillips. For the transcript."

"Yes," Phillips spat out.

"Could it have been as short as two minutes?"

Phillips breathed deeply and closed his eyes briefly, as if to calm himself. Then he looked away from Bratt and toward the jury.

"No, that's way too short. I know that for sure. It was way longer than two minutes."

Bratt pulled out a stopwatch from underneath his robe and held it up for everyone to see.

"Mr. Phillips would you indulge me? I'd like you to describe the events of last June 14 once more. Tell us what happened all over again, starting from the moment you heard the door slam, and try to keep your story as close to real time as possible. Could you do that for me?"

Again, Phillips looked toward Parent. This time the Prosecutor looked like he wanted to object to this demonstration, but he held back. Bratt gave him a sly little smile, because he knew, as Parent surely did, that the jury would want to see how this experiment turned out and would wonder why anyone objected to it.

"Mr. Phillips? Can you do that?"

"I can do that."

Dramatically, Bratt held the stopwatch up high and looked knowingly at the jurors. He kept his eyes on them, noting their attentive and expectant faces.

"Are you ready, Mr. Phillips? OK, begin now."

Bratt began the stopwatch and Phillips retold his story, speaking slowly and with great deliberation.

"I was watching TV and I could hear Indian talking to these two guys. Then, suddenly the door slams shut and I turn to see them all just inside it. The tall guy yells out, 'I'm here for your shit, so nobody fucking move.'

"Then he pushed Indian down on the floor and I see the guns they have. He shoots Indian real fast, Bang! Bang! He looks up and sees me staring at him, and he points the gun at me and starts walking at me. He yells, 'Get the fuck on the floor, or I'll shoot you.'

"All this time he's walking straight at me. It's maybe ten, twelve feet. He's coming from my left and a bit in front of me, and I slide off the sofa, onto my knees. My hands are up in the air and I'm looking right up at his face as I lie down on my stomach. Then he's standing right over me and he asks me if I have a gun, and then he pulls on my belt from behind. I look up at him quickly and see that he's bending low over me, that's when I saw the gap in his teeth. I look back down into the floor and then, that's it."

"That's it? The last thing you remember?"

"Yeah."

"OK. So I'm stopping the stopwatch…now."

Bratt held the now-stopped timepiece up in the air for a few more seconds, letting the tension increase, then slowly brought it down and held it directly in front of the witness's face. Phillips's eyes widened in surprise.

"Can you tell the jury what the time on the stopwatch is, Mr. Phillips?"

"Fifty-two seconds," he whispered.

"For those who didn't hear his answer, he said fifty-two seconds. The judge will correct me if I'm wrong. So, less than one minute. Not way more than two. Not three. And certainly not the four to five minutes you led us to believe yesterday."

"Is there a question there, Mr. Bratt," Green interposed.

"Yes, My Lord, a question. Would you not agree, Mr. Phillips, that you had much less time to observe your assailant than you have claimed until now?"

"It seemed longer."

"Yes. It must have seemed like an eternity."

"A question, Mr. Bratt," Green raised his voice only slightly.

"Many questions come to mind right now, My Lord, and I hope the witness will be able to answer some of them one day."

"Right," Green pushed his chair back impatiently. "Time for lunch, the lawyers are clearly in need of a break."

Bratt kept his eyes on the jurors as they filed out, avoiding looking at Green because he knew the judge had been clearly irritated by his little off-the-cuff remark. Once the jury was out of earshot Green scowled angrily at him.

"I expect that to be the last time you grandstand in my courtroom, Mr. Bratt. Is that understood?"

Bratt still felt pumped up from his cross-examination and he had half a mind to answer Green back defiantly, but he knew this wouldn't help Small's case. He breathed deeply, and bowed his head as contritely as he could.

"Sorry about that. Got carried away with myself."

Green looked mollified, and a maybe even a bit surprised, by Bratt's quick retreat.

"There was certainly no reason for it. See that it doesn't happen again. Have a good lunch, gentlemen."

With that, he turned and walked off the bench. Bratt smiled broadly at Kouri, looking like a child who had gotten caught with his hand in the cookie jar, but then was allowed to eat the cookie anyway. As he turned to pick up his notes his eyes fell on Nancy and he was momentarily surprised at seeing her there. He had been so concentrated on Phillips's testimony the past two days that he had hardly noticed her presence.

She didn't look in his direction but simply followed Parent out of the courtroom and was soon gone.

Just before 2:15 p.m. Bratt was standing in the hallway outside the courtroom, looking down its length while Kouri held the door open for him.

"You know she only comes after the testimony begins," Kouri said.

"I know," Bratt replied, craning his neck in the hope of catching a glimpse of the elusive Jennifer Campbell. "She's turned into a bit of a holy spirit this week, the way she metabolizes out of thin air. That lady is unusual, to say the least."

"Maybe she just doesn't want to disrupt your concentration."

"Well her plan backfired, then, hasn't it? This sneaking in and out of court business has really gotten on my nerves."

"You could always just phone her."

Bratt turned toward the courtroom without responding and headed for his seat.

I get the feeling that anything she might have to tell me I don't want to hear over the phone.

"Mr. Phillips, you remember the gun the taller assailant pointed at you, of course."

"Yeah, well, I had a good look at it, I guess."

"Yes, I'm sure you did. And that's exactly what I want to talk to you about. You have testified that when he advanced toward you his arm was stretched out straight in front of him, with the gun pointed right at you. Yesterday you made a motion with your hand, which obviously wasn't picked up by the court's audio recording system. Could I describe it by saying that the assailant held the gun at eye level, almost as if he was looking down the length of his arm, aiming at you over the gun sight?"

"Yeah, that's exactly what he did. He was walking at me and the gun was sticking straight out from in front of his face."

"And it must have felt like you were staring right down that big gun barrel."

"It didn't just feel that way. I *was* staring right into that gun barrel. It looked like a cannon pointed at my head."

"A cannon that could have gone off and killed you at any second."

"That's right."

"That certainly must have held your attention."

"You bet it did."

"Because I did notice that you weren't able to really describe the gun itself, even though you were staring right at it."

"I wasn't looking at the gun to admire it. All I could see was the mouth of that barrel, and I started thinking a bullet was going to come right out of there and kill me."

"Couldn't take your eyes off it, could you?"

"I was scared to look away. Like I thought he wouldn't shoot me if I kept my eyes on it."

"And all this time the gun is held out in front of his face. And you're sitting down, looking upward at that gun, is that right? You're really concentrated on it."

Phillips opened his mouth to answer, then shut it tight. In his eyes there was a look of dawning realization.

"Mr. Phillips, isn't that how it was?"

"I could see his face looking at me over the gun."

"Mr. Phillips, you were staring up right into the barrel of this cannon. You didn't see anything else. Your mind could think of nothing except whether a bullet was about to be fired out of that gun and into your head."

Parent jumped up, with a bit more urgency than his prior objections, to cut Bratt off.

"My Lord, defense counsel isn't asking questions, he's testifying for the witness."

"I certainly didn't hear any questions, Mr. Bratt. Want to try again?"

"Certainly, My Lord. Mr. Phillips, everything I just said: isn't that the truth?"

Parent harumphed loudly and sat down hard, clearly not satisfied with Bratt's response to the judge's direction.

"I didn't see *only* the gun. It wasn't like that."

"Well how was it then? In your own words, 'all I could see was the mouth of that barrel.' You just finished telling us you were too scared to take your eyes away from it."

"A question please, Mr. Bratt," Green intoned.

"Isn't that true, Mr. Phillips?" Bratt asked.

Phillips paused again. He could barely disguise his rage at the lawyer, or his confusion at the questions that were being asked of him.

He finally managed to squeeze a few words through his clenched jaw. "Could you repeat your question?"

"Certainly. Isn't that true, Mr. Phillips?"

From the jury box there came a noise like a surprised laugh that was quickly muffled. Green, however, found nothing humorous in Bratt's question.

"I think he'll need a bit more than that," he grumbled. "Take it from the top."

Bratt turned, smiling, to the judge.

"Never mind, My Lord," he said, having decided to not give Phillips the chance to answer his question. "I'll go on to something else."

"None too soon, I may add," Green said under his breath.

"Mr. Phillips, you mentioned yesterday that when the taller assailant approached you he pulled on the back of your belt."

"Yeah. He asked me if I had a gun."

"And you said you looked up and could see his face from real close. Had he bent far over you at that point?"

"Like I said, his face was very close to mine, so I got a good look at him."

"Here's something I'm curious about, Mr. Phillips. You said that you slid forward off the sofa to your knees, then lay straight out from the sofa on your stomach. Perpendicular to it, isn't that right?"

"That's right."

"And the man with the gun was walking toward you from your left?"

"Yeah."

"Could you look at pictures 17 and 19 in Exhibit P-3."

Phillips picked up one of the albums of crime-scene photos and flipped over to the pictures that Bratt had enumerated. Judge and jury did the same with their own copies. Bratt leaned over and pointed to the sofa on the right side of the first picture. Directly in front of the sofa and parallel to it was a rectangular coffee table at least four feet long. Then he showed the witness the second picture: a large pool of blood was clearly visible between the sofa and the coffee table, and about five feet to the right from where Phillips had said he was sitting.

"Mr. Phillips, was that coffee table there when you were sitting on the sofa?"

"I don't remember."

That's the first time he's admitted to not remembering something, Bratt thought. *But, this time, it's to his advantage to remember as little as possible.*

"Well, could it have been somewhere else than there?"

"I have no idea."

"Could somebody have brought the table in and put it there after the shooting?" Bratt asked, raising his eyebrows incredulously to the jurors.

"Anything's possible, I guess."

"You really think that's possible?" Bratt exclaimed. "You think maybe one of the police officers decided to put the table in front of the sofa, just to give us a pretty picture? Or is it more likely that the coffee table had always been in front of the sofa, as coffee tables so often are?"

"I guess that's likely," Phillips conceded.

"Much *more* likely?"

"Pretty damn likely!"

Green raised his eyes to the witness again, but said nothing this time. Bratt was glad the judge had stayed silent because it was obvious that Phillips had been provoked to the point that he was getting careless with his answers.

"Well, if it was pretty *damn* likely that the coffee table was always there in front of the sofa, how could you have lain down the way you said you did? Straight out from the sofa, perpendicularly, as I said."

"I know what the word means," Phillips snapped back. "I can't explain how I did it, but I know that's where I lay down."

"Did you lie down under the coffee table?"

"I never said that."

"No, you didn't. You also didn't say you lay down on top of the coffee table, but that seems to have been the only other choice."

"A question, Mr. Bratt," Green said.

"Sorry, My Lord. Here's a question, Mr. Phillips. See all that blood there in pictures 17 and 19? Whose blood is that next to the sofa?"

"I guess it's mine."

"You guess it's yours. Well, are there any other pools of blood in the living room, which may indicate where you were shot?"

"No, that's it."

"Yes, that is it. And can you tell us why that pool of blood is inches from the sofa, a body length to the right of where you said you lay down?"

"No, I can't."

"You can't? Could it be that when you slid off the sofa you didn't go down forward, but you turned *away* from the gunman and, with your back to him, lay down along the length of the sofa, between the sofa and the coffee table?"

Parent objected again: "My Lord, multiple questions."

"I'm sure your witness is smart enough to understand them," Green answered. "Please sit down."

Phillips's voice had gotten huskier with his anger, even as he tried to keep it low and under control.

"All I know is I slid down straight in front of me and I never took my eyes off him the whole way down."

"So the pool of blood just magically appeared several feet away, did it?"

"I can't explain why it's there."

"Don't you think a perfectly good explanation is that you lay down facing away from him? That you had your back turned to the taller assailant when he advanced to the sofa?"

"No."

"If you turned away from him you wouldn't have gotten as good a look at him as you've been telling us, isn't that right?"

"I didn't turn away from him. I kept my eyes on his face the whole time."

"The whole time? Isn't it true that when the taller assailant advanced-"

Phillips suddenly interrupted Bratt, "Why do you keep calling him that: the 'taller assailant?' His name's Marlon Small and you know he shot me!"

Green banged his hand hard on his desk to get the witness's attention.

"Mr. Phillips, you stop right there."

"Why? He keeps saying 'assailant' and shit when he knows Small's the guy in the apartment."

"That's enough out of you. That's an issue for the jury to decide."

Phillips turned toward the jury and raised his hands, palms upward, in supplication.

"I'm the one that was there. You all know I saw him."

Green's face was beet-red with anger as he jumped to his feet and leaned on his desk, yelling down at Phillips.

"I said that's enough! Mr. Parent if your witness says one more word I'm going to order a mistrial, so you better get him under control. Ladies and gentlemen," he turned to the jury, "you will disregard the outburst by the witness. Those remarks do not constitute any sort of evidence and you will not take them into consideration. It is up to you and you alone to determine who the author of the shootings was."

Green paused to catch his breath and control his anger.

"I think that's enough for all of us today. We'll pick up where we left off tomorrow morning."

The jurors reluctantly got up and began filing out, keeping their eyes on the witness to see if he had anything more to say. But Phillips stayed quiet, his eyes locked on his hands folded in front of him. Once the jurors were out of earshot an angry Green turned back to the equally-seething young man.

"I don't know where you think you are, so let me make it very clear to you. You are in a court of law. More than that, you are in *my* courtroom, and I will not allow anybody, witnesses or lawyers, to fly off the handle and spout whatever they please in front of the jury.

"Whether you like it or not, that man," and he pointed at Small, while never taking his eyes off Phillips, "has the right to a fair trial and you can be certain I will make sure he gets it. If this is too hard for you to understand I suggest you have a long talk with Mr. Parent in the corridor. Next time you step into my courtroom you will not open your mouth except when you're answering a question. I'm not even going to ask you if I've made myself clear."

With that Green spun around and stomped down the stairs from his dais, showing more energy than anyone might have thought he had.

All this time Bratt stood, leaning motionless on the front of the prisoner's box, his eyes fixed on the witness. Seeing him get yelled at by the judge didn't cheer him in the least. He knew that this would be irrelevant to the jury. They had heard Phillips loud and clear: he was present at the shooting, they weren't. He had the best seat in the house, and he alone knew the identity of the shooters. Green could admonish them all day about ignoring his outburst, but Bratt knew it was something that would stick in their minds.

His chin resting in the palm of his hand, he watched as Phillips slowly headed out of the courtroom. Parent quickly caught up to him and put his arm around his star witness's shoulders. Bratt couldn't tell if the gesture was meant to console Phillips, or to congratulate him on a job well-done.

I wouldn't put it past him, Bratt thought.

"Monsieur Bratt! Monsieur Bratt"

Bratt and Kouri turned on their heels at the same time and saw a well-dressed, slightly chubby woman wearing dangerously high-heeled pumps chasing after them across the courthouse lobby. Bratt waited impatiently for her to catch up to them, in a hurry to get back to his office to work on the next day's cross-examination.

"Can I help you?" he asked as she stopped in front of them and put her hand on his arm as if to prevent him from escaping.

"I'm sorry to go yelling out your name like that. I'm Carmen Champagne. I don't know if Senator Madsen told you about me."

"Senator Madsen?"

"I'm on the Cabinet's Judicial Selection Committee. I came in from Ottawa last night. Have to show my face to the constituents now and then you know, and when I read about the trial I thought I'd also come and see you in action."

Bratt's mind was still on Phillips and he only half-understood what she was saying. He blinked at her several times, as if to see her more clearly.

"I'm sorry, you read about the trial?"

"Of course, in the newspaper," she laughed loudly. "What did you think? If I know old Roger Madsen you probably know you're on our shortlist. Oh, don't worry," she held her hand up at his expression of surprise. "I know it's all confidential, but that's the way things are done in Ottawa, aren't they? I just thought I'd enjoy a first-hand view of your work, so here I am. I hope you don't mind."

"Shortlist? Of course," Bratt almost shouted, suddenly seeing the light. "I'm sorry, I must seem so dense. I've been so preoccupied with this trial I really wasn't sure what you meant."

"I understand completely, and I don't want to keep you from your work. I'm sure you have a lot on your mind. I just didn't want you to find out later that I had been here and think I was spying on you."

"Well, as long as you only send back glowing reports to your committee."

She laughed again, squeezing his arm as she did so.

"You can be sure that I'll only have positive things to say. I find your work so fascinating, and I must say you do it so well."

"You caught me on a good day."

"Now that's just false modesty, and there's no need for it. I'm sure the way things are going you're going to win this trial. I just regret I have to leave town tomorrow and can't watch more of it. Good luck. We'll be in touch. Not that anything's been decided, you understand."

She reached to shake his hand, then noticed that both his hands were full with his briefcase and courtroom apparel, so she squeezed his arm again instead. She laughed breathlessly as she did so, gave Kouri a short wave and rushed out into the winter afternoon.

"What the heck was that?" Kouri asked.

"The face of the future," Bratt said tonelessly. "Pretty scary, eh kid?"

They continued on their way back to the office but Bratt said nothing more about the surprise visitor.

It was midway through Friday morning's court session that Bratt decided he didn't really dislike Dorrell Phillips. As a matter of fact, he felt quite sorry for the young man. Not for the terrible trauma he had undergone, although that was bad enough, but because the focus of his testimony had been turned away from that trauma and was now aimed squarely at his inability to recount what had happened in a believable manner.

The lawyer wondered what it must be like to get two bullets in the base of your skull and then be treated like a liar. No wonder Phillips's anger and resentment colored every answer he gave.

"You were in the hospital for six days before you picked Marlon Small's picture out of that high school yearbook."

"Yeah, I said that before."

"And in your statement of June 23, three days after you selected that picture, you gave a physical description of your two assailants, although you had already given some descriptions to the police on two prior occasions."

"Mr. Bratt, do you have a question?" Green muttered, looking bored.

"Mr. Phillips, why didn't you mention that the person who shot you had a gap between his teeth until after you saw that gap in the high school picture?"

"I don't get your meaning."

"You don't get it? Let me make it clear, then. Between the shooting on June 14 and the statement you made on June 23 you met several times with homicide detectives, correct?"

"*Correct.*"

"On none of those occasions, either by word or in writing, did you mention the very distinctive gap between your assailant's teeth. It was only after you saw the high school picture of Mr. Small, where he's got a big, gap-toothed grin, that you suddenly added that to your description. Why is that?"

"I don't know. I guess that's when I remembered it."

"Didn't you testify earlier this week that he brought his face close to yours and that's when you saw the gap in his teeth?"

"Yeah."

"You were facing certain death at the time and yet that gap was so obvious that it struck you and stuck in your memory. How could you just forget it in the following days, when the police were desperately trying to come up with something to identify your attackers?"

"I can't explain that."

"Isn't it true that the man who shot you had no gap at all between his teeth? Didn't you just add that particular little feature to your description when you saw it in the picture of Marlon Small?"

"No, I always knew the guy who shot me had those funny teeth."

"And when were you planning to tell the police about it?"

Phillips shook his head silently, but didn't answer Bratt's question. Green looked at him for a few seconds before turning to the lawyer.

"Do you want an answer to that question, Mr. Bratt?"

"No, My Lord, I don't expect an answer at all."

"I didn't think so," Green said, burying his head in his notebook again.

Bratt looked over at Parent's unhappy face. It was one more little mystery that Phillips had been unable to clarify for the jury and the prosecutor could see that now even the judge had gotten into the act. Some witnesses could get away with saying the dumbest things at times, but responding to a question with silence was a near-fatal path for anyone to take. Unfortunately for Dorrell Phillips, stubborn silence was where he constantly retreated when faced with hard questions.

Bratt glanced up at the clock and saw that it was just past noon. Less than half an hour until Green adjourned for lunch. Just enough time to finish with the last few questions he had for Phillips.

"Mr. Phillips, did you ever have any doubt about what your assailant looked like?"

"Never. I always knew it was him."

"You didn't hesitate at all when the police showed you his picture?"

"Not even a second."

"You didn't see any other pictures that might have been your assailant."

"No, I didn't. Well…"

"Well?"

"There was a mug shot of a guy that I thought might have been him, but I wasn't sure. I think I said that the other day."

"Yes, you certainly did."

Bratt rifled through some papers and pulled out a color copy of the pictures in the mug book that Phillips had been shown at the hospital.

"Mr. Phillips, these are the mug shots shown to you by the police last June 17, are they not?"

Phillips flipped through a few of the pages that had been placed in front of him.

"They look like it."

"Do you remember writing any comments on any of those pages, anything about people you thought you recognized?"

"Like I said, I thought one of them was maybe the guy who shot me, and I wrote that."

"As a matter of fact," Bratt paused as he turned the pages until he reached the picture in question, "what you wrote was, 'Number three. He's the one who shot me.' Isn't that your writing?"

"Yeah, that's what I've been saying all along."

"Is there a difference in your mind between saying number three is the one who shot you and saying number three *looks like* the one who shot you?"

"I don't know. I guess so."

"You didn't write that you *thought* number three was the one who shot you, nor that he *looked* like the one who shot you, did you? You wrote that number three *is* the one who shot you. Sounds like you were pretty certain it was number three, doesn't it?"

"It looked like him. That's what I meant."

"Can you show me if anywhere, on any of these pages, you corrected yourself and told the detectives that he only *looked* like your assailant?"

"You know I didn't write anything like that."

"Did you say anything to the police about it?"

"No, I was still intubated at the time."

"That's right, you were. If I tell you that nowhere in any of the detectives' personal notes nor in their official reports do they mention that you ever indicated that number three only *looked* like your assailant, would that surprise you?"

"No, I guess not."

"You guess not. Is it not then possible, and even likely, that when you saw that picture you were certain that number three was the man who shot you?"

"No way. I only meant he looked like the guy who shot me. I never said I thought it was him."

"Well, well. That's settled then. But tell me another thing, Mr. Phillips. How old would you say the man shown in picture number three is?"

"I can't tell."

"Would you say he looks older than you? Maybe closer to my age?"

"Yeah, he's old, like you."

"Thanks a lot," Bratt gave a sarcastic smile. "Would you agree with me that Mr. Small, who is all of twenty-one years old right now, looks much younger than number three?"

"Yeah."

"In the picture, the man's lips are slightly parted. Look carefully and see if you can spot any gaps in his front lower teeth."

Phillips glanced briefly down at the picture, already knowing the answer beforehand.

"No, there's no gaps."

"And, as you've so correctly pointed out, Mr. Small does have a very noticeable gap between his teeth, doesn't he? All right, other than the age difference and the missing gap in the teeth, can you tell us if there are any similarities between Mr. Small and the man in picture number three?"

This time Phillips studied the picture a little harder, although the result was the same.

"They don't really look like each other."

"Not even a little bit?"

"No, not even a little bit."

Bratt made a show of scratching his head in puzzlement and looked a little longer at the picture, then over at Small in the prisoner's box.

"OK, maybe you can help me here, because I'm a little confused. You're telling us today that when you saw picture number three you told the homicide detectives that the man in the picture *looked* like the man who shot you. Yet you've just admitted that Marlon Small doesn't look anything at all like the man in picture number three. How can you claim today that Marlon Small shot you when you've told us that he doesn't even look like the man who shot you?"

"That's not what I said. You're twisting my words."

"Yes, well defense lawyers are known for that, aren't we? So let's put it in your own words. Does the man in picture number three look like the guy who shot you?"

Phillips retreated into silence again and just stared at the picture. This time, though, Bratt didn't want to leave the question unanswered.

"Mr. Phillips. Isn't that what you told the police last June? Isn't that what you just finished telling us a few minutes ago?"

"Yeah," Phillips forced himself to answer.

"Yeah, what?"

"Yeah, number three looks like the man who shot me. Is that what you want me to say?"

"Only if it's the truth, Mr. Phillips. You are telling us the truth, aren't you?"

"You know I am."

And they say the truth will set you free, Bratt thought. *It just might, if you're Marlon Small.*

To Phillips he said, "And is it not also the truth that this same number three, the one who looks like the man who shot you, doesn't look anything at all like my client?"

Phillips glared at the lawyer without answering for several seconds. Then, just when Bratt thought he'd have to repeat his question, Phillips finally spoke up.

"No. He doesn't."

Bratt nodded thoughtfully, and paused for a few seconds to collect his thoughts. He knew he had come to the perfect place to stop.

"Thank you, My Lord," he said. "We'll have no more questions for this witness."

With that, he sat down, flipping his robe dramatically behind him as he did so. His face beamed a smile of perfect contentment toward judge and jury, and for added effect he lightly tossed his pen onto the desk in front of him and crossed his arms. His work there was done.

It was past seven o'clock and Bratt was starting to feel hungry. He sat alone at his desk, savoring the silence and solitude at the end of his hectic week. Kouri had headed home about an hour earlier, but Bratt was in no rush to leave, still feeling the need to wind down from the daily adrenalin rush he had been experiencing.

That afternoon, after they had had their lunch, they put aside whatever feelings of accomplishment Phillips' cross-examination had brought them, along with all their notes concerning his testimony. There was still work to do, and they turned their attention to Marcus Paris, who would be called to the stand on Monday morning. Their minds still full of Phillips and his testimony, they tried to concentrate on their cross-examination strategy for the next witness.

They spent the afternoon reviewing the questions Bratt would have to ask Paris, making some changes based on what Phillips had said over the last three days. Finally, feeling mentally drained, Bratt had told his assistant to put everything away until Monday morning. There were only so many times they could go over the same points before they began burning themselves out.

Bratt looked at his watch again and put his stockinged feet up on his desk, his favorite position for relaxing and contemplating the twists and turns he was navigating on the road to what seemed to be his final destination of being named a judge. He smiled to himself, allowing a feeling of contentment to wash over him.

The weekend ahead looked to be fairly uneventful and he intended to forget all about the Marlon Small trial, if only for a little while. He wondered if he shouldn't call up Jeannie, or maybe even Nancy, but mostly he looked forward to enjoying some peace and quiet at home.

From his seat he heard the front door of the firm opening and footsteps entering softly. He thought it must be Kouri coming back for some forgotten item, so he called out to him.

"What's the matter, Pete? You miss the place already?"

There was no immediate answer, but he heard the footsteps slowly approach his open door and pause for a second or two just outside his office. Then Dorrell Phillips walked in.

Bratt sat up abruptly, as if he were seeing a ghost. His first thought was that Phillips had come there to kill him and he hadn't even waited until the trial was over to do it. But Phillips made no move toward him and, within a few seconds, Bratt could see that violence was the furthest thing from his mind.

The young man stood in the doorway, looking nervous and totally lost, as if he had no idea how he had gotten there, or what he meant to do. Bratt slowly relaxed, let out the breath he was holding and calmly spoke, taking charge of the situation.

"Dorrell? You shouldn't be here."

Upon hearing his name spoken aloud Phillips moved forward with a start, his eyes focusing on Bratt.

"I wanted to talk to you a minute. Is that okay?"

"I guess so. Strictly speaking you're not a Crown witness anymore. But why are you here?"

"I wanted to tell you something. You're a hell of a lawyer."

He's the last person I would have gone to for compliments, Bratt thought, saying nothing in reply. *But he's clearly got a lot more than flattery on his mind.*

"Mr. Parent was pretty pissed at me," Phillips continued, "because I didn't answer your questions very well."

"He shouldn't blame you. Getting up on the stand is never an easy thing to do."

"You made me look like some kind of liar. Twisted everything around until even I didn't know what was the truth anymore."

Bratt had an uncomfortable sense of deja-vu, as he heard Jeannie accusing him of the same thing a few weeks earlier. He tried to ignore her voice in his head. Dealing with this unexpected visitor was hard enough.

"It was my medication," Phillips stated matter of factly, as if in answer to a question that only he had heard.

"I'm sorry?"

"In the hospital. The first week or so they had me under heavy medication, cortisone and stuff, and I couldn't see the mug shots too well. I couldn't think too clear either. I was real scared in court, and pretty mad at you too, and when you asked me about that picture I chose, I guess I forgot about the pain killers."

Bratt realized that Phillips was trying to justify his performance on the stand, and to explain to Bratt what he had been unable to explain to the jury. It wasn't such a bad explanation either, but it was too little too late.

"Listen, Dorrell, I don't want you to take this the wrong way, but what you're telling me really isn't going to change anything. Maybe Parent should have asked you more questions about your physical condition, but that was his job."

Phillips shrugged, regaining the sad and lost look he had had on the first morning he had testified, before his dislike of Bratt had begun influencing his answers.

"It really was Small, you know."

"I know that you honestly believe that. I never tried to imply you were lying about it, and I'm truly sorry if that's how it felt. Anyway, it's not something I can discuss with you now."

Phillips seemed to be trying to take in what Bratt was saying for a moment, before blurting out, "My brother Dexter really fucked up his life, even before Small killed him. But my dad still loved him. He was the oldest boy in the family."

Oh God, he's going to lay a guilt trip on me, Bratt thought, unable to stop a lump from rising to his throat. He wondered if Phillips was supposed to be some version of the Ghost of Christmas Past.

"After I got home from the hospital," Phillips went on, "I'd lie in bed when I couldn't sleep at night and I'd hear my dad go by himself into Dexter's room. My bed was right next to the door and the walls are pretty thin. And I'd hear my dad sitting there and crying, almost every night. He sounded like a girl when he cried. In the daytime I never saw him cry, you know. He was always taking care of me, protecting me. But, at night, I'd just listen to him cry for his boy that your client took away."

Son of a bitch's going to make me cry now too, Bratt thought in alarm. *Get him out of here before he actually does it.*

"Listen, Dorrell," Bratt stood up, clearing his throat, "this is inappropriate, especially since the trial's still going on. I'm going to have to ask you to leave."

Phillips nodded without saying another word, and turned to head back out. Bratt felt he had to say something to show that he wasn't totally heartless.

"I'm really sorry about your brother," he called out, as he chased after Phillips into the reception area.

Phillips turned to him with a look that questioned his sincerity.

"I really am," Bratt repeated. "Whether Small did it or not, I know what it's like to lose someone you love, and I do feel bad for you and your father."

Phillips looked at him for a few more seconds before speaking again.

"It ain't normal for a father to bury his son," he said, then turned and left Bratt standing there, feeling angry, but unsure who he should be angry at. He had no idea why Phillips had decided to come see him, and he didn't know what it was supposed to change.

Maybe it was just to remind me that sometimes I don't like this job after-all, he told himself, turning back and stomping toward his office. He violently kicked a metal trashcan that was in his path, sending it crashing into the wall behind it, leaving a nasty gash in the plaster. He glared wordlessly at the trash can, as if blaming it for being part of some sort of conspiracy to make him hate himself and his work.

Shit, it's like Jeannie at the courthouse all over again, he raged wordlessly. *I thought I was past all that. I didn't need to hear this crap right now.*

In his office he fell onto his sofa, looking helplessly at the desk where he had been sitting, happily daydreaming about becoming a judge only minutes before. Those few moments of happiness, that feeling of self-worth that he had regained over the course of the trial's first week, were gone now. They had been stolen by Dorrell Phillips and the vision of a father mourning his murdered son.

"Goddamn Dorrell Phillips and his father," he said out loud, and slammed his fist into the sofa's soft cushions. "Goddamn Marlon Small! And goddamn *me*!"

Chapter 11

Early that Monday morning Bratt lay on the sofa in his office, trying to get a grip on the simmering anger that had often threatened to overtake him during the weekend. For two days he hadn't been able to shake the mental image of Dorrell Phillips's father, sitting alone in a darkened bedroom, mourning his oldest son Dexter. And the more he thought about it, the angrier he had become.

At first he was angry with Dorrell for having given him the image in the first place. It had taken away what little pleasure he had been able to derive from his work in the trial. Eventually, his anger turned toward Small, for perhaps having been involved in the killing of the young man, as well as for just being such an unlikable client. Every now and then his anger was even aimed at Jeannie for having triggered his uncharacteristic soul-searching in the first place, without which stories like the one Dorrell Phillips had told him would have just been shrugged off as so much melodrama.

Running like an undercurrent throughout this river of bitterness, he was mostly angry with himself. He knew he should never have let Dorrell's obvious emotional manipulation affect him the way it had, and he derided himself for his weakness. But he also blamed himself for being willing to work for people like Marlon Small in the first place.

He tried to imagine a job, a life, where interacting with murderers and rapists wasn't part of his everyday routine. Was there really such a world beyond the walls of the courtroom? And had he become so used to his world, so enured to the pain and suffering that filled it, that he had lost the capacity to be affected by it? If he had ever thought this might be the case, these past few weeks had proven him wrong.

He had no idea how long he had been laying there, trying to clear his mind so that he could concentrate on the trial he was supposed to fight that morning, when John Kalouderis knocked on his door and walked in without waiting for an invitation. Bratt lay unmoving, his eyes covered with his forearm.

"Christ, you've gone and turned into me," Kalouderis said as he flopped into Bratt's chair and put his feet up on the desk. "Does this mean I have to go win that murder trial for you?"

"If you're not too busy," Bratt mumbled in reply, his eyes still shaded from the light streaming through the window.

It occurred to Bratt, with only a small pang of regret, that if he really had turned into his friend he might at least have had the cold comfort of some alcohol to get him through the past two days. As it was, he hadn't had a drink since their binge nearly two weeks earlier. He had spent the weekend stone cold sober, keeping company only with the disembodied voices of Jeannie and Dorrell Phillips, both of whom seemed to have taken up permanent residence in his head and his apartment.

"Pete says the trial's going pretty well so far," Kalouderis said.

Bratt sighed and slid his arm off his face. He slowly got up into a sitting position and rubbed his face. He looked at his friend, but said nothing in reply.

"Am I missing something here?" Kalouderis asked. "Did something happen?"

"Nothing happened. The trial's going about as well as I could have hoped for. I'm just tired, I guess."

"Looks like you haven't been getting enough sleep. You and that lady cop make up, finally?"

"I wish," Bratt said, unwilling to tell Kalouderis the cause of his sleepless nights. "I guess I'm just not finding this case to be much fun."

"Come on, what's not to like? A juicy double murder, all the papers talking about the way you ripped into that Phillips kid. It should at least take your mind off J.P., if that's what's got you down."

If Kalouderis's words were intended to raise Bratt's spirits, they had the opposite effect. Considering what Dorrell Phillips had suffered the previous summer, the last thing he had needed was to be ripped apart on the witness stand. Having given way to that thought Bratt couldn't help but dredge up the memory of Claire Brockway and what had happened to her in court.

Why the hell do I keep going back to her? As if it isn't bad enough that I blame myself for Marlon Small's crimes. Do I have to feel bad about what all my clients may have done?

"Shit," he exclaimed, and jumped up from the sofa.

A surprised Kalouderis also jumped up, uncertain what had come over his friend. Bratt gave him no explanation, putting on his coat in preparation for the walk to the courthouse. He knew he had to get a grip on his racing thoughts or he'd drive himself crazy. Moping around wasn't doing him any good, not with a trial still to fight. As for the voices in his head that were castigating him, they would just have to wait their turn and keep the damn volume down in the meantime.

If Dorrell Phillips had the universal sympathy of everybody who had listened to his tragic story, Marcus Paris would have been lucky if he was just intensely disliked.

Every prosecutor who ever had to make a deal with one criminal in order to catch another knew he was really making a deal with the devil. That morning, as Paris stood in the witness box before them, several jurors may well have wondered if, in fact, the prince of darkness himself hadn't incarnated in front of them. Even Francis Parent stood at a certain remove, looking at his young witness as if he was afraid to catch the plague from him, while he questioned him about the events of June 14, 1999.

The slightly built young man had testified about his arrival at the apartment in Little Burgundy, allegedly with Marlon Small. After describing the shooting of Indian, he came to the point where he had come across a stoned Dexter Phillips coming out of the bathroom. Then Parent asked the question that Bratt had been waiting for all morning.

"And what did you do then, Mr. Paris?"

"I got the guy down on his stomach and I shot him in the back of the head."

Bingo, Bratt thought, looking over at the jurors, most of whom now sat with their mouths agape. *The Crown's honorable witness is a cold-blooded murderer, ladies and gentlemen. Maybe Dorrell should be here to get a look at the guy who actually shot his brother, instead of dumping his heartbreak on my back.*

"Can you describe how you shot him, Mr. Paris?"

"I was standing by his feet and I shot him three times, just above the neck."

Several jurors shifted uncomfortably in their seats and continued to stare openly, both at Parent and Paris. Even Judge Green was now looking at the two of them with an obvious expression of disdain.

Bratt wondered what the jurors found more shocking: that Paris admitted he had killed Dexter Phillips as casually as if he were stepping on a bug, or that Parent had called him as his witness? The prosecutor had asked them to keep their minds open and believe Paris when he implicated Small as his accomplice, but by the looks on their faces, Bratt didn't think they were going to cut him a lot of slack.

He should have been enjoying his rival's predicament, just then, but joy was no longer a feeling that he could call up at a moment's notice. Instead, he had found a new target for his anger.

"What happened after that?" Parent continued.

"Nothin'. Brando kicked him to make sure he was dead, then I heard some people running around out in the hall, and we just booted it by the back door."

"Did you take anything with you when you left the apartment?"

"Nah, we had to get out of there too fast. The whole thing was a big waste of time."

Bratt glared angrily at Parent, feeling as if it was his own child's pointless death that was being talked about in such a trivial fashion.

Your wonderful witness just described shooting three innocent people as a big waste of his time, Bratt wanted to yell at Parent. *Hope this makes you feel as shitty as I have these last two days.*

Parent's own face showed his revulsion at Paris's cavalier attitude toward his crime. He lowered his eyes to the papers in front of him and shuffled them around as if looking for something important. From Bratt's vantage point, though, he could tell that the prosecutor was just trying to compose himself after his witness's last remark. Nancy, sitting beside him, seemed equally unnerved by the heartless young man.

Parent didn't seem to be in any hurry to get back to Paris and he kept shuffling his papers until Green finally spoke up.

"Mr. Parent, did you lose something?"

Yeah, thought Bratt. *His self-respect.*

Parent looked up, his face flushed, and cleared his throat before turning back to face Paris.

"Did you do anything particular after leaving the apartment?"

"Yeah. We ran round the corner and threw both guns into a big garbage bin, behind some warehouses near there."

"You say "we". By that you mean…"

"Me an' Brando. Marlon Small. We both threw our guns away there. That was the plan from the beginning."

Parent turned to a table behind him and opened one of a half-dozen cardboard exhibit boxes that were on it. He pulled out two plastic evidence bags, each containing a handgun, and laid them in front of the witness.

"Do you recognize these, Mr. Paris?"

Paris looked at them indifferently, then pushed at the smaller of the two with the forefinger of his right hand.

"That's the one I shot him with, the snub nose." His tone was flat and emotionless when he spoke. "Brando, he used the automatic."

Bratt went through the chronology of events in his mind: the cops had found the guns the morning after the shooting, just before the week's scheduled garbage pick-up. Paris's fingerprints were all over the small revolver, but, as he had no record, they hadn't been able to match them to him at first. The prints on the 9mm automatic were too smudged to be of any use, though, so there would be nothing to connect Small to that gun except Paris's say-so.

Once Dorrell Phillips had selected Paris's picture out of the 1999 Dorset High yearbook, the police quickly brought the suspect in. His prints matched those on the gun that fired the bullets found in Dexter Phillips's skull. With that evidence in hand there was no need to be concerned that Dorrell's identification might be faulty. Paris was cooked and he had known it.

That the Crown had agreed to let Paris plead guilty to second degree murder in return for his testimony meant that someone on their side doubted their ability to convict Small on Dorrell Phillips's evidence alone. So, Francis Parent, that holier-than-everyone paragon of virtue, found himself allied with an unfeeling killer on this Monday morning, and he clearly didn't like it.

Bratt watched with great interest as Paris testified, outlining the minimal planning that had gone into the robbery/murder, and demonstrating to everyone how little effect the violent deaths had had on him. Bratt was amazed at how easily the decision to kill had been made. He had no doubt that the jury would care very little for this witness, but they could still believe his claim that Small was his accomplice.

Parent came to the end of his direct examination just before the court was to adjourn for lunch, and the expression of relief on his face was obvious. As for Paris himself, he seemed to pay him no heed as the prosecutor gladly handed him over to Bratt for cross-examination. He had hardly looked Parent's way throughout the first half of his testimony, and he didn't seem to be overly concerned at the prospect of being questioned by Bratt.

Bratt reflected on the cold indifference that Paris was displaying and wondered if it was all just an act. He would get the chance to find out at the outset of the afternoon session, but he sincerely hoped that it wasn't.

"He looks like a tough nut to crack."

Kouri stated the cliché as if it was the result of some deep analysis. Bratt just continued to lean back quietly on the metal bench outside the courtroom as they waited for a constable to come unlock the doors.

"I don't know that you're going to be able to shake him up," Kouri continued, still looking for a response from the senior lawyer. "I guess you'll have to spend a long time with him."

"Heaven forbid," Bratt answered, although he sounded as if he were speaking to himself.

Kouri said nothing in reply, but clearly looked puzzled. Bratt turned to him and smiled, although there was no sign of happiness in his eyes. Kouri's expression showed even more befuddlement now.

"What? What am I missing?"

"How important a witness is he?" Bratt asked, sitting up and gaining a little spark now that he had decided to impart his wisdom to his assistant once more.

"Well, I would have thought pretty important."

"What if *I* don't think he's important at all? Don't you think the jury might be happy to learn they could just dismiss that scumbag from their thoughts?"

"What're you going to do?"

"Spend as little time on him as he deserves. I'd really like nothing more than to spend a couple of days going at him, hammer and tongs, but that would tell the jury we're scared of him. So, I'm just going to shrug him off like a minor irritation, kind of the way he acted when he shot Dexter Phillips."

"Ah, so that's your secret plan."

"I know it doesn't seem like much of a plan," Bratt said, although he liked its backward logic. "But I'm not going to let that punk enjoy his moment in the sun for one second longer than necessary."

The jurors filed back in, Green limped up to his seat, and Marcus Paris, almost strutting despite wearing shackles around his ankles, was escorted to the witness box by a prison guard. Bratt thought of a speed-chess tournament he had seen in a park once. Hit and run, don't give your opponent time to think, score as many points as fast as you can. He picked up his legal pad with its pages of prepared questions, opened his briefcase, dropped the pad inside it, and closed it with a snap. He had something else on his mind.

Paris stood staring at the wall behind the jury, totally disinterested in Bratt's presence. Bratt decided to get his attention.

"Tell me, Mr. Paris," he began in as casual a tone as he could, "how many people have you killed?"

From the jury box Bratt heard several breaths quickly sucked in at the question.

Paris's look darted to Bratt's face and for a moment the young man's confusion was evident. His eyes finally pulled away from Bratt's, and he stretched his frame up on his toes as he breathed in deeply.

Answering the question as casually as Bratt had asked it, he said, "Just the one guy, that I shot myself."

"Dexter Phillips."

"Yeah, whatever."

"Didn't seem very hard for you to do. Feel bad about it?"

"Not really."

"He had it coming?"

"His fault for being there. Wrong place, wrong time."

"So why's he still the only one? If it didn't bother you more than that, I mean?"

"Dunno. Cops caught me a couple weeks later, you know."

"Are you implying they cut your career short?"

Paris sneered, as if he found the thought funny.

"That's okay, I'm still young."

Bratt paused briefly. He was intentionally giving Paris enough rope to hang himself, but the young killer's braggadocio was helping his case all the more. With each answer, Bratt felt his internal thermometer creeping closer to the boiling point.

"Besides," Paris decided to add on his own, "I only got nine years and a bit left."

Good, Bratt thought. *Make my point for me, you little shit.*

"Beats twenty-five to life, doesn't it?" he asked.

"Goddamn right it does."

Bratt glanced up at Green, but the judge said nothing to the witness about his language. He was surprised to see that Green wasn't even taking notes, but simply sitting back in his chair, staring at Paris with a look of dull anger. Bratt allowed himself a brief look at the jury and found similar expressions of distaste on their faces as well.

Okay, so you all hate him. Let's make sure that translates into points for our side.

Bratt turned and looked at his client in the prisoner's box for a moment, thinking that it hadn't been so long ago that Small was the sole object of his ire. He turned his attention back to the witness.

"So, why's Marlon Small the lucky lottery winner?"

"He shoulda knowed better," Paris turned to face Bratt now, a thin smile playing on his lips. "I was barely eighteen."

"So it was all his idea, right? You were just going along for the ride?"

Paris didn't answer this time, just shrugged slightly and stared off into space again.

"No," Bratt continued, "I guess you're not a guy to ride on somebody else's coattails, are you?"

"I'm my own man."

"A big man?"

"You know it."

"But not big enough to do the time for what you did, are you?"

"Hey, I'm still in jail."

"That's right. All of nine years and four months left. And two men dead."

"I didn't make the law, man."

"No, but you did make the deal, didn't you?"

Again, Paris just shrugged, but the thin smile reappeared on his lips at the mention of the plea bargain.

"It must have been hard on you to accept the Crown's offer."

"Hell, no. Why should I spend more time than I got to in jail?"

"So, you were even willing to testify against a close friend."

"The fool's no friend of mine."

Bratt feigned surprise at this news.

"You mean you guys don't even like each other?"

"Like him? Man, what shit's he been telling you?"

Green cleared his throat loudly at the expletive, but still said nothing.

"Isn't Marlon your sister's boyfriend?"

"No, he just thinks he is. He's the guy who raped her, is who he is."

"He didn't really rape her now, did he?"

"He took advantage of her and she was just a little girl. She was only fifteen when she had his baby."

"You don't seem too happy about that."

"Damn straight. I shoulda shot him too, but Karen begged me not to."

"So, you would have liked to kill him?"

"And he knew it too."

"But you still went ahead and did this holdup with him."

"Business is business."

"Something heavy like that, don't you have to trust the man you're working with?"

"I know."

"So, you hated him and wanted to kill him, but still you trusted him enough to put your life in his hands?"

"I won't make that mistake again."

"No, I guess you won't. But you're also telling us that he knew you wanted to kill him and he still went along with you, putting his life in your hands."

"That was his problem."

"Any chance that you wouldn't have done such a foolish thing?"

"Whaddya mean?"

"I mean was there any chance that the man you were with last June 14 was not Marlon Small?"

"I think I woulda knowed if it was somebody else."

"Oh, I'm sure you did know."

"You saying I'm a liar?"

Now he's got the idea, Bratt thought. His control on his temper loosened just enough to raise his voice a notch or two.

"I'm saying you and someone else went to that apartment and shot those three young men."

"You're way off."

"Marlon Small was nowhere near the crime scene. You just decided you'd take him down with you and save yourself at least fifteen years of jail while you were at it."

"No way, man. Whatever he's been selling you, you shouldn't be buying it."

Bratt stepped closer to the witness and leaned aggressively closer.

"And just what are you selling us?"

"I'm telling it like it went down."

"And we're supposed to believe you?"

"It's how it happened."

"So you say. Why should we believe you?"

Now Paris looked flustered for the first time.

"I'm telling it like that other guy told you."

"What other guy? The one who managed to survive your killing spree?"

"Yeah, him."

"He's got a name," Bratt said, his voice rising. "Don't you even know it?"

"They told me, but I forget. Anyway, I know he says it was Brando shot him."

"So the only reason to believe you is because you're repeating what Dorrell Phillips said?"

"I never said that's the only reason."

"So let me repeat my question: why should we believe you?"

"Why would I lie?"

"Why *wouldn't* you lie? You hate Marlon Small and would love to see him dead. Twenty-five years to life is pretty close to dead, isn't it?"

Paris didn't answer, but his constant sneer had begun to waver.

"You're saving yourself fifteen years in jail," Bratt continued. "Great for you, too bad for the guy you hate, isn't it?"

"I'm just lucky, I guess," Paris's voice dripped with sarcasm.

"Yes, you are lucky. Dorrell Phillips picked out the picture of your worst enemy and gave you a chance to save yourself while getting rid of him. Isn't that what happened?"

"I wouldn't lie about it."

Bratt laughed, surprising himself as well as the rest of the courtroom. As he continued, though, it was anger, not humor that came through in his voice.

"You wouldn't lie about it? Gimme a break! You want us to believe you wouldn't lie to get the biggest break of your miserable little life?"

"Mr. Bratt," Green finally spoke up, albeit mildly and looking a bit like he just woke up from an unhappy dream. "Please calm yourself."

Bratt tried to control the trembling in his voice caused by the rush of hatred filling his mind.

"Maybe I'm a bit slow. Can you explain why you say you'd gladly kill him, but you don't expect us to think you'd lie to put him away for good?"

"It's not the same thing."

"Of course not. After all, you may be a cold-blooded murderer, but you're not a liar."

Green cleared his throat again, making a half-hearted attempt to protect the witness.

"Just answer me this one simple question," Bratt said, lowering his voice. "Are you saying that you would *never* lie to get Marlon Small convicted *and* to save yourself fifteen years in the pen?"

Paris sneered again, trying to regain his earlier arrogant attitude. He looked around the courtroom and could surely feel how unwelcome he had become.

"Yeah, I'd lie," he bragged, in defiance of the obvious hostility that surrounded him. "I'd do whatever I had to to put that motherfucker away."

"Mr. Paris," Green exploded, but the witness just ignored him.

"Getting fifteen years less is just a bonus for me."

His point made, Bratt sat down quietly, although his heart was racing. He vaguely heard Green berate Paris for his foul language in court, and from the corner of his eye he saw Parent standing up, attempting to apologize on his witness's behalf.

But Paris seemed to be paying no attention to the commotion he had caused. His eyes were glued to Bratt's, and they looked cold and lifeless. Bratt looked at the thin smile on Paris's tightly pressed lips and shuddered. He wondered if that was how he had looked at Dexter Phillips just before shooting him. In his mind Bratt saw the image of a shark about to calmly rip into its prey, and thought that Paris would be flattered by the comparison.

That was the end of Marcus Paris's brief moment in the limelight. Two prison guards led him through the box where Marlon Small sat, and into the detention area. Neither of the chained young men looked at each other. They both seemed to be denying the role that each played in the other's ultimate fate. In the courtroom, nobody looked happier to see the witness being led away than Francis Parent, who began to breathe palpably easier once the door to the cells were closed behind his witness.

Parent now found himself with a problem: he had expected Bratt to spend several hours questioning Paris, as he had done with Phillips the week before. But Bratt's uncharacteristic brevity had caught him off-guard because the pathologist, whose turn to testify was next, had only been subpoenaed for the following day. Judge Green, looking very much like someone who wanted to get this trial over with as soon as possible, begrudgingly adjourned for the rest of the day, giving everybody the afternoon off.

Despite being satisfied with how things had gone Bratt fumed quietly all the way back to his office, hardly noticing the wet snow that clung to his glasses like spilt soup. Kouri, sensing how angry he was, kept his mouth shut.

Once back at the firm Bratt greeted nobody, but strode straight into his office. Kouri, ever the dutiful assistant, signaled to Ralston and Kalouderis that they would be better off leaving their irascible friend alone for a while. He then followed Bratt in and gently closed the office door behind him, all the while maintaining his silence. Bratt saw this, but said nothing.

They had both been sitting silently for several minutes, their winter coats still on, when there was a timid knock at the door. Kouri jumped up to answer it and found Sylvie on the other side. Bratt heard them whispering, then saw Kouri back away from the door and let her in.

"What?" he glared at her.

"There's a woman to see you. She doesn't have an appointment."

"If she doesn't have a damn appointment why're you bothering me?"

Sylvie seemed stunned by his reaction and looked to Kouri for help. He stepped quickly forward and took her gently by the arm, as if to reassure her, then turned to Bratt.

"It's Detective Morin."

Bratt knew he'd had no reason to snap at Sylvie, and tried offering her a weak smile in apology.

"OK. I'm sorry, Sylvie. You can let her in."

Kouri followed the receptionist out the door and after a few seconds Nancy appeared in the office doorway, hesitating and looking unsure whether she had done the right thing by coming there.

"Hey," she whispered. "You all right?"

He hadn't expected her to be worried about him and he stood up to show her he was all in one piece.

"Yeah, great. I just wasn't expecting you."

"I've wanted to talk to you for a while now. You get my note?"

"I did, and it really took me by surprise. I wasn't too sure how you'd react to my message."

"Oh, I'm not so sure about that. I think you knew exactly how I'd react. Anyway, between your feeling so bad and my having to listen to St. Jean and Parent ripping into you behind your back, I began to wonder where my own priorities were. I'm sure there's more to it than that, but I can't really express it any better right now." A brief look of sadness flickered over her face. "It seems there are assholes even on the good guys' side and I don't want them controlling any part of my life."

"Fair enough," he said, not wanting to push her any further than she wanted to go just yet. "Although since the note you haven't exactly been, um…accessible."

"I still think we should take things slow for now, particularly with this trial. Maybe I'm not as self-assured as you might think I am."

"But you're here now."

"You had me worried today. I never saw you so angry before."

"I didn't think I was *that* angry."

She stepped slightly closer to look into his eyes.

"Believe me, you were. When did you begin letting your personal feelings affect how you did your job?"

"I thought I did pretty well today."

"Yes, I'm sure the jury thought you were defending your client with great passion. But don't tell me you suddenly fell in love with Marlon Small over the weekend. There are some things I'm not ready to believe."

He leaned back against his desk. *How do I tell her that my anger at Paris was on behalf of Dorrell Phillips, and not my own client?*

"I guess I just don't like stool pigeons," he answered.

"You're not the only one. Parent's probably showering in disinfectant as we speak."

They both smiled at the image and looked at each other silently.

"How was your weekend?" she asked unexpectedly.

He shrugged in response, realizing that the conversation risked taking a very serious turn, and unwilling to bring up the images Dorrell Phillips had left to haunt him the previous Friday.

“Oh God, now you’re giving me the silent treatment,” she smiled, not looking at all concerned that this might be the case.

“No, not at all. I’m still just getting used to having you here.”

She approached, still smiling as she leaned toward him, and reached her face up to kiss him lightly on his lips.

“You’ll get used to it. But I have to go now.”

“No. Stay.”

“I can’t. We’re having a little strategy session to talk about how it’s going.”

Bratt smiled slyly.

“It’s not going too well, is it?”

“Don’t get too cocky. The jurors only have to like one of our witnesses to put your guy away for life.”

“Uh-oh, we’re slipping into shop talk again. Maybe you should go before I reveal any defense secrets.”

She touched his cheek lightly and looked again into his eyes, searching for any residue of his earlier anger, but it all seemed to have dissipated.

“I’m glad to see you smiling again. I’ll see you in court tomorrow.”

Bratt had to admit her arrival had helped him get over much of his anger at Paris, and he continued smiling as she quickly left.

Now that I’m over Paris I can go back to hating Small, he half-joked to himself.

He stepped out of his office and headed for the reception area where Kouri and Sylvie were huddled.

“Grab your coats, kiddies. I think I owe Sylvie a nice dinner.”

“It’s only four o’clock,” she protested.

“So, we’ll have a few drinks first. Uh, soft drinks, perhaps. Put the phone on the answering service and let’s go. I’ve got some cobwebs to shake off.”

As simply as that he had buried all thoughts of Marcus Paris deep in his mind, where they could fester and grow quietly in the dark, while at least giving him a few hours of peace.

The next two days of the trial were a pure joy compared to what had gone before. Bratt let Kouri take over much of the cross-examination of the next few witnesses. There was the ballistics expert who explained which guns had been used against which victim, as well as the directions and distances from which the shots had come. The fingerprint expert confirmed that other than Paris's prints on the small revolver there were no other usable prints found on either of the guns or anywhere in the apartment. The pathologist explained which bullets were fatal (in the case of Dexter Phillips any of the three bullets which struck him could have caused his death, testifying to Paris's accuracy with a gun, as well as a tendency toward overkill.). There was testimony from members of the hospital staff who treated Dorrell Phillips, removing bullet fragments from the base of his skull and somehow managing to keep the young man alive.

Finally, there was S/D Philippe St. Jean, who told the jury of the difficulties the police had faced in their investigation, with little in the way of clues to go on until the famous "anonymous phone call" had led them to the Dorset yearbooks. He testified about the various statements and descriptions that Dorrell had given investigators over time, unable to deny the fact that the surviving victim had provided very few details about his assailant until after he spotted Small's picture among the class of 1996.

Bratt cross-examined St. Jean himself, and as much as he would have enjoyed provoking and toying with the detective, especially with memories of their run-in at the bar still fresh in his mind, he was able to control the more mischievous side of his nature. St. Jean was probably quite surprised at how politely Bratt asked the few questions he had for him. Bratt took only the time that was necessary to get St. Jean to confirm some of the weaknesses in the identification process, before letting the detective go off to enjoy his retirement.

At that point it was late Wednesday afternoon and Francis Parent stood up to announce that the case for the Crown was closed. With that, the hardest part of Bratt's work was done. He no longer had to plan attack strategies against witnesses, or react on the fly to any unexpected answers they might give. All that remained was to call his own witnesses and hope that the time spent in their preparation, particularly by Kouri, paid off.

He stood up and announced to the jury that he would present his defense beginning the following morning, and the person they most wanted to hear from, Marlon Small, would be the first witness on the stand. Their eyes turned en masse to the prisoner's box where the long-delayed star of the show sat, gazing calmly back at them like they were all just passengers with him on a bus. Bratt held his breath for a moment, suddenly certain that something disastrous was about to happen, but nothing did. Judge Green adjourned the court, the jurors filed out, and Marlon Small remained an enigma to them for one last day.

Bratt and Kouri squeezed into the tiny cubicle in the courthouse basement. Across a glass partition from them sat Small, in an equally tight space. Bratt reflected on how they had first met under similar circumstances at R.D.P., and how loud and cocky his client had been then. Over the past ten days Small had hardly said a word to them other than a grunt of greeting at the beginning of each court day. Now, he looked tense and apprehensive, fully aware that the ball was about to be handed off to him and his lawyers could do nothing to help him if he should fumble it.

Bratt had little new to tell his client, but knew this visit was necessary as a morale-booster for Small, so he avoided showing any impatience with him.

"How're you feeling, Marlon?"

"OK, I guess," Small shrugged. "Looked like it went pretty well."

"About as well as we could have hoped for. All that's left is for you and your friends to put us over the hump. Just keep your temper in check. Copping an attitude like Paris did won't help you a bit."

Small's expression changed at the mention of Paris's name, and he was back to the street-tough punk they had first met at R.D.P.

"Don't worry, I know better than that bitch. I saw how you led him right where you wanted to, an' that was real good. But I'm smarter than he is, so I'm gonna keep my story simple and nobody's gonna rattle me."

Bratt nodded thoughtfully. Maybe a little feistiness from his client wouldn't be such a bad thing. There was no point letting Parent steamroll over him.

"How's your mother doing, by the way?"

"She's OK. Why?"

"She's been going out of her way to avoid us the past couple of weeks. Any idea why?"

"Ah, she's just superstitious, that's all. She's pretty happy about how the trial's been going, though."

"Yeah? Good. All that's left, then, is for you to do your part."

There was another long pause, with little happening except for Small nodding his head occasionally as if agreeing with some voice that only he could hear. Bratt knew that the time for chitchat was over and it was time to leave Small alone with his thoughts. He stood to go, considered placing his palm up against the glass partition to wish his client well, but couldn't get himself to do it.

"We'll see you tomorrow," he said, and squeezed past Kouri and out of the tiny room. He heard Kouri whisper a few words of encouragement to their client and then follow him out, his face showing signs of nervousness. Bratt squeezed his assistant's shoulder.

"Relax, Pete. Tomorrow we throw him in the deep end and see if he can swim."

Small's defense was deceptively simple. There were only so many ways he could deny that he had committed the crime, after all. His alibi was almost idiot-proof. He was playing basketball in the park and only heard about the shooting the next day on the news. The only facts he had to remember were who was with him and how long they stayed there. The fewer opportunities there were for him to make a mistake or contradict himself, the better.

Bratt knew it was the type of defense the prosecutor would hate, because the only way to attack the witness's credibility was by trying to trip him up on minor details, and that was rarely what impressed a jury.

It took the defense lawyer barely thirty minutes to have his client tell the court how he had spent the night of June 14, 1999, then he sat down with a satisfied look on his face. There seemed to be little for Parent to work with.

The prosecutor stood and looked at Small for several seconds before asking his first question.

"So, Mr. Small, I understand you like having sex with fifiteen year-old girls."

Holy shit! Bratt's mind screamed, the question jolting him out of his complacency.

"Objection!" he shouted, jumping to his feet. "What kind of question is that?"

Green was barely able to disguise his displeasure at Bratt's outburst.

"This isn't a rodeo, Mr. Bratt. There's no need for you to go whooping in my courtroom."

Bratt tried to compose himself, realizing that his reaction had drawn some smiles and even snickers from the jury box.

"Sorry about that, My Lord. But you have to admit that my colleague's question was clearly intended to shock."

"And is that all you're objecting to? You've been known to push the dramatic buttons yourself on occasion."

"I've got nothing against drama. But the question is totally irrelevant to this case, and you certainly shouldn't allow it."

Green's eyes narrowed and his face reddened. He jabbed the pen he was holding in Bratt's direction.

"I don't need advice from you on how to do my job." His voice was almost cracking. "As long as you're not up here on the bench, and that might still be a while yet, don't you forget your place."

Bratt was embarrassed at having his judicial ambitions mentioned in open court, but he didn't sit down.

"I've made an objection, My Lord," he stated, trying to remain outwardly calm. "Would you please rule on it."

Green glared at him for several seconds before finally turning to Parent, who had been quietly enjoying Bratt's discomfort.

"Mr. Parent, your question is irrelevant…for now."

Parent turned to Small and smiled.

"Well, now that that's settled, tell us, Mr. Small, what's your relation to Marcus Paris?"

"His sister Karen's my baby-mother."

"Baby-mother, yes," Parent spoke the words as if they were somehow unclean. "And she was how old when you got her pregnant?"

"I never asked."

"I hear she's sixteen now, is that possible? So, she was probably all of fifteen when you got her pregnant."

"I guess so."

"Maybe fourteen?"

"Maybe. But I don't think so."

"I see. Marcus Paris says you raped her. Did you?"

Bratt was on his feet again, but managed to maintain his composure this time.

"I object. My colleague can't ask the accused if he committed a crime that he was never even charged with."

"My Lord," Parent responded, "I thought it might be relevant for the jury to know exactly why he was never charged with raping that fifteen year-old girl."

"My client never raped anyone!" Bratt came close to yelling.

"Calm down, Mr. Bratt," Green said. "You know you can't answer on behalf of your client." He turned to speak to the jurors, who seemed to be very interested in Small's relationship with Karen Paris. "The jury will disregard the defense lawyer's last comment. If I decide to allow the question it is up to the witness to deny the allegations…if he so wishes."

Bratt was stunned into silence. He had fallen into Parent's trap. They both knew that Small had never raped Karen Paris but now, even if Green over-ruled the question, the jury would think that maybe he had and then somehow managed to get away with it. He sat down slowly, regretting the overconfidence that had prevented him from seeing this coming.

Kouri reached over and grabbed his arm.

"Hey, he can't-"

"Yeah, well he just did. Forget about it. We gotta let him score some points."

Parent, not surprisingly, had nothing to say in defense of his question and Green promptly disallowed it, admonishing the jury to disregard any implications that Small may have raped Karen

Paris, as there was no evidence of this crime, nor was it an issue before them.

And just because he's a rapist, doesn't mean he's a not a nice guy, Bratt thought sarcastically to himself. *I'm sure that's just what they're thinking.*

Parent, looking more self-satisfied than he had for days, continued his cross-examination.

"Mr. Small, do you think Marcus Paris hates you enough to falsely accuse you of this murder?"

"Sure looks that way."

"You must have really done something bad to his sister for him to hate you."

"I didn't rape her, if that's what you mean."

"I know, I know. Please don't think I'm implying that you did. She was perfectly willing, wasn't she?"

"That's how it was."

"She was barely fifteen years old and she did whatever you wanted her to, is that right?"

Kouri leaned over to Bratt again.

"Why don't you object? They can't attack an accused's character."

"Calm down," Bratt whispered, well aware of how the judge would respond. "I'm the one who raised this issue first, with Paris."

"The girl knew what she wanted," Small was saying to Parent, remaining calm in the face of the intrusive line of questioning.

"And you weren't too much of a gentleman to say no, were you? Not to a pretty fifteen-year-old girl. I guess they're hard to resist."

Again Kouri grabbed Bratt's arm.

"He's making him look like a scumbag."

He is a scumbag, Bratt was tempted to reply. He patted Kouri's hand in understanding before removing it from his arm.

"Tell me, Mr. Small," Parent was saying, "if you didn't rape his sister is there any other reason that Marcus Paris might hate you so much that he'd falsely accuse you of murder?"

"Not that I'm aware of."

"Did you ever steal from him?"

"No, never."

"Did you maybe lie to him, or betray his trust somehow?"

"No, I was always straight with him."

"So, if you were always straight with him and you never raped his sister, why would your lawyer suggest that Marcus Paris was ready to lie to this court because of his deep hatred toward you?"

This time Bratt did stand up to object, but he knew that it was already too late.

"Objection. The accused can't be asked to comment on his lawyer's cross-examination of prosecution witnesses."

"I agree totally," Parent magnanimously conceded, having already gotten his point across to the jury. "I withdraw the question."

Bratt sat down slowly, irritated that Parent was trying to put ideas into the jury's head by tossing out inadmissible questions, with no expectation that they be answered. At the same time, Bratt had to admit a grudging admiration for the prosecutor's strategy.

Have your fun for now, Francis, Bratt wanted to tell him. *But you're going to have to deal with his alibi sooner or later.*

Parent, though, had obviously decided that his best chance to score points against Small was not in questioning him on the details of his alibi. Instead, in the Marlon-Marcus-Karen triangle, he found a subject that he was going to milk for all it was worth. All Bratt could do was make sure he kept his questions legal.

"Isn't it true," Parent went on, "that Karen Paris was jealous about your several other girlfriends and she complained to Marcus about it, and that caused the rift between you?"

Bratt was quickly back on his feet again.

"My Lord…"

"I know," Green replied before he could finish his objection. "Multiple questions, Mr. Parent. You know better than that."

Parent breathed in and tried again, as Bratt sat back down.

"Could that be the reason Marcus hated you?"

"Could what be the reason?" Bratt jumped up again.

"Mr. Parent," Green spoke as if he were lecturing an undergrad, "if I have no idea what you're asking I don't expect the accused to be in any better a position. Make your questions clear."

Parent said nothing in reply, but simply bowed slightly, before turning to face Small again.

"Was the conflict between you and Marcus due to the fact that you had several other girlfriends Karen's age and she was very jealous?"

Bratt couldn't believe that he had to object again already, and he was quickly back on his feet.

"That's as bad as the other one."

Green sighed deeply, trying not to lose his patience.

"Mr. Parent, I'm starting to get a sore throat. Will you just break it up into separate questions?"

"I'll try to do better," Parent said with a solicitous grin, although Bratt doubted that he intended to do any such thing.

Parent was trying to draw the ugliest possible picture of Small's character for the jury, and he knew his questions didn't have to be allowed by the judge to succeed. Bratt objected whenever it was necessary, but was well aware of the impression being made on the jury. Green warned the jurors several times to ignore whatever he disallowed, but there was no way to be sure they did.

As the morning wore on, though, Bratt began to notice a change in the attitude of several jurors. They had stopped listening as intently to Parent's lurid insinuations. Instead, they began looking bored. Most of them stopped taking notes. Their eyes wandered and several yawned openly.

Bratt realized that Parent's strategy had hit a wall. There was a limit to how long he could hint that Small had a hidden dark side without actually offering any proof. The jurors were surely expecting him to confront Small on his alibi at some point, and since he seemed to be purposely avoiding the topic, he was losing their interest. As for Small himself, his responses had been calm and courteous in the face of what were often embarrassing questions, and Bratt thought the accused might have started to look good in the jury's eyes.

By the time the morning drew to a close Parent's expression showed that he knew he had gone as far as he could with his attempt to discredit Small, and had only had limited success. He was going to have to rethink his strategy, but Bratt wasn't going to repeat the mistake of feeling too confident yet.

There's always this afternoon, he told himself. *We'll see what Francis has up his sleeve then.*

They were only ten or fifteen minutes into the afternoon session when Bratt realized that Parent didn't have any hidden reserves at all. It was as if he had tried everything he could think of in the morning and had nothing new for the afternoon.

When he finally got around to questioning Small about his alibi his questions were simple and straightforward. Small was confident and well-prepared, and he had no difficulty answering everything that was asked of him. Parent's approach was so indifferent that Bratt wondered if the prosecutor had any fight left in him at all.

Maybe you smell your own defeat, Francis, Bratt reproached Parent in his mind. *You never could handle a little adversity.*

Parent spent an inordinate amount of time flipping through his pages of notes after each of Small's answers, perhaps hoping to uncover that one key question that would shatter the witness's self-confidence. Even Green tapped his fingers impatiently on his desk at the stalling tactics.

"Isn't it possible that you left the park before midnight?" Parent finally asked.

"No. Like I said before, nobody's allowed in the park after twelve, and a couple of city security guys came and told us to leave."

"And you're certain that was the night of June 14?"

"Yes."

"There's no doubt in your mind about it?"

"No, there isn't."

Bratt grabbed at his notepad, but only because he wanted to pass a note to Kouri. He was shaking his head internally at Parent's weak-willed performance and needed an outlet for his frustration.

"He's totally disheartened," he scribbled. "He knows there are no chinks in our armor."

He slid the note over to Kouri and sat back.

Somehow Parent managed to fill the entire afternoon with questions that didn't come close to shaking Small up, or poking any holes into his story. When the cross-examination was over, Small turned out to have been as good a witness as Bratt could have hoped for. With Sims and Jordan scheduled for the next day his earlier optimism about this trial now looked justified.

The court adjourned for the day, and Bratt began packing his briefcase while watching Parent out of the corner of his eye. The prosecutor's face was drained, and his movements were slow and uncertain.

Kouri slid over to Bratt's side.

"He looks like shit."

"He's a coward," Bratt snapped, surprised at his own vehemence. "He talks big when he thinks he's got you on the ropes, but score a few points on him and he's ready to throw in the towel, just like a schoolyard bully. That's why I could never work for him."

Bratt dragged his heavy briefcase off the desk, picked up his overcoat from where it lay on a chair in the corner of the room, and headed out with Kouri.

Once outside, he turned to see Nancy coming out of the courtroom. Parent was nowhere in sight.

"What happened to Francis?" he asked.

"Honestly, I think he's pretty tired of this case. Ever since he called Marcus Paris to the stand he's been feeling almost revolted. That's just how he is."

"Oh, I know how he is, and I don't think it has a lot to do with Paris."

"So what do you think it is?"

"Does the expression 'airtight alibi' mean anything to you? He sees the case slipping though his fingers and he just doesn't have the heart to put up a fight."

"Don't be so smug, Robbie. You should know better than anyone that a lawyer can't always love the case he has, …or the client."

She raised her eyebrows knowingly and turned to join Parent who had finally appeared in the hallway. His shoulders slumped, he walked past them without a glance. Nancy looked at Bratt a last time, shaking her head, then caught up with Parent.

That hit close to home, Bratt thought, his heart still beating hard. *Not that I'm ready to feel any sympathy for Parent.*

He thought of Dorrell Phillips and how his visit the week before had affected him. He wondered how Phillips would feel seeing the man who was supposed to get him justice slinking away, almost ready to admit defeat before the trial even ended.

If that's not as ironic as it gets, he told himself. *Now I'm the one concerned about the victim's feelings.*

Chapter 12

On Friday morning, Vernon Sims, the first alibi witness, was called to the stand to testify on Marlon Small's behalf. This day was to be Kouri's true coming-out party. He had spent hours preparing Sims and Jordan for their testimony on his own and he would undertake their examinations in chief. Bratt wasn't totally free to sit back and relax, though, even if this was supposed to be Kouri's show. He was going to have to stay alert in case Kouri, who was displaying a strong case of nerves that morning, had any problems with either Parent or Judge Green.

Sims, as a witness, turned out to be everything that Bratt had expected. He spoke well, remained calm and polite at all times, and retained a good grasp of the facts he had to recount. At times, when Kouri's inexperience got him off track, it was Sims who brought the testimony back into line. Bratt, sitting next to Kouri, tugged on his robe from time to time, just to slip a word of encouragement or advice into his assistant's ear. But it was clear that it was Sims that Kouri relied on to give the right answers, even when his occasionally awkward questions were not clear.

At the end of the examination in chief, which had lasted well over an hour, Kouri sat down, his face red and sweaty. Bratt patted him on his back. It had all gone quite smoothly: nothing spectacular, no disastrous mistakes.

As for Parent, it seemed that he wasn't in any more of a fighting mood with this witness than he had been with Small.

Once again, he went through the alibi, detail by detail, but in an uninspired and desultory fashion. He made no attempts to attack Sims's character or reputation. Kouri had prepared his witness for far worse and Sims was able to answer all the questions without hesitation.

There were the engineering courses he had switched, meeting Everton Jordan at the Metro station, the undercooked hamburgers his friend had eaten. All the stories were told and retold. Their arrival at the park, who they had played basketball with, Jordan's taking ill and being taken home. Sims never came close to contradicting himself on any of the details. The time of their return to the park, Small's presence throughout, and his eventual defiance of the midnight curfew. Parent questioned Sims on everything, but there were no obvious lapses.

By the time the lunch break came around, the prosecutor looked about ready to pack it in. Bratt began feeling the excitement as he saw the finish line getting closer and he could almost taste victory. In the jurors' eyes he could read their confirmation of the probable outcome. They no longer scowled when Small's name was mentioned and they stopped averting their gazes from him in the box. He was no longer the cold-hearted killer that they were sworn to condemn. They had been given Marcus Paris, after all, on whom they could focus their righteous anger.

Everybody in the courtroom is on the same page, Bratt told himself. *Even Parent, although he'd never admit it. Maybe I should call up Madsen tonight and tell him to let his buddies in Ottawa know they've got their next Superior Court Judge lined up right here.*

When the court had emptied, and only he and Kouri remained, he couldn't restrain himself from giving the younger lawyer a big bear hug.

"Did a hell of a job, Pete. I'm not one to count my chickens before they're hatched, but unless they blow up the courthouse over the weekend you're about to have your first victory in a murder trial."

They left their files behind them in the courtroom since there would be nothing for them to prepare or work on over lunch. Jordan would be the last witness heard in this trial. It would surely go as smoothly as Sims's testimony had, and they would have more than enough time over the weekend to prepare their final arguments.

They walked down the courthouse corridor with huge smiles on their faces, Kouri humming "We Are the Champions" as if the verdict had already been rendered. Turning into the lobby, Bratt spotted Jennifer Campbell standing alone near the Notre Dame Street exit on their left. He saw her facing them and he slowed his pace just slightly, expecting her to avoid him as had been her habit throughout the trial.

But she did not turn away. She continued to look at him from across the open space, nervously shifting her weight from one foot to the other.

He signaled Kouri to take the door leading out onto St. Laurent Boulevard and go to the office ahead of him, then he walked toward her.

He was only a few feet away from her when she finally made a move as if to walk away.

"Mrs. Campbell, don't go."

She stopped in her tracks, but she didn't look back at him.

"Don't worry," he said. "Things have been going so well I don't think our talking is going to jinx anything."

Now she turned to face him, but she didn't seem to have understood his meaning.

"Jinx what?"

"You know, the trial. Marlon said you were a bit superstitious, but I have to admit I'm pretty amazed you've been able to avoid me for so long."

Her eyes widened at his words, and she sounded indignant when she spoke.

"I don't have a superstitious bone in my body. The Good Lord doesn't deal with luck or jinxes."

"Then why the vanishing act these past two weeks?"

Her face took on a nervous expression and she took a step back, looking like she was thinking of running away again.

"I can't say I'm enjoying my first experience in a courtroom," she said, not looking at him.

"I know it can't be easy listening to the things that were said about your son, but now it's our turn and it's going even better than I could have hoped for."

"None of this is easy," she said, her voice dropping almost to a whisper. "I pray every day…"

Her voice trailed off, leaving Bratt puzzled at her attitude. He might have expected her to be concerned about the possible verdict, but something else seemed to be on her mind.

"Mrs. Campbell, what are you worried about? Is there something I can help you with?"

"They're all swearing on the Bible in there."

"Well, yes, that's how it's usually done."

"But they lie anyway."

"You don't have to worry about the lies. I think our defense is going over very well."

She sniffed impatiently and looked at Bratt with a shake of her head. When she spoke again she sounded as if she was speaking to a child who just wasn't getting the point.

"Mr. Bratt, do you know the story of Saul of Tarsus?"

Oh brother, not with the Bible again, he thought. The one thing he hadn't missed about talking to her was her religious zeal, and he couldn't help but be flippant when he answered her.

"Wasn't he the Christian-hating Jew who became a Jew-hating Christian?"

"Well, that's not exactly how it's written in the Bible," she replied, looking offended by his disrespectful tone, "but we seem to be talking about the same man."

"What about him?"

"He spent his life persecuting the followers of Jesus, as you seem to know. Then one day everything changed, and he realized that everything he had ever believed in or stood for was a lie. He suddenly hated the man he once was."

Her words hit Bratt like a slap in the face. It was as if she had been reading his most secret thoughts over the previous month and had now drawn them out into the open. Surely the reference to a man who questioned his life's work was nothing but a coincidence.

"What's that got to do with me?" he asked, dreading her answer.

"Oh, it's not just you. It's me too. When the scales fell from my eyes I knew I was a coward and I ran away from the truth. But you don't even run away, Mr. Bratt. You just keep holding on to those scales, preferring to be blind than to see what you should know."

"Hold it, hold it," Bratt said, unclear about what she was talking about and unable to disguise the irritation this was causing him. "You've really lost me with your religious mumbo jumbo. If you're unhappy about some aspect of the defense I've presented for your son, why don't you just come out and say it?"

She looked deeply into his eyes now, and he could see that she was feeling a great deal of sadness and confusion. When she spoke, though, her words were straightforward.

"For such a smart lawyer you play dumb very well. Maybe this helps you lie to your heart."

Bratt said nothing, unsure if she was trying to provoke him into anger.

She bit her lip to keep herself from speaking further, and looked around them for several seconds, before finally saying, "I have to go eat something to keep my strength up. Have a good lunch."

Bratt couldn't believe she was going to just walk away after her cryptic pronouncements. On top of that he was bothered by her suggestion that he knew something when he had no idea what that something was.

She left the building and he trotted out the door after her. He caught up with her on the sidewalk, where the sting of the icy wind made continuing their conversation particularly unpleasant.

"Listen. I have no idea what you're talking about, so I don't even feel insulted about being called dumb. I just wish you could be a little clearer in whatever it is you're trying to tell me."

"Ananias can remove the scales from your eyes, if you really want him to."

"Anna who? For crying out loud, is that supposed to be clearer?"

"He was a disciple in Syria and God sent him to give Saul his sight back, so that he might believe and spread the word. Go speak to your own disciple if you truly want to see. Now, please leave me in peace."

With that she walked off, quickly disappearing into a crowd of people that were braving the bitter cold on the way to their favorite lunch spots. Passersby, trying to squeeze between Bratt and the snowdrifts, lightly jostled him as he stood in their path.

He was far from certain what she had meant, but he could tell that underneath her holier-than-thou attitude she was clearly distressed. She seemed to expect him to feel the same way. He told himself that he didn't know what was bothering her, even if she seemed to think that he did and was just refusing to admit it.

The cold began digging into his bones and he started back toward the office at a fast pace. As he walked he thought of the conversation he had had with Marlon at R.D.P. several weeks earlier, when the line between what a lawyer really knew and what he didn't know had gotten blurred. Wasn't that what she was saying now? He would have to seek out his own "Syrian disciple" it seemed. That was about the only part of her obscure ranting that he had understood.

Back at his office Bratt had no appetite for lunch. He watched Kouri, eating, talking on the phone, trading stories with Kalouderis, and he wondered what it was that his assistant could reveal to him. Despite Jennifer Campbell's exhortations, he couldn't get himself to ask.

It had been several weeks since he had first begun putting his life and his career under the microscope. In the middle of his self-analysis he had decided to put his questioning aside because it was going to be a distraction from the murder trial he had taken on. Now the trial was almost over. Victory was a strong possibility and after it there would come the reward that could put an honorable end to his now-unhappy legal career.

He decided he would have to get through the trial first, before approaching Kouri in search of enlightenment. Only then would he have the nerve to find out what secrets his assistant held.

That afternoon in court Bratt's mind was on autopilot as his body went through the motions with which it was so familiar. Parent wrapped up his cross-examination of Sims, getting no further with the witness than he had that morning. The frustration on his face was clear for everyone to see, but Bratt felt no particular satisfaction from it. Despite his earlier commitment to himself that he would see the trial through to a successful conclusion, his mind kept harking back to Jennifer Campbell's cryptic words.

He glanced in her direction at the back of the courtroom, but she didn't seem to be looking at him. Her face maintained the passivity it had shown over the previous two weeks, as if their conversation just two hours earlier had never occurred.

She was probably wondering if he had spoken to Kouri as she had instructed him to, but her face held no clues. He didn't know how she managed to get into his head the way she did, but his lack of concentration over the trial was proof that she had. If it had been him, instead of Kouri, who was questioning the alibi witnesses, the afternoon would have been a total disaster.

As it was, he hardly listened while Kouri took their next witness, Everton Jordan, through the events that constituted Marlon Small's alibi for June 14, 1999. There was the occasional glitch, a few leading questions that Parent objected to, but overall Kouri was proving himself to be an able attorney.

There's an ironic twist, Bratt thought. *He's got the trial well under control, while I can't even get a grip on my own thoughts.*

Jordan's examination in chief ended at nearly four-thirty and Green suggested Parent cross-examine the witness on Monday morning. The judge looked at the prosecutor like he thought the weekend's rest would do him good. Then, with a curt, "Have a good weekend," he stood and followed the jurors out of the court.

Bratt had barely gotten into the corridor when he stopped and turned to Kouri.

"Come here," he said, directing Kouri into an empty interview room. There was no way he could wait out the weekend before clearing the air of the fog Campbell had filled it with. If speaking to Kouri was supposed to somehow change things in his life, then so be it.

Besides, he told himself, *I still know the first rule of cross-examination. I never ask a question unless I already know the answer.*

"What's going on, Pete?"

"What? Did I screw something up?"

"No, no. You did great. But she's right, something's going on and we really need to get it out in the open."

"Who's right? Did I really do great?"

"Forget how you did, this is important. Jennifer Campbell told me you'd remove the scales from my eyes, so that I could see what I should have known all along."

"Are you pulling my leg, Mr. Bratt? Because I can take a joke now."

Bratt shook his head impatiently, but he saw traces of surprise and fear in Kouri's eyes.

"This is serious, Pete. Campbell's all twisted up on the inside instead of being happy with how well her son's trial is going. She's an odd bird, but not that odd."

"So why're you asking me about her?"

"Because you're my Syrian disciple, aren't you? You know whatever it is that I'm supposed to know. You know what's eating away at her insides."

It's been eating away at me too, Bratt admitted to himself, feeling a sense of inevitability about what he was about to find out. *I just need to hear him say it out loud.*

"OK, enough of this beating around the bush," Bratt's voice suddenly got loud in the face of Kouri's continued silence. "You and her have been holding out on me and I think you better tell me what's going on."

Kouri's face showed the fear openly now, and his eyes looked around the small room in search of an escape route. Finding no way to avoid a confrontation his shoulders sagged slightly in resignation.

Head down, he mumbled, "Don't you think Small is guilty?"

"Look," Bratt said, getting exasperated, "I'm asking *you* the questions."

Kouri's voice sounded petulant as he answered. "I'm trying to answer you, all right? I just want to explain what I did and it's not that easy. So, please let me do it my way."

"Fine, go on. Just make it quick."

"OK, OK. From the first day we met Small you thought he was guilty, right? The more time we spent on his file, the more certain you became that he was guilty. And that's not just my opinion. She knew it, too."

Kouri hesitantly looked Bratt in the eyes now, and Bratt saw that the young man was still half-expecting him to jump down his throat. He simply nodded, encouraging him to go on with his explanation, yet already having a good idea of what it was.

"So, what did it matter who his witnesses were?" Kouri said. "You had already decided that they were going to be lying, no matter who they were or what they said. The only thing you cared about was that they look good in front of a jury.

"Remember that day in R.D.P. when you all but told him that you didn't care if his witnesses were liars, as long as they were good?"

Bratt wanted to answer that he had never told Small anything of the kind, but he kept silent. Kouri had obviously been listening between the lines that day.

"I was so shocked at the time," Kouri went on, "but then I realized that you were right. It didn't matter if the witnesses were going to lie or not. Because if Small was innocent then we had to do whatever we could to get him off, even if it meant getting people to perjure themselves. Better than seeing an innocent man convicted of first degree murder, right? That's how I saw it, at least. But since you always thought he was guilty it didn't matter to you where we got the witnesses. Because you had to think that they were all going to be liars anyway."

Kouri paused to catch his breath, and rubbed his suddenly cold hands together. He shrugged his shoulders, in response to an internal argument.

"And so Mrs. Campbell and I got you what you wanted," he continued. "Marlon had given Sévigny a bunch of names, and there were a couple he thought could pull it off. You got your good witnesses that would help you win the case. And he got the witnesses who'd save him from going to jail for a crime he didn't commit."

Bratt stared at him, unable to believe that Kouri was confirming the suspicion that had lingered in the back of his mind from the day of Leblanc's heart attack.

What kind of twisted logic is this? Pete went out and found a couple of guys whom he could make into witnesses? Whether Small is guilty or not, does he really think he can actually justify what he did? Christ, that better not be his defense at his disbarment hearing. Make that our *disbarment hearing!*

"Oh boy, Pete. What the hell did you do? Did you ever stop and think that maybe if there were no *real* witnesses it's because Small was never in that damn park? Don't you see this guy killed those people and he got you to help him get away with it?"

"You don't know that he killed anyone."

"YES, I DO KNOW, DAMMIT!" Bratt shouted now, heedless of who might hear them in the hallway. "I know it with every bone in my body. That's probably what's making his mother nuts. She must have realized it too and now she hates herself for helping him. But I understand why she did it. She couldn't *not* help her own son. Now you're the only one who still believes him, even if it's so obvious to everyone else. He killed those guys."

"Well, I'm sorry if I don't just blindly accept your say-so. But, even if he did do it, what does that change?" Kouri was almost in tears now. "That's our job, isn't it? We're paid to get the murderers off."

"Not this way we're not," Bratt said, reacting angrily to how close to the truth Kouri had come with his answer. "We give them the best defense that we can, that's all they're entitled to. But you didn't just do that. You went out and suborned perjury."

"No, I didn't," Kouri said, looking unexpectedly defiant even though his lower lip still trembled. "*You* did."

"What? Are you nuts?"

"You did. You called two alibi witnesses for what you always thought was a false alibi. You couldn't have believed they were telling the truth if you thought Marlon was guilty, but you let them testify anyway because you knew they could help you win. As far as you were concerned they had to be lying if they claimed he was in the park with them, but that didn't stop you from putting them on the stand. Well, you were right, so why the hell are you so mad at me now?"

Kouri's eyes brimmed with tears and his lower lip quivered uncontrollably. Bratt felt a touch of pity for the young lawyer, mixed with anger at what he had done. He had to find some way to show Kouri that he had totally twisted around what a lawyer's job was, yet he was worried that he might not be able to find the words.

"Jesus, Pete, you're turning everything upside down. That's not how it works. Just because I think he's guilty it doesn't mean I'm going to encourage him to perjure himself. Nor am I going to go get people to come and say they were witnesses to something they weren't.

"If the client says he has an alibi then we present an alibi defense. That's what our job is, no matter what we may feel personally. But that's all it is. Then it's up to the jury to decide if they believe him or not. It's not our place to decide for the jury what it should or shouldn't believe. And we sure as hell don't *knowingly* let anybody lie on the stand."

"You hypocrite!" Kouri yelled out, his tears flowing freely now. "Maybe you wouldn't have let them testify if I had told you they were going to lie. But as long as nobody told you anything you gladly put them on the stand, even though you were sure they *were* lying. What the hell's the difference between the two?"

"Dammit, there is a difference," Bratt said, still refusing to accept the blame that Kouri was trying to lay at his feet. "It's the difference between being a lawyer and being an accomplice to perjury. It's the difference between doing your sworn duty and committing an indictable offense. It's bad enough that his crazy mother tried pulling this off. You had no business getting involved."

"But why is what I did so wrong? You never really believed Sims and Jordan. From the first day you said they were too good to be true. But you were still willing to close your eyes and hold your nose and ram through their testimony, all the while hoping that nobody would be the wiser. You didn't give a shit about their honesty from the very beginning. So how come I'm the only one who's at fault here?"

"Because I can defend everything I said and did when we get called up before the Bar for this and you can't. Maybe I am a hypocrite, but I at least know how to cover my ass."

Bratt hated himself for saying that. He was certain that the issue was much more than just covering their asses, but that was all he could think of just then.

"If Small was going to bring us witnesses," he continued, his own voice starting to crack with emotion, "then we had to keep our own hands clean. Let him get them to lie if he wanted to, but we couldn't have anything to do with it. That's where you went wrong. You stopped acting like his lawyer and you began acting like his friend. I don't know why you felt he needed a friend, dammit, but it wasn't supposed to be you."

They stood face-to-face, their tear-filled eyes locked on each other. Bratt thought that anybody who peeked through the window in the door would think they were two lovers having a quarrel. Then again, their voices had been loud enough that passersby in the corridor could have heard every word they had yelled at each other.

Kouri's voice was so low when he spoke again that Bratt almost didn't hear him ask, "Now what?"

"I don't know. Thank God it's the weekend. We at least get a couple of days to think about it. We'll see."

"We could always just do nothing. Maybe you're wrong about him and he is innocent. Nobody would know what we did."

"I would know."

"Yes…"

The way Kouri let his voice trail off suggested that Bratt might be ready to live with their little secret, especially if he received the reward he was expecting from Small's acquittal. That suggestion hit Bratt in his very core, even while he recognized that it made a lot of sense. Kouri had begun to know him too well. He knew what motivated him almost as well as Bratt did himself.

"We'll see," he said gruffly, then opened the door and stepped out.

The stale air in the courthouse corridor tasted fresh compared to that in the interview room, and he gulped in a huge lungful as if he had been suffocating.

I have *been suffocating*, he told himself. *Now I have to find a way to get out from under before it's too late.*

He threw his coat over his shoulders and walked out of the courthouse, passing by the taxi stand without giving the cabs a second thought. He turned north and headed in the direction of his home. It was about a half hour walk in the cold wind, and he would need every frozen minute of it to clear his mind.

Later that evening Bratt stood under a hot shower trying to rid his aching body of the numbing cold that seemed to have dug permanently into his bones. He lingered as long as possible behind the frosted glass door of the shower stall, allowing it to cut him off from the day's events, finding in his temporary isolation a tenuous sense of security. But the steam rising around him was little defense against the news that Kouri had dropped on him earlier in the day.

He still couldn't believe how his assistant had stood before him and tried to defend his actions, as if perjury were just a matter of opinion, or a question of degree. But the bottom line was that it was he, Robert Bratt, who had done everything to give Kouri just that impression. He had simply chosen to look the other way when the truth was there for any thinking lawyer to see.

After a lifetime of bending the truth it really hadn't been that hard for me to do. Kouri seems to have known me better than I knew myself. So am I really going to change now? When all it'll take to get onto the bench is to let this one little lie stand?

It certainly wasn't his first lie, he knew, and maybe if he just forgot about it he could make it his last. The problem was that it had become too easy to lie to himself, to convince himself that he didn't know the truth when he really did. Suddenly his own glib justifications about how he exercised his profession weren't so easy to swallow.

He thought of Sims and Jordan. He was certain there had been a brief moment when he had honestly been against using them. But, that was when life, and then death, had gotten in the way. First, there had been the temptation of that seat on the Superior Court, just waiting for him to win this trial. Then Leblanc's death had thrown him for an emotional loop, giving him an excuse to avoid making any hard decisions.

He rubbed his face hard under the harsh stream of water, trying to shake himself out of his wishful thinking. His feeble attempts at justifying what he had done just didn't wash, no matter how many excuses he tried. He had willingly closed his eyes and let himself be manipulated, because the only thing he had cared about was the final result. Winning was the best drug he knew of, and ever since he had gotten hooked on it he couldn't imagine living without it.

Had his cynical attitude rubbed off so easily on Kouri, though? And why did Kouri still cling so tightly to the illusion that Small was innocent?

Bratt knew that there had to be more than just his own influence at play on his assistant. If anyone could have convinced Kouri that Small was innocent it was Jennifer Campbell. Bratt was sure that she had drawn Kouri into this cockamamie plan, what with her religious fervor and soul-deep sincerity. From the beginning she had wanted a lawyer who would do anything to get her son out of jail, and this twisted, illegal scheme seemed to be just what she was looking for.

"Holy shit!" he exclaimed out loud, as the realization dawned on him. "She knew he was guilty from the beginning!"

It was suddenly very clear to him: she hadn't come to him hoping he could save her falsely accused child, although that was what she may have led Kouri to believe. Nor had she just recently realized that Marlon was guilty of the murders. She had known the truth all along.

His mind raced back to their talk at the office, the day of Leblanc's funeral, when she had wondered out loud if it might not be God's wish that Marlon be acquitted. She had gone so far as to say that in the greater scheme of things the court verdict didn't really matter, only God's did.

At the time he thought she had been preparing herself for the possibility of Marlon being found guilty despite what she believed to be his innocence. Now he saw that she was trying to justify getting her son out of jail even if he had committed the murders. She had all but said that if God's final judgment against him was going to be the same anyway, then Marlon should at least enjoy the brief time he had to spend here on Earth, and not waste most of it locked away in a jail cell.

Christ, I thought Kouri's logic was twisted, he told himself. *Those two characters could plead anything, and better than a lot of lawyers I know. Her only problem is that her conscience is stronger than her love for that son of hers. No wonder she's been unable to face me the last two weeks. She was probably afraid she wouldn't be able to keep her secret in, but all along it was eating her up on the inside. If there's anything I know about these days, it's how guilty feelings can gnaw away at you.*

Bratt wondered why she had come to him during that day's lunch break, why she had pushed him to get the truth from Kouri. Did she just want him to share in her complicity and her misery? Or had she been looking to him for some sort of help?

He thought wearily, *Help her? I gotta help myself first.*

Shaking his head he turned the shower off just in time to hear his phone ringing. He briefly considered making a wet, mad dash to answer it, but decided to let his machine get the message and reached for a towel instead.

Stepping out of the shower as he dried himself he wiped the fog off the bathroom mirror with one hand and leaned in to look at his vague reflection. He tried to find in it some shred of honesty or self-respect, but the steam quickly covered up his image again.

You're not much to look at right now anyway, he told himself as he stepped back, feeling disappointed. *Not half as smart as you thought you were.*

He wrapped the towel around his waist and padded into his bedroom. Once there he pressed the "play" button on his answering machine. The tape rewound quickly, then it was Jeannie's voice that he heard.

"Excuse me, is this the residence of the soon to be Judge Bratt? If you haven't gotten too big for your britches perhaps you would condescend to a lunch appointment tomorrow with a couple of lovely young ladies, namely Claire and myself. She says *she'd* like to see you again, although for the life of me I don't know why. Call us soon, Daddy-o."

Bratt felt no joy at the sound of his daughter's voice. He stood staring at the machine like it was a snake about to bite him. It had hurt to hear her refer to him as a judge, knowing the things he was having to do to get there. So many of his actions in this trial seemed to have been intended to prove her accusations right.

And the thought of facing Claire still scared him. Maybe she didn't hold what had happened to her against him, but he realized that in his heart he still felt responsible. He would have to do something to set things right before he could ever face her again. There would have to be some act of atonement to make up in a small way for some of the things he had done in his past…and in this trial.

He asked himself if he was really going to throw everything he had worked for away so easily. He saw his answer in the image of Jennifer Campbell, standing on the icy sidewalk outside the courthouse, struggling with her guilty conscience.

Maybe she does need my help, he thought. *It looks like we're in the same sinking boat and I'm going to have to save us both from drowning.*

On Saturday morning he woke up early, feeling refreshed from a surprisingly good night's sleep. He felt strangely at peace with himself. The previous day's events, capped off by Jeannie's phone message, had shown him the path that he would have to take. Whatever self-doubts had haunted him earlier had disappeared in the face of his resolve to take charge of matters and undo some of the wrongs he had committed. He would have to beg off his daughter's lunch date, but that would be made up for soon enough.

He jumped out of bed and strode to the bathroom to relieve himself. He still wasn't sure how he was going to go about it, but he knew he couldn't let Small get away with the perjured witnesses. Defending his client's best interests was the last thing on his mind now. Small had broken the rules of Bratt's game, rules that were so flexible Bratt had thought that actually breaking them would be impossible to do.

He couldn't let that stand. He had once told Kouri that he didn't know how far he would go to defend a client, but it looked like he had finally found his answer. He was relieved to learn that he did have some limits, after all.

Bratt turned to the sink and began brushing his teeth, his mind racing through the different options that lay ahead of him.

Of course, Small hadn't been alone in his little plot, and Bratt would have to take that into account in whatever he decided to do. Bratt knew he wasn't above reproach in this whole scenario, despite his brave words to Kouri the day before. Once everything was out in the open he might be lucky enough to avoid any criminal accusations, but the Bar Ethics Committee would have its own way of looking at things.

When all was said and done, he realized that he could kiss the Superior Court goodbye. Exposing Small might even spell the end of his career as a defense attorney, but somehow he felt little regret over that. It was a high price to pay, but it seemed to be the going rate for self-respect these days.

As for Kouri, obstructing justice in a murder case was a definite invitation to a long jail term, and Bratt couldn't let that happen to his favorite new sidekick.

Then there was Jennifer Campbell. Even though she had lied to him from the beginning, now he believed that she sincerely regretted what she had done. He also wasn't so secure in his own self-righteousness that he could let her drown in the quagmire she had helped create. As she would probably say, "Let he among you who is without sin…"

So, he'd have to find a way to cover up for all three of them, no matter what he decided to do. There was no turning back for him now. Tomorrow was Sunday, and for the first time in a long time he planned to go to church.

It was a small Episcopalian church in Cote des Neiges, where Jennifer Campbell was a parishioner. As far as saving souls went, he was a raw amateur, so he was going to let her show him the way, whether she wanted to or not.

Bratt sat outside a small, nondescript brick building that he thought looked as much like a church as Montreal's Olympic Stadium looked like a baseball field. It might have housed a corner store once, but now it was Jennifer Campbell's spiritual home, and that was all that mattered.

He had arrived shortly after the services had begun, snuck in the back for a few seconds, just long enough to make sure that she was there, and then returned to his car. The faded printing on the old glass door said the service let out at eleven and he hoped she had no plans to stick around for any coffee hours afterward.

He had nothing to worry about. At a few minutes after eleven the door opened and the few parishioners who could fit into the storefront prayer center began filing out. Campbell was one of the last among them. She spoke to nobody, but walked quickly down the sidewalk, her headscarf wrapped around her face against the damp morning air.

Bratt put his car into gear and crossed the intersection. He quickly pulled up alongside her, leaning across to roll the passenger window down as he did so.

"Mrs. Campbell, over here," he called out.

She turned her head and her look of surprise at being accosted this way was quickly replaced by fear as she recognized him. She didn't answer, but stepped up her pace.

"Mrs. Campbell, I just want to talk. Please, stop."

She finally stopped walking, but refused to look in his direction. He parked his car and got out.

"I hope I didn't frighten you. I just want to talk for a minute."

"It's Sunday," she replied, as if this forbade conversation.

"Please come in the car," he said, ignoring her response.

She hesitated several seconds, then looked behind her, afraid of anyone seeing her enter this stranger's car. Finally, bowing her head in defeat, she opened the passenger door and got in. Bratt took his place behind the wheel.

He had no particular place he wanted to take her, but felt a need to keep the car in motion until they had cleared the air between them.

Bratt had spent much of the previous day coming up with an argument that might convince her to turn against her own son. He would have to speak to the only thing that may have mattered to her more than her love for Marlon. He only hoped that he hadn't read her wrong.

They drove in silence for several minutes until Bratt reached the highway. It was only once they were away from the safety of the residential streets where she lived that she looked at him.

"Why are you here?"

"You know that as well as I do," he answered coldly, feeling this was no time to let her play the innocent. "The scales have fallen from my eyes. Peter saw to that."

"What did he tell you?"

"The truth about what you and he did, just like you knew he would. Why are you pretending to be so ignorant of everything?"

"You're not the only one who's been lying to himself, Mr. Bratt," she whispered.

He felt a brief pang of shame at her words. He knew that that was exactly what he had been doing. It seemed that he had managed to fool nobody but himself with his charade.

"We have to do something," he told her, hoping that she would already have something in mind. "The time for self-deception is over."

"Do something? The trial's over. There's nothing to do."

"It isn't over yet. We can't let him get away with this."

"You're talking about my son, who also happens to be your client, and you're supposed to be defending him."

"Well, I'm not defending him anymore. I don't care if he is your son. He lied to us and used us both, so cut out the offended-mother routine."

Her eyes opened wide, but with pain, not with anger, as she answered.

"He didn't lie to me," she said in a voice so low that Bratt barely heard her.

He said nothing, still finding it hard to believe she had fooled him so well for so long. He wondered if he could ever be certain what she was really thinking.

"I'm sorry I was dishonest with you, Mr. Bratt."

"You know, Mrs. Campbell, I'm used to my clients being dishonest. But, with you, it never occurred to me that you were anything but what you seemed."

"And what did you think I was? I was just a mother, wanting desperately to save her son from jail."

"Your son killed two people."

"Should I hate him then? There are enough people out there who hate him right now. He needs me to keep on loving him. And to forgive him."

"You could have done both without concocting this elaborate lie of yours."

"I'm not so foolish to believe my love would have been much comfort for him in jail, Mr. Bratt. I spoke to him a great deal about what he had done, to try to understand it. I can't rightly say that I do understand, even today. But, I prayed for him. He prayed with me, and I think he's on the right road."

"The right road to where, for Christ's sake?"

"Sir, do not take the Lord's-"

"Cut the crap," he yelled, furious now. "I've listened to that sanctimonious routine of yours long enough and, since you can't even live by your own rules, quit shoving them down my throat."

She turned toward the window without answering and didn't move for a long time. He could tell she was crying and he was glad. He didn't like being used, even if he had gone along willingly, and if he couldn't take out his frustrations on Marlon Small, then his client's mother was a good substitute.

They continued a while in silence, taking the ramp onto the Villa Maria Auto-Route, heading toward the downtown core. Things weren't going quite the way he had hoped. Instead of convincing her to help him, he was having difficulty reaching out to her through his own anger.

He tried to soften his tone.

"Mrs. Campbell, can't you see what this has done to the both of us? I'm at my wit's end right now. I hardly know where to turn. And look at how you've been acting the past two weeks. It's not so easy being a party to perjury, is it? Not when you have to watch supposed witnesses swear on the Bible."

She didn't answer, nor did she even turn her head. He only hoped she was still willing to listen to him.

"If you came to me on Friday, it wasn't because you were happy with what you did. I think you've been avoiding me all this time because you were afraid you couldn't keep the lie going. In the end that's what happened, isn't it?"

Still no answer, but he wasn't going to let his temper flare again.

"You can't feel very good about the way you suckered Pete in, either, can you? I mean, I'm an old hand at all this double-talking, right? It's what I've done all my life. But Pete's an original innocent. Even with those two phony witnesses, he still thinks Marlon didn't shoot anybody.

"I just wish you hadn't dragged him into all this. Like I told him, I can cover my ass. That's second nature for me by now. But he's up shit's creek, if you'll excuse my French. He knows he's going to get disbarred for this, but I don't know if he's aware he's going to jail."

This time she did answer him.

"Nobody has to go to jail."

"No? You don't think they put people in jail for this kind of stunt?"

"You wouldn't turn him in. You'd face the same thing."

"You're not listening. I can cover my ass. You're *my* alibi. You kept me in the dark the whole time, and the only ones who are facing jail time for this are you and Peter."

"So that's what you've decided! Betray my son, turn Peter and me in, all the while protecting yourself? Can you live with that?"

"I could if I had to, but that's not my plan at all. If you're willing to trust me the only person who's going to jail is Marlon."

"But I don't want him to go to jail. Haven't you understood that yet?"

"Yes, I have. But I would have expected you to have other concerns for him. Aren't you supposed to be worried about his eternal soul right about now?"

"Oh, you can mock me if you like, but I have thought of nothing but his soul and mine since the beginning. But why should I leave him to waste away in jail by himself, when we are both damned anyway?"

"It doesn't have to be that way."

"Please, Mr. Bratt, when it comes to the law of God, you are not an authority."

"But what happened to forgiveness? Aren't you supposed to seek forgiveness for your sins? I learned a lot about confession when I was in Sunday school and if that's not good for the soul…"

He let his words trail off, afraid of sounding insincere, and hoping she could see what he was getting at. She sat gazing at him quietly for several seconds, and he turned his head to look at her.

She allowed herself a small smile and said, "I was just trying to picture you in Sunday school."

"I'm afraid it was wasted on me."

"Perhaps not."

Bratt wondered if he was better off pushing her harder or hoping she could come to her own decision.

You never won anything waiting for the witnesses to come up with answers to their own questions, he reminded himself. *Let's see how much of my catechism I remember.*

"If you help Marlon get away with this than you are definitely condemning his soul to hell. As much as you hate the idea of him in jail, are you willing to do that?"

"You don't think killing those boys was enough to damn him?"

"I don't know. He could repent, couldn't he? Wouldn't God forgive him if he accepted his punishment and honestly repented his crimes?"

"I can't answer for God…but that is what I've always believed."

"Well, how do you expect Marlon to seek forgiveness when he's going to avoid responsibility for what he did? If he thinks he's gotten away with murder, he'll never regret anything he did."

"That's not necessarily so."

"Oh, come on. Do you think that after he walks away a free man, by getting people to falsely swear to his innocence, he's going to turn around and honestly feel bad about everything he did? You're still lying to yourself if you do."

She sat quietly, seeming to take all this in, so he kept up the pressure.

"His only chance, maybe not a big chance, but the only chance he has, is to take responsibility for what he did and serve his jail sentence. Maybe then, somewhere down the road, he'll realize how horrible what he did was, and have a chance to save his soul. He could change, you know. He wouldn't be the first killer to find God in jail. But the way you're acting, it's like you don't believe God would ever be able to forgive him. I would have thought that was a major no-no for you."

"He would never forgive me."

"God?"

"Marlon. If I turned him in, I'd lose my son forever."

"You've already lost him. He was taken away by a cold-blooded killer, who cares as little for you as he did for those boys he shot. If he walks away free from what he did, the Marlon you've loved all your life will be as good as dead to you."

She bowed her head and began crying again, not turning her face away from him this time. She pulled a tissue from an endless supply that seemed to fill her purse and wiped at her tears. She was weakened, and it was time for Bratt to conclude his argument.

"You have a great faith in God, Mrs. Campbell. Something that you've shown me has been sorely lacking in my life. But you seem to have forgotten about it somehow. This is a chance for you to redeem all of us, including me. We've all twisted the truth beyond all recognition. I feel bad about it, and so does Peter. But we can't set things right without your help. Marlon also needs your help, or he'll go on living the way he has, with no chance to return to God's grace. And for all your prayer and love of God, you're damning yourself to hell too.

"Help me now. Help yourself at the same time, and help Marlon. After tomorrow, it'll be too late for all of us."

She didn't answer, but Bratt didn't need to hear her say anything. By the way she looked straight ahead out the windshield, trying to steel her resolve, he knew he had gotten his point across.

He headed for the nearest exit and got off the highway. They were near the eastern half of the city now, and he turned north and took the road that led to Nancy Morin's home.

Bratt had often fantasized that his first time inside Nancy's apartment would have been under more romantic circumstances. Now, he watched quietly as Jennifer Campbell sat alone in the small, neat living room, sipping tea, while Nancy tried to reach Francis Parent on the phone.

Bratt had called her from his car just after they turned off the highway, and gave her a brief rundown of what had happened. She had been about to step out, but his news had stopped her in her tracks

Now he stood next to her in her kitchen as she spoke to Parent's aged mother, with whom the prosecutor lived. She left a message that Parent should call her as soon as he came in, then hung up.

"He's been up at the family cottage all weekend," she said as she hung up. "When he goes up there it's mostly to sulk, and he takes the phone off the hook."

Bratt leaned his head back against a cupboard and rubbed his face. *This is only a minor setback,* he told himself.

"Robert, are you feeling all right?"

He lowered his hands and smiled at Nancy.

"Believe it or not, I feel pretty good. It's like the weight of the world is off my shoulders. For the first time in weeks I know exactly what I want to do."

They rejoined his client's mother in the living room, and Nancy went and sat next to the worried-looking woman. Bratt stood over her, wondering what the next twenty-four hours was going to bring.

"We can't reach him," he told her. "It's possible that you won't get a chance to speak to him before tomorrow morning at court."

"And, boy, won't he be surprised," Nancy added.

"I'll say, but that's not necessarily a bad thing. He won't have much time to think things through, so he's going to have to do this my way. You're going to have to keep a lot of what you heard here under your hat, Nancy."

"You're asking a lot of me, Robbie."

"You want a conviction, you do it my way. Make sure Parent knows that too, before he starts asking too many questions. If he even gives her or Peter a dirty look I'll see to it that she's never allowed on the stand. I'm, *we're*, trying to do the right thing here, but crucifying those two is not an option."

Jennifer Campbell looked up at him, her eyes red with sadness.

"I don't want to hurt Peter. But, I can't fix all the lying I've done by adding more lies to them."

"No, no. Don't look at it that way. You *are* going to tell the truth, but only about what Marlon told you he did, not about getting those witnesses. There's no reason to get yourself or Peter in trouble. He's the one who committed the crime."

"And what have I done?"

"You've acted like a mother trying to protect her son, remember? Nobody's going to blame you for that."

Bratt glanced over to Nancy as if for confirmation and she nodded, albeit hesitantly, and said nothing.

"But lying is what got me here in the first place. How will it help me make things right?"

"Look, trust me on this. Everybody's been doing what they think is best from the beginning, but nobody's been asking my opinion. Forgive me if I sound a bit vain, but I *am* the lawyer here. And I really do know what's the best solution for everybody. So it's my turn to make the decisions, OK?

"You *are* going to tell the truth, but only the truth about Marlon. He's on trial, you're not. Your role in this scheme is irrelevant to the jury, so nobody's going to ask you about it and you're not going to talk about it. Please tell me that's clear."

She looked unsure, but finally nodded.

"I'll do whatever you say, Mr. Bratt."

"Very wise decision. Now, Nancy, I need you to do the right thing here. She's been through enough. You guys don't need to look for any scapegoats."

"OK, I'll keep my mouth shut. This time you get your way. And may I say that your nobility is a very attractive character trait?"

"Thanks. For now, we cross our fingers," he looked over at Jennifer Campbell's tired face and added, "and pray for guidance."

Chapter 13

On the last day of Robert Bratt's legal career he saw his first bird of the late-arriving spring and thought that it must be an omen of some sort, although he had no idea what. It didn't matter. Today was not a day for superstition, but for practical matters, getting his hands a little dirty, taking back control of this trial and getting things done.

Kouri was sitting alone in his office as Bratt entered. He looked up nervously, and Bratt realized he was probably still wondering what was going to be done about the alibi witnesses. Bratt had considered filling him in on what he had asked Campbell to do, but finally decided against it. He wasn't sure how the young lawyer would react, especially if he still persisted in his belief that Small was innocent.

Bratt also thought that Kouri had taken part in more than his share of shady deals in this case already, so there would be no need to involve him in this one. If things didn't work out the way Bratt hoped, Kouri would be in enough trouble without being an accomplice to this cover-up as well.

"Happy days, Pete," he said, without hinting that it meant something totally different for him than it did for his assistant. "After Jordan's cross-examination today, that'll be it for our defense."

Kouri rose from his seat without saying a word. As they set off for the courthouse he looked relieved, yet uncertain if he should be. He maintained his silent, pensive mood as they made the short walk in a warming sunshine.

Once there they met Jordan outside the courtroom, and the young witness looked self-assured. Bratt had no doubt that Sims had informed him about how weak a challenge Parent's cross-examination had been, despite a court order forbidding them from discussing their testimony.

No matter, thought Bratt. *If Francis hasn't totally lost what balls he had, he'll take a very different approach with this one.*

He entered the courtroom to find Parent already in his seat, with Nancy sitting beside him. Nancy had obviously already filled the prosecutor in on Bratt's plan, because Parent looked like he had strong doubts about agreeing to anything the defense attorney had in mind.

Bratt and Kouri had just taken their seats when Judge Green and the jury entered. The jurors' faces showed that they knew the end of the trial was near, and they would be back to their normal lives before too long. Jordan was sworn in and Bratt's heart beat a little faster as Parent stood up to cross-examine him.

"Mr. Jordan, isn't it true that this alleged alibi is nothing but an invention, concocted by the accused, Marlon Small?"

Without missing a beat, Jordan replied, "Not at all, sir."

Bratt glanced at Green and saw the judge raise one eyebrow, as if to say, "That didn't prove much."

Just wait and see. We'll give you a story to remember in your retirement.

"Mr. Jordan, is it not a fact that the accused asked both you and Mr. Sims to lie to this court, by providing him with a totally false alibi?"

Again, Jordan took the accusation in stride. "No, sir."

"Mr. Jordan, is it not true that the accused admitted his guilt for these crimes in your presence?"

"No, he never did."

"Mr. Jordan, is it not true that you told the accused's mother, Jennifer Campbell, that you were glad to help your friend get away with these crimes by lying to this court?"

Jordan paused slightly before answering, wondering where exactly these questions were leading. Then, once again, he said, "No, sir."

"Mr. Jordan, is it not true that you, the accused, and Mrs. Campbell had a three-way telephone conversation in which the accused stated, and I quote, 'I didn't plan to do those Phillips boys. They just shouldn't have been there;' end quote?"

Jordan's eyes jumped to Kouri's face, an expression of confusion evident at having heard this direct quotation. He took several seconds to gather his thoughts before answering and, during this time, Bratt saw the jurors perk up noticeably, as if the trial had just gotten interesting again.

"I, I never heard Mr. Small say that…sir."

"You never heard Mrs. Campbell say in reply, 'I pray for all those boys every night,' to which the accused commented, 'It's me you should be praying for. So that my guys can pull this off'."

"I never had any conversations with both Mrs. Campbell and Marlon at the same time," Jordan stated firmly.

"Never?"

"Never."

"Thank you very much, Mr. Jordan," Parent said, sounding truly grateful, and sat down. He looked toward Bratt and nodded almost imperceptibly. Bratt breathed a sigh of relief that the first part of his plan had been successfully completed, and stood up to address the court.

"My Lord, ladies and gentlemen of the jury. The defense rests."

He sat back down and Kouri reached over and gave his arm a congratulatory squeeze. Bratt didn't turn to look at him. He felt he was being a hypocrite toward his assistant, even if it was for his own good.

Parent stood up, eliciting a small look of surprise from the judge, who surely thought the final witness had been heard.

"My Lord, having heard the defense witnesses, the Crown will be calling one witness in rebuttal."

"Not something you forgot to put in your evidence in chief, I presume," Green grumbled, clearly skeptical about the Crown's strategy.

"No sir. A new witness that I only learned of this morning. And she will be called on to rebut certain statements by the last defense witness, which were not in any way foreseeable by the Crown."

"Really? How dramatic. And just who might your rebuttal witness be?"

"The accused's mother. Jennifer Campbell."

The courtroom almost exploded at this announcement. Small and Kouri jumped simultaneously to their feet, and shouted in unison: "What?"

Green himself looked dumbfounded and for a few moments allowed the loud buzzing and arguing go on in the courtroom unabated. The jurors talked excitedly among themselves, like children who had just learned of the surprise visit of a favorite relative.

The two calmest people in the courtroom were Bratt and Parent. The defense attorney ignored his client's repeated calls to turn around and explain this sudden turn of events. He sat with his back to the prisoner's box, suppressing the smile he felt growing on the inside. As for Parent, he seemed to be breathing easier than he had been of late, regaining his grasp on the victory that had been slipping away from him until today.

Finally, Green got over his shock and stood up, slamming his hand down on his desk.

"Everybody calm down! I want quiet or I will clear this court!"

The buzzing died down, although probably not as fast as he would have liked. The jurors turned their attention back to him, as did Parent. Kouri sat back down next to Bratt, looking confused and angry. Only Small continued standing in the prisoner's box, keeping silent with obvious difficulty.

"Mr. Parent," Green began, glowering at the prosecutor over his glasses, then opening his mouth to continue, seemed to lose track of what he wanted to say, and so closed it again. The anger seeped out of his face and was replaced by a look of wonder at what Parent intended to do. All he could ask was, "Really?"

"Most definitely, My Lord," Parent answered, his confidence having returned to his voice.

"And Mr. Bratt, what do you have to say?"

Bratt stood slowly and shrugged, feigning indifference.

"I guess I'll wait and see what he's trying to prove."

This obviously wasn't good enough for Small who looked on the verge of panicking as he yelled out, "I GOTTA TALK TO MY LAWYER NOW!"

Green turned to scold him for speaking out of turn, then again his features softened.

"Yes, I'm sure you would want to. We'll take a ten-minute recess while Mr. Parent readies his witness. Mr. Bratt, you may speak to your client there in the box once the courtroom is cleared."

Small paced along the side of the ten-foot long box, his cuffed hands opening and closing as if he were strangling somebody in his imagination. Once the courtroom had emptied there were only his two lawyers and a guard sitting at the end of the box left with him. The guard didn't even try to look like he wasn't listening to their conversation, but this was only a minor concern to the accused at that point.

"What the hell's going on?"

Bratt shrugged again, knowing full well that his indifference would only serve to aggravate his client even further.

"They can call rebuttal evidence if it's to answer something that came out in the defense case and they had no way of foreseeing it beforehand."

"But if it's to prove an out of court statement by Marlon," Kouri argued, "it has to be in their evidence in chief."

"Not if they can show they never knew of this witness or that statement before now."

"And how the hell do they know about her now," Small demanded. "Who told them to go speak to my mom?"

Bratt considered telling him the truth, but thought Small would probably fire him on the spot. He would have been more than happy to walk away from this case, but it could have caused delays in finishing the trial and he was worried that Jennifer Campbell might lose her nerve in the meantime.

"We'll just have to wait until she gets on the stand to see what she says about you and about showing up here today."

"Shit! Is that all you can tell me, wait and see?"

Again Bratt shrugged, looking anything but concerned. The effect on his client was predictable.

"Fuck you," Small hissed.

The ten-minute break stretched out to half an hour, but Green finally got back on the bench. The jurors looked excitedly from Parent to Small. Their wide-eyed anticipation was responded to with a sullen glare from the accused.

Parent seemed to have grown several inches, he was standing so tall now, but Bratt was past the point where he needed to mock his rival's pride. He had no problem with the prosecutor reveling in his moment of glory, as long as everything went according to plan.

The courtroom door swung open and a uniformed police officer stepped in, followed close behind by Jennifer Campbell. She walked slowly forward, focused on the witness stand to avoid accidentally making contact with her son's eyes. Bratt thought that she looked so much older now than when he had first met her. As concerned as she had been for her son's fate, it had been her role in the perjury that seemed to have taken its greatest toll on her.

She stepped through the small opening in the witness box and positioned herself in front of the Bible that rested on the counter in front of her, gazing at it with a mixture of sadness and affection.

When she was sworn in, her voice was so low that Parent had to ask her to speak up, and he did so with great gentleness, like she was a fragile crystal.

"Mrs. Campbell. Are you Marlon Small's mother?"

She swallowed before answering, this admission clearly difficult for her now, and kept her eyes only on the prosecutor as she spoke.

"Yes. I am."

"You are aware of what he was accused of last summer?"

"Yes, of course."

"Did you know he claims to have been in a park in LaSalle, playing basketball, at the time of the shootings in Little Burgundy?"

"I was aware of that."

"Do you know anybody who was willing to place him in the park that night?"

"Yes, two boys. Vernon Sims and Everton Jordan."

"And how did you first find out about them?"

She stretched a little and looked at the judge now, her head held high.

"Marlon asked me to call them, to see if they would be willing to be his alibi witnesses. Actually, he asked me to speak to several people, to see who would make the best witnesses."

Bratt squirmed in his seat. He saw that she was on the borderline of admitting her own participation in the perjury plot and hoped that she hadn't decided to punish herself too, after all.

"And these were people who were with him in the park on the night of June 14, 1999?"

Now, for the first time since she had entered the courtroom, she turned and looked at her son, who sat staring back at her in disbelief.

"Not at all. My son…my son told me he was never in the park that night. He asked me to help him find at least two people who could testify convincingly that he was. But it was a lie."

Aw, shit, Bratt thought. *Why'd she have to go and do that to herself? She just had to be a martyr.*

Even Parent seemed unprepared for her admission of complicity and he took several seconds to gather his thoughts.

"You mean you were aware the alibi was false?"

"I mean I was as responsible for the false witnesses as my son was."

From behind him Bratt could hear Small mumbling, "no, no, no," under his breath, and he felt like joining him.

"And was anybody else in on this plan to fabricate an alibi?" Parent asked, staring right at Bratt as he did so.

Son of a bitch is out to get me, Bratt thought.

"No," she answered, to Bratt's relief. "There was only Marlon and me."

I guess she wants to go down with her ship alone, Bratt thought regretfully. *After all these years protecting clients from themselves, I still couldn't get her to listen to me.*

"And why did you think it was necessary to fabricate an alibi for your son?"

Again she hesitated and looked at Small before answering.

"Because he told me that he had shot those boys."

Everyone in the courtroom seemed to suck in their breaths in surprise at this revelation. Small kicked the wall of the prisoner's box.

"SHIT, BRATT. STOP HER!" he yelled out.

Bratt didn't respond and Green paid no attention to this outburst. The judge began questioning the witness himself.

"Are you saying the accused admitted to you his guilt for the crimes he's accused of?"

"Yes," she answered calmly, a tear forming in one eye the only evidence of the emotional strain she was under. "We talked about what he did on several occasions. He told me that him and Marcus shot all three of them. He thought he had killed Dorrell Phillips too…but God spared the boy."

Bratt heard Kouri's labored breathing and looked over at him, half-expecting him to be about to jump up in protest. But his assistant only sat staring down at his hands in his lap, a look of understanding growing on his anguished face.

Better late than never, Bratt thought.

"Did you and the accused ever speak with Everton Jordan via a three-way phone call from jail," Green continued.

"Yes, at least twice. Once with Mr. Sims too."

"Did you discuss the false alibi during these conversations?"

"Yes."

"Did he make any admissions of guilt during any of those phone calls?"

"Yes. I remember one occasion when he said it was too bad they had to shoot the two young men who had been in the apartment. The man they called Indian was the only person he had expected to find there that night. I suppose you could say he was their original target."

Green sat back and let his breath out slowly. Parent just stood there beaming, not needing to say anything else. Bratt caught Nancy's eye and she nodded to him slightly to let him know he had done the right thing. For a moment Bratt thought that they would be the only ones who were aware of his role, but Green still had some questions he wanted answered.

"Tell me, Mrs. Campbell. Why did you come forward now?"

She looked down, as if discussing her own feelings of guilt was something too shameful to face in open court.

"I loved…I *love* my son. But I hated myself for what I had done. I couldn't lie anymore to protect him from the awful thing he'd done. I only hope that one day he'll realize that my coming here was as much for him as it was for me."

"YEAH, RIGHT!" Small called out angrily.

"Quiet, you!" Green snapped at him, looking at Small like he was something less than human. Then he turned to the witness and continued his questioning.

"What I'd like to know, madam, is why you chose now to come forward. Why didn't you tell this to the police before the trial?"

"I really hoped to take this awful secret to my grave, but I couldn't. Not after what I'd heard here in this trial. I had to tell someone or my heart was going to burst. I needed someone to advise me on how to heal this wound in my soul."

"Whom did you speak to?"

"Mr. Bratt."

Well, this is what I wanted...and feared, Bratt told himself, sensing that all the eyes in the courtroom were now on him.

"*Really*," Green almost sang the word. "And could you tell us about *that* conversation?"

"I told Mr. Bratt…well, the same thing I've told you. I told him that I felt very bad about what I had done. And that I wanted to set things right."

She glanced over in Bratt's direction and allowed herself a small, grateful smile, which he couldn't help but return.

"He told me that I had to speak with Mr. Parent, here. That I had to tell the truth, which I guess is what I've wanted to do all along."

Feeling quite happy with himself, Bratt looked past the witness to the prosecution table and wondered why Parent and Nancy's faces wore looks of surprised horror.

Then Nancy jumped up and yelled out, "*Robert*," just as the small chain of Marlon Small's handcuffs was pulled across Bratt's throat. He was dragged backward toward the prisoner's box where his enraged client was leaning over the railing, swearing loudly and trying his best to strangle his lawyer.

Just before he lost consciousness Bratt looked up into Small's hate-filled face glowering down at him, and the thought occurred to him that his client should really get his teeth fixed while he was in jail.

Chapter 14

On Monday, April 3, Robert Bratt sat in his office, his stockinged feet up on his desk, and spoke to his daughter Jeannie on the phone.

"The movers'll be here any minute now," he said, running his fingers over a cardboard box that contained some of the personal memorabilia that had decorated his office for so many years. His voice was hoarse, his throat still tender from where the chain had almost cracked his windpipe a week earlier. "Ralston's drawn up the papers. He's good at that stuff. I just want to sign it and get out of here."

"I can't believe you're actually going to Costa Rica without me," Jeannie said from the other end.

"Well, maybe we'll go down again when school lets out. You know we've got a standing invitation from that old, uh, friend of mine."

"I guess you and Nancy don't want me hanging around you when you're down there this time."

Bratt laughed, but only briefly. Laughing still hurt his throat the most, although it surprised him how much he had found to laugh about since Marlon Small had been convicted of murder. For good measure, his former client had also been charged for the courtroom assault on his lawyer, as well as on one of the guards who had wrestled him to the floor of the prisoner's box. Bratt, though, wasn't planning to hang around long enough to testify against him. How much more than a life sentence could they give Small, anyway?

There had been a brief moment when he had considered staying on to defend Jennifer Campbell against the obstruction of justice charges that Parent had insisted on laying. But he knew that was not what she wanted for either of them, so he had left her to her own fate.

As for Peter, right after the verdict he announced he was taking a sabbatical to contemplate his future. Bratt wasn't sure if he'd continue in defense, or even stay in law at all. He was still young, though, and would have lots of time to recover from his mistakes.

While Jeannie nattered on about how dull the rest of her semester was going to be compared to the sunny climes he was headed for, Sylvie came timidly to his door and he waved her in.

"There's a Mr. Madsen here to see you," she said.

Crap, he thought, *of all the people I didn't want to see now.*

He lowered his feet and slipped them into his loafers, telling Jeannie he had to go but would see her at home later. He had barely hung up when Senator Roger Madsen walked in, his stiff, military bearing almost failing him when he looked around at the empty office walls. Without saying a word he pulled his forlorn gaze back to Bratt.

There was what felt like an eternity of awkward silence, then Bratt spoke up.

"Senator Madsen, how nice of you to drop by."

"I just had to see it with my own eyes. You're actually leaving."

Bratt could think of nothing to say, so he just shrugged and smiled. Madsen shuffled over to the sofa and sat down with a sigh.

"Twenty years, Robert. You did a lot of good work."

"Some of it was good."

"You're really going to give all this up?"

"I don't think I have much choice, even if I wanted to stay."

"Oh, that Bar inquiry's a lot of hogwash, you know that. They can't blame you for acting like an officer of the court."

"I know. But that's not much of a selling point for potential clients. Besides, I need a change."

"You could have been on the bench. That should have been change enough for any man."

"It would have been nice. But the price was too high."

Madsen jumped up to his feet, too agitated to remain seated. He began pacing, looking like he was practicing an army drill, marching up and down a square.

"Good thing your father's not around to see this."

"He never liked what I did much, anyway."

"Maybe, but I'm not so sure. I do remember he was damn proud of you the day you graduated law school."

"You say it like that makes him special," Bratt sniped back, instantly regretting his insolent tone.

Madsen turned away.

"Listen, Robert," he said with his back still to Bratt. "I know you're tired, so take some time off, enjoy life for a while. I'm sure in a few weeks you'll be raring to get back in the game."

"I'm sorry, Senator, but you don't seem to understand what's happened. I've burned my bridges. There's nothing to come back to. I'm not even wanted here, friends or no friends. I've become a pariah for the office clientele. And the truth is, that's just fine with me."

Madsen turned back to look at him and Bratt was surprised to see he had tears in his eyes.

"I just want to make sure you'll be all right, Robert. This is all so sudden."

"No, Senator. It really wasn't that sudden. Like all divorces, it's been brewing for a long time. This was just the right time to leave."

He put his arm affectionately around the older man's shoulders and walked with him out the office toward the elevator. They stood silently as they waited for it to arrive. When the doors finally opened, Madsen paused before entering.

"You still have that lovely old Jag?"

"Mm-hm."

"I thought I saw it pulling up outside. There was a pretty young lady driving it."

"That would be Nancy. She's…*a friend.* If she's here the movers won't be far behind."

Madsen silently mouthed the word "movers" and nodded solemnly, before getting in the elevator.

"Don't be a stranger, Robert," he called out as the doors slid closed.

Bratt only smiled to himself. As fond as he was of the old man, he didn't expect to see him again for a long time, if at all. There were many old friends he would have to get used to missing, but fresh starts didn't work if they came with old baggage.

Before stepping back into the office he paused to look at the shiny new sign on the heavy wooden doors: "Ralston, Kalouderis, Attorneys at Law."

They didn't take very long to get it up there, he thought, with only the slightest pang of regret.

ABOUT THE AUTHOR

Gabriel Boutros practiced criminal law for 24 years in Montreal, where he lives with his wife and two sons. He has previously published two short stories, neither of which have anything to do with the legal profession. This is his first novel.

Made in the USA
Charleston, SC
26 April 2013